Blue Light Yokohama

Nicolás Obregón was born in the UK to a Spanish father and French mother and grew up between London and Madrid. As a travel writer, Nicolás has had in-depth experience of Japan, but the beginning of his fascination with the country came from watching Japanese cartoons as a young boy. The inspiration for *Blue Light Yokohama* came during his first trip to Japan, when he discovered an article about a real-life crime which was to haunt him. Sixteen years after this atrocity, the case remains unsolved.

Nicolás is a graduate of the acclaimed Birkbeck Creative Writing Masters and a former bookseller.

www.obregonbooks.com
Instagram@obregonbooks
Facebook.com/obregonbooks

Blue Light Yokohama

NICOLÁS OBREGÓN

MICHAEL JOSEPH
an imprint of
PENGUIN BOOKS

MICHAEL JOSEPH

UK | USA | Canada | Ireland | Australia
India | New Zealand | South Africa

Michael Joseph is part of the Penguin Random House group of companies
whose addresses can be found at global.penguinrandomhouse.com.

Penguin
Random House
UK

First published in Great Britain by Michael Joseph 2017

001

Copyright © Nicolás Obregón, 2016

The moral right of the author has been asserted

Set in Garamond MT Std 13.5/16pt
Typeset by Palimpsest Book Production Limited, Falkirk, Stirlingshire
Printed in Great Britain by Clays Ltd, St Ives plc

A CIP catalogue record for this book is available from the British Library

HARDBACK ISBN: 978–0–718–18404–9
TRADE PAPERBACK ISBN: 978–0–718–18702–6

www.greenpenguin.co.uk

MIX
Paper from
responsible sources
FSC® C018179

Penguin Random House is committed to a
sustainable future for our business, our readers
and our planet. This book is made from Forest
Stewardship Council® certified paper.

For my mother, for Lela. Hasta el cielo de la calle.

At the foot of the lighthouse, darkness reigns.

Proverb

1996

The cable car pulled away, carrying one last load of tourists up into the warm dusk. It climbed higher and higher over the bay, the seaboard unfurling below. To the east, Hideo Akashi saw the grimy docks – microchips, fish and bleach were being loaded on to trucks, bound for the city. Japan's cities were always hungry.

Akashi turned to his wife. Yumi's eyes were closed, her lips hiding. He took her hand and squeezed gently.

'I don't like heights,' she whispered.

'I know. It'll be over soon.'

Around them, elderly tourists cooed at the panorama. Honeymooners posed for photographs. The cable car attendant reeled off cheery facts about their altitude and the city below. Akashi kissed Yumi's freckled shoulder and, as he did so, he saw the woman. She was sitting at the back of the cable car, alone and silent. Her filthy clothes were too heavy for this weather. She did not take in the view, nor did she snap any pictures. She just stared at the floor. A little girl stood near her, possibly her child, but there was nothing maternal about this woman. There was a listlessness about her gaunt face that unnerved and excited Akashi. Beneath her youthful exterior there was something he couldn't look away from.

'Hideo?' Yumi whispered.

'Yes?'

'You're hurting my hand.'

'Oh. Sorry.'

Akashi forced himself to look away from the woman and reached for his camera instead. He took a step back and framed his wife's face. Yumi smiled, squinting in the setting sun.

Click.

He was about to take another but something stopped him. At the back of the cable car, something was happening, something was wrong. The attendant was pleading, his white gloves outstretched.

'Madam, please. Step away from the door.'

The woman in the heavy clothes stood before the attendant.

Thud.

There came a spluttering noise and now the woman held a knife aloft, her thin hand glistening with blood up to the wrist. At her feet, the attendant writhed, gurgling like a baby. Trembling, the woman pointed the knife at the crowd. Her eyes locked on to Akashi's.

'You stay *away* from me.'

The crowd lurched backwards in the car, clumping together in bovine fear. The woman wiped her bloody hand on her coat, painting red faces, forehand and back. With the butt of her knife she smashed the glass panel of the emergency stop button. Cables groaned, then squealed, until the car finally shuddered to a halt. To the west, the sun was setting, this day being swallowed for ever.

An automated message played over the PA system.

Ladies and gentlemen, we are experiencing minor technical difficulties. Please remain calm. Our engineers have been notified and you are perfectly safe in the cable car.

There was a shaky hush in the car. The attendant had fallen silent, his face now pale. The woman stepped over his body and stood before the doors. Closing her eyes, she gripped the lever and took a breath. Hideo Akashi's instincts finally kicked in. Yumi reached for him but he was already gone, fighting through the torsos.

'Police! *Move!*'

The woman pulled the lever, the doors jolted open and a deafening wind raged in. Akashi's legs felt weak as he staggered towards her. There was too much saliva in his mouth, no space in his head for thoughts. The woman kicked off her shoes, threw off her jacket and said something Akashi couldn't hear in the wind. He pushed the little girl out of the way and threw out a hand.

Then the woman was gone.

A moment of silence.

No lifetimes flashing by, only silence.

Akashi reached out of the car and caught her by the wrist. He felt an overwhelming agony as her weight wrenched him to the floor. The pain arrived long before the realization. By one blood-soaked wrist, he held the woman over the abyss. Her hair cartwheeled in the wind. The void beneath them yawned, infinite and blue.

She lifted her head and blinked. Her mouth opened and fragile words fell out, the last droplets from a closing tap.

'I see elephant clouds . . .'

Akashi bellowed but his muscles were ripping. Bile was rising in his throat. His arm was breaking. And then he saw it – the tattoo on her bloodied wrist. In deepest ink, a large, black sun.

He looked at it. It looked back at him. Hideo Akashi let go.

Fifteen Years Later

1. Boxes

Iwata woke from a falling dream again. Drenched in sweat, struggling for breath, he went to the window. The Tokyo cityscape stretched out below him, cities within cities, angles incalculable. Thirty-five million existences crammed into circadian rhythms of concrete and cables. Immense infrastructure, never-ending networks – all of it delicate as hummingbird heartbeats.

The lights of the city are so pretty.

Iwata crossed his sparse apartment to the kitchenette and poured himself a glass of water. He saw the large cardboard boxes stacked in the corner and looked away. Wrapping himself in a blanket, he sat down by his stereo system and put on headphones. He closed his eyes as the opening notes of Schubert's Impromptu in G flat major, Op. 90, No. 3 filled his disquiet and the nightmare dissolved in the music.

Grey morning haze had seeped through the blinds by the time Iwata had made up his mind to leave. He drank coffee in silence, showered rigorously and dressed in jeans and a thick grey cashmere pullover. Picking up the newspaper addressed to the previous tenant, he took the elevator down to the car park and unlocked his 1979 Isuzu 117 Coupé. He plucked a handwritten note from the windscreen offering cash, scrunched it up and put it in his pocket. The leather had cracks and she'd hardly ever seen a garage, but Iwata found notes like these every other week. Clearly, he had a covetous neighbour.

He started the car but left the radio off, enjoying the rare quiet of the Tokyo roads. At the southern entrance of Shibuya Station, the first few street vendors had assembled, sharing bags of hot nuts and flasks of tea as they conspired. Payday-loan shops and cell-phone dealerships were opening their shutters. On the roof of a department store, the news played on a giant LED screen. Mina Fong, a famous actress, had been found dead in her apartment. A well-known heiress had broken up with a promising Yomiuri Giants pitcher. A popular cookery show had been cancelled. And there was a new number one single in the pop charts. The broadcast ended with an insurance company's slogan:

THIS IS WHAT JAPAN SHOULD BE

Iwata turned off the main roads and found parking in an overlooked lot behind an arcade. He stuffed his hands in his pockets and made his way along the chilly backstreets. Spring was not just late this year; it had seemingly given up on itself.

Iwata went into a large department store and spent an hour buying highlighters, workbooks and plastic dividers. In the café, he ordered a gum-syrup coffee and a fruit salad. There was no Wi-Fi here but Iwata liked the view. He sat among exhausted night-shift workers and sipped his coffee, looking down at the high street. Shibuya was now throbbing with flustered commuters and bleary-eyed students. Traffic cops frantically waved at inching traffic and pedestrians bristled at the red lights.

Iwata opened the newspaper and turned directly to the classifieds. He ignored oblique offers for discreet massage, dining company from middle-aged women and French tuition. He stopped at the storage-space section and scanned through carefully. After a few minutes he circled an ad, then folded the newspaper under his arm and left.

Outside, the fog had momentarily lifted and the sky was a cold, exquisite blue. Iwata got back into his car and called the number from the ad. A drowsy voice answered.

'This is Matsumoto here.' The man coughed then lit a cigarette. 'Your storage problems are my passion.'

Iwata stated his interest and Matsumoto reeled off an address, agreeing to meet in an hour.

Driving north, past Harajuku, Iwata parked up near the subway station. He walked along Takeshita Street with its knock-off T-shirts, Hello Kitty and plastic fads. Tourists gawked at the chichi neon and manufactured cheer. Posters of the latest idol groups clung to all available wall space. Cheap speakers played happy pop and teenage girls cutting class weighed up prices. Iwata hated this place but there was a nearby noodle bar he favoured for its breakfast tamago-yaki. Usually it was half-empty but today, for some reason, it had attracted a large queue of smoking salary men. Iwata swore and returned to his car.

He drove south-east, along the grand, tree-lined avenue of Omotesandō, where wealthy housewives browsed designer Italian labels. Iwata turned on to Aoyama-Dori, and fifteen minutes later, he turned off Meguro-Dori. He found space in an empty lot between houses. As Iwata got out, he looked up at the sky. It would rain tonight.

From a hole in the wall, he bought a paper plate of vegetable and shrimp dumplings. The old cook complained about the game last night and Iwata nodded along while he ate. When he was done, he promised the cook he would come back again.

At the end of the street, a short, fat man with a ponytail stood outside a shabby shop, its windows covered in faded newspaper. The man was smoking anxiously as he glanced up and down the street. Seeing Iwata, he pinched his cigarette between his lips and stuck out a hand.

'Are you my guy?' The cigarette bobbled as he spoke.

Iwata nodded and they shook hands.

'Let's open her up for you, then.'

Matsumoto stepped over a mound of junk mail. The room was narrow but Iwata liked the gloom. The walls were lined with lockers of varying size. At the back, there were also several deposit boxes.

'What you thinking, mister? You like it?'

'I like it fine.'

'What you using it for?'

'I just have some boxes. I've got about sixteen of them, about this wide and the same high.' He held his palms fifty centimetres apart.

Matsumoto whistled.

'I can give you the whole back room, but it'll cost you.'

'How much?'

He looked at Iwata sidelong.

'Mister, if you don't mind me asking, why not just keep them at your place?'

'I do mind you asking. How much?'

'All right. You're looking at thirty-five thousand a month.'

Iwata shook his head.

'I'm going to make you an offer instead: eighty thousand for three months. But, for your flexibility, I'll pay you up front.'

'*Eighty*.' Matsumoto puffed out smoke and squinted one eye. 'Up front?'

'That's right.'

'What are you, some kinda loan shark?'

'I just need a space for my boxes.'

'So why me, why not just store them at one of the big places for less?'

'I don't like forms.'

Matsumoto shrugged. 'Fuck it. You got yourself a deal.'

At the bank, the cashier politely reminded Iwata how little insurance money would remain but he ignored him. Outside, Matsumoto slipped the fat envelope into his pocket and tossed over a set of keys in return.

'Guess I'll see you in three months.' Matsumoto winked.

He turned away, his ponytail swishing down the street. Iwata returned to his car, and in the distance, he heard thunder.

Iwata reached the airport-sized maze of Shinjuku Station a little after 1 p.m. He bought a ticket for the bullet train to Nagano and boarded Asama 573. The seats were clean and the temperature was optimal. Staff bowed as they entered and left the carriage. The silent car was absolutely silent.

As the train pulled away, Iwata watched Tokyo recede. He flew past commuter towns of new-build complexes and man-made lakes. Young professionals lived here, eating the right food, getting enough exercise. Iwata had been like them once. Before there was any need to make this journey. He couldn't remember the last time he had taken this train. Nor did he want to.

The lights of the city are so pretty.

When the concrete of Tokyo's sleeper cities finally ended, there were only dead fields and pylons. In the distance, green hills swelled like lovesick sighs.

Arriving at Nagano Station, Iwata bought an evening newspaper and a tasteless lunchbox. He had appetite for neither. He boarded an old train, too ugly for vintage, bound for the mountains. At its own pace, the limited local express passed through green flatlands, then up forest ridges.

Through the window, Iwata observed mundane details of

mundane towns. A woman at a red light scratched her elbow. Schoolchildren painted over a graffitied wall. An old lady on a bench watched cellophane wrapping rolling past her in the breeze. A mistaken bee butted against the window of a closed pharmacy. A car alone in a rice paddy, its security alarm blinking needlessly.

A little before 5 p.m., Iwata arrived at his destination – a nothing town near Lake Nojiri. He got into the only taxi outside the station and asked for the Nakamura Institute. He passed derelict factories and long-failed businesses scheduled for demolition; the last remaining blots of the old way. The driver was listening to a radio report regarding a deepwater drilling conglomerate that had defrauded a mid-sized bank. His white-gloved hands hardly moved on the wheel.

Iwata looked up through the sunroof at the deepening dusk. In the distance, cranes were motionless, a profitable future waiting to be built. He made out a slogan:

CREATING TOMORROW TOGETHER

Iwata stopped at the only shop near the institute to buy fresh fruit and several pairs of thick socks. The old lady at the till smiled at him.

'Visiting?'

Iwata nodded and left. The path up to the institute was steep and long. Despite the chill, he was sweating by the time he reached the main entrance. The receptionist recognized Iwata and bowed. As she led him through the secured corridor, she looked down at the disinfected floor.

'I'm sorry to mention it, but it appears that you're seven weeks behind on your payments . . .'

'Forgive me, I must have made an awful miscalculation. I'll rectify this as soon as I get back to Tokyo.'

The nurse nodded apologetically.

'She's outside for sunset. Please go through.'

Iwata thanked her and stepped into a large, well-kept garden. Patients were planting flowers at the far end. Papier-mâché flamingos and elephants swayed in the breeze. Colourful pinwheels spun. From an open window, he heard a woman practising her vocal scales. At the other end of the garden, near the tree line, Iwata saw her. Cleo was lying on a sun bed, covered in a blanket.

The lights of the city are so pretty.

His stomach lurched as it always did when he saw her. It had always been this way, but it was a different kind of lurch these days.

I'm happy with you. Please let me hear.

He took a white plastic chair and sat down next to her. Cleo was Iwata's age, mid-thirties, her blonde hair recently cut into a rough, short bob. Her skin was paler than he remembered. Her dark blue eyes were fixed on the distance.

'Hello.' He spoke in English.

Birdsong fluttered through the dusky branches above them.

I walk and walk, swaying, like a small boat in your arms.

He reached out for her hand and gripped it sheepishly, his lips trembling. It was small, its warmth faded like a pebble plucked from the beach.

I'm happy with you. Please let me hear.

Realizing he must be hurting her, Iwata let it go.

'I bought you some fruit. Some socks, too. They always lose yours.'

She said nothing as he placed the bag beside her.

'I'll ask them to stitch your name in. They won't get mixed up that way.'

She still considered the horizon, as though she had decided to do only this for the rest of her life.

'You look strong, Cleo. You look . . . well.'

I'm happy with you. Please let me hear. Those words of love from you.

Iwata began to sob into his hands.

'You fucking bitch. You fucking bitch. You fucking bitch.'

It was after 1 a.m. when Iwata reached his apartment in Motoyoyogicho. In the corridor, he stepped over tricycles, bundles of newspapers and fallen mops. The microwave's clock bathed his apartment in weak green. Seeing his boxes heaped in the corner, he looked away. He would have to move them soon. But not tomorrow.

Iwata did his crunches while he watched an English-language TV show. The impossibly cheerful host congratulated her guests on their terrible pronunciation. The word of the day appeared on-screen in jaunty yellow letters:

UNEXPECTED

Iwata switched off the TV and laid out his cheap futon. He got in and opened the curtain a crack. Below him, Tokyo's neon aurora. Infinite function and enterprise, every square metre scheduled for expansion and redevelopment. The clouds were heavy and low, though he could not tell their colour. Trying not to think of Cleo, he closed his eyes. Iwata hoped for dreamlessness.

2. Hungry Work

'I'm just saying, in any other country in the world, four prime ministers in four years would be a crisis.'

'He hasn't gone yet.'

'Pah! It's just a matter of time. But the sad truth is, for Japan, it won't be a crisis. Just another resignation and the political automaton will rumble on, running on empty. And who is there to care about it?'

'You're talking about political apathy?'

'Exactly that. Voter turnout at the last election was less than 50 per cent. How are we ever going to change anything when half of Japan doesn't care?'

'But maybe there's just nothing to be done about it, apathy or no.'

As Iwata looked through the blinds at the murky dawn, he imagined volume dials on radios all over Tokyo being turned down. It wasn't that the hosts didn't raise the occasional interesting point, it was their self-satisfaction that irritated him. One was practically squealing now, enraged that the other disagreed – contractual though it was.

'How can they care? Take schoolkids. They are not taught to ask why, or to disagree, or to learn through debate. They get taught to sponge up and fit in. The ones that don't? Put them on the baseball team. Let them learn their place that way. Somewhere along the way, every other Japanese just learns to accept for the sake of accepting –'

Iwata switched stations to a local frequency.

'– time is 5 a.m. and if you're just tuning in, today's topic is Theta – the fastest-growing religious organization in Japan. Some call it a new and enriching way of life, while others say it's a money-making scam. Some even go so far as to describe it as a cult. What do you think?

Perhaps you have questions for today's panel? Call in now, we would love to hear –'

Iwata flipped stations until he stopped at rolling news.

'– specially designed blue LED lights were installed overnight above the platforms of dozens of Yamanote Line stations in Tokyo in an effort to combat ever-increasing rates of passenger suicide. While there is scant scientific evidence that blue lighting will reverse this worrying trend, many experts in colour therapy believe the colour blue may have a calming effect. Sumiko Shimosaka reports.'

The sound of a train's horn resounded, followed by the footfall of commuters and shrill service announcements. Iwata liked good production value.

'Japan's soaring rates of suicide have been exacerbated in recent years by the economic climate.' Shimosaka's voice was childlike but defiant. *'Tragically, this is an issue that has been seen time and again on the platforms of Tokyo's busy Yamanote Line. East Japan Rail Company's response to this? According to Professor Hiroyuki Harada of the National Research Institute, who was heavily involved in the project, the blue lights are associated with the sky and the ocean, giving those suffering with agitation a calming effect. But with little evidence behind them and coming at great cost, will they actually work? This morning I spoke to a spokesperson for East Japan Rail Company.'* The broadcast cut to the middle of an interview. *'Mr Tadokoro, the fact is, there is no evidence to suggest the lights will actually help. Given that the cost of this project is fifteen million yen, are you concerned that these blue lights will be seen as nothing more than a gimmick?'*

There was a ripple of embarrassed laughter. *'It's very simple. People are dying, and it is our responsibility to try to help. This is why the system has been rolled out across all twenty-nine stations on the Yamanote Line. And that's just the start. Fifteen million yen is a small price to pay if the situation can improve.'*

Shimosaka came back in. *'A company line confidently toed. But as the end of the financial year approaches, certain realities — and losses — will have to be confronted by Tokyoites. Perhaps it is no coincidence, then, that March is traditionally the peak month for suicide, or that 2011 is already predicted to be the fourteenth consecutive year to exceed thirty thousand suicides, according to preliminary figures from the National Police Agency. As for the blue lights, it remains to be seen what effect they will have on Tokyo's commuters. This is Sumiko Shimo-saka, reporting for —'*

Iwata turned the radio off. He showered, shaved quickly, then dressed in a dark suit. He looped an old black tie around his neck and left his apartment.

Cramming on to the 51 bus, Iwata spent the journey watching commuters play games on their phones. He got off one stop before Shibuya Station and passed a nameless canal which hid behind cramped, overpriced apartment blocks. In these backstreets, failing restaurants lived on the lonely lunch hours of salary men. Walls were latticed with graffiti and rotting billboards advertised vague concepts:

DVD

SET-MENU

REMEDY

Tokyo rain brought out the smell of sewage. Beyond that, there was only soy sauce and exhaust fumes.

Iwata emerged on to Meiji-Dori and Tokyo Metropolitan Police Department Shibuya HQ came into view. It was a fifteen-storey beige block built in a V-shape, looking more like the headquarters of an insurance multinational than a police station. Iwata crossed the rain-slick road with a volley of commuters and hurried up the steps to the main entrance.

Inside, expressionless Tokyoites sat blinking in the filthy

waiting area. Parents chewed their nails, young women denounced gropers, commuters reported stolen bicycles – the daily bread of the TMPD. Skipping the queue, Iwata approached the front desk and identified himself. A balding cop handed over a temporary pass.

'Elevators. Far end, up to the twelfth.'

The elevator was wall-to-wall with mugshots and missing persons. No music played. A large poster for tourists outlined the steps to follow when calling 110.

1. STATE WHAT HAPPENED.
   – 'THERE IS A ROBBER.' = 'DOROBO DESU.'
   – 'THERE WAS A TRAFFIC ACCIDENT.' = 'KOTSU JIKO DESU.'
2. STATE YOUR LOCATION.
3. STATE YOUR NAME & ADDRESS.

The doors slid open to a large open-plan office awash with loud telephone conversations and cigarette smoke. The halogen panels overhead gave faces an ugly pallor. A huge digitized map of Tokyo took up the entire back wall, lights flashing wherever there was an incident. The city was black, the lights were red. Beneath it, rows of monitors flickered green like tired eyes. Iwata could smell air freshener, a poor attempt at the kinmokusei flower which failed to hide the stench of sweat.

Everyone was working. In the centre of the room stood the only exception to this – a pack of men in poorly cut suits eyeballing crime scene photographs. The tallest one, hands in his pockets, puckered thick lips and snorted.

'Don't fucking lie to us, Horibe.' His voice was adenoidal and composed. 'Given half the chance, you still would.'

The others fell about laughing while Horibe feigned good

humour. Iwata left them behind and stopped at a door at the end of the office. Above it, the sign read:

SENIOR INSPECTOR ISAO SHINDO

He knocked firmly and entered. The office was a featureless cube, the window blinds were down. Shindo was a tall, balding man in his fifties. Clearly, he hadn't showered in several days, shaved in several weeks, nor seen a running track for several years. Iwata bowed before him and shifted a stack of papers from one of the guest seats. Shindo rubbed his long-broken nose as he inspected the new arrival. Iwata pretended not to notice, instead looking around the room.

There were no personal items here, no photographs, no awards, and no infantile drawings. Just filing cabinets, case documents and coffee stains. Iwata could respect that.

'So.' Shindo's voice was parched and tired. 'You're my new inspector?'

'Yes, sir.'

'*Iwata*, then?' He took out a personnel file and flipped through.

'That's right.'

'You studied in America?'

'Political Science at UCLA. Then Peace Officer Standards and Training at San Diego Miramar College.'

'That might be enough to be police in America. But what have you got that counts for something here?'

'Training and qualifications at National Police Agency in Fuchu.'

'No other studies in Japan?'

'After high school, no, sir. It should all be right there in the file.'

'I can read, Iwata. But right now we're talking.'

'Yes, sir.'

'Tell me something, do you consider yourself Japanese?'

'I was born here, sir. Same as my parents. My passport has a chrysanthemum flower on it, just like yours. I am Japanese, whatever I might consider myself to be or not.'

Shindo grunted and leant back in his chair. 'Actual police experience?'

'Four years. Chiba Prefectural Police. Chōshi PD.'

'The quiet life by the ocean, eh?'

'I was with Homicide for three years, sir.'

'And did you get any actual homicides? I'm not talking suicides or traffic here.'

'Several. Including the Lake Hinuma murders.'

'Oh, that was you?'

Iwata nodded.

'Yes, I think I remember reading about that, made one or two of the papers.' Shindo checked himself and leafed through to the end. 'And you've been signed off work for . . . fourteen months?'

'Yes, sir.'

'It's not my business but it's my business, you under-stand?'

Iwata nodded and Shindo flipped the file shut. He'd seen enough.

'Well, I have to ask. Are you sure you're ready for Tokyo? It takes a certain kind of cop to stomach Division One. This wouldn't just be *returning*, this would be like going up two or three levels, you get that?'

'I'm ready, sir. I assure you.'

Shindo drummed a silent tune on his lips.

'OK. I'm going to be honest with you. I'm not a fan of people transferring in here. Anyone who steps up to bat for Division One ought to *know* this pitch, not just have a good swing.' Shindo shrugged. 'But you have good studies. Good references from Chōshi PD. You speak English. You've cleared cases. Those things matter, I suppose.'

Iwata glanced at the tower of thick case files on the desk. Shindo had collected a roll of napkins in a Tupperware container. His only cutlery seemed to be a knife.

'All right, then,' Shindo said, mostly to himself. He picked up the phone. 'Sakai? Yeah, come through.' He hung up and sighed with what Iwata read as buyer's remorse.

There was a knock at the door and a woman in her late twenties entered. She wore a grey suit and a crisp white blouse. There was an empty beauty about her and her smile was indifferent. She was only a few inches shorter than Iwata and she wore a thin gold butterfly necklace. She bowed sharply but Shindo waved away the formality.

'Sit.'

As she sat, Iwata caught a snatch of her perfume. It contained no flowery notes, only function.

'Sakai, this is the newly appointed Inspector Iwata. He will lead this investigation and you will assist him. Welcome to Homicide, kids.'

She glanced sidelong at Iwata for a moment. If she was impressed, it didn't show.

'What about the Takara Matsuu case, sir?' Her voice was a surprising contralto.

'You've just graduated from Missing Persons. That creep will turn up in the mud sooner or later. Any other questions, Sakai?' Shindo's tone made it clear that the question was rhetorical.

'No, sir. Thank you for this opportunity.'

Shindo took a case file from the top of the pile. It was marked with a large, stark label:

Before passing it over, he aimed a rotten banana of a finger at them.

'Now I want you both to tread with care. This case belonged to Hideo Akashi until he threw himself off a fucking bridge four days ago. That man was an institution here, just so you know the size of the shoes you're trying to fill. Added to that, the Mina Fong thing has brought a fucking shit storm down on us. We're still playing this as accidental or suicide for now, she's an actress after all, but the press already smell bullshit. Anyway, to the matter at hand. Do your best but don't expect help from the other departments. The family were Korean, so not exactly front-page news. Especially not when a sex symbol turns up dead in her own apartment.'

He tossed the file across the desk and Iwata opened it. After a moment's reading, he looked up.

'The whole family?'

Shindo smiled worn teeth.

'Like I said, son. *Two or three levels.* Now get going. They were killed sometime over Valentine's night, so this case is already overripe.'

Iwata and Sakai both stood and bowed.

'We'll do our best, sir!' Sakai barked.

'Let's hope so.'

Sakai opened the door and led the way through the office without looking at her new partner. She marched confidently towards the elevator, ignoring what Iwata assumed were habitual glances from the desks. The group of men standing by the water cooler fell silent as she passed. A few paces ahead, an elastic band whistled past Iwata's ear and pinged off Sakai's back. She didn't slow her stride but Iwata saw her cheeks darken. He turned back to see the tallest of the men smile. His face was sallow, his buzz cut fresh and his dark lips wet. Seeing Iwata, a smile formed on his lips – presage or playfulness. Beneath the lips, canine teeth.

The Lord is my light and my salvation.
Whom shall I fear?

'You have a *real* productive day,' he called.

Iwata turned away.

Sakai was waiting for the elevator with folded arms. The doors slid open and Iwata followed her in. In the TMPD car park, Sakai approached the security booth, showed her badge and signed out a maroon-coloured Toyota Crown.

'It's in your name.' She slung Iwata the keys. 'So drive good.'

As he pulled out on to Meiji-Dori, rain engulfed them. Sakai pressed a button and the turret lights flooded the street with blue. The siren began to wail and traffic parted. Iwata headed west, towards Setagaya.

Though one of Tokyo's most populous wards, Setagaya was quiet today. Only the patter of raindrops through the zelkova leaves could be heard. The streets were empty from the downpour. In the distance, a slow train lumbered towards the city.

Iwata and Sakai got out of the car. The parking lot was an exposed, mostly empty space wedged in between the Tama River and a fringe of trees, which acted as the boundary to the university grounds. Zipping up her black raincoat, Sakai led the way down concrete steps that gave on to the edge of the river. Iwata paused.

'Sakai.'

'What is it?'

23

'There should already be police here to secure the area and canvass for witnesses. These cars should be checked out.'

'Yeah, well you heard what Shindo said about resources.'

Iwata took out his new notebook and jotted down the registration plates of the three vehicles. When he was finished, they followed the river south, its surface flecked with premature cherry blossoms. A few hundred metres up the path they came to a stairway that led up to a gated complex.

A miserable police officer huddled against the rain. White breath seeped out from under his hat.

'Sorry, no press.'

Sakai smiled tepidly and pulled out her police ID. The officer apologized, lifted the police tape and opened the gate for them. Inside, the housing complex was a muddy swamp of malachite puddles. Abandoned hardhats collected rainwater. Construction vehicles lay dormant. A large sign read:

VIVUS CONSTRUCTION – *THE GOOD LIFE*

Not much of the complex remained. Demolition work had claimed every home except for the one at the far end. Sakai swore as she crossed the sludge but refused to slow her pace.

'Come on,' she called over her shoulder. 'Don't dawdle.'

Except for its size, the Kaneshiro family house was an unremarkable two-storey concrete affair surrounded by a small partition the demolition company had provided. It was well maintained, with a garage and a small balcony on the upper floor. It might once have been a desirable address but its distance from the street and the looming wall of trees behind gave it a private solitude. All the curtains were drawn and all the windows closed. Except for one.

Two cops in high-vis raincoats stood under the awning, flipping through a lurid exposé of the Mina Fong death.

SUICIDE? SOMETHING MORE SINISTER?
SENSATIONAL DETAILS INSIDE!

The taller of the cops was skinny with no chin, while the shorter one had dyed orange hair and a mole just above his eyebrow. That mole cocked up now as he caught sight of Sakai.

'Who are you?'

Sakai held up her ID and checked her trousers for flecks of mud.

'Open the door,' she said flatly.

The chinless cop smirked and went back to his newspaper. Mole noticed this and reddened. He licked his lips before replying.

'You mean *you're* the investigators?'

Sakai looked up at Mole for the first time and at once he recognized his mistake.

'Do you think we're delivering pizza, asshole?'

'No, I just –'

'What's your name?'

'Hatanaka but –'

'Well, Hatanaka, I asked you to open the door but for some reason, we still seem to be having a conversation about this. So I'm going to threaten you. But I want to be very clear here. My threat doesn't entail protocol. It entails your disgusting fat ass, a roomful of bull queers and adult nappies for the foreseeable future. I hope you understand me because I doubt nappies come in your size.'

Hatanaka paled as he nodded. She turned to the taller one and slapped the newspaper from his hands.

'Now *you* will have the parking lot secured and have learned the names of the car-owners by the time I'm done in here or I'll fucking paralyse you. I know a lot of bad men who'll take a lump hammer to your spine for my pretty please with sugar on top. Do we understand each other?'

Both men bowed sharply.

'Peachy. Thank you, officers. Now fuck off.'

Chinless immediately hurried towards the lot as he fumbled with his radio while Hatanaka fished out the house keys from his pocket. Iwata bit the insides of his cheeks to suppress his smile and pointed to the front door.

'Was this locked on discovery?'

'Yes, sir.'

'Who found the bodies?'

'The wife's mother.'

'Where are the bodies now?'

'With the Medical Examiner's Office, sir.'

Hatanaka unlocked the door and Sakai stepped in without hesitation, following the safe path marked out by blue tape on the floor. The smell of incense wafted out after her, faint at first, then the earthy tang overcame Iwata, as though he had ripped up a clump of forest moss and pressed his face into that secret smell beneath.

I'm happy with you. Please let me hear.

'Inspector?' Hatanaka was frowning uncertainly.

'What?'

'I asked if there's anything else you need from me.'

Iwata cleared his throat and gathered his thoughts. 'First, you'll give me your number. Then I need you to canvass the local area thoroughly. I want to know if this family had any feuds, any debts, any enemies, anything at all like that. And don't forget to look for passion as a motive. These murders happened on Valentine's night. Affairs, old flames, you know what I'm saying.'

'Yes, sir.' Hatanaka wrote his number on a piece of paper, bowed and closed the door behind him. The hallway was gloomy and silent. The genkan was packed with shoes. Photographs hung on the walls. A normal family home.

He is happiest, be he king or peasant, who finds peace in his home.

Iwata stood in the hallway next to Sakai, who was flipping through the case file.

'Ready?' she asked.

'Ready.'

'OK, then. Fred Flintstone was found upstairs in the master bedroom. Everyone else was found in there.' She nodded towards the lounge.

'Hatanaka confirms the front door was locked.'

'So maybe the killer had a key. Or maybe he knows them.'

'But the upstairs window is open and the file says no prints were found on the front door.'

'He's a glove-owner, then. Hey, look at that, our first lead. Now, shall we?'

'Yes, ma'am.'

'Ladies first.' She held open the lounge door.

He closed his eyes for a moment, took a breath, and entered.

I walk and walk, swaying, like a small boat in your arms.

The room was lit by powerful lamps. The bodies of the family were no longer present but a sticky stench lingered in the air. Iwata knew it by heart. Carbohydrates, proteins and fatty acids broken down by microbes. Gases emitted by dead bodies. Connective tissues broken down and, as the phases of decomposition shifted, intestines starting to liquefy. The daily bread of Division One.

'Lovely blood spatter.' Sakai nodded at the red mountain range on the wall. 'I mean is this guy a regular Picasso, or what?'

'You mean Pollock.'

'Who?'

'Never mind.'

Iwata stepped over blood-soaked homework. On the front cover of a *Good Housekeeping* magazine, a fleck of gore had landed on the smiling model's nose. A small bonsai tree had shed its leaves and was slowly dying on the windowsill. Sakai pointed to the three distinct lakes of dark blood on the carpet.

'Meet Wilma, Bamm-Bamm and Pebbles.'

Sakai passed him several photographs from the case file. The mother lay spreadeagled in the centre of the room, disembowelled, her throat slashed. Her teenage son had died against the wall, a deep wound to his oblique abdominals, his right eye socket destroyed. Lastly, in the corner, the young girl had been murdered. Her shoulders were hunched, as if mystified by death.

The lights of the city are so pretty.

'This is how it plays out.' Sakai cracked her knuckles. 'The killer threatens the children, the mother doesn't resist. She's killed there and then. The son jumps up in her defence. He's a big boy, strong, probably throws a few punches. This is why his first stab wound is a defensive blow. Lastly, the child has its throat cut. She's cowering the whole time.'

Iwata nodded. Dead children and rotting flesh were all part of the job, no different from waiting at red lights and filing reports.

'You have a good eye, Sakai.'

She ignored the compliment and scanned the case file.

'Picasso didn't leave a single print behind here, either.'

'Let's move on.'

They searched the ground floor, finding nothing out of place. When they were done, Sakai led the way upstairs. On the landing, they paused at the bathroom door. Above the toilet, the window was open, a cold wind whispering in. Iwata

pulled down the toilet seat to reveal part of a muddy footprint.

'This isn't in the file, is it?'

Sakai shrugged.

'At least now we know how he got in.'

They returned to the hallway and checked the children's
bedrooms. There was nothing in the file relating to either
room and they noticed nothing out of the ordinary. They
cleared the balcony and then the garage downstairs. The
Kaneshiros seemingly owned no car, despite some grease
stains and an old bottle of antifreeze.

'Where's the car?' Sakai asked.

'Hasn't been in the garage for a long time.'

'They sold it?'

'One second.' Iwata dialled Hatanaka. 'Yeah, it's me again.
One more thing, I need you to check on a family car registered to the Kaneshiros. If their money situation wasn't
great, they might have sold up. Or it could have been reported
stolen. When you find out, let me know.'

Iwata hung up and Sakai winked at him.

'Good thinking.'

'What's left?' he asked.

'Just the study and the master bedroom.'

'OK, in that order, then.'

They returned upstairs. The door to the study was wide
open. The family PC was still on and a tub of mint ice cream,
now melted, had been left by the keyboard.

'Strange,' Iwata said quietly.

'Could be him. Murder is hungry work.'

'No spoon.'

Sakai passed him the case file, sat down at the computer
and snapped on a rubber glove. She opened up the internet
search history.

'Look at that.' She scratched her head. 'The guy spent hours online.'

'Definitely him?'

'It's well after the family's time of death. He looked up theatre groups, baseball news and eventually got round to searching for flights to Korea. Nothing in the file about computer records, but I'm sure we could have the tech boys spend twenty minutes on this.'

Iwata shook his head.

'This makes no sense, Sakai. He kills an entire family without leaving a single print or clue but then gives us his browsing history?'

'You're saying you think he did this deliberately?'

Iwata shrugged.

'Everything else was done in such a fashion.'

Sakai mulled this over.

'Could be. This Picasso is too clever for his own good, then.'

Iwata flipped through the pages of the case file.

'Sakai, doesn't this file seem a little slim to you? A little vague?'

'Not surprising, given the circumstances surrounding Inspector Akashi. Come on, one room left.'

They left the study and stopped at the blood spatter outside the master bedroom.

'OK.' Sakai pointed at the bedroom door. 'So Fred is in bed, feeling unwell or whatever. He hears something coming from the bathroom but he comes out to check. Why does he come out to check? Why not assume it's just his wife having a crap?'

'Maybe the noise is very loud. The footprint was scuffed, right? Maybe the killer slipped and fell.'

'Yeah that makes sense. Either way, he comes out, sees

Picasso and they clash. The killer debilitates him, the main threat is neutralized and then our guy is free to work the others.'

Iwata hunched down over the blood pool.

'The father *was* badly injured, but we know he died in the bedroom.'

'So?'

'If he was still conscious out here, he might have heard his family being killed downstairs.'

'God, I love my job.' Sakai scratched her nose. 'You ready?'

Iwata nodded. She opened the door to the master bedroom and there was the blood of Tsunemasa Kaneshiro.

The lights of the city are so pretty.

Iwata knew the practicalities of murder. And he knew the practicalities of death. The father would take ninety minutes to cremate. His son, Seiji, roughly the same. His wife, Takako, would take forty-five minutes. His six-year-old child, Hana, a little over twenty minutes. An afternoon's work for somebody.

Iwata saw a sunset over cliffs. He saw rocks below. He staggered for a moment.

I'm happy with you. Please let me hear.

'Iwata, you OK?'

'Fine.' He was in control again. 'We need light.'

Sakai peered at the pond of blood on the bed. Iwata opened the curtains, bathing the room in harsh light.

That's when he saw it.

Sakai hadn't yet noticed. She was absorbed in a photograph of the dead father.

'Clearly, this was the most brutal killing. Stab wounds everywhere, additional to the first attack sustained in the hallway. I'm guessing Fred was Picasso's muse.'

In the photograph, a large hole gaped open beneath Mr Kaneshiro's ribs.

'He took his heart,' Iwata whispered to himself, still look-ing up at the ceiling. 'These killings were ritualistic, Sakai. Taking the heart *meant* something. See how he only took the father's? The rest he left alone.'

'Ritualistic? Isn't that a bit much? Maybe the killer was after money or revenge. Or we're just talking about a psycho who sees an open window and goes from there. You're not saying anything; what is it?'

Iwata pointed up to the ceiling in reply. Sakai covered her mouth.

'Oh my fucking God.'

There, in sooty smudges, was a jagged black sun.

3. I Am Here

Doutor café was packed with the lunchtime crowd. Gossiping housewives gasped behind the rims of their coffee cups and salary men sitting alone absently chewed on doughnuts. Sakai was shaking her head as she sipped her hot chocolate. Printouts of the internet search history from the Kaneshiros' family PC were splayed on the table between them.

'Just because he didn't book the flights there and then at the house, doesn't mean he didn't do it later. Or maybe he did it over the phone. Do you really think that this asshole is going to go to the trouble of looking up flights to Seoul for twenty minutes if he's not going to go?'

'I do think so, yes.' Iwata was biting a nail, tapping his foot and peering at the sketch of the black sun that he had made.

'Why?'

'Maybe he knows that if we're given a logical line of inquiry, we'll usually take it.'

Sakai laughed.

'You *have* been a cop before, then.'

'Reserving a flight from the Kaneshiro computer would have meant giving away his name. And that's a death sentence.'

She licked chocolate from her upper lip.

'Maybe he wasn't thinking straight after slaughtering a whole family? Maybe he pulled out because he got spooked?'

Now Iwata shook his head.

'He killed the family around 10 p.m., and by 8 a.m. he had eaten the food from their refrigerator, filled out the sudoku

33

in their newspaper, listened to their CDs and looked up flights to Korea on their computer. You think a guy that can stab a child to death and take a man's heart out is going to spook at a slamming door?'

Sakai pondered this then gestured for another hot chocolate. Iwata shook his head.

'Maybe the grandmother's incessant phone calls freaked him out,' she said.

'Could be. But think about it, he left in broad daylight. He was comfortable enough to know that if he was seen, he wouldn't be recognized.'

'Look, all I'm saying, just because he wore a pair of gloves and drew some symbol on the ceiling, doesn't make him a genius.'

Her chocolate arrived and she snapped some butter biscuits into the cup.

'Your teeth will fall out, Sakai.'

She narrowed her eyes in spiteful pleasure as she drank. 'So go on, why is he such a sharp tack?'

'Statistically speaking, the evil genius is essentially one in a million. But there is a chance he'll be above average intelligence, yes.'

'Well, fuck him. Your brain doesn't seem defective and I'm bright as a button.'

'It's not his IQ that worries me, Sakai. What's troubling is that, so far as I can make out, he hasn't left behind a single worthwhile clue. Obsession, meticulous planning and a cold-blooded readiness to act on his fantasy – whatever the collateral. He has the makings of an organized serial killer.'

'*Serial killer!* And how do you know he's one of those? Aside from the family, I mean.'

'The FBI definition is a killer with four or more victims. He already qualifies.'

'You were in the FBI?'

'No, that's just a standard definition. You learn them in police training over there.'

'Why are you so sure he's not finished?'

'The symbol. He didn't just put it there for fun. It means something. It represents his work, or his world, or his manifesto. You call him Picasso. If an artist signs his painting, it isn't because he's only going to paint once.'

'All right, so what does the symbol mean?'

'No idea, but I know what it's saying to us.'

'And what's that?'

'*I am here. I am not finished.*'

Sakai downed her chocolate then used her spoon to fish out the last crumbs from the cup. Iwata finished his coffee and paid the bill, making sure to keep the receipt for his expenses. He hoped he could claim the money back soon. Outside, the drizzle had thinned, but Sakai still hurried to the car. Iwata pulled away and headed for the Medical Examiner's Office. He guided them up to the expressway as Sakai went through the case file again. After a few minutes, her phone began to ring and she answered without greeting.

'All right, thank you.' She snapped her phone shut and shook her head. 'That was the Ninth Floor. They're saying it'll be impossible to lift DNA from the ice cream. And the footprint from the bathroom was too vague to show much. One thing it does reveal, however, is that the killer has big feet. Twenty-eight centimetres.'

Iwata looked at her.

'*Twenty-eight?*'

'Seems we're looking for a giant.' She grinned.

Tokyo's Medical Examiner's Office was one of the largest buildings in Bunkyō, a large, white L-shaped structure that cast shadow over a children's playground across the street. In the lobby, proud statistics were displayed on the walls.

EACH YEAR, WE RECEIVE 20% OF TOKYO'S DEAD WE PERFORM OVER 13,000 MEDICAL EXAMINATIONS WE CONDUCT OVER 2,650 AUTOPSIES

Iwata knew that this morning, it had already conducted four.

At the reception desk, Sakai showed her badge and they were buzzed through the security doors. They took the elevator down to the basement and the doors slid open to reveal a short, middle-aged woman in a lab coat. Her hair was pulled back in a ponytail, she had written reminders on the back of both hands and the tips of her fingers were yellow from tobacco. She was whistling 'Greensleeves'.

'I'm Doctor Eguchi. You're here for the family, yes?' She had a smoker's voice.

'Right, I'm Sakai and this is Iwata.'

'You're early. Those that come down here are usually late.'

The detectives looked at each other.

'Never mind,' Eguchi said. 'Pathologist humour.'

She led the way.

'It's been three or four days, I was beginning to think nobody was coming for the bodies.'

'There's been a hold-up due to a change in TMPD personnel.'

Eguchi hoisted an eyebrow but said nothing.

She led them into a large and gleaming dissection room with beige walls and five metallic tables.

The lights of the city are so pretty.

The halogen strip lights flickered into life. The autopsy room was starkly lit now and every surface was spotless stainless steel. Four of the autopsy tables were occupied by the bodies of the Kaneshiro family.

'Well,' Eguchi said, 'I think we can safely list this one as multiple homicide. All of them stabbed to death. Some more thoroughly than others.'

She glanced up, smiling hopefully.

'Your predecessor had more of a sense of humour.'

Eguchi gestured towards Tsunemasa and Seiji Kaneshiro, as though she were indicating the power outlets in an apartment she was letting.

'The father and the son both struggled with the aggressor, though neither drew blood; nothing under the nails.'

The father and the son looked much alike, though the former had sustained far more severe punishment. He had been slit open like a fish. His heart had been accessed through a massive slash under his lower rib. His eyelids were torn. Cream-coloured fragments of skull jutted through his forehead.

'The wounds show that the killer is left-handed. Also, given the damage to the underlying bone and the manner in which the heart was removed, your killer is, I'd guess, extremely strong.'

Eguchi swept a hand towards the mother and the girl, clearly less interested.

'None of the victims were interfered with sexually, I should add.'

The girl's lashes were long, her mouth open, her cheeks a waxen yellow now. Beneath her small chin, a long, deep cut ran across her throat, curved like a cat's smile.

'Doctor, any information on the murder weapon?' Iwata asked, looking away from the child's still, white shell.

Eguchi smiled enigmatically.

'That's the interesting point, Inspector. We can normally

have a good guess at the exact kind of blade, model of knife and what have you. Each knife or scalpel leaves behind telltale signatures or imperfections.'

'But that's not the case here?'

'We have extensive records but, to be honest, this family was killed with something I've never seen before.'

'Sorry, Doctor. What exactly do you mean?'

'I mean that they were all stabbed to death. But not with any knife on sale in Japan. The cuts are too perfect, too *sharp*.'

'You think it could be some kind of scalpel?' Iwata asked.

'These wounds are simply too large for a scalpel. These are more consistent with a machete of some kind. Perhaps a small sword.'

Iwata and Sakai looked at each other. The doctor continued as Sakai began to scribble down notes.

'The results of the tests on the blood, urine and gastric contents will be ready tomorrow morning. All the bodies had traces of some kind of black soot on them, too. The father had the most; he actually had it on the forefinger of his left hand, though he was right handed. Perhaps he was forced to touch it.'

'The black sun,' Iwata whispered to himself. 'Kaneshiro was forced to make the symbol.'

Doctor Eguchi led them out of the room again.

'Now, how to put this delicately. The bodies –'

'The grandmother is handling the arrangements,' Sakai said. 'The bodies should be removed by tomorrow afternoon.'

'All right. We open at 8.30 a.m. tomorrow morning; I'll have the results for you by then.'

'This is my number.' Iwata tore out a page from his notebook and handed it across.

The detectives both bowed and made their way out of the building. As they got into the car, Sakai's phone rang.

'Oh it's you . . . Yeah? That's good. And have you got a name?' She clutched the phone with her shoulder and jotted something down. 'OK, what else have you got for me? 2010? All right, good. And what about your boyfriend, did he get those registration plates from the car park? Yeah, well that doesn't interest me. Look, it's now two o'clock. I'm going to call again at five and I want those names. Your friend is off the hook. You've just inherited his little errand. Do you understand?'

Iwata caught a smile of pleasure sail across Sakai's lips.

'Oh, and Hatanaka? You remember what I said before? Just keep in mind that I'm a woman of my word.'

She hung up.

'That was that asshole cop with the mole.'

'Hatanaka.'

'That's the one. Two things. Firstly, the family did have a car. Honda Odyssey 2010. No info on a sale or theft, though.'

'Well, whoever has that car now is worth speaking to.'

'I think so too. Second thing, Hatanaka got a name from the locals.' She held up her notepad.

'Kodai Kiyota?' Iwata read out loud.

'Neighbours say it was well known that he had bad blood with the family. Apparently he has links to the development company doing the demolition around the Kaneshiro house.'

'He wanted them out; they wouldn't go?'

'Very possible.' She shrugged. 'But get this, the guy has past links to the yakuza as an enforcer. And not only that, but his police records show he's one metre eighty-eight.'

'Then I want this guy found, Sakai. I'm going to drop you at Setagaya PD. You find him, you call me.'

'Where are you going?'

'The father worked at a call centre in Keiō-Tamagawa and the mother worked at a nearby university. I'm going to talk to colleagues, see if I can find out anything.'

Sakai yawned and looked at Iwata now.

'So where are you from?' she asked.

'Miyama. Out in the sticks. Not too far from Kyoto.'

'I heard you were American.'

'I spent some time there when I was young, that's all. College. What about you?'

'Kanazawa.'

Iwata laughed.

'That's funny to you?'

'No, I just didn't exactly picture you wandering over Flower-viewing Bridge in Kenroku-en garden. Is that where you're from, then?'

'I just got my badge there.'

Iwata glanced at her. She seemed to bite her tongue and looked out of the window. Cheap chain hotels and anonymous corporations flanked the grey of the expressway. Love hotels stacked behind the road, overpriced apartment blocks stained with years of exhaust.

I'm happy with you.

'Who was that this morning? On the way to the elevators,' Iwata asked.

'Who?' she said distantly, still looking out of the window.

'The one that flicked the elastic band at you.'

She turned to face him now. Her eyes searched his for a moment before she answered.

'His name is Moroto.'

'What's his deal?'

'Moroto is . . . look, just avoid him.'

Seeing the green sign for Central Setagaya, Iwata turned off the expressway.

'Well, first impressions and all that, but seems to me that Moroto is an asshole.'

She looked back out of the window.

'You know, Iwata, for a Kansai region guy, you're not such a prick.'

They smiled at each other for the first time and the rest of the journey to Setagaya Police Station passed in silence.

Happy Cloud Communications was on the second floor of a squat building in the shadow of the multistorey car park. Iwata walked alone, passing a Korean restaurant and a tiny dental clinic, until he found the side entrance. He pressed the buzzer and an overweight man in a dirty cardigan opened the door. Iwata showed him his police ID.

'Ah, you must be here about Kaneshiro?'

Iwata nodded.

'I'm Niwa, the manager. I'll show you his desk.'

Iwata followed him into a windowless room with yellow walls and plastic pot plants. Around thirty employees were sitting at their terminals, all locked into bright telephone conversations. A young man with long hair and a soft face looked up at Iwata, and then away sharply. He stood and left the room.

'Did Mr Kaneshiro have any problems here, Mr Niwa?'

Niwa chortled over his dandruff-laden shoulder.

'Problems? The guy hardly said a word to anyone. He just did the IT stuff for me. He had little contact with the employees. Maybe a "hello" in the mornings, and a "goodnight" in the evenings but not much more than that. This was his office.'

Niwa knocked on the door ironically.

'No one's in.'

'You can leave me here, Mr Niwa.'

Iwata made a few mental notes as he looked around the cramped office. It was set back from the main room and shared a side door with Niwa's office. The blinds were drawn on the window, which gave out on to the back alley below. Iwata saw only litter, a skulking cat and, for some reason, a dirty old megaphone on the floor.

Iwata snapped on a glove and unlocked Kaneshiro's computer. He spent some twenty minutes going through the man's emails but could find nothing even remotely connected to a dispute of any kind, much less a family homicide. He searched through the hard drive and found only work. Iwata locked the computer again, noticing the family photograph on the desk. Four smiles in a sunset, a picnic devoured.

Please let me hear.

Iwata checked the drawers of the desk but found nothing interesting. On the floor beneath the swivel chair there was some old, faded blood spatter.

Maybe a nosebleed. Maybe something else?

The hook on the back of the door supported a single raincoat but its pockets were empty. On the wall there was a small calendar from the nearby Korean restaurant. Iwata flipped through the weeks, seeing nothing but perfunctory appointments, school meetings and family engagements. He got back to the beginning of the year before he saw something that stood out. On 4 January, Kaneshiro had an hour after work blocked out with the note *Meet I.*

Iwata left Kaneshiro's office, thanked Niwa and left the call centre. He stopped at the 7-Eleven across the road and bought two rice balls and a banana jelly drink. He returned to the Toyota, devoured his food, then called Sakai.

'Yes?' Her voice was impatient.

'Sakai, it's me. I'm at the father's office. Listen, it's probably nothing but I need you to look into something.'

'One second.' He heard her shuffling through her bag. 'OK.'

'On the fourth of January of this year, Tsunemasa Kaneshiro met someone called "I".'

'That's it?'

'Kiyota is a good bet for the murders, but I want more than one horse in this race. You keep Hatanaka out there knocking on doors. If anything for "I" comes up, you call me.'

Sakai sighed.

'Speaking of Kiyota, no location on him so far – he seems to have dropped off the map. But you'll like this more. He has convictions for violent crime relating to yakuza enforcement. And not just that. He's also got links to Nippon Kumiai. Heard of it?'

'Some kind of nationalist party.'

'Right. Looks like Kiyota wanted to fashion himself a career in activism. Oh, and I almost forgot. One of the Vivus construction workers says he saw a man near the house on the morning after the murders. A man with a limp who seemed to be talking to himself.'

'OK that's good. Listen, I need something else. I need you to get permission to access Mr Kaneshiro's bank account from the start of the year. There's nothing on this in the case file, which is surprising. Anyway, anything out of place, you call me.'

'What I said about you not being a prick? I spoke too soon.'

'I'll meet you at Setagaya in about an hour.'

Iwata hung up.

He was about to pull away when someone knocked on the window, making him flinch. The long-haired employee from the call centre was standing there. Iwata wound down the window.

'Yes?'

'Are you police? Here about Tsunemasa Kaneshiro?'

Iwata nodded.

The young man looked up and down the street.

'Niwa told you there were no problems at work, didn't he?'

'Why do you ask?'

'There was a girl . . . *young* . . . I don't know her name. But she had a grudge against Kaneshiro. She stood outside his office for hours at a time, screaming obscenities over a megaphone. *Screaming*. "Cockroaches. Cockroaches. Kill the cockroaches."'

'Why?'

'She knew Kaneshiro was Korean. It was mostly racist stuff. Honestly, I don't think I've ever seen someone . . . so angry. The police were called a couple of times but she always came back. And then a few weeks ago, Niwa ordered Kaneshiro to go down and deal with the girl once and for all. He came back a few minutes later with a big gash on his arm.'

'You said she looked young?'

'No more than eighteen. Sixteen, I'd say. Around one hundred and fifty-two centimetres. Dyed hair.'

'Name and number, please.' Iwata tore out a page from his notebook. 'I may be in touch.'

The man wrote down his details quickly, looking up and down the street again.

'Kaneshiro was a good man.' He passed over the scrap of paper. Then he was gone.

4. Irises

Iwata parked near the old Olympic stadium and headed towards the main campus of Komazawa University. It was 3.30 p.m. At the entrance, an old stone carving with the university's name dated back to the 1590s. The motto ran beneath:

TRUTH. SINCERITY. RESPECT. LOVE.

The rugby team was out training on the playing fields, the university mascot, a magpie, emblazoned on their chests.

One for sorrow.

At the main reception, Iwata explained that he was investigating the murder of Mrs Takako Kaneshiro. The receptionist immediately sent for the facilities manager. It took only a few moments for an elderly, pudgy man in a worker's uniform to appear. Iwata held up his police ID and the man bowed deeply.

'I'm the manager, how can I help, Inspector?'

'Mrs Kaneshiro worked for you, correct?'

'That's right, she was a cleaner. Mainly in Radiological Sciences and Business Administration.'

'Did she have a work station?'

'No, sir. Just a locker.'

'Please show me.'

The manager led Iwata along the polished corridors, descending several levels to the employees' changing rooms. At the back of the dingy room used by the female workers, he pointed to the locker with wreathes of flowers beneath it.

Two for joy.

It was secured with a large padlock, twice the size of all the others.

'Did Takako ever have any problems here?'

'No, sir. She was a model employee, never late or sick. A wonderful worker and a wonderful person. What happened is . . . awful.'

'Sir, forgive me. If she had no problems here, do you mind telling me why she had such a large padlock?'

'Well, there was an . . . incident at the beginning of the year. Takako complained that her locker had been broken into.'

Pipes shuddered and groaned above them.

'What was taken?'

'That was the strange thing – only her worker's uniform. It made no sense; those are issued by the university. It's just a cheap uniform. Replacements are frequently given.'

'Takako had no enemies, then, that you can think of?'

'She was a quiet woman. I can't imagine her having enemies. Who could hate such a person?'

'Do you have a key for this locker?'

'Just one moment.'

He rustled through a large ring of keys until he found the duplicate and unhooked it. Iwata unlocked the padlock and the door creaked open. The locker was empty.

Three for a girl.

Four for a boy.

'You said Mrs Kaneshiro had the theft problem at the beginning of the year, correct?'

'That's right.'

'Would you be able to tell me exactly when?'

46

'I have records in my office.'

He led Iwata along an unlit corridor that reeked of disinfectant. There was a soft scuttling in the darkness. The office held little more than a desk, a chair and some shelves packed with binders. The manager grunted as he reached for the right folder.

'Here we are.'

He unclipped a page dated January 2011. Iwata could see the heading:

TAKAKO KANESHIRO COMPLAINT OF THEFT FROM LOCKER

Iwata noted down the date.

'Were the authorities called?'

'No, sir. It was dealt with internally.'

'Did you discover who was responsible?'

'A young Iranian woman who worked with us for a short time was dismissed.'

'She admitted to the theft?'

The manager laughed uneasily.

'The process was rather more . . . informal, Inspector.'

'She lost her job *informally*?'

'Several of her fellow employees voiced their concerns about her trustworthiness and the woman in question made no fuss.'

Iwata nodded.

'An Iranian immigrant would be unlikely to, don't you think?'

The manager turned red.

'Inspector, I assure you that –'

Iwata waved the protest away.

'What was her name? That's all I want.'

'Saman Gilani, I'm not sure if that's the correct pronunciation.'

Iwata ran his finger along the page, scanning the characters mentally.

'Do you have any employees here with criminal records?'

The older man thought about this.

'It's quite possible, I suppose. However, I deal only in low-level workers, you understand. We don't have those kind of checks in place any more. Everything is outsourced now.'

'All right. Well, thank you very much for your time here.'

The older man bowed and showed him out of the office. Iwata walked alone through the dark corridor, the scuttling gone now, the shuddering squeals of the pipes and gasps of steam replacing it.

At the bottom of the stairwell, Iwata dialled Sakai.

'What now?' she huffed.

'I think I might have found a couple more horses. Are you at a terminal?'

'Yep, give me a name.'

'First of all, Saman Gilani, though I'm not hopeful.'

Iwata spelled the name out and there was a pause.

Five for silver.

'OK. Iranian national. She was deported a couple of weeks ago. She arrived after the employment treaty in the nineties and seemingly never went back. Has a child with a Japanese citizen. Looks like the kid ended up in care. But what's she got to do with this?'

'Nothing. Now cross-reference the next search with the criminal records database. Any current employee of Komazawa University.'

Iwata heard her fingers run over the keyboard, then a clucking sound from her tongue.

'OK, two hits. First up we've got a guy with several delinquency charges some ten years ago, nothing on him since then except parking fines. Then we have Masaharu Ezawa. Hm, he's got a nice spread of sexual harassment, peeping in female toilets and theft of underwear. No address on him for the last three years –'

Six for gold.

Iwata was already sprinting back towards the manager's office. He ripped open the door and the old man flinched.

'Masaharu Ezawa, he works here?'

'Y-yes.'

'Address?'

'Well, yes, but –'

'I need it *now.*'

He opened a plastic wallet and then passed over a single-sheet file. It outlined Masaharu Ezawa's address, national insurance number and shift timetable. Iwata looked up.

'He's on shift now?'

The manager nodded, a worried expression on his face.

'Take me.'

Moving faster than he had for many years, the older man hurried up to street level with Iwata cursing him forward. They cut across lawns and through buildings until he pointed. His finger was aimed through a bank of trees, to a crouching man. In a quiet corner, Masaharu Ezawa was slowly and diligently tending to a strip of irises.

Seeing them, Ezawa stood. He was a short man with a long, feminine mop of thin hair hiding one eye. His worker's uniform hung off him like a child wearing his father's clothes. His lips were full, his teeth were small and his nose was puglike. He looked like a boy put to work on a man's job.

Iwata gestured for the manager to leave them.

'Mr Ezawa.'

'Who are you?' His voice was soft but strained.

Iwata took out his badge in reply and Ezawa immediately looked down at the flowers.

'Oh.'

Three paces from him, Iwata looked down to put his ID away. As he looked up, he caught only a snatch of Ezawa's hand in his pocket.

'Hey, come on –'

A muddy rock hit Iwata's face. Staggering back, he tried to claw soil from his eyes. Snarling, Ezawa crashed down his trowel on Iwata's skull.

'Fuck!'

Ezawa was already running, running as fast as he was able, but something was wrong. His stride was pathetic, his ankles at odds. Iwata was on his feet now – swearing and bleeding but closing on Ezawa's weak, limping stride.

'Stop!'

Ezawa glanced over his shoulder, his face desperate.

Iwata's body tackle was hard.

Seven for a secret, never to be told.

On the seventh floor of Setagaya Police Station, Iwata sat across from the interview rooms pressing a bandage to his scalp. Through the two-way mirror he watched Ezawa, who was sitting alone at a metallic table.

'You need to change that bandage.' Sakai sat next to Iwata and handed him a vending machine coffee.

'I'm fine. This coffee is more dangerous than he is.'

'An arrest and a beating from a midget on your first day – that has to be a record.'

'Go home, Sakai.'

She laughed softly into her coffee.

'I've got some news that will cheer you up, though.'

'Really?'

'You don't sound convinced.'

Iwata rested his head on the wall behind him, closing his eyes.

'Occupational hazard. Did you pick up Kiyota?'

'No, but that note from Kaneshiro's calendar? Well, it turns out we might have an "I". Guy by the name of Ijiri – moneylender in the local area.'

'He lent to Mr Kaneshiro?'

'Well, the guy won't speak to us. So I brought him in for refusing to cooperate.'

Sakai gestured to the second interview room with her plastic cup. A large man with a beard and a red suit was pacing the room, smoking impatiently.

'He looks like a real charmer.'

'I like a man with panache. Shall we?'

Iwata groaned. Sakai slung her coffee in the wastebasket and stood. She nodded to the guard and the door opened. Iwata watched as she sailed in, her white blouse the only clean thing in there. He saw Ijiri's face twist into a smile as he registered the woman before him.

'You're in for a real surprise,' Iwata whispered.

He closed his eyes and tried to wait out the throbbing pain screaming inside his skull. Iwata looked into his cup of coffee and saw his face in the black circle.

'Fuck it.'

He threw the cup and the yellow-red bandage into the wastebasket, then nodded to the guard outside Ezawa's interview room. The door clunked open and heat hit Iwata in the face. Ezawa did not look up. He was hugging his own shoulders, a sad mime in a cell. He rocked slightly back and forth in his chair.

Iwata turned on the tape, reeled off his name, the date and the name of the interview subject. He sat down before Ezawa and spread his hands on the table. He said nothing for a while, the only noise in the room the fleshy sound of Ezawa chewing his lips.

'Coffee?'

Ezawa shook his head.

'Smoke?'

Another shake.

'OK, Mr Ezawa, I need to ask you some questions and I need you to be honest with me. It's very important, do you understand?'

Ezawa kept his eyes on the table.

'I understand.'

Iwata nodded.

'All right, good. Now, I'd like you to help me understand why you ran from me earlier. Did you just panic?'

Ezawa looked up.

'I don't know you.'

'You saw my badge.'

'Not properly. I was scared.'

'Why?'

'I don't know.'

Iwata sat back in his seat now and pinched the bridge of his nose.

'You've been in trouble in the past, haven't you?'

Ezawa flinched, breathing hard through his nose – the face of a scolded boy.

'Yesss. But that isn't –'

'Ezawa, you ran because you thought I was coming to arrest you.'

'I haven't done anything wrong.'

Iwata's head throbbed.

'You knew Takako Kaneshiro, didn't you?'

Ezawa looked away now, as though Iwata had placed a rotten fruit on the table before him by mentioning her name.

'Everyone knew her.'

'You know what happened to her.'

He nodded.

'But despite this, you saw a policeman and you assumed I was coming to arrest *you*.'

There was no reply.

'Ezawa, you realize that doesn't look good.'

A shrug.

'Tell me, does your manager know about your past?'

Ezawa chewed his lips furiously now, shaking his head.

'OK, so tell me something else. Did you know the Iranian woman, Saman Gilani?'

'. . . Not really.'

'She has a child, you know.'

Ezawa looked away.

'She lost her job. Without work, she was deported. Her child is still here, in care. Think of what growing up without a mother does to a child. Do you understand?'

Ezawa was rocking again, harder now.

Iwata smacked the table hard with his palm.

'Answer me, Ezawa. Do you understand what you've done to this child? Tell me why the Iranian woman lost her job.'

'I don't know.'

'Don't lie to me. Not to *me*. Now you tell me why she lost her job.'

'For stealing,' he whispered.

'Yes.' Iwata leant back in his chair again and watched the blades of the fan above them stir the heat like an empty merry-go-round. He had ahold of his anger now. 'For stealing.'

'Please can I go?'

'Ezawa, you ran from me because it was you who stole from Takako's locker. That's the truth of it, isn't it? You have her panties, don't you? That's why you ran from me. Tell me the truth.'

Ezawa's eyes were closed, his lips wet, his body trembling.

'Tell me, Masaharu, so that we can clear your name of suspicion. Take responsibility for what you have done to the Iranian woman – to her small child. Tell me that you took Takako's clothes. You took them, didn't you?'

There came a small, childlike nod.

'Now tell me why you did that. Why did you steal her panties? Was it because you wanted to jerk off on them?'

Ezawa looked up now, face pink, the same hidden snarl from earlier.

'No!'

'Then why?'

'I . . . I just wanted to have something that belonged to her. But she was never careless, she never left things behind, not like the others.'

'The other what, crushes?'

'No!'

'She was more than a crush, wasn't she? Masaharu, be honest with me. You loved her, didn't you? You loved Takako.'

He looked away, his expression screwing into pain.

'That's why you killed her, isn't it? Sniffing her panties was no longer enough for you. The fantasy of Takako had to become reality. Only it didn't happen, did it? She rejected you because you're a small, ugly cripple and the rejection obliterated you. So you sought to wreak vengeance on her and her family. That's why you reserved such special attention for her husband, isn't it?'

Ezawa was on his feet, in tears.

'No!' he shrieked. 'No!'

'Sit down.'

Ezawa obeyed, his face twisted with revulsion.

'Where were you on the night of the fourteenth of February?'

'At work, at home . . . I don't remember.'

'You don't remember where you were a few days ago? Masaharu, we have a witness saying they saw a man with a limp like yours leave the crime scene. You have a motive, you have no alibi, and we know that if we search your house we will find evidence of prior criminality against one of the victims. I can walk out of this room right now and wash my hands of you. How do you think things will turn out for you?'

Iwata clutched his tie and pulled it taut above his head in a mock hanging. Ezawa looked at him with trembling loathing.

'I would never hurt her. I would never hurt anyone . . .'

'Like you would never hurt me?' Iwata leant forward to show his lacerated crown.

Ezawa was quietly crying now, his limbs sagging like parched petals in the heat.

Iwata sat up straight, his palms flat on the table. 'You attacked a cop, kid. You ran from the police. You have the possessions of a dead woman in your house.'

'. . . I didn't touch her.'

'If you didn't kill her, what did you do?' Iwata leant forward again and stroked Ezawa's sweat-soaked head. The young man's eyes closed in disgust or gratitude.

'Masaharu,' Iwata whispered. 'Just tell me. What did you do?'

'I took pictures . . . Oh God. I took pictures of her . . .'

'Where? Where, Masaharu?'

'At the university . . . sometimes at her gym . . . sometimes outside her house.'

Iwata sat back and checked his watch.

'You didn't kill her? You didn't hurt the Kaneshiro family?'

Ezawa was on his knees now, snot streaming down his chin.

'Never, never, never. I'd never hurt Takako.'

Iwata reached forward and turned off the tape.

'All right, Masaharu. You still have more questions to answer and you will face the consequences for what you have done. But we'll call this a free pass.' Iwata pointed to his head.

Still on his knees, Ezawa was repeating Takako's name under his breath over and over again as he wept.

'Must be your lucky night,' Iwata said as he stood.

5. A Million Cities

Sakai was outside the police station, smoking as she squinted at the darkening skyline. Iwata emerged from the main doors and followed her purple trail. She eyed him sidelong then returned her gaze to the moon.

'You look like shit, boss.'

'You've got a good eye, Inspector Sakai.'

'So you keep saying. Did the kid sing?'

'From the rooftops. But he's no killer. How about Ijiri?'

'It wasn't his first time in a police station, that's for sure. But I grilled him pretty hard all the same.'

'Of that, I have no doubt. I'm sure he wasn't banking on your soft skills.'

She curled up a smile with a puff of smoke and offered Iwata her packet. Iwata took one and lit it from hers. Their smoke mingled up into the cold night.

'He says he knew *of* the family, the father even made a few inquiries some years back, but he never lent them a single yen.'

'And you buy it?'

'I think so. He keeps detailed records, which we can look at if we get the permissions. However, I did get access to Mr Kaneshiro's bank account a little while ago. Turns out he deposited over one and a half million yen into his account on the fifth of January.'

'The day after meeting *I*. Interesting.'

'It's a lot of money. Car sale?'

'Could be.'

'Certainly enough to keep the construction firm from their gates for a while.'

'Enough to kill an entire family for?'

Sakai shrugged and stubbed out her cigarette.

'Come on.' Iwata threw his down too. 'I'll take you home.'

'You're all right to drive?'

'I won't win at Suzuka, but I'll get you there.'

'Then shoot for Nishi-Azabu.'

Iwata got into the driver's seat and set off at a slow speed eastwards, following the signs for Metropolitan Expressway Number 3.

'Oh by the way.' Sakai reclined her seat. 'I spoke to Shindo earlier. He wanted a report, as he was getting static from Setagaya about us. He sounded pleased with what I told him.'

'Shindo sounded "pleased"?'

'Well, more like he didn't sound pissed off with us yet. Said you should collect your permanent techou and gun tomorrow. Looks like he doesn't want rid of you just yet.'

'Hey, I bled for that badge.'

Sakai laughed a tired laugh.

'You got hit by a shrimp with a small gardening tool.'

She closed her eyes and Iwata turned on the radio, both of them done with any further conversation.

'Almost one week after the death of young actress Mina Fong and mystery continues to shroud the incident. Few details have been released at this point, though it's understood her agent has requested privacy for her family at this time. Gossip columns leading up to Fong's death were rife with rumours of drug abuse and possible breach of contract with her production company relating to her role in the popular soap opera Cherry Generation. *Estranged boyfriend and idol Riki Noda described Fong's death as 'a shocking tragedy'. Her remains are due to be cremated and buried in Fuchu Catholic Cemetery on Friday.'*

The news shifted to the increasing likelihood of the prime minister resigning and the unseasonably cold weather.

'Hey, Sakai, who has that Mina Fong case?'

'Moroto is leading it.'

'Is he top dog, then?'

'Something like that. Akashi's heir apparent. Upstairs love him.'

The traffic was surprisingly sparse for 9 p.m. The car sailed along the rise and fall of the expressway. The turn-offs and junctions curved outwards and inwards like grey tentacles, lit up by rows of white and red lights. On either side of the expressway, waves of indistinct glass and concrete. Countless billboards, countless windows, countless fire escapes, countless Tokyo.

'You ever hear that thing people say about this city?' Sakai murmured. 'That Tokyo is a million cities and one city all at once?'

'Yeah.'

'You ever wonder if maybe some of those cities are good and some of them are bad?'

'Maybe so. Sakai, can I ask you something?'

'Mm.'

'What happened to Inspector Akashi?'

Sakai opened her eyes and looked at Iwata now, her face stern.

'Akashi jumped off Rainbow Bridge. What else is there to say?'

'You were close with him?'

She looked out of the window.

'I knew him. That's all.'

He glanced at her.

'What?'

'Nothing.'

'Then why are you looking at me?'

'I'm not.'

'Why so curious about Akashi?'

'I just have this nagging feeling that maybe he saw something early on. Something that we might have missed.'

'Anything he saw would be in the case file, surely?'

Iwata drove along the length of Gaien-nishi-Dori in silence, turning left down a side street just before the Nishi-Azabu crossing. They passed various embassies of countries home to dictators and jungles. The streets were lined with tiny bars and three-stool noodle shacks. The first queues for nightclubs had formed, prostitutes lit tentative cigarettes and tourists gathered outside a restaurant that had featured in a Tarantino movie.

Iwata stopped in front of a six-storey white apartment complex. It looked more like a cheap beachfront hotel than anywhere Sakai would live. But then picturing where Sakai would live was like meeting an extra-terrestrial and picturing their home planet based on the address alone. She stepped out of the car and hunched down to look at him. The rain hissed around them, illuminated by the headlights. It felt like a relieved goodbye after an underwhelming date.

'Well,' she said, 'get some sleep, Inspector.'

And then she was gone, clicking away, her heels still dirty with mud.

I'm happy with you. Please let me hear.
Those words of love from you.

Iwata woke from another falling dream. He had left the window open during the night and rain had blown in. Today's grey sky threatened yet more. The pain in his head was no longer a blaring horn, but he still bared his teeth when he stood up. He went to the mirror and parted his hair to see a dark, deep gash. In doing so, Iwata noticed his first greys.

Cleo invaded his thoughts, making him stumble and grip the sink.

She runs her fingers through his hair, lightly grazing his scalp with her nails.

'Your hair is so dark.'

Iwata slapped himself in the face, spat in the sink and controlled his breathing. From a sparse wardrobe, he took out a white shirt and a grey suit. He dressed, made himself a cup of black coffee and went over the morning newspaper, looking for the Kaneshiro family murders. The front page was dominated by two stories: the prime minister's defiant comments regarding his position and the death of Mina Fong. Iwata found a brief article in the crime section that spoke in broad terms about the Kaneshiro murders. Only Tsunemasa's name was used and the ages of the children were incorrect. There was no outrage or urgency to the piece, just a perfunctory listing of facts as if the writer were dealing with an upturn in tuna prices instead of a murdered family. Iwata closed the paper as his phone began to ring.

'Inspector, this is Doctor Eguchi.'

He checked his watch. 8.32 a.m.

'Ah yes, Doctor. Thank you for calling.'

'The tests on the blood, urine and gastric contents all came back completely normal. No traces of anything in their systems that shouldn't have been there. However, some of the blood on the father's body was turkey blood.'

'Turkey blood?'

'That's right!'

'You sound almost excited, Doctor.'

'Well, it's a puzzle, isn't it?'

'Anything else?'

'Yes. All of the victims had inhaled some kind of smoke or incense.'

'Interesting.'

'Oh, and that soot I mentioned on the father's fingers? It's just plain old charcoal. You'd have to check with your forensics division, but I would assume it's the same substance on the ceiling of the crime scene.'

'Thank you, Doctor.'

'Inspector, there was one more thing. I don't even know whether to mention it, actually. But the father did have a six-inch laceration on his left forearm that doesn't fit. It was on its way to healing at the time of his death.'

'I think I can answer that. I spoke to a colleague of Tsunemasa Kaneshiro who said that a young girl had a grudge against him. Apparently there was some kind of altercation a few weeks ago and when he came back to the office, he had a gash on his arm.'

'Well now, that does fit. The wound is two to three weeks old and clearly applied with nowhere near the level of raw force in the actual murders. But that niggles. Who gets stabbed and doesn't report it to the police? Doesn't that seem suspicious to you, Inspector?'

'Not if the police treat you like the shit on their shoe.'

'Hm. Anyway, that's about the shape of it, Inspector.'

'You've been very helpful, thank you.'

'Aha.' Her voice had a jolly lilt to it. 'Good luck.'

Iwata hung up and grabbed his keys. The Toyota was in a spare bay behind the apartment complex. As he turned the ignition, he dialled Sakai.

'Iwata. You're still alive, then.'

'And what a lovely morning it is.'

'Oh every day on the TMPD is a glory.'

Iwata filled Sakai in on the incense, the turkey blood and the charcoal.

'OK,' she huffed. 'It's official. Picasso is a weirdo.'

62

'That's not all, Sakai. The father had a stab wound on his arm that was three weeks old.'

'Shit. You think that's our guy? Has to be, right?'

'Eguchi doesn't see it that way. Nor do I. A colleague mentioned a young girl with a grudge against Mr Kaneshiro, maybe against Koreans in general. Apparently she attacked him a few weeks back. Something we'll have to look into.'

Sakai laughed bitterly.

'A giant and a little girl. What a fucking case. Listen, the registration plates from the parking lot near the family home came back. Nothing particularly interesting, all nice people with nice alibis. But you'll like this more – the bank got back to me this morning with someone slightly more competent. Told me that Tsunemasa Kaneshiro asked for quotes from various law firms. Not only that, he'd actually been billed by one of the best property-dispute lawyers in Tokyo.'

'So Kaneshiro *was* in the money.'

'I called the lawyer this morning and he made it clear that he had no inclination to talk to us. But he did throw me a bone.'

'Tsunemasa wasn't of a mind to sell to Vivus?'

'Bingo.'

'Good work, Sakai. I'm on my way.'

The automated gripe of the windscreen wipers hurt Iwata's head and he swore at the frequent red lights that caught him. The drive to Shibuya HQ took much longer than it should have.

In the underground car park, Iwata showed his temporary pass. The man in the booth signed him off and buzzed open the security doors. They opened on to a narrow corridor with Arctic blue walls and countless faded papers with mug shots, descriptions and warnings. Iwata walked this thin ventricle deeper into the station. He passed more elevators, toilets and changing rooms. He ignored the bawdy laughter spilling out of the changing rooms and followed the sound of Beethoven. At the end of the corridor, Iwata came to an armoury. Behind the bulletproof glass, an old man with white hair and a weathered face looked up from his newspaper.

'You're Iwata?'

'That's right. Symphony No. 7?'

A slow smile spread across the old man's face.

'A man of culture. I'm Nakata. One moment please.'

The old cop went into a back room and returned a while later. He opened the slider and pushed through a black leather techou, some handcuffs, a shoulder holster and a small, black SIG Sauer P232. Iwata put on the holster and felt the weight of the gun in his palm.

'Seven rounds,' Nakata said. 'And she's a good size.'

'Next time someone attacks me with a trowel, I'm ready.'

'A trowel?'

'Don't ask.'

Iwata slid the gun into the holster under his blazer. It was the voice of God at his side, yet he felt nothing but a pleasant weight.

'You ever shot one before?'

'Only in training.'

'Say, Inspector. Where's that accent from? You from Kyoto too?'

'I'm from Miyama. Small village not far from Kyoto.'

'Good walking? Fishing?'

Iwata saw bunk beds, dead fields and crows perched on power lines. And somewhere deep in a forest, a whispering whirlpool.

'I . . . haven't been there in a long time.'

Nakata smiled politely and nodded at the gun under Iwata's blazer.

'Well, let me know if she misbehaves for whatever reason.'

'Thanks, I'll do that.'

'One more thing. Don't let these Kantō assholes get you down.'

He smiled and bowed. Nakata went back to his paper and his Beethoven. Iwata returned to the elevators and pressed the call button. As he waited, he opened the leather pocket-book. On one side, his name, rank and photograph. On the other, a gleaming badge with a gold-wreathed silver emblem and two gold bars. The symbol of the Tokyo Metropolitan Police Department. The mark of justice.

As the elevator pinged, Iwata heard shouting from the changing rooms behind him.

The lights of the city are so pretty.

In among the noise, he heard Sakai's voice. Instinctively, Iwata hurried down the hallway and ripped open the changing-room door. The smell of sweat and piss hissed out. Horibe and the rest of Moroto's goons encircled Sakai. Moroto himself held Sakai's sports bag high over his head. Sakai's face was red with fury.

Iwata stepped forward. 'Give the bag back.'

'And what the fuck do you care, Mickey Mouse?' Moroto smiled, his rubbery, smacking voice ricocheting around the cramped changing room.

Iwata took another step forward. 'Give the bag back.'

Moroto glanced around his cohorts in mock offence. 'Ms Sakai is just goofing around with her colleagues, *buddy*. Why don't you go arrest someone?'

'Iwata, forget him.' Sakai's voice was pleading.

Iwata was now nose-to-chin with Moroto. 'Give her back the bag. Last time I say it.'

Moroto smirked and the others passed around smiles. 'Last time he says it. And with that fucking polite Kyoto accent too. You know what I like about you, *Yankee*?'

Iwata punched him in the gut. Moroto doubled over, eyes bulging, the air in his lungs imploding. Iwata snatched away the bag and pushed Moroto hard to the floor in the same motion. Three men were around Iwata now: Tatsuno, Yoshida and Horibe, static in their confusion. The latter, first to defend his leader, stepped forward. Iwata looked him in the eye and shook his head.

Horibe stalled. Passing the bag over to Sakai, Iwata knelt down by a wheezing Moroto.

'Listen to me, Moroto.' The words contained no pageantry. 'Don't ever come near her again. I hope you understand me.'

Moroto coughed incredulously, still holding his stomach. '. . . You don't know who you're fucking with.'

Iwata tapped Moroto on the side of the head, the little spikes of black growth stabbing his finger.

'But I do, Moroto. I'm fucking with you.'

Iwata stood now eyeing each of Moroto's men. He left the room with Sakai close behind. The elevator was quick. The ascent to the twelfth floor passed in silence. The elevator doors slid open to an identical scene from yesterday morning. The loud phone calls, the sickly light, the commingling of cigarette smoke across the low ceiling. Sakai stopped at the door of the toilet.

'Iwata?'

'Yes?'

'You shouldn't have done that.'

'Is that your version of "thank you"?'

She sighed and let go of the door. Iwata crossed the office, knocked on Shindo's door and went in. Shindo was staring at the grey blur of his window, a fixed grimace on his face.

'Inspector, come in.'

Iwata shifted a fresh pile of papers from a chair and sat down.

66

'Kid, I just got off the phone with Setagaya's chief. He says the moneylender is being cut loose but they're keeping this Ezawa character. What's your view?'

'I don't think Ijiri has any kind of connection to this. Ezawa, however, is definitely guilty of a variety of offences. No real alibi, probably a vague motive in there too and plenty of stink about him – yes. But he didn't kill this family, I'm certain.'

'What about the witness who saw a man with a limp?'

'A limp doesn't really prove anything. What does is the fact that Ezawa simply wouldn't have the strength to kill an entire family like this. And even if he did, to be honest, he doesn't have the brains to do it without leaving behind a single clue.'

'All right. We have another twenty-two days to hold him without charge. Let's play it safe and keep him for the time being?'

'No arguments from me.'

Sakai opened the door and bowed. She was wearing a navy blue trouser suit and a light blue blouse now, but her hair was up in a hasty ponytail.

'Sit down, Sakai. Your partner was just saying how he thinks the moneylender and Ezawa are innocent of the murders, interesting characters though they may be. You agree?'

'Yes, sir.'

'Are there any other angles I should know about?'

Iwata nodded.

'An employee who worked with Tsunemasa Kaneshiro informed me that a young girl was harassing him at his work – shouting obscenities over a megaphone and the like. Apparently, a few weeks ago, there was some kind of confrontation and Kaneshiro returned to the office bleeding. This explains the secondary laceration. But all we have is a vague description of the girl. I would like to ask Officer Hatanaka to look into her, if possible.'

'The kid from Setagaya you've got running through hoops?'

'That's him.'

Shindo shrugged his OK.

'And so I take it both of you want to pursue this Kiyota, then?'

Sakai nodded.

'He hasn't yet turned up, sir. However, last night I spoke with an official at the Civil Aviation Bureau and described our suspect – tall, male, twenty-eight-centimetre shoe, likely travelling alone, possibly with a limp. They told me that in a two- or three-day window, we were looking at anywhere up to seventy-five flights to Seoul or Bangkok.'

Shindo whistled.

'OK, Iwata, where do you want to go from here?'

'Setagaya PD badges are canvassing the Kaneshiros' neighbourhood; I think that should continue. In my view, the best course of action for Division One would be to pursue Kiyota. He has links to Nippon Kumiai, so we start there. If anyone knows where he is, I'm betting it's them. From what I've seen, Assistant Inspector Sakai is more than capable of carrying out this task.'

Sakai glared at him.

'Sir –'

Shindo silenced her with a hand.

'And what about you, Iwata?' he asked.

'Kyoto University. I have a contact there, an old friend with expertise in symbols.'

The older cop made a diamond beneath his chin with his fingers.

'Why?'

'Sir, these murders are ritualistic. The black sun symbol the killer left at the Kaneshiro house underpins the act – I'm almost certain.'

'This isn't Hollywood, Inspector. I told you about resources.'

'I spoke with the coroner this morning. One of the bodies was smeared in turkey blood, they had a strange incense in their lungs, there was a symbol left behind, the father had his heart removed – all of that points to a ritualistic killer. He may be a serial killer. The sooner we understand his motives – how he chooses victims – the faster we can narrow down his identity. Understanding that symbol should have been my first step, really.'

Shindo looked out of the window and rubbed his old, broken nose.

'Be back here by tomorrow morning, then. No travel expenses.'

'Thank you, sir.'

'Sakai, take two uniforms with you to Nippon Kumiai. Let those assholes see the blue.'

'Sir.' There was a quiver to her voice.

Iwata and Sakai left Shindo's office. Moroto and his goons were nowhere to be seen. They crossed Division One and called the elevator. As soon as they stepped inside and the doors closed she wheeled around and hissed.

'You could have sent any asshole to knock on doors. You cut me out after *one day*? Did I not give you everything you needed?'

'You did. But assholes miss details, Sakai. You, on the other hand, have a good eye and a fierce tongue. That's precisely why I want you chasing down Kiyota.'

'Bullshit.'

She held out her hand for the car keys and Iwata passed them over. In the car park, she headed for the Toyota without a word. Iwata took the stairs up to street level, left the station and crossed the street to the subway.

6. Lovers Cannot See

The Nippon Kumiai office was located on a backstreet in Takadanobaba, a plain three-storey structure that could have been a travel agency or a language school. Sakai told the police officers accompanying her to wait outside. She showed her police ID to the young man at the reception and ignored his protests as she made her way to the office at the back. She knocked once and opened the door to a room latticed with framed black-and-white photographs. The room smelled of cigar smoke, aftershave and feet. A small, smiling man in his fifties with thick black hair, slicked back, sat at a bureau too big for him. His spectacles were too small for his wide, coin-like face.

'Yes?'

His voice was inquisitive, pleasantly surprised at the young woman standing before him. When Sakai held up her police credentials, his expression did not change.

'Assistant Inspector Sakai. Division One.'

'My name is Gorō Onaga. Please sit.'

Signed portraits of Jean-Marie Le Pen and Saddam Hussein sat on Onaga's desk, facing outward towards the visitor. Another photograph showed Onaga warmly embracing the former Minister for Security. Above his chair, a huge portrait of Yukio Mishima, handsome and muscular, looked down at Sakai. Beneath the author's folded arms ran a quote of his in severe, dark text:

PERFECT PURITY IS POSSIBLE IF YOU TURN YOUR LIFE INTO A LINE OF POETRY WRITTEN WITH A SPLASH OF BLOOD.

Onaga cleared his throat.

'Division One?'

'The Homicide Unit, Mr Onaga.'

The man's eyes widened theatrically as he sat back in his chair.

'So, what can I help you with, Assistant Inspector?'

Sakai gestured around the room.

'What is it you do here?'

'Nippon Kumiai retains the fundamental character of our nation.'

'I see.'

Her eyes settled on a long rack in the corner which supported T-shirts and windbreakers of all sizes. They all bore the Nippon Kumiai logo.

'Is that why you came here, to ask me that?'

'I think you know the answer to that question, Mr Onaga. I'm just curious about your . . . organization, that's all. I've heard certain things.'

He leant forward, a delighted grin on his face.

'May I ask what things?'

'That you seek to justify Japan's role in World War II. That you reject its war crimes.'

'What I reject is self-hate. I reject the self-flagellation taught in schools to our children. I reject the pacifist constitution foisted on us by America. I reject the limp-wristed lack of patriotism in our youth. And I'm not the only one to question "conventional wisdom" when it comes to our history.'

'I see.'

'You don't sound convinced, Inspector.'

'Occupational hazard.'

Onaga laughed but his eye twitch belied his displeasure at her quip.

'Go to any bookstore in this country and you will find all manner of freely accessible literature questioning our role in the war and supposed "crimes". In the West, this would be shocking – even unacceptable. But we're invisible to the West. So why pander to it? Why let others define us? Forgive me, but I am free to judge my own nation's character as I see fit.'

Sakai leant forward, picked up one of the framed photographs and inspected it. It showed a large group of Nippon Kumiai members smiling in front of a baseball diamond. Evidently a team-bonding exercise.

'It's interesting, Mr Onaga. The constitution that you have just rejected so freely is the very thing that protects your ideology.'

Onaga laughed an unpleasant laugh, marbles being mixed in a bag.

'We live in a puppet state, Inspector Sakai. A puppet state from which my group demands independence. The error of post-war democracy is unforgivable.'

'You're a fool if you think you can ever achieve that.'

Onaga chortled.

'Inspector, do you realize that my group has swollen to over fifteen thousand members? In the last year alone, we've staged over one hundred demonstrations all over the country. Many, many more are active online. Japan is at a turning point, Inspector. And I will die seeing it return to the old way of life.'

Sakai took out a notebook, signalling the end of the debate.

'What you will do, Mr Onaga, is very simple.' She turned the photograph around and pointed to Kodai Kiyota's long face. 'You will tell me where this man is.'

For the first time since she had entered the room, Onaga's smile dropped.

'Why are you asking me about him?'

'Do you think I'm paid to answer *your* questions? I asked you where Kodai Kiyota is. That's all.'

Onaga's face darkened.

'I don't know where. In any case, that man is no longer part of our organization.'

'Why not?'

'Because he left.'

'Why?'

Onaga mulled this over. Sakai was used to this pause, the search for the right words, the search for clean answers.

'Mr Kiyota was a very promising member in our organization. I thought he might go on to achieve great things. He had a talent for . . . getting people to listen to him. But in the end, it didn't quite work out that way.'

Sakai stopped writing for a second and looked up at him. Onaga sighed and sat back in his seat.

'You're here about the dead Korean family, I assume? Look, that family's pigheaded stance over the housing project became somewhat of a thorny issue in the local area. The Vivus project would bring jobs, infrastructure and wealth to Setagaya. Yet this one family was too obstinate and selfish to care.'

Sakai waved this away.

'Get to the point. Where does Kiyota come into it?'

'Mr Kiyota had only recently joined us and had achieved good results. He asked me if he could deal with the family personally. Of course, I made it clear that he could only talk with them peacefully and lawfully.'

73

'But the Kaneshiros wouldn't budge.'

'They started legal proceedings which would be extremely costly for us. I then made it clear to Mr Kiyota that we had to know when and where to pick our battles but he wouldn't let it go. It created tension within the group. And it was at that time when trusted members pointed out to me his own . . . unsavoury tastes.'

'Don't be shy, go on.'

'His drinking was out of control and his criminal past was becoming irritating. It gave us all the wrong associations. The left-wing press had more and more mud to sling at us.'

'*Kiyota*, talk to me about Kiyota. So he was a drinker with a criminal record, what else? You said "unsavoury tastes".'

Onaga met Sakai's eyes.

'There was also his girlfriend. But she was . . . very young.'

'Name?'

'She was also a Nippon Kumiai member, I can arrange for her details to be given to you when you leave.'

'I'd like those details now, please.'

There was a long pause before he picked up the phone and requested the necessary file.

'It won't be a minute, Inspector.'

'Thank you.'

'You know, I must say, I have the utmost respect for you. Police, I mean. A noble undertaking. Not necessarily in *this* case, you understand. Here I think you are wasting your time, but generally speaking, a most commendable undertaking.'

'You don't think a murdered Korean family merits investigation?'

He smiled.

'I didn't say that. I mean a waste of your time by coming here. But then again, maybe it was providence that brought you here. Perhaps you might come again. For further discussion?'

74

'I deal in homicide, sir. That's all. Frankly, I think the only one wasting their time is you.'

Onaga's smile faded then twisted into a snarl.

'There are over a million of those cockroaches living in my country, Inspector. You say you deal in death? Well, let me be frank – Nippon Kumiai deals in hatred, nothing more. Nobody does anything about injustice. But for hatred? People have no limits for their hatred.'

'Very rousing. But I came here for Kodai Kiyota.'

'I cannot say where Kodai Kiyota is, nor what he did or didn't do. If he is involved in those murders then, of course, I condemn it. But let me say this to you, Inspector Sakai. Whoever *did* kill that family must have had their reasons.'

The receptionist entered holding the file. Sakai plucked it from his hands and opened it. It contained a single typed page concerning a female named Asako Ozaki. In red ink, a word had been stamped across the page:

EXPELLED

Onaga shook his head gravely.

'Her father killed himself when she was very young after being forced out of his laundry business. Guess who moved in to clean up and steal customers at half the rate? Her mother married another man and Asako was left, more or less, alone. She never forgot those Koreans who moved in. By the time she came to us, she was more vitriolic than many of our most hardened members. To be honest, she was a PR dream. I was sad to see her go. She was so dedicated. But what can I say? Love is blind and lovers cannot see.'

'Why was she expelled, Mr Onaga?'

'She refused to follow our code of conduct. She was

consistently in trouble with the authorities and then this relationship with Kiyota, well, we had to let her go.'

Sakai ran her finger down the page.

Are you Iwata's girl?

'Inspector, you think that we're simply racists, don't you? I can see that. But this word, it does us a disservice – simple racism robs us of logic and integrity. It implies an *irrational* disgust or fear. But it's not the right word. No, we choose, in all logic, to fight back against this small but powerful minority. And if that makes us racists, then so be it. If that leads to condemnation in the liberal media, so be it. We are already fighting greater, more insidious battles.'

Ignoring him, Sakai reached the bottom of the page. Asako Ozaki lived in Shin-Ōkubo. She was fourteen years old.

Sakai stood up.

'Mr Onaga, I hope we cross paths again. I do.'

Smiling, Onaga stood and offered his hand.

'Oh yes, Inspector. It was a pleasure.'

'No, I think you misunderstand my meaning.'

She left the room.

7. In Praise of Shadows

Iwata wanders aimlessly through the Californian dusk. People huddle in blankets on the beach beneath emerging stars. Slim palm trees rustle in the breeze. Orange and black waves lap at the glassy shore, blinking bubbles left behind in the shingle. In the distance, Santa Monica Pier twinkles on the water, its big wheel slowly revolving. Iwata hears music now, sad but defiant.

The lights of the city are so pretty.

He leaves the beach behind and follows the melody.

I'm happy with you.

On the corner, a little shop has its door propped open, music spilling out for the pleasure of all passing by.

Please let me hear. Those words of love from you.

Iwata walks in and sees her.

'Hello,' she says.

'Hello,' he replies.

The woman smiles.

I walk and walk, swaying, like a small boat in your arms.

'I know this song,' he says.

'It's beautiful. Do you know what she's saying?'

Iwata nods.

'So what's she saying?'

'Sad things.'

They regard each other for a moment.

'I'm Cleo,' she says.

Her skin is a mellow tan, her woven friendship bracelets frayed.

I hear your footsteps coming. Give me one more tender kiss.

Soon they will be bare in her broken bed, surrounded by damp and freshly cut flowers and music. She will correct his English and make eggs most mornings. She will always sleep on her side. In the pre-dawn, Iwata will run his hands down her ribs, a breeze over sand dunes.

How did I find you?

In the warm half-dream, he will only be able to answer that by whispering, 'A miracle.'

Days will pass into years – car journeys, struggles, entire weekends in bed. Cleo will play records and burn toast. She will quietly encourage her old car in the mornings and shout at the news in the evenings. She is the only one allowed to break her own rules. Cleo becomes the only authority in Iwata's life. Walks along the ocean, throwing sticks for an imaginary dog.

Hubris. Hubris. Hubris.

Cleo, ablaze in the setting sun, looks over her shoulder and smiles.

'It's so pretty here.'

A different sun, a different country, and in brilliant white above her – the lighthouse. Casting never-ending shadow.

Iwata pulled over on to the hard shoulder and swung open the car door. He jumped the expressway barrier, ran to the nearest tree and vomited. He blinked out tears, gasping.

'Fucking bitch. Fucking bitch. Fucking bitch.'

Then he kicked and punched the tree and didn't stop until he felt nothing in his bleeding hands. Stillborn cherry blossoms landed on his shoulders for a moment, then fluttered down to the dirt.

'Kyoto University is one of Asia's oldest and most prestigious.' The elderly security guard led Iwata through the beautiful gates, hands behind his back, smiling proudly as though he had laid these bricks himself. 'Eight Nobel Prize laureates, two Fields medallists and one Gauss Prize. And some twenty-two thousand students in any given academic year.' He pointed to the information post. 'There we are. You'll be looking for the Department of Psychology.'

Iwata thanked him and crossed the campus green. It was a sunny afternoon and groups of students were sitting out on the grass. The old camphor tree, which was the university's emblem, stood in the shadow of the redbrick clock tower of the Centennial Hall. The terrace café was packed with students enjoying iced tea and gossip in the sun.

Iwata skirted the skipping rope team's practice and made his way to the eight-storey building behind the old hall. He was about to enter when something caught his attention. A repeated dull thwacking and grunting could be heard nearby. Iwata followed the sound and glanced around the corner. On a shaded strip of grass behind the faculty building, two men were sparring. The younger man, muscular and squat, held up boxing pads. The other man was in his forties, powerful and tall. He rained down a flurry of blows with precision and economy. The younger man was struggling to keep the pads up, as though holding up a newspaper to a water cannon.

Iwata concentrated on the shots and saw that the older man was left-handed. It was soon over.

The younger man laughed, his face red.

'Professor Igarashi,' he panted. 'That jab cross is brutal.'

The professor looped a paternal arm around his shoulders.

'It's not what it used to be.'

'I'd better not be late on your assignments!'

Igarashi laughed.

'Come on, I owe you a beer.'

Before he could be noticed, Iwata left his spot. Entering

the building, he took the stairs to the third floor and knocked on the door marked FORENSIC PSYCHOLOGY / SEMIOTICS.

A woman answered.

'Come in.'

Iwata opened the door to a cramped room with four desks and dying pot plants. A woman roughly Iwata's age looked up from her papers. Her hair was mid-length with a long fringe. Her face was heart-shaped with a strong jaw. She wore silver and turquoise stud earrings and a loose green cardigan.

'Can I help you?' It was a warm, steady voice.

'I'm looking for Professor Schultz.'

'He should be back any minute. May I ask who you are?'

Iwata held up his ID. She raised her eyebrows.

'Whenever we get police here they're usually looking for me, not David.'

'Oh?'

The woman pointed to the plaque at the end of her desk.

DR EMI HAYASHI – CRIMINAL PSYCHOLOGY

'Maybe next time,' Iwata said.

'Please take a seat.'

As she gestured, Iwata noticed her Mickey Mouse watch. She caught his glance but he looked out of the window. The lawn where Igarashi had been sparring was now empty.

'Would you like a coffee while you wait, Inspector?'

'No thank you.'

'You're sure? I happen to have a rather fancy espresso machine in the staff room.'

'I'm fine.'

'David should be back any moment.'

Iwata recognized his friend's characteristic chaos of papers and books around the desk. A Pittsburgh Steelers flag was

Blu-tacked to his monitor. By the phone, there was a framed photograph of a slight woman with red hair. She was holding a small child in her arms.

The door swung open and David Schultz huffed into the room, struggling with a stack of papers. His red-and-white gingham shirt was dark with sweat and his jeans were two sizes too tight.

'Holy shit. Kosuke?'

The two men embraced.

'You got fat,' Iwata replied in English.

'Fuck you, man. Japanese diet.'

Doctor Hayashi collected her papers and stood.

'No, Emi. Stay. I'll be back later,' Schultz said.

She smiled a neat smile then went back to her work. Schultz fished out his wallet from his desk drawer and led Iwata back to the terraced café by the clock tower. He greeted several students warmly in near faultless Japanese, then chose a secluded table away from the chatter. He ordered them two coffees and they quickly fell into discussion regarding Schultz's career, recent divorce and long-distance parenthood.

At the first lull in conversation, Schultz looked up to the dusky sky and his face turned grave. A silence of birdsong and youthful laughter.

'Iwata, I know I haven't seen you since, uh, what happened. I just wanted to say I'm sorry. Fuck, I'm so sorry. I know there's nothing else to say.'

Schultz clapped a thick hand on Iwata's shoulder. He looked away and saw golden pillars of sunlight through the branches of the camphor tree. A girl was reading a book beneath it, leisurely moving her bare feet in the breeze.

'We don't have to talk about it, Dave.'

Schultz nodded vigorously.

'No, no. Of course. It's just good to see you, Kos.'

Iwata opened his bag and laid a plastic folder on the table. He waited for the waitress to set down the coffees before opening it. Schultz looked aghast.

'Tell me you're not working again.'

'I need to ask you a favour.'

'How did I know you hadn't come all this way just to see an old friend?'

'Because you're a very smart man.'

Schultz's smile dimmed.

'Seriously, though, are you sure you're ready for this? Maybe you should take a while to –'

Iwata held up the photograph and the black sun silenced Schultz. He saw the fascination swallow him whole.

'You bastard.'

Iwata grinned. The photograph framed the jagged smears of the black sun on the ceiling in a harsh flash, darkness at the contours.

'What was it drawn in?'

'Charcoal. The killer forced the victim to paint it with his finger before ripping out his heart. Killed the wife and two kids as well. I've got more photos I'd like to show you.'

Schultz sighed and looked up at the now bloodshot sky.

'What do you want to know?'

'One. Is it a symbol or a sign? Two. What does it *mean*?'

Schultz rolled his eyes.

'Kos, I'm a semiotician, not Hercule fucking Poirot.'

'I went out on a limb coming all the way out here on limited time. I need to go back with something, Dave.'

'That was on you.'

Schultz looked at the photo for a moment then shook his head in defeat.

'All right.'

'You're a good man, David.'

'I'd call you a cruel bastard but that's implicit in your race.'

High up in the green-and-red hills, Iwata and David Schultz sat on a bench. Far below, Kyoto shimmered like it gave off warmth.

The lights of the city are so pretty.

'Nice spot,' Iwata said.

'I come here when I need to clear my head.'

'Does it work for you?'

'Sometimes.'

'Beats Pittsburgh?'

Schultz laughed.

'Hey, you ever read any Jun'ichirō Tanizaki?'

Iwata nodded.

'Emi leant me one of his books and there's this line I can't get out of my head. "Beauty lies not in objects, but in the interaction between the shadow and light created by objects."'

'*In Praise of Shadows*,' Iwata said.

'Just keeps going round and round in my head, I don't know why.'

'I know what you mean.'

Schultz gave a wan smile and stuck out his hand.

'Go on, then. Show me the fucking photographs.'

Iwata opened his bag and passed over the plastic wallet. Schultz slowly shuffled through the images, his face revealing only the slightest of twitches. He was seeing the black sun fully now, from various angles and its position in relation to the brutalized body of Tsunemasa Kaneshiro.

Schultz put the photographs in the plastic wallet and gingerly passed them back.

'How do you get used to seeing that sort of thing?'

'I just let my eyes sweep over it.'

'Kos, all this.' He gestured to the slaughter in the photographs. 'Are you really sure you're ready to handle it? I mean what happened to you is –'

Iwata held up a hand.

'Dave, please. Just, please.'

Schultz nodded.

'OK.' He exhaled. 'OK.'

'Thank you.'

'You asked me if it's a symbol or a sign. My guess is it's a symbol.' Schultz pointed at the hazard sign in front of them before the drop to the rocks below.

'Now a sign means something – *stop, go, walk* et cetera. The sign thinks for you. It commands you. A symbol, on the other hand, *represents* an idea, a process, or a physical entity. But the important word here is *represents*. The symbol represents something else, something beyond what you are looking at – whereas the sign means only *this*. The Christian cross doesn't just mean a dead guy crucified, it represents sacrifice, faith, hope, whatever – an entire religion. Where the sign thinks for you, the symbol asks you to do the thinking – abstract versus the literal, I guess.'

'So you don't think the black sun is a direct command or a warning?'

'This is all guesswork, but no, I would say that the *killings* themselves mean something. Whatever this person's objective was, I think it's possible that the death of the family was not the goal in and of itself. The symbol could mean that the murders are not the end product. They could mean *something else*.'

'You're saying the murders are . . . somehow subordinate to the sun?'

'Kos, I think the murders belong to it. Maybe the killer does, too. You never know, man. Reality to survive, fantasy to live.'

There was no trace of the dusk now, only a cold night and a thin nail of moon high above it.

'You also asked me *what it is*. That's the sixty-four-million-dollar question, isn't it?' Schultz puffed the air out of his cheeks. 'Fuck, it's like asking a mathematician what the significance of the zero is. I mean, where do you want me to start?'

'Wherever makes sense.'

'OK. You're looking for a murderer, I guess. One possibly obsessed with this dark symbol. So look, maybe it could be read as an absence of light that is driving him – the black sun as the end of all life, eternal darkness, Satan blah, blah, blah. The black sun has a rich tradition in the occult, not to mention esoteric Nazism.'

'Esoteric Nazism?'

'We should have gone somewhere that serves beer. Look, I don't know how much detail you want here but basically, you're talking about a semi-religious and mystical interpretation of Nazism starting around the 1950s. The black sun was seen as a kind of a mystical source of energy capable of *regenerating* the Aryan race. There's a long-standing literature connecting the Aryan race with this black sun, or mystical sun. Helena Blavatsky's *Theosophy* talks of a "central sun". Thule or Hyperborea, for the ancient Greeks, was a place where the "people beyond the North Wind" lived. Other interpretations see it as the ancient seat of the original Aryan race. Oh, and Himmler was a big fan of the *Oera Linda Book*, which is sometimes referred to as the "Nordic Bible", and frequently referenced when discussing esotericism and "Atlantis" literature. Anyway, Himmler was alleged to have commissioned an old "Aryan symbol" for Wewelsburg Castle. You can guess what he chose. This is all academic, though.'

Schultz did up the last button on his coat, looking out at the horizon without blinking.

'You mentioned this family was ethnic Korean, Zainichi, so you must have considered some sort of racial hatred or purity complex at play here? I mean I couldn't tell you explicitly *what* the connection with the black sun is but it's certainly worth thinking about it if you make a Nazi link. That said, your killer could just as easily turn out to be some kind of satanic nut job or fundamentalist.'

Schultz scratched his stubble before continuing.

'Now, Kos, we've just been speaking last century here. You should know that the black sun symbol crops up in pretty much every ancient culture there is, all over the world, essentially from day one. The Egyptians, the Sumerians, the Aztecs . . . It was a sacred symbol connected to creation stories, apocalyptic legends and the like. But you'd need historians to go down that route. Anyway, that's about all I can tell you. But I can do some reading for next time.'

'David Schultz, you're luminous.'

Back in the car, they wound down the shadowy hills, mostly in silence, half-listening to a radio report on Japan's booming elderly care industry and dwindling birth rate. Iwata drove at a languid speed, his thoughts caught up in dark symbols. At the campus gates, Schultz opened the passenger door and the interior light came on.

'I'll call you if I think of anything else, all right? Next time just come without dead bodies.'

They embraced briefly. Schultz got out, turned and ducked his head into view.

'Max Weber once said, "Man is an animal suspended in webs of significance he himself has spun." My gut feeling? Whoever it is you're looking for is suspended in that black sun. It's not a calling card. I think it's his whole web. He lives and breathes it.'

Schultz patted the roof of the car and tossed the door shut with a metallic clunk.

8. Honey

Iwata left the Meishin Expressway, switching on to the Tomei for Tokyo. He kept his eyes on his lane, not looking beyond the cones of light on either side of the road. Though his head ached badly and he needed sleep, Iwata sensed a change coming. He turned on the radio and heard a young man laughing modestly.

'No, of course I don't see myself that way. I don't even see myself as a particularly worthy man. I'm only interested in personal growth. If I have started something which helps people to achieve their own growth, then I'm very happy. But guru? No, certainly not. I'm just a man conscious of the emptiness inside people. The uncertainty that gnaws away. The doubt that presses down. And I'm interested in talking about that. I'm interested in clarity and well-being. And, above all, I'm interested in people.'

'If you're just joining us, tonight's guest is Akira Anzai, interim leader of controversial and much-discussed spirituality group Theta. *As ever, we want to hear from you. Mr Anzai is happy to take questions. Our number is –'*

Iwata switched the radio off and, on a whim, dialled the number for the Shibuya armoury. After a long while, an old voice answered uncertainly.

'Yes?'

'Mr Nakata, it's Iwata from this morning.'

'Yes, I remember you. I don't get many phone calls down here.'

'I was wondering if I could ask you a favour. I need the address of a colleague.'

'I have access to those records. Who are you looking for?'

'Inspector Akashi.' Iwata said the name casually.

Nakata paused and Iwata could hear Mahler softly playing in the background.

'Hideo Akashi?'

'That's right.'

'. . . One moment, please.'

Iwata heard a metallic clank of a filing cabinet before the old man came back on the line.

'Do you have a pen?'

Iwata jotted down the address and thanked Nakata warmly. He programmed it into his satellite navigation system and saw that Akashi had lived almost an hour outside of Tokyo, in Chiba.

Iwata made the turning and a few moments later, his phone started to ring.

'Are you at home?'

'I'm driving, Sakai.'

'Where?'

'Just going for a drive.'

'A drive. Sure. With no particular destination, I presume.'

'Why, are you lonely or something?'

'Dream on, dickhead. Anyway, I already have a man in my life.'

Iwata leant forwards.

'Kiyota?'

'The very same. Well, I have a good lead, at least. Nippon Kumiai hadn't seen him in weeks but the asshole has a four-teen-year-old girlfriend – Asako Ozaki. I'm betting that's the girl Tsunemasa Kaneshiro's colleague was talking about har-assing him. We find her, we find Kiyota.'

'Great work, Sakai.'

'Gee, thanks.'

*

A bleak, foggy day was dawning as Iwata reached Chiba. The GPS had guided him to a large, empty space strewn with litter. Building sites in the distance had been abandoned. A half-completed highway overpass ran south. To the east, several derelict structures stood isolated. The wind blew through a silent pachinko parlour. An empty business centre was falling apart, unsold houses were being consumed by weeds. Life had been seeded here but it had not taken root. To the north, a few kilometres away, Iwata saw rusty train tracks. The land was flat and brown, stretching out into a prosaic distance. Crows flapped up from the mud, into the thick fog.

Iwata double-checked the address. He got out of the car and noticed a dirt track leading away from the road, to the centre of a desolate field. Squinting through the mist, he saw a jagged shape. Iwata walked towards it uncertainly. At the end of the path, the fog relented and he saw the burnt-out wreckage of a small cottage. A simple brick foundation was still standing but the wood and plaster had been devoured by flame. Only a spindly black framework remained like scorched bones. Iwata smelled the burning – a stench that would never fade. Local police had erected a sign warning off passers-by. Iwata knew they would have figured this for a simple delinquency.

He went through the space where the door would have been and the house caught its breath.

Pillars of light stabbed through the destroyed roof and rainwater leaked down the walls. Charred household objects quaked under Iwata. The merest of touches sent puffs of ash flaking up into the air. Strange objects made up the floor – twisted and distorted shapes, having lost all form trying to escape from the flames.

Iwata looked for improbable points of ignition at the front door and the exterior walls. He checked the plug sockets and sniffed surfaces for flammable liquids. He could not make out the origin of the fire. He looked for signs of drug use but found nothing.

He is happiest, be he king or peasant, who finds peace in his home.

There was a sadness to this place. The house creaked quietly in the wind, glad to have been burnt down. Iwata tried to picture a home here, he tried to see a life in this place – between the abandoned, the residuum and the half-formed. He could not see Hideo Akashi living in such a place, beneath the highway overpass, in an old hut built on a muddy desolation. He tried to gauge the man's frame of mind at the end.

Did the fog seep through your thin walls? Did it soak through your house and absorb your mind in the days before death? Did you go through the motions, saying what you were required to say? Did you feel relief as you jumped?

Iwata felt the loneliness of the dead man and a cutting sympathy for him. He had to crouch to get his breath back.

Whosoever is delighted in solitude is a wild beast or a god.

Iwata filled his lungs resolutely and stood back up. And as he did, deep in the char, he saw something. Beneath drooping nails, burnt wood and twisted plastic, it glinted up at him. Iwata sunk his arm into the detritus and plucked it up. It was a small, glassy glob of amber – honey-like and hard. He blew ash from its surface and held it up to the light. Golden bubbles were captured inside it, minuscule termites and flecks of dirt preserved for ever.

'What are you doing here?'

Iwata closed his eyes. Outside, he could hear something was coming.

When the wicked came upon me to eat up my flesh, they stumbled and they fell.

He pocketed the stone and stepped outside into the swirling grey fog. A rumbling grew near.

Iwata took several steps forward and heard a whining squeal.

The Lord is the strength of my life. Of whom shall I be afraid?

The fog turned pink now and headlights pierced the mist. A black car broke into view, travelling fast, already on him. Iwata reacted, struggling for balance as he dashed back to the house. The car was in touching distance but Iwata leapt through the window frame of the house. He heard a simultaneous metallic crunch into the bricks.

Blink.

Blink.

Blink.

Iwata was on the floor, blood from his reopened head wound seeping into his eyes – a jagged pipe cutting into his ribs. He scrambled to his feet and fell back down hard, a shooting pain in his ankle drawing a yelp from his throat. Iwata forced his head up and saw the car had crashed into the foundation of the house. Blood dripped loudly from his nose into his lap. It sounded like applause. Stark headlights bathed the wreck of the house and exhaust mixed in with the fog. A car trying to get into a house, it seemed almost comical. The car's gears were grinding violently now. Iwata drew his gun and forced himself to stay on his feet. He squinted through the pungent smoke, trying to see the driver.

'Get out of the car with your back to me and your hands up!'

A moment of stillness and trembling. A silhouette through the smoke, watching Iwata.

Then the car shot off in reverse, the lights shrinking in the grey. Iwata struggled out from the filth and hobbled away from the wreckage. He felt blood streaming down his ribs and face, his ankle was pounding – an interminable distance to the Isuzu. A brief sequence of blackouts punctuated his journey to the car. Then he was on the back seat, struggling with his phone. Iwata dialled Sakai's number but she didn't pick up. Gasping for breath, he called the emergency line and gave his ID.

'Black Honda 2010 Odyssey model . . . damage on the rear of vehicle . . .'

'Hello? Inspector? Hello?'

'Just attempted to run over a police inspector . . .'

'Hello? Inspector? Hello? Are you there, Iwata?'

Iwata could only see the dashboard clock, darkness and fireflies spreading across his vision.

Faltering breaths slowed.

His eyes closed.

Atomization.

9. Galatians 6:9

Cold.

It is the first day of 1986.

The bus station is big and very busy.

The clock face shows 8.20 a.m., which is an easy one to work out.

Kosuke holds his mother's hand tight, though he cannot keep up with her.

She is looking in all directions and there is sweat on her forehead.

Kosuke has never seen that before.

He looks in all directions too, though he doesn't know what he's looking for.

'What you're looking for? I'll help you look,' he says up to the black tangle of her hair.

She doesn't hear him.

Her jaw is moving as she grinds her teeth.

Kosuke knows he has to be careful when she is like this, he knows he shouldn't ask questions. Buses come in and out of the station.

Families are waiting to be put together with their missing parts.

Kosuke knows he has no missing parts.

His mother takes him to the back end of the station, where the parked buses wait.

There is a strong smell of petrol.

She sits him down on a bench next to a drinks machine that doesn't work.

She puts his Captain Tsubasa backpack next to him.

She looks around, her eyes moving quickly.

The tiny pink strings in the corners are shiny and wet.

'Kosuke, your mother needs to go and do something, do you understand?'

Kosuke's mother never says *I*.

He nods *yes*, though he feels sick without knowing why.

'Look after your bag, you hear?'

Kosuke nods *yes*.

His mother turns to go.

She pauses.

She turns.

She comes back.

She crouches in front of him now, and he can smell her sweat.

'. . . Kosuke, you stay in plain sight. You remember the rhyme?'

Kosuke nods *yes*.

'Go on,' she says.

'One for sorrow . . . two for joy . . .'

'Good boy, carry on.'

She smiles and bites her lips at the same time.

She is very beautiful and Kosuke has noticed that people find it hard to look away from her.

It's the same when people see an accident on the road.

Or if they see a crazy person in the street.

She takes out some money from her bra and puts it in the back pocket of Kosuke's jeans.

'Do good things, boy. Good things.'

Then she stands and leaves, her head down.

He watches her mix in with the people until he can't see her any more.

Kosuke plays with the zip on his bag, making rip-rip sounds.

He looks inside and sees sandwiches and clothes.

He swings and swishes his feet and waits for his mother to come back.

They had to wake up early and Kosuke is tired.

It was still dark when she shook him awake.

'Three for a girl, four for a boy . . .'

He rubs his eyes now and lays his head on the backpack.

He can't help it but he falls asleep.

When Kosuke wakes, he knows something is wrong.

Too much time has passed and there are hardly any families at the other end of the bus station.

His mother told him to stay in plain sight.

Nobody can see him here.

Kosuke picks up his bag and wanders to the other end of the bus station.

People look at him and smile but he tries not to look at them.

Outside the station, it is getting dark even though the clock only shows four o'clock.

It's very cold and Kosuke wishes he had brought his mittens.

A man in a long, dark jacket stoops down in front of Kosuke now.

'Hello.' He pats Kosuke's head. 'You look like you're hungry. Do you like plums?'

Kosuke does not look at the man and he says nothing.

His mother has told him about that before.

The man looks around and then leaves.

Kosuke goes back to his bench.

Maybe he shouldn't have wandered off.

What if she had come back while he was away?

Kosuke knows he has to be careful with her.

Now that he has realized it's cold, he can't stop thinking about it.

95

Kosuke lays his head back down on his bag and closes his eyes again.

After a long time, a man nudges Kosuke.

He is tall and old and wearing a uniform.

This is a policeman.

Kosuke has always trusted policemen, but now that he is looking at one, he sees only a man.

'What's your name?'

Kosuke mumbles his name.

'You're lost, right?'

'My mother said I should wait here.'

'When was that?'

'The clock said 8.20 a.m.'

The policeman hides his lips for a second.

'How old are you?'

'I'm ten.'

'Is that true?'

Kosuke doesn't say anything.

'You ever ride in a police car before?'

Kosuke shakes his head *no*.

The policeman takes his hand and leads him out of the station.

The police car smells like lemons and cigarettes.

The policeman straps Kosuke in and then makes a call on his radio.

It's chilly but the policeman turns on the heating.

Warm air blows out with a loud moaning.

Kosuke sees the bus station get smaller in the mirror as they go faster.

The roads are very dark and the trees are white in the headlights as they flash by.

They are driving higher up a mountain.

The radio crackles and a fuzzy voice talks very quickly.

Then the policeman picks up the receiver and just says: *Understood.*

Kosuke looks at the ocean of stubbly trees crawling down the mountain.

Watching them swish by silently makes him sleepy.

The warm air is making his cheeks hot.

After a long time, the police car stops outside a small house on the edge of a steep forest.

The policeman opens the door for Kosuke and puts a hand on his shoulder.

'You'll stay here tonight. Tomorrow, we'll see.'

The porch stairs sigh and insects circle the bare bulb.

The policeman hangs his hat on a peg.

'Wait here.'

The policeman disappears for a short while as Kosuke smells the smell of other people's home. He comes back holding quilts and leads Kosuke to a side room.

He lays out the quilts in the corner.

The policeman pats him on the head and Kosuke smells a woody, smoky smell.

Then he goes.

Kosuke isn't tired any more.

He whispers to himself.

'Five for silver, six for gold.'

He sits up playing with the zip of his backpack.

Rip. Rip. Rip.

The next day is grey and wet.

Kosuke realizes that mountain days are much shorter than city days.

The bedroom door opens and an old lady with an angry face and a mess of grey hair is standing there.

She closes it and he hears her footsteps marching away.

Soon Kosuke hears the policeman's low voice, slow and sad.

'He's just a little boy.'

The woman is whispering very loudly.

Her voice sounds like soft wheels over gravel.

'Well, how long *for*, Eiji?'

Kosuke can't hear what the policeman says now but the woman talks over him.

'Well! He still needs feeding, doesn't he? He still needs clothing. He needs *things*, Eiji. You're too giving. They won't pay you for looking after him, will they? It's *cruel*, that's what it is. You think you're being kind, but actually it's the opposite.'

The door slides open and a chubby girl, a little older than Kosuke, walks in.

She closes the door behind her and sits in front of the TV.

'My grandmother,' she says over her shoulder. 'Always complaining.'

The girl turns on her SEGA Mark III and the shiny blue logo appears in the blackness.

Automatically, Kosuke sits quietly behind her.

She skips through the options menu and the title sequence but Kosuke already knows it.

This is *Bare Fist 2*.

Metro City was once a peaceful place until one day . . . an evil crime syndicate, headed by the mysterious Mr Z, moved in and took over. Gripped by a violent crime wave, the city was plunged into chaos and the police force has been corrupted. With no one else left, only you can save Metro City now . . . with your BARE FISTS!

The girl chooses Flame – the judo expert – and Round 1 begins.

She is good at this, hardly taking damage as she KOs wave after wave of bad guys.

Her cheeks glow blue from the TV.

Kosuke spends all day watching her mash buttons, taking back Metro City, one punk at a time.

It's not until late afternoon that he sees the policeman again.

The arguing in the hallway stopped a long time ago.

The policeman stands in the doorway, wearing his hat.

Kosuke picks up his backpack and waves goodbye to the girl.

'Bye,' she says, without looking over her shoulder.

The policeman puts Kosuke back in the police car and straps him in.

They set off back down the mountain.

'Are we looking for my mother now?'

The policeman looks at Kosuke in the rear-view mirror but says nothing.

He just drives.

Only the heating makes any noise.

Kosuke hopes he hasn't done anything wrong but he vows to be careful.

The last of the sun is sinking behind the mountains.

Kosuke wishes he could eat a mushroom and grow to be twice his size.

Kosuke wishes he could eat a power flower and throw fire from his hands.

Kosuke wishes he could watch the girl play SEGA for ever.

The drive is long and it's pitch black when the policeman stops the car.

Behind tall gates, a big building with tall windows stands in the middle of an empty field.

The sign reads:

SAKUZA CHRISTIAN ORPHANAGE –
KITAKUWADA DISTRICT

'Where are we?'

'Nearest village is Miyama. Wait here for me, son.'

Leather squeaks as the policeman swings out of the car.

As he passes the headlamps he lights up like the SEGA logo.

Then he disappears inside the building.

Kosuke waits and waits and realizes he is very hungry.

He takes out the sandwiches from his bag and begins to eat them.

He is thirsty and he needs the toilet.

He thinks about his mother but it makes him feel sick so he looks at the building again.

Behind it, a mountain rises up like a wave on pause.

Forest stretches out all around it.

The policeman comes back out with a woman in a black-and-white uniform.

She is wearing a black hood and a long silver cross bounces on her stomach as she walks.

The policeman opens the car door and Kosuke feels the cold.

'Come on, son.'

Kosuke steps out of the car and slips on his backpack. He can hear a river somewhere nearby.

'Thank you, Officer Tamura.'

The woman's voice is very strange.

She is tall and her skin is very pale.

The policeman nods, then without saying another word, he gets back into the car.

He reverses away, looking over his shoulder.

When the car is swallowed up by the dark, the woman takes Kosuke's hand.

'I'm Sister Mary Josephine, I'm the head nun here. You must be tired.'

She leads him through the wet grass towards the big building.

Inside, she smiles down at him as she locks the door.

Kosuke feels strange in his stomach, like an animal is digging down to get away.

The corridor is lined with pictures of a dying man.

In some he wears a nice blue yukata.

In others, he is almost naked, bleeding everywhere, his eyes rolled back.

In this dark, the floor is shiny like a frozen river.

Their footsteps are loud.

The woman clears her throat gently.

'You must be very tired, Kosuke.'

Kosuke doesn't know if he's tired or not.

She leads him up creaking stairs.

As they pass the windows, the moon illuminates her pale face.

She doesn't look down at Kosuke, she just stares straight ahead.

There is a slight smile on her lips.

Kosuke can't see her hair, or her feet.

She looks like a shadow with a woman's face.

At the end of the corridor, she stops and takes out her keys.

She leads Kosuke into a room of smelly feet, cold snot and fragile sleep.

She points to an empty bunk and Kosuke takes off his shoes.

He puts his backpack under his pillow and climbs into the bunk.

The nun turns to go, and this is when Kosuke realizes his mother has abandoned him.

This is when Kosuke realizes his mother is not coming back.

This is when he realizes that the policeman isn't looking for her.

Kosuke screams.

Faces rise up out of their slumber, some laughing, some angry.

They are grey smudges in this milky light.

Kosuke is holding up the money his mother gave him in both hands.

He's holding it up like treasure.

'PLEASE NO! PLEASE NO! DON'T GO! PLEASE!'

Kosuke is struggling to breathe.

Fear is eating him whole.

Voices are heard in the corridor now.

Lights are being turned on.

Kosuke grabs hold of the nun's ankles.

'Child, let go –'

Kosuke cannot let go.

'I WASN'T CAREFUL ENOUGH! I WASN'T I WASN'T I'M SORRY I'M SORRY!'

The other boys have descended on the small wad of money that Kosuke's mother gave him.

The nun is angrily trying to kick him off.

Someone is passing round his sandwiches.

The moon is smirking behind its cloudy fingers.

Mr Uesugi is prowling through the pews, his eyes sweeping over the tops of the little heads.

Kosuke feels the cold, hard stone on his knees.

He puts his hands together like the others do.

The words begin and he closes his eyes.

They are strange words.

If you close your eyes they sound like magic.

'Let us NOT!'

Mr Uesugi's voice is booming.

His footsteps echo loudly through the chapel and Kosuke peeks at his big shoes.

They shine like aubergines.

'Let us *not* become weary of doing *good* . . .'

Mr Uesugi checks that his children are kneeling well, their backs straight, their hands even.

He irons out those who are not with a kick.

'For if we do not *give up*.' Those last words drip with disgust. 'Then at the proper time *we will* reap a harvest. Galatians 6:9.'

Mr Uesugi's footsteps stop by Kosuke.

He rests his palm on Kosuke's small head.

'Oh, boys,' he sighs happily. 'Look out of the window.'

They all turn to look out of the window.

'Look at what the Lord God has given us. Remember these words, boys. *Our glories float between earth and heaven like clouds which seem pavilions of the sun.*'

A cold wind whistles and the wooden walls of the chapel tense up.

Kosuke imagines that wind looking down on them.

A little painted box in snow and grass, surrounded by naked trees.

'And REMEMBER!' He grins up at the stained-glass Christ. 'Here we are *together*. We are together and therefore we are joyous. *For whosoever is delighted in solitude is a wild beast or a god*. Aristotle.'

Mr Uesugi looks over the silent, kneeling children, their hair recently cut, still as stones at the bottom of a well.

Kosuke cries at night.

The other boys are used to ignoring tears and covering their ears.

So Kosuke is not expecting it when, some nights after arriving, two feet swing into view.

A boy called Kei drops down to the floor and lands like a cat.

Kosuke freezes, trying to bury a sob in his pillow.

Kei pats him over on the mattress and Kosuke turns to face the wall.

He feels warm arms loop around his shoulders.

He tries to squirm away but Kei does not let him, he is too strong.

'Shush.'

Kosuke falls quiet, sucking in breath in quick threes.

Then twos.

Then steady.

10. A Great White Shark

Iwata couldn't breathe through his nose.

He opened his eyes.

A hospital room.

Where?

He looked down and saw his patient ID on his wrist – *Chiba University Hospital.*

Dead petals from long-gone flowers lay by the window. Outside, the brown tube of the canal curved out eastwards. It was raining.

'Rise and shine, Inspector.'

Sakai was sitting across from the bed, papers splayed out around her.

'How long have I been here?'

'Twenty-four hours. Some blood loss. Twisted ankle. Busted nose. Couple of stitches for your fun. Want to tell me what it was all in aid of?'

'Did you find the black Honda?'

'Nothing turned up.'

Iwata registered something beneath her words.

'What is it, Sakai?'

She looked down at the pages around her.

'There's been another one.'

'Him?'

'Looks that way.'

Iwata swung his feet out of bed. His head was a rung bell. His ankle was cracked porcelain.

Sakai threw a plastic bag on the bed containing cheap, no-brand clothes and underwear from a supermarket.

'Your clothes were ruined, I threw them away, except your jacket.'

Iwata hobbled behind the screen and changed. When he was done, Sakai opened the door and her heels clicked down the busy corridor loudly. Iwata struggled to keep pace.

'Something isn't right,' he mumbled.

'What do you mean?'

'I mean someone tried to kill me in broad daylight.'

She paused in the corridor and turned to him.

'*Someone.* In a black Honda Odyssey.'

'I'm confused as to why you sound dubious, Sakai.'

She sidestepped him and carried on walking.

'Iwata, it's obvious that you haven't been sleeping or been eating right. Now you were hit pretty hard on the head the other day –'

He laughed harshly. 'That's sweet of you, but I know what I saw, Sakai. If I were half a second slower, I'd have bigger problems than a poor sleeping routine.'

They reached the elevator and Sakai punched the button.

'You saw the driver? You get the registration?'

'No.'

'Then it could have been anyone.'

'Sakai, you know as well as I do who was driving that car.'

'You think it was the killer. But you can't prove it was the killer. You don't even know it wasn't some drunk, too smashed to have even seen you.'

'In reverse? In the middle of nowhere? What would he even be doing there?'

'I was thinking of asking you the same thing.'

They stared at each other until the doors slid open.

'Suit yourself, Iwata. But Shindo's pretty pissed off. You

think it will escape his attention that instead of working our case you were snooping outside a dead colleague's house? And I'm sure you'll be able to bullshit him later, but you have no reason to hold out on me.'

She hit the button and the elevator began its descent.

'All right. Fuck it. I think that Akashi could have known more than what's in that case file.'

Sakai shook her head, a husband tired of this line of complaint.

'Even if that were true, what difference would it make now?'

'*Think* about it, Sakai. Why did Akashi kill himself all of a sudden? Why is his house burnt to the ground? And why does someone try to kill me when I snoop there?'

'Chiba PD says local delinquents use the place to get high – probably what caused the house fire. As for your hit and run, they're assuming it's the same little gang.'

They reached the car park and Sakai led them to the Isuzu.

'Do you mind driving?' Iwata nodded down at his ankle.

'You drive like a grandmother anyway.'

'Sakai, I checked that house from top to bottom. There was no drug paraphernalia present. "Delinquent" is a cosy word which saves people work. But someone burnt that house down. And someone went for me when I looked.'

Sakai corkscrewed them up to street-level and waited for her opening in the traffic.

'OK, let's say Akashi did know more than the contents of our case file. What would that prove? He clearly wasn't well. A guy thinking straight doesn't throw himself off Rainbow Bridge.'

'Or maybe he does.'

'What does that mean?'

Iwata shrugged and looked out of the window. Rain started to drum on the roof of the car. They drove in silence for a while. Iwata kept his eyes closed and tried to ignore his pains.

'Where we headed?'

'Sagami Bay,' she replied. 'Victim is a Yuko Ohba. Widow in her late seventies. No children or known family. Heart removed, just like Tsunemasa Kaneshiro. Kanagawa PD has sealed the scene for us.'

'Did they establish time of death?'

'Two nights ago. But no traces of Kiyota so far, if that's what you're thinking.'

Sakai made the turning to join the expressway.

She drove south, skirting Yokohama, bound for the tip of the Miura Peninsula. Sagami Bay, the Bōsō Peninsula, the Uraga Channel. Iwata knew these place names from history lessons. A century ago, beneath Izu Ōshima Island to the south, the Great Kantō Earthquake had awakened. It devoured Tokyo, Yokohama, and the surrounding prefectures. Some 100,000 died.

Today, the sea was a calm expanse of tinfoil grey. Grass fluttered along the coastline. On the sandy slopes leading down to the water, crinum lilies grew like white stars. Farther along the coastline, Japanese black pines stood guard over nesting cormorants. They squawked in and out of the cold water and huddled together when the wind blew.

Sitting beyond these pines, almost completely enveloped by bushes and creeping ivy, was their destination: 6082 Misakimachi Moroiso. Dust coated the windows and the paint on the exterior walls of the house was curling away. The telephone wires above were now just green vines. Piles of rubbish and old furniture strewn on either side. There would have been a beautiful sea view but the brambles had not been cut back in years. It was not a long walk to the neighbouring property, a large, modern white structure, but the thorny bushes and rubbish marked its isolation. Today, the road had been cordoned off.

Sakai parked and got out of the car, narrowing her eyes as the ocean breeze buffeted her. Iwata hopped out and buttoned up his jacket to the top. A portly cop in his fifties broke off from the police huddle and approached them.

'Whatever you need, I'll take care of it.'

'Sergeant, I'm Iwata. This is Assistant Inspector Sakai. Division One.' He nodded at the house. 'I'm assuming we have no witnesses?'

'I'm afraid not, sir.'

Sakai cut in.

'Did you speak to the neighbours?'

The sergeant seemed taken aback by her tone but he nodded.

'They arrived this morning for the weekend. They've holidayed here for ten years and never once saw the victim. They thought her house was abandoned.'

'Signs of forced entry?'

'No, ma'am. Though the back window to the kitchen was open.'

'Who found the body?'

'The delivery boy. He was her only contact with the outside world. Though even then, the kid says he hardly ever saw her. She'd leave the money, he'd leave the food and collect her trash.'

'Kid?' Iwata asked as he surveyed the house.

'He's fifteen.'

'Does he have an alibi?' Sakai asked.

The sergeant flashed a wolfish smile, misreading her question for humour. He immediately realized his error and cleared his throat.

'He was home all night. With his parents.'

They reached the front door and Sakai waved the man away with curt thanks. His face darkened but he left as instructed. Iwata sighed and ducked under the police tape. Large lamps illuminated a gloomy hallway full of dusty newspapers, phone books and packaging from the convenience store. To the left, the shōji was open, revealing an empty room. Inside, there was only an ornate Butsudan shrine in the corner. Next to this was an old black-and-white photograph of a man with white hair and large bags beneath his eyes. He wore the black robes and white neckpiece of a judge. On his wrist, an expensive gold watch with a sapphire face.

Iwata could smell incense in the room but it was not the same odour as from the Kaneshiros' house. It was too flowery, too sweet. Sakai turned left into the kitchen and gagged. The room had been abandoned to the filth long ago.

'Sakai? You OK?'

She answered covering her mouth.

'Just rotting food, I think.'

Iwata hobbled up the stairs. Countless photographs of the old couple hung on the walls. There was a great variety in both the quality and the backgrounds of the photographs, as well as in the changing faces of the subjects as they aged.

Iwata saw the door of the master bedroom was open. It framed two bare legs. The skin was a translucent papyrus of purple veins and discoloured splotches. Beyond the legs, silver light from the bay windows flooded in. Iwata could smell faeces. Above that stench, now he did recognize the smoky, citric, earthen smell that had also lingered in the Kaneshiros' house.

You again.

Standing in the doorway, Iwata saw the whole scene. The woman was spreadeagled in the middle of the floor, the sheets and blankets beneath her showing she had been dragged. Her eyes were fixed on the sea, two old marbles. She had the same gaping tunnel to her heart. The same black staining on the fingers of her left hand. On the wall behind her was another black sun symbol, as tall as Iwata.

Iwata heard the soft ticking of the gold watch he had seen in the photograph. Mrs Ohba kept it on her bedside table.

'Oh this is very chic, I love what they've done with the wallpaper.' Sakai appeared beside Iwata and handed him rubber gloves. He avoided the blood spatter and crouched down over the body, steadying himself with his free hand. Peering into the cavity beneath the old woman's ribs, he took out his flashlight and shone it into the bloody hole.

'No heart.'

Iwata stood and peered closely at the symbol on the wall.

'There are differences in size and shape – the old woman's trembling could have affected it – but this is the same symbol as before.' He moved in closely and sniffed the air. 'And he used charcoal?'

Sakai stood next to him and sniffed the symbol.

'. . . Something else,' she murmured.

They looked down at the floor. A funeral urn was upturned, its contents making a small, grey dune.

'What's the betting that's the late Mr Ohba on the wall?' Iwata said.

Sakai wrinkled her nose and crouched down by the body. She delicately held up the old woman's left index finger. It was the same grey as the pile of ash.

'He made her draw the symbol with her husband's ashes.' Sakai chewed her bottom lip. 'Then he took her heart. Same as Tsunemasa Kaneshiro. But why not the others?'

'He was there for the father – for his heart. The others had to die, but only because they were in the way.'

Sakai folded her arms.

'OK, so what's the connection between Tsunemasa Kaneshiro and Mrs Ohba?'

'Don't forget *Mr* Ohba.' Iwata smiled.

'Surely you can't include a dead man on a list of murder victims?'

'I'm including him on a list of connected people. He's part of the ritual too.'

Sakai patted her cheek with the butt of her pen. She clucked her tongue.

'I fucking hate this guy.'

'Sakai, you're going to have to work your charms with the local PD and make sure they've combed her background thoroughly. The husband too – if he was a judge, there's a nice ripe patch for revenge motives there.'

Sakai grinned.

'Perp gets out after a thirty stretch and wants to take it out on the asshole that put him there – then he finds out the old crow died so he takes it out on the wife?'

'So how does the Kaneshiro family fit?'

'Witness testimony?'

Iwata nodded an open-ended nod.

'Get on to judicial administration in Tokyo – see if we can dig that sort of information up. Then you hit the records, Sakai.'

'What do you want?'

'Answers. Did the Kaneshiro family and the Ohbas ever live in the same neighbourhood? The same town? Same car dealer? Doctor? Did they ever shop at the same supermarket? Bank? Phone record cross-checks. Anything.'

Sakai nodded.

'What's wrong, Iwata? Why are you making that face?'

'Because this makes no sense. This woman hasn't left her

house in a decade – how did the killer know she was here? They can't have been friends.'

Sakai shrugged.

'Maybe he didn't. Maybe he thought the place was empty and she winds up dead.'

Iwata shook his head.

'What does he want with this place, then?'

'Money.'

Iwata nodded to the bedside table.

'But he leaves the antique gold watch and ignores the huge house up the road? No, he knew she was here, just like he knew where the Kaneshiros were.'

Sakai nodded softly.

'Two secluded houses . . .'

'Both the father and Mrs Ohba were forced to make a black sun. Both had their hearts removed. But why? If we connect them, we take our first step forward.'

Sakai looked out of the window. A crowd had formed.

'Oh shit.'

'What is it?'

'Shindo is here.'

'You go now, Sakai. I'll call you later.'

She nodded once, searched for words, but left the room with just a sigh. Iwata heard her greet Shindo at the entrance of the house. There was no response. Heavy footfalls swallowed stairs. The two men came eye to eye in the gloomy corridor. There was only the noise of Shindo breathing through his nose.

'Is the victim in there?'

'Yes.'

Shindo passed the master bedroom and opened the door to a small, cramped room. The legal textbooks, academic papers and newspaper clippings said this was Mr Ohba's old study. One corner had been taken over by his wife – sudoku magazines were arranged in neat piles and a half-knitted scarf lay in its own entrails on the crowded desk. There was an old leather seat which Shindo pointed to. Iwata sat as directed and Shindo closed the door. His words were quiet.

'You saw the local press are out there?'

'No.'

Shindo punched the wall above Iwata's head and plaster showered down.

'They're standing there with their dicks in their hands, going berserk for the first story to hit this fucking place since 1923. And let me tell you, they won't stay local for long.'

'They won't have any details yet.'

'Details?' Shindo started to pace the small room. 'Let me tell you about details. Yesterday morning, some smug fuck from one of the nationals calls me, threatening to run with police ineptitude on tonight's front page if I don't give him a little more meat on his plate. Quite understandably, I tell him to get fucked and hang up, safe in the knowledge that the cerebral Inspector Iwata is on the case. But, the call has left me a little flustered it has to be said. So just to make myself feel better, I go ahead and call the reliable Assistant Inspector Sakai anyway. Imagine my surprise, then, when Sakai tells me that instead of doing what I fucking told him to do – hitting the ground running and putting a fucking investigation together – Iwata has, in fact, visited an old buddy and managed to get himself involved in a fucking traffic accident. Well, I say to myself, there must be some reason for this odd behaviour. And *then* I'm informed that one of my more senior inspectors has been physically assaulted over a misunderstanding – assaulted by none other than Inspector . . .'

Iwata shifted.

'Shindo, hold on –'

'So *now* I'm sat there with serious doubts. I ask myself, what has the TMPD got to show for its trust? So I make a list: a retard pervert in bracelets, a missing drunk and some fucking graffiti on a wall.'

Silence throbbed between the two men for a moment.

'I can't close a case like this in a week. As for Moroto, he's lying.'

'Fuck Moroto, he's an asshole. But *you* . . . Well, Inspector, you deserve all the gold stars. Fucking bravo.'

'Boss, what do you want me to do?'

'Two hours ago I get the same journalist fuck calling me up to tell me that he's heard there's been a grisly homicide in Sagami Bay. Word gets around externally and internally. Do you know who Fujimura is?'

Iwata gestured *upstairs* with a forefinger.

'That's right, *Superintendent* Fujimura. He calls me upstairs for a chat. He wonders how long it will take the press to connect this judge's wife with the Korean family. He asks me what I think we should do to improve the situation, bearing in mind the Mina Fong murder is now hitting the international press and we haven't found a single fucking clue. So now I'm sat there thinking how maybe this is all Inspector Iwata's fault. I get to thinking maybe he's not so fucking cerebral after all. And then the solution becomes obvious – I should just sack him.'

Iwata held up his hand, his head pounding, his airways blocked.

'I get there's pressure, Shindo. I understand. But headlines will happen.'

The older man's laugh was incredulous.

'Are you fucking kidding me?'

Iwata was shaking.

'Shindo, please listen to me. The Black Sun Killer has murdered five people in five days and left behind nothing that he didn't intend to leave behind. He's a great white shark, Shindo. He's bigger than Mina Fong, or any press attention. You need to give me a chance to catch him.'

Shindo pointed to the bedroom next door.

'And get a couple more like that you mean? No, fuck your glib remarks, Iwata. You talk to me about sharks, well I've got an office full of them hungry for the work.'

'I can get him.'

Shindo sighed as he picked shards of plaster from his knuckles.

'If this asshole is so fucking special, give me one single reason to make me think you're able to get him.'

Iwata pinched the bridge of his nose. He tried to contain the burning in his forehead and the churning in his empty stomach. Shindo jabbed a finger into his shoulder.

'*One.*'

'The killer works fast.' Iwata exhaled shakily, he knew he was on the ropes. 'That means our trail stays warm. Also, he's not afraid of us. That's clear. And I think that's a weakness we can use against him. Sooner or later he'll slip. Shindo, I'm smart enough and I'm quick enough. Give me the chance.'

Shindo raked his stubble for a long while, then leant back against the desk and shook his head.

'Kid, I came here to fire you.'

'Please.'

'There are no feelings here. Hard or otherwise.'

Iwata held his head in his hands.

'I need this.'

'What?'

'I *need* this,' he shouted.

Shindo regarded his subordinate. Struggling. Weak. But

sharp. He exhaled, then cursed Iwata.

'All right. I'll say only this. Find him, Inspector. You find him. I want day-to-day progress.'

'Thank you,' Iwata said quietly.

'I must be crazy.'

Shindo stood and blew the last of the plaster from his knuckles.

'Iwata, listen. There are certain people in the department who aren't comfortable with your . . . approach.'

'What do you mean?'

'Just do me one favour.' He sighed. 'Take care of yourself.'

'What are you saying?'

Shindo left the room and Iwata listened as the older man creaked down the stairs. He could hear it was raining outside. Above him there was a photograph of the Ohbas on holiday in Pompeii. They were smiling amid the ruins. Sakai appeared at the door.

'You OK?'

Iwata nodded.

'Well, chin up, some good news at last.' She grinned. 'They've found our girl, they found Asako Ozaki.'

11. The Whirlpool

Tsukuba-Kita Police Station sat on a lonely tract of State Road 125, in the shadow of the mountain. There was a large blue frog mascot by the parking lot. The Japanese flag fluttered on the roof. If it weren't for the patrol cars outside, the building could easily be mistaken for a second-hand car dealership. Behind the station, green rice paddies stretched to the horizon, interrupted only by the occasional pylon.

Down in the guts of the holding cells, Kodai Kiyota cowered in a corner. He clutched his head between gnarled hands. His face was long and horse-like, his cheekbones prominent. When he grimaced, he showed large, square teeth. On his temples, veins struggled to the surface like worms. Kiyota was too thin for a man of his frame.

This was his second night in the cell and he still didn't know why. Gasping in pain, he stood, covering himself in the sodden blanket. From the barred window, he could see the roadside sign:

MOUNT TSUKUBA – IBARAKI'S MOST
FAMOUS SON

He closed his eyes and tried to remember the myths his grandfather told him as a boy.

Thousands of years ago, a god descended from the heavens and asked Mount Fuji for a place to spend the night in return for blessings. With its great summit and almost perfect cone, proud Mount Fuji refused. The god then asked our own Mount Tsukuba, who humbly welcomed

him as an honoured guest, even offering food and water. Today, Mount
Fuji is a lonely and barren place, while our mountain bursts with vege-
tation and the changing colours of the seasons.

Kiyota vomited violently in the toilet. Hearing this, the
policemen outside slammed on his door with their nightsticks.
When Kiyota was finished, he forced himself not to sob.

We told you you would end up here again.

Good to see you after all this time.

Welcome home.

The first of the day's trams trilled through the Setagaya
streets. Bakeries cast warm light on the rain-slick pavements.
Umbrellas sprouted like sea anemones. Hatanaka was waiting outside Setagaya HQ, his face sullen. He caught sight of
his own reflection in a puddle and looked away.

'Look who it is,' Iwata called.

Hatanaka greeted the detectives with his eyes on the floor.

'Where did you pick the girl up?' Sakai asked.

'Outside the Kaneshiro family house,' Hatanaka replied
quietly. 'She was spray-painting the walls. Racial insults, that
kind of thing.'

Iwata and Sakai looked at each other.

'Did you get a call?' Iwata asked.

Hatanaka shook his head.

'I've been back to the house a few times. I was there on a
whim. I guess I got lucky.'

'Where is she?' Sakai asked.

'The canteen. I didn't want to put her in the holding cells.'

Sakai brushed past him but Iwata clapped a hand on his
shoulder.

'You did good work, Hatanaka.'

Even at this early hour, the canteen was a rowdy din
of clattering plates and guffawing, the ceiling blanketed in

cigarette smoke. Soon to be on-duty officers drank coffee and read newspapers. None of them found it strange that a fourteen-year-old girl might be among them.

In the corner, Asako Ozaki kept her eyes on the floor. She wore pink eye make-up, vivid green contact lenses, an oversized Babymetal T-shirt and tartan knee-socks. On her feet, she wore battered old Converse, the only thing about her that looked childlike and vulnerable. The rest of her was ironic cutesy. They sat on either side of her, Sakai placing a hot chocolate on the table.

'Asako.' She cleared her throat. 'I know you don't want to talk to us, so we can do one of two things. We can call your little stunt last night minimal juvenile delinquency and you can walk out of here in ten minutes. Or we can call it a "hate crime", which, as I'm sure you know, carries consequences. Up to you. But think about it. A cute, fourteen-year-old ultra-nationalist desecrates the home of a murdered family? If we go down that road, the news networks will be all over you. You will not enjoy it. Any secrets you ever had become public property. Believe me, Asako. I don't want to go down that route. I want you to talk to us.'

Asako Ozaki blinked.

'About what?'

'Kodai Kiyota.'

The girl folded her arms.

'It is a risky matter to discuss a happiness that has no need of words.'

Iwata snorted.

'Quoting Mishima won't impress us, kid. If you think shacking up with a man old enough to be your father is paradise then fine, but you're not protecting Kiyota by not speaking to us. You're only hurting yourself.'

Sakai shot him a look.

'We just want to talk to him.' Sakai smiled. 'Get things straight.'

Ozaki laughed bitterly.

'Sure you do. Look, I don't know anything about any murdered family.'

'Really.' Iwata raised his eyebrows. 'You don't know the Kaneshiro family?'

'Yeah I know them. So?'

'You're telling me you didn't attack Tsunemasa Kaneshiro?'

Ozaki regarded Iwata scornfully.

'That fucking cockroach humiliated Kodai. That's why he left Tokyo. Do you think I would let that go unpunished? I might not be much to look at but that Zainichi pig underestimated me. Kodai had nothing to do with it.'

Iwata shook his head.

'I'm sorry, you expect us to believe that *you* murdered an entire family?'

'Who said anything about murder? That's what you're talking about. I stabbed him, that's all.'

'So you mean to tell me you didn't know the Kaneshiro family were murdered? Maybe you don't read the papers.'

Ozaki looked from Iwata to Sakai.

'I didn't know. I figured they had finally left the house.'

'So where did you attack him? When?' Iwata pressed.

'Outside his office. A few weeks ago. Sounds like you already know that much.'

Sakai cut in.

'You said Kiyota left. Where to?'

Iwata bristled at Sakai's shift in direction.

'Ibaraki. His parents live near Mount Tsukuba. Go find him, I don't care. I woke up. He'll die realizing he shouldn't have tossed me away so easily. Hey, you know what I realized the only difference between them and us is?' Ozaki jutted her chin towards Iwata.

'We're both assholes, it's just that their kind spends less time feeling sorry for themselves. So fuck Kodai. I hope he falls down a well. But he didn't kill anyone, I can tell you that much.'

Sakai chewed away a smile as she knelt down and undid the girl's handcuffs. As Ozaki adjusted her plastic wristbands to cover the red marks, Sakai stood over her.

'If you've lied to me, I'll be pissed off.'

Ozaki grinned.

'Something tells me I don't think I'd want to see that.'

'Go on, get out of here. And quit the dumb shit.'

Asako Ozaki shuffled away as though she had just left one boring lecture, bound for another.

Sakai sipped the untouched hot chocolate.

'You're staring at me.'

'What was that?' he asked.

'Prioritizing.'

'Not sentimentality?'

'Fuck off, Iwata. She gave us what we needed.'

'She admitted to a hatred of our victims. She admitted to trying to *stab the father*. She's part of an ultra-nationalist group. Is graffiti the only threat she poses?'

'Fine. You tell Shindo you suspect a child, I'll go find Kiyota.'

Iwata swore under his breath and stood up. He followed Sakai to his car and got in on the passenger side. Ignoring Sakai's whistling, he reclined the seat and was asleep within seconds.

After prayers, Kosuke has a free afternoon. It's Sunday. The other boys are outside playing table tennis, or downstairs in the main hall betting on cards. Kosuke is in the dormitory, lying on his bunk, reading a book. He has been here for more than two years.

Kei walks in, hands in his pockets, whistling.

'Wanna see something?'

'What?'

'Well, do you, or not?'

Kosuke hides his book under his pillow and follows. At the perimeter, they hop over the low brick wall and they dash for the forest.

Once they get to the treeline, they are safe. That's what Kei says and Kosuke trusts him. The other boys don't talk to Kei but it doesn't matter to him.

He watches Kei walk deftly along a fallen log, his arms out like a tightrope walker.

'Why don't they let you come to this forest?'

'Me?' Kei smiles over his shoulder and hops down. 'You mean *us*, Iwata.'

'OK, *us*.'

'Because of the bear. That's what they say, anyway.'

'Bear?'

Kei shows his incisors. The thin branches above them creak under the weight of last night's snow. The hill is carpeted in brown leaves and rocks. White breath webs out over their shoulders. Their cheeks are bright, red mushrooms. A stream gurgles nearby.

'Kei? You think there's a bear?'

'Maybe there is.' One shoulder skips up. 'But that fuckin' nun talks about it all the time just to keep us from acting up.'

They reach the top of the hill and it's a sheer drop down to the silver gush of the river. The height makes Kosuke feel like his legs are melting. He imagines how it would hurt to fall.

They carry on along the ridge, following the river. Kei leads, sending avalanches of dead leaves hissing down the hill. Kosuke traces the footsteps, smelling the perfume beneath the mud. The sky darkens and a light rain begins to trickle through the leaves.

'Maybe we should go back,' Kosuke calls.

Kei spins round, his hands behind his back, and he strides around in a circle. The imitation of Mr Uesugi is crude but undeniable.

'The Lord is my light and my revelation! Whom shall I fear?' He kicks his boots high up into the air, a crazed look on his face. 'The Lord is the strength of my life! Of whom am I afraid?'

Kosuke joins in now, laughing, marching in his own little circle of righteousness.

'When the wicked came upon me to eat up my flesh, they stumbled and they fell,' he joins in gleefully.

Kei climbs a rock and looks around the forest as though it were his chapel.

'Let us NOT . . . fear the bear! For he who trusts in the Lord can never be eaten up by any heathen bear.'

Kosuke falls against a tree trunk laughing, holding his ribs.

Kei looks the proudest and highest he has ever seen someone look.

Then they huddle under an outcropping and wait in silence for the rain to pass.

By the time it's finished, the day is almost gone.

They carry on along the ridge which has thinned to half its width now.

Kei holds on to branches as he goes.

This deep into the forest, it's always cold and there is never much light.

Kosuke can hear a strange sound getting louder now – a crashing sound with a murmuring underneath that.

Ug.

Ug.

Ug.

'Kei?' Kosuke calls.

Kei doesn't look back.

'We're almost there,' he says.

The end of the ridge is very narrow, just wide enough for them to stand side by side.

Kei stops. He points down and Kosuke looks over his shoulder.

The eye of the whirlpool is blinking up at them.

Iwata wants to run away and never come back.

Kei stares down at it, enthralled.

'Sometimes,' he whispers, 'I dream about it.'

It swirls.

It swirls.

It smiles.

12. Orange

Iwata and Sakai arrived at Tsukuba-Kita Police Station at 6 p.m. The cop behind the front desk looked up from his manga.

'Shibuya. Division One,' Iwata said. 'We need an address for the parents of Kodai Kiyota.'

'You won't need to bother them. He's downstairs. We pulled him for a domestic disturbance at his parents' house.'

Iwata and Sakai looked at each other, smiles spreading over their faces.

In a tiny subterranean interrogation room, Kiyota was shivering badly. Small, grey jewels of sweat clung to his stubble. He was handcuffed. Sakai paced the room like a jaguar before feeding time. Iwata, the tired zookeeper, sat across from Kiyota and lit a cigarette. He pressed record on the tape.

'Friday, 25 February 2011, 6.09 p.m. Interviewee is Kodai Kiyota, forty-five years of age. No counsel present.'

Then there was only the tiny sound of paper crackling as Iwata smoked. Kiyota was hunched, his head in his hands.

'You OK, mister?' Sakai asked.

'Fine,' he bleated through gritted teeth.

'It's just that you look like total shit.'

'Mr Kiyota.' Iwata smiled glass. 'What are you doing in Ibaraki?'

'I'm from this town.'

'You live in Tokyo.'

'Seeing the folks, seeing the sights. Are you going to tell me what the fuck is going on?'

Sakai kicked the back of Kiyota's chair hard and he flinched.

'Like he doesn't fucking know,' she snorted.

Kiyota turned to look at her, his eyes pink.

Iwata snapped his fingers.

'Don't look at her, look at me.'

'What's her fucking problem?'

'Kiyota, don't make me repeat myself. Now we were having a nice, respectful conversation. Tell me about Nippon Kumiai.'

Kiyota waved the concept away.

'I'm not part of that any more. It's bullshit, anyway.'

'Why?'

'All talk, no action, everything needs agreement. Funding disappears down black holes. Fucking waste of time.'

Sakai huffed.

'They said the same thing about you. With the added detail that you're a fucking useless drunk and a pervert.'

Kiyota stiffened but didn't reply.

Iwata cleared his throat.

'Do you know Yuko Ohba? Her husband, Terai Ohba?'

'Nope.'

'Do you know the Kaneshiro family?'

'Yeah, the Zainichi family. So?'

Sakai tossed her police ID on the table.

'Read that out to me.'

Kiyota opened the black wallet.

'Noriko Sakai, Assistant Inspector. So?'

'And what does it say underneath?'

'Tokyo Metropolitan Police Department.'

'Correct. Tokyo Metropolitan Police Department. Which, interestingly enough, is an anagram for KIYOTA GETS FUCKED IN THE ASS.'

'Let me spell that out for you.' Iwata snatched the ID and quickly buffed it with his sleeve before handing it back to Sakai. 'We can charge you with obstruction of justice, meaning another twenty-three days in here . . .'

'I'm not obstructing –'

'That's in addition to the twenty-one days these guys have left with you for breaching the peace at your folks' place. Now, even your average guy doesn't want that, but *you*? With your shakes . . .'

Kiyota kicked the table leg.

'I'm not fucking obstructing anything! Just tell me what you need.'

Sakai sat on the table.

'*Come on*, Kiyota.' She grinned. 'Just tell us.'

'Tell you *what*?'

'You killed them, didn't you?'

Kiyota laughed out loud.

'Who! That fucking family? Yeah, I cut them up in little pieces. Lock me up and throw away the key.'

Iwata stubbed out his cigarette.

'You don't sound surprised to learn that they're dead, Mr Kiyota. You don't look like a man who reads the papers, though.'

'You're Homicide, you're asking about them – I'm not that fucking simple.'

'You deny having anything to do with their murders?'

'Of course I fucking deny it.'

Sakai hopped off the table and began to circle him.

'Let me tell you a little story, Kiyota. Sometimes, when we get liars, we suggest they take a polygraph test. Now these look very official, what with all the wires, the technician and whatnot. But you know what gives the liars away?'

Kiyota said nothing.

'We lie to *them*. We tell them that sweat interferes with the test so we ask them to go wash their hands. Then we all rush into the CCTV room for a good laugh. The liar turns on the tap, stands by the hand-dryer, you know – they make a big show of it. But of course, the liars never wash their hands. So what I'm saying to you is that we fucking *know* liars. We smell them out for a living. And you fucking stink.'

A wave of hatred washed across Kiyota's face. He struggled to keep his voice level.

'You don't know me.'

'No?' Sakai's smile was beautiful. 'Aged nineteen, you are booked into this very station on petty delinquency charges. It would be the first of four occasions. On the last, the charge is rape. You serve an eight-year stretch, which seems a little harsh to me. When you come out, you move straight to Tokyo – a fucking bumpkin like you, and yet you manage to carve out a life in Shinjuku. And with your new gangster friends, you fall off the face of the earth for a decade. Next time you show your face, you're wearing a suit and have a megaphone in your hand. You realize that with politics you can finally put your talents to good use *and* make a difference. Besides, you've always been a proud nationalist, why not do something about these foreign assholes? You jump from group to group until you end up with the comparatively respectable Nippon Kumiai. It's around this time that the Vivus mixed-use construction project is announced in Setagaya, where you're now living with your wife – sorry, *ex*-wife. The project will be good for local commerce, good for Setagaya – good for Japan. But, as usual, the fucking Zainichi element is getting in the way. The Kaneshiro family don't want to sell up. Nippon Kumiai needs some firm action, so you say you'll handle it. You stake your reputation on it. *Good ol' Kodai Kiyota can be relied on. He'll be able to frighten those bastards out of Setagaya.* Only, they don't frighten. They don't sell. In fact, you start to look like an asshole. So much for the ex-yakuza mystique, eh? Things get embarrassing in NK and things get ugly with the wife, don't they? Especially when she finds out about that teenager you've been fucking, am I right?'

Kiyota turned to Iwata.

'I don't have to listen to this –'

'*Maybe* that's the moment you decide to take matters into your own hands, eh? Only that stubborn bastard Kaneshiro isn't listening, is he? Maybe it's then that all your helplessness and impotence finally erupts and you slaughter the guy just because he wants to protect his own home and his own family. What a fucking model citizen.'

Kiyota shook his head incredulously.

'She's fucking crazy.'

Iwata tapped on the table for concentration like a conductor.

'Kiyota, did you know Mr and Mrs Terai and Yuko Ohba?'

'I told you, no!'

From his inside pocket, Iwata produced an old local newspaper article:

LOCAL BOY CONVICTED OF RAPE

Flanking the article was a grainy picture of Judge Terai Ohba.

Iwata leant forward.

'You do remember him now, don't you?'

'So I couldn't remember the judge's name. Big deal. You can't keep me here without –'

Sakai kicked Kiyota's chair again and he flinched.

'Stop that!'

'I'll stop when you talk to me.'

'What do you want?'

'Eight years for rape . . . Probably seemed a little steep to you. Very steep. Time like that can really change a man.'

Kiyota was practically in tears of anger.

'What *is* this shit, man? What's that got to do with anything?'

'Everything, honey. Because maybe after you got done annihilating the Kaneshiro family, you got to thinking how different it all might have been if you had been treated more fairly from the start. And what have you got to lose at this point? You think you might as well get even, give back a little judgement of your own. Only then you realize that you waited too long and the old bastard has died. It's just the old widow who's there. But you're angry. You've come all that way, after all. You'll have your vengeance. Vengeance is all you have left, isn't it, Kiyota?'

'This is bullshit –'

'You killed the Kaneshiro family. You killed them and you enjoyed it. Then, free of inhibition, you travelled to Sagami Bay and you killed Mrs Ohba. A fucking rapist, a child molester and a gangster. Now a murderer too. That's why you ended up here, back at the start of things, drinking yourself into oblivion. That's why you're back to square one. Because you have nothing left, and nowhere to go. Isn't that the truth?'

Kiyota shouldered away a grubby, resentful tear. Rage trembled on his lips. Iwata glanced at Sakai.

'So you see, Kiyota, you were wrong.' Finished, she leant back against the wall. 'I *do* know you. And it took me two minutes flat to comprehend the whole fucking mess of your worthless life.'

Iwata spoke quietly now.

'Where were you on the night between the fourteenth and fifteenth of February?'

Kiyota looked up.

'I'm fucking glad! I'm fucking *glad* they're dead!'

He struggled with his handcuffs and spat on the floor.

'Did you kill them?'

'I didn't kill anyone!'

'So why the little party, Kiyota?' Sakai sneered.

'Because I'm dying, all right? You fucking bitch, I'm dying.'

She looked at Iwata. Kiyota caught it.

'Call my oncologist, see if I'm lying.'

He turned to Iwata.

'And, Inspector? Do me a favour when you find whoever did these murders? Make sure they get a fucking pat on the back from me.'

Iwata stopped the tape and Sakai blinked, as though she had been snapped out of a hypnotic state.

She called for the guard to open the door. He did so, then unshackled Kiyota from the table and led him away.

Night had come. Cold rainclouds enveloped the mountain like a gloomy Saturn. Only occasional cars lit up the long road, candles cupped by hands in a dark corridor.

Beauty lies not in objects, but in the interaction between their shadow and light.

Across from Tsukuba-Kita Police Station, Iwata and Sakai were sitting in a lonely ramen restaurant. They were hunched over their bowls at the counter, slurping soba in silence. The waitress topped up their plastic cups with green tea and returned to her game show on a flickering TV. Iwata drained his broth and looked around. He saw only policemen and drivers, all of them by themselves, all of them here transiently, none of them by choice.

'For a moment,' Iwata said, 'you almost had me convinced in there.'

'Much of what I said fits.' She pushed away her bowl.

'And a lot doesn't. No trace evidence of Kiyota at either scene. And he's right-handed.'

'But he is physically *capable* of carrying out these murders and he's got a history of violence. Trace evidence might yet still turn up at the scenes. And I'll call that oncologist to confirm his story. Could be bullshit.'

Sakai paid, pocketed the receipt and they left. They hurried across the road to the police car park.

'It needs a wash,' Sakai said, getting behind the wheel of the Isuzu. 'Actually, you just need a new car. This is a piece of shit, Iwata.'

'But it's a classic.'

'That's just another way of saying you're hanging on to the past.'

He looked out of the window and watched the mountains recede into lacquer.

Kosuke is thirteen today. He sits on the bench by the driveway, wearing his best clothes. He keeps his eyes on the mountain. His mother has telephoned and she wants to take her son out for the day.

'*Are you excited to see me?*'

'*Yes.*'

'*You don't sound it.*'

'*I am.*'

'*It's been a long time, I understand you might feel strange.*'

'*Where do you live?*'

'*We'll talk about that. Your new father will be coming too. He's a wonderful man. Very respected. An American.*'

'*American?*'

'*You must dress smartly, Kosuke. Do you hear?*'

There's a rumbling excitement in his stomach but also a whirling fear below it.

It is a beautiful day and pollen drifts across the fields like fairies. Up until now, Kosuke has ignored visiting days. Everyone ignores them. They always end in the same way: a wailing child and a parent rushing out, Uesugi snivelling after them. Nobody at Sakuza Orphanage likes to think about the 'before'. You are here now and that's that.

A pebble hits the wall behind Kosuke and he looks up. Kei is balancing, arms out, as he tightrope walks across the orphanage wall.

'Had to see this for myself,' he says, pointing to Kosuke's ill-fitting suit.

Kei teeters, regains his composure then jumps down. He sits next to Kosuke, splits an orange and passes half of it across.

'How did you get out of class, then?' Kosuke garbles the words as he chews, juice spilling down his chin. Kei squints in the sunshine. He swallows, grins and shrugs.

'What's your mother like?' he says.

Kosuke sucks his fingers clean, then fiddles with pith.

'I would say she's just normal. But then I suppose she left her kid in a bus station.'

Kei smiles and tosses away the peel.

'I would have left you too.'

They watch the clouds roll, unfurl and split across the blue panorama before them. Flies zip up and down from the red ping-pong paddles on the table across from them.

'And yours?' Kosuke asks.

'She's dead. I have a few memories but I can't separate them out, you know? Just pictures, really. I think she was nice, though.'

Kosuke doesn't know what to say so he checks his watch. His mother is an hour late.

'What did Uesugi say, then?' Kei dangles his shoe from one toe.

'Not much.'

'Well, if she takes you into town, you better share any contraband, asshole.' Kei stands up.

Kosuke nods and returns his gaze to the road. He wants to see his mother before she sees him.

'She'll come,' Kei calls before disappearing inside the orphanage.

The wind blows.

Hours later, Sister Mary Josephine calls Kosuke in, wrapping her arms around him. She keeps telling him not to worry, there's a perfectly good reason, of course, but Kosuke shows no emotion.

She leads him to the chapel and asks him to recite Psalm 27. He kneels and the words fall out of his mouth fluently.

'The Lord is my light and my salvation. Whom shall I fear? The Lord is the strength of my life. Of whom shall I be afraid? When the wicked, even mine enemies and my foes, came upon me to eat up my flesh, they stumbled and fell. Though an host should encamp against me, my heart shall not fear. Though war should rise against me, in this will I be confident. When my father and my mother forsake me, then the Lord will take me up. Teach me thy way, O Lord, and lead me in a plain path, because of mine enemies. Deliver me not over unto the will of mine enemies: for false witnesses are risen up against me, and such as breathe out cruelty. Wait on the Lord, be of good courage, and He shall strengthen thine heart. Wait, I say, on the Lord.'

The nun places her hand on his crown.

'Good,' she says warmly. 'In the years to come, those words will see you through.'

Kosuke feels a deep certainty that these words mean absolutely nothing.

13. Black Smudge

Iwata stood by his window, drinking coffee, looking down at the street. Night had fallen on Motoyoyogicho like a stumbling drunk. Israelis were selling fake designer watches. A prostitute checked her watch as though she were waiting for someone in particular. Having missed the last train home, only the most desperate businessmen hurried past now. Iwata watched their lips move, muttering excuses under their breath, trying them out for authenticity.

The lights of the city are so pretty.

He turned to look at the space where the cardboard boxes had been stacked, before putting his cup in the sink. He was glad they were gone. The refrigerator hummed in the dark like a monk in his sanctuary.

I'm happy with you.

Iwata took off the clothes that Sakai had bought him, trying not to provoke his injuries. He pictured her going through the racks of clothes, attempting to gauge his size. Was it a gesture of affection? Attraction? Practicality? He knew Sakai was a woman that would love through action, not words. If she wanted a man, he knew it would be a pragmatic and impersonal conclusion. Iwata thought about her beauty, a simple composition of soft and brutal lines. Had her good looks been an inconvenient appendage throughout her life? Or something she had learned to live with and eventually use to her advantage? Iwata wondered what had made her the way she was. There was an anger deep inside her that seemed to fuel her. It gave her conviction, a willingness to suffer and cause suffering to achieve her goals. He had seen that anger overflow, and it had scared him on some level. He would never know what made Sakai the way she was. But then he didn't need to.

Please let me hear. Those words of love from you.

Iwata kicked off his shoes and took off his trousers. He threw his jacket at a chair in the corner and it just caught hold of the frame. He fell on to the futon and stretched each limb in turn. Doing crunches was out of the question but Iwata realized his pain had become bearable – he just needed sleep.

He closed his eyes and heard a small, muffled thud.

On the outskirts of his senses he realized what had caused the noise. Iwata forced himself to stand. His jacket had fallen to the floor. He searched the pockets and plucked out the amber stone. Collapsing back on to his bed, he held it up, turning it between his thumb and forefinger. In the darkness, he could not see what colour it was. Iwata pictured the black sun on the wall, shifting and gurgling. He thought of the car in the fog, its red lights hazing into nothing. His fingers closed around the amber.

'I'm coming for you.'

The next morning, Iwata examined his injuries. His cuts were puffy, his nose was swollen and a green bruise had formed under his left eye. Everything was sore but he was in working condition.

He did a passable job of changing his bandages and cleaning away dried blood. Iwata saw his grey hair more clearly than before. He noticed his knuckles were also cut and raw, though he could not remember why.

As he brushed his teeth, there was a knock at the door. A muffled voice outside.

'Inspector?'

Iwata waited for a few moments. Then the phone rang, which he let go to voicemail.

'Inspector Iwata, are you there? . . . This is Inspector Yoji Yamada from the Cults and Religious Groups Division . . . I'm outside your door.'

Despite a jolly voice, there was a clear unease to the man's words.

'Well, the reason I'm calling is that I happened to get my hands on a copy of your Black Sun Killer case file . . .' He sighed. *'I'd like to offer my help on any possible cult or ritualistic angles to the case. I think I can offer you some insights here. You'll find me in the TMPD basement or you can reach me on this number. Good day.'*

A card was slipped under the door. The message ended and Iwata heard soft footsteps lead away.

'Help,' Iwata echoed. 'Sure.'

He deleted the message, threw away the card and called his partner.

'Sakai, it's me. I just got some guy called Yamada at my door claiming to be from the Cults Division. You know him?'

'Sure, he's like the resident black sheep.'

'Think he could be connected to Moroto and the others?'

'Unlikely, he's harmless. To be honest, I've always kind of had a soft spot for him.'

'I didn't think you had those, Sakai.'

'There aren't many people worth having them for.'

'Touché. Anyway, I want you to continue to look for any links between the Ohbas and the Kaneshiro family.'

'Suppose this means you're not buying my Kiyota revenge angle?'

'Terai Ohba sentenced thousands of men in his time – I just don't see Kiyota as the one to seek revenge. He committed a crime, served out his sentence and started a new life on the other side of it. What would be the point of revenge after all this time? Plus, there's the small matter of not having a single crumb of evidence against him.'

'Then the exciting world of Public Records awaits.' She sighed. 'Where are you going?'

He held up the amber stone to the weak morning light and sniffed it gently.

'To follow my nose.'

Iwata dressed in jeans, a grey sweater and a suede jacket. In the kitchen, he rifled through a drawer and fished out an old address book.

'There you are.'

He found the right page and tapped on Cleo's small, slanted handwriting.

Junzaburo Hyuga - Incense

Iwata tore out the address, grabbed his keys and left the apartment. At the wheel of the Isuzu, he tried out his ankle on the pedals. The pain was tolerable.

It was only a ten-minute drive to Aoyama but the morning traffic was ponderous. The low cloud that hugged the cityscape had split in places, showing snatches of blue sky for what seemed like the first time in a long time.

At 9.10 a.m. Iwata parked in a small lot on the corner. Hyuga Incense had an understated wooden sign over a small doorway. The roof of the building was the traditional blue-glazed clay tiling of which little remained in Tokyo. Inside, every wooden shelf contained trinkets or plants. The glass counter was packed with brightly coloured boxes of incense. Framed calligraphy and traditional Japanese watercolour landscapes adorned the walls. A grinning fortune cat waved rhythmically. Iwata smelled a delicate, leafy perfume in the air.

'Can I help you, sir?'

Iwata held up his badge to the young woman behind the counter. Iwata had known cops who enjoyed causing the stir – the sudden manifestation of greater purpose in the little people's lives. He was not one of them.

'Police. Is Mr Hyuga here?'

'Just one moment.'

She picked up the phone and announced his arrival.

'Please go through.'

Iwata walked into a surprisingly large office, a zoo of fragrances hanging in the air. Behind a desk, an elderly, bird-like man with bright eyes looked up. An uneven white moustache curled up into a smile. Iwata held up his ID again, and took the seat across from Hyuga at his request.

'Mr Hyuga, I'm Inspector Iwata of Shibuya Homicide. I need your help.'

'I'll certainly do my best.'

Iwata took out the little amber globule and slid it across the desk like a chess piece.

'May I?'

Hyuga perched some old spectacles on his nose, turned on his lamp and narrowed his eyes as the light soaked through the specimen's resinous innards. He peered at the stone for a few seconds then nodded.

'I presume this is connected to an investigation?'

'That's right.'

'Well, well. More than fifty years in this business, but this is a first.'

'Is it amber?'

'No, it's copal. The cheap variety too. The more expensive kind is a milky white colour. It's sometimes called Mexican Frankincense, or Young Amber. But you can easily tell them apart thanks to amber's lighter, citrine colour.

Also, its surface becomes tacky with a drop of chloroform or acetone.'

'Please continue.'

'Well, it's a tree resin used by pre-Colombian and Meso-american cultures. Later on it was used as an effective varnish – Western train carriages, expensive portraits, that kind of thing.'

'Where can it be found?'

'Japan, for starters. But New Zealand, Central America, East Africa, South America . . . I'm sure there are other places.'

'Mr Hyuga, there was an acrid, earthy smell at my crime scenes. In your opinion, could that be the result of burning copal?'

'Inspector, if you have smelled copal, you would be unlikely to confuse it with anything else. What you have described does indeed sound like copal. I could give you a demonstration? Though you will lose it in the flame.'

'That would be helpful, please go ahead.'

Hyuga placed the copal in a stone burner, laying it on charcoal tablets mixed with sand. Under the flame, the globule softened, then gelled, then turned into a translucent golden spittle. Within moments, he recognized the Black Sun Killer's scent.

'Thank you, Mr Hyuga. In your opinion, how many places in Japan would sell copal?'

The old man put out the flame and shrugged.

'A handful, no more than three or four at a guess. Of course, there's also the internet. But I can tell you that it's not a common purchase in this country. The smell is too strong for Japanese noses.'

He chuckled.

'Did you ever sell copal here?'

'I believe so. Years ago.'

'Would you have records for bulk buyers, frequent customers and so on?'

'No, I'm afraid not.'

Iwata stood and held out his hand. Hyuga had a surprisingly firm grip.

'Inspector, have we met before? I can't shake the feeling I know your name.'

'My wife used to have an account here.'

'*Ah*.' Hyuga chuckled with the satisfaction of a solved mystery. 'She's American, yes? Came down from Chōshi, if I remember correctly?'

'That's right.'

'Her Japanese is very good. Is she well?'

'Fine, thank you. I'll pass on your regards.'

'Her orders were always well put-together. She was a delightful conversationalist, too.'

'Thank you for your help, Mr Hyuga.'

They shook hands again and the old man tapped himself on the head.

'I've just had a thought. There *was* a gentleman that sometimes came for copal . . . yes that's right. I would run into him at trade fairs and conventions and the like. Specialized in ancient South American cultures, he said. Something along those lines.'

'Do you have a name?'

Hyuga held up a finger and shuffled through his bureau. He surfaced with a business card.

'Keep it. My networking days are behind me.'

'Thank you.'

'A bit of advice, Inspector?' he smiled. 'Always follow your nose. The nose never lies.'

Outside it was a bright, windy morning on the verge of change. Iwata got back in his car and smelled the copal on his fingers. As he did this, he glanced at the business card

142

Hyuga had given him. His breath caught. Iwata knew the name on the card. He had heard it before.

Excitement belted through his stomach as he screeched out of the lot, dialling Sakai's number.

'Sakai, I need you to get on to Surveillance. There is someone we need to look at.'

'Does this someone have a name?'

Iwata looked back down at the card. Its black text was simple, the font tasteful:

PROF. YOHEI IGARASHI – CURATOR /
PROFESSOR OF ANCIENT CULTURES

Iwata approached Ueno Park from the south, along Chuo-Dori. Parking in an underground lot across from Shinobazu Pond, he tried to contain the instinct that told him he was closing in on the killer.

A killer who had left nothing behind. A killer who knew what police would look for. A killer who accounted for all eventualities. But no man was smart enough to account for dumb luck.

Even so, Iwata had to contain his certainty. He could not allow it to be transmitted to Igarashi. He did not want to disturb the man's habits. It had to seem as if this were just a routine inquiry and Igarashi just another citizen to chalk off the list. But Igarashi's routine would be Iwata's now. Like lines from a script for an actor to learn, he would pore over this man's existence and search for fault. If Igarashi was the killer, then all hope was lost for him – his only chance had been his anonymity. Once Iwata had tasted the scent, he would never let go.

His phone buzzed.

'Give me good news, Sakai.'

'OK, so still nothing linking the Kaneshiros with the Ohbas but I do have plain-clothes guys outside Igarashi's house already and two men are en route to the museum. We've been given four days. I've also contacted Legal and they're working on telephone and bank records – we should be able to get that by tonight. Without a charge or any evidence against him, I think that's as much as we can hope for.'

'You're a star.'

'You're thinking about the note in Kaneshiro's calendar, aren't you? *Meet I.* Igarashi.'

'It crossed my mind.'

'Need me to come down?'

'No, don't worry.'

'Iwata, I'm not a fucking secretary. You know you could use me.'

'Look, I'm already here. I'll call you when I get out.'

'Well, I hope you're right about this guy. We don't have much time left.'

He hung up and locked the Isuzu. On the north-east corner of Ueno Park, the Tokyo National Museum loomed over a fringe of trees like a great ark. Tourist coaches jostled along the street facing the museum, trawlers trying to sell their catch. Iwata skipped the line and held his badge up to the guard at the security gates. He ignored his own reflection in the grey pool outside the museum and hurried towards the entrance.

The foyer was carved out of cream marble with a large, split staircase. Off to the left, he cut another line to the information desk. The young man behind the counter began to protest but Iwata casually flashed his police credentials and asked for Professor Igarashi. He nodded and picked up the phone but Iwata halted him with a diluted smile.

'Actually, we're old friends. I'd prefer it if I could surprise him.'

The man printed Iwata a temporary pass and directed him to the Aztec and Mayan exhibition – a temporary exhibit on the third floor.

Iwata ignored the national treasures, Greco-Buddhist art and long-dead civilizations. Today, he was looking for the living. He was searching for a tall, likely left-handed and powerfully built man who wore a twenty-eight-centimetre shoe. The same man, Iwata felt, he had seen at Kyoto University, raining down blows on his opponent.

He came to a door bearing a single word:

CURATOR

Beneath it, Igarashi's business card had been affixed. Iwata steeled himself and ran a succession of images through his mind – the Kaneshiro children on the metal slabs, the widow's pale legs, the black sun in the gloomy bedrooms. They were jumbled radio waves.

They have to be coming from this room.

Iwata knocked once, then turned the handle. It did not give. He heard heavy footfalls. The door tore open and Igarashi peered down at Iwata.

'Who are you?'

Iwata held up his badge and watched for facial twitches. Igarashi gave off surprise, perhaps even interest, but Iwata smelled no fear on him. His eyes were far apart and his nose was long, but he had a pleasant enough face. His hair was mid-length and very recently styled. His thick eyelashes gave his face a gentleness that the inspector did not trust. Iwata smelled a subtle aftershave. It contained lemons, perhaps. Zest. Spices. Wealth.

'Professor Yohei Igarashi?'

A bemused smile surfaced on the man's lips.

'That's right.'

'May I come in?'

Igarashi stepped aside and offered Iwata a seat on the bank of sofas in the corner. The office was spacious and light, wall-to-wall with books. The large window framed Ueno Park below. A sleek white desk held neat stacks of paper, a Spanish/Japanese dictionary and photographs of Igarashi standing in a jungle somewhere. Beneath the desk, a small suitcase contained meticulously folded clothes and plastic folders.

'Nice office,' Iwata remarked. 'Sure beats my desk in Shibuya.'

Igarashi laughed, seemingly without reaction to the mention of a police station.

'I would offer you tea, but I'm in a bit of a rush I'm afraid. Forgive me.'

He nodded towards his suitcase.

'That's quite all right, this shouldn't take too long.'

'Of course, I'm happy to help . . . Inspector, have I seen you somewhere before?'

'Kyoto University, I believe. I was there recently, visiting an old friend.'

Igarashi grinned.

'Of course, I saw you walking with David.'

'Actually, I saw you too. You were sparring. Quite a left you have on you under all that tweed, Professor.'

Igarashi batted away the compliment.

'Far weaker than my right.'

Iwata took out his notebook, though he didn't aim to note much down. Igarashi's eyes rested on it for a second.

'Not a natural southpaw, then?'

'No.' Igarashi laughed. 'I'm surprised that wasn't obvious.'

Iwata mirrored the laugh but noted the taut facial muscles

146

on this man. To the casual glance there would be no hint of the power beneath the man's English-cut suit.

'Not in the least.'

'You're too kind. And what about you, Inspector? Do you box?'

'Not since the academy.'

'And those?'

Igarashi gestured towards the black eye and the wounds on Iwata's knuckles.

'Work.'

The men shared a smile. Birdsong lilted through the window.

'Professor, I do have a few questions and I don't want to take up too much of your time.'

'I'm sorry, I've been blathering. What can I help you with?'

'Copal,' Iwata replied abruptly.

Igarashi met his eyes and Iwata studied them. They were large eyes, with an intelligence about them. So far, however, Iwata could only register curiosity, not deception.

'Copal?'

'That's right, Professor. I was looking into copal and I was given your name, actually.'

'I used to burn it to give exhibitions a little authenticity. I don't think the visitors ever cared – beyond wondering what the funny smell was, of course.'

'Let me be honest with you, I'm investigating a series of murders where copal was burnt at the scene.'

Igarashi's lips tightened. Iwata continued.

'The hearts of the victims were removed. Turkey blood was found also. The lacerations were done with an incredibly sharp blade. I was hoping you might be able to shed some light on copal use.'

Igarashi looked out of the window for a moment and discomfort seemed to wash over him. His eyes were dark pools. He bared his teeth.

'Are you all right, Professor?'

After a few seconds, Igarashi nodded.

'Quite all right, sorry. I just have some digestive problems, that's all. Now, copal? Well, it was primarily used to cleanse in Mexican and pre-Colombian cultures. Sometimes it was used in a remedial way, or to make an offering suitable for sacrifice.'

'Sacrifice?'

'Well, what you've described sounds like a crude sacrifice, yes. The turkey blood, the hearts, the copal – all of that sounds in imitation of human sacrifice as per ancient South American cultures.'

'Why would someone do that?'

'Today? No idea. Historically speaking, human sacrifice was widespread for a long time. Broadly, it was often a blood-debt to the gods in order for ancient peoples to avoid plagues and natural disasters. They sacrificed animals, too. And, of course, let their own blood.'

'So it was a form of atonement?'

'You could say that. The Aztec legend of the Five Suns says that the gods sacrificed themselves so that mankind might live. In a way, life could only exist if fed by death. There was a central belief among the Mesoamerican peoples that a great, ongoing sacrifice sustains the entire universe. Everything is *tonacayotl* – a sort of "spiritual flesh-hood" on earth. And earth, the crops, the moon, the stars and all people – everything – all of it sprung from these sacrificed gods. Humanity itself is *macehualli* – "those deserving and brought back to life through penance".'

'So they lived to repay their debt?'

'Put simply. It was commonly used as a metaphor for human sacrifice – a sacrificial victim was someone who "gave his service".'

'And if the debt wasn't paid?'

'Then the sun would turn black and the world would end. But I'm not sure if any of this is relevant to your murder investigation, Insp—'

'Funny thing is —' Iwata opened his bag and took out the crime scene photographs of the black sun. '— it would seem it *is* relevant.'

Igarashi squinted at the symbols.

'Hmm, a black sun? Or some kind of eclipse, perhaps?'

'They were drawn by the perpetrator.'

'How strange.' Igarashi glanced at the clock. 'Well, Inspector, I really must get going if I'm to make my flight.'

'Of course. Are you going somewhere exotic?'

'Beijing. It's just a series of talks. I'll only be gone for a few days. I'm sure we can meet again to discuss this further.'

'I'd appreciate that. Driving to the airport?'

'I have a taxi booked.'

'I'll walk you.'

Igarashi finished packing his suitcase and then led Iwata out of the office. They walked side by side through the museum, weaving through school groups and tourists.

'Professor, can you tell me what kind of blade was used in these rituals?'

'Usually an obsidian blade.'

'Obsidian?'

'It cuts with incredible precision. Certain surgeons today are starting to use obsidian scalpels, in fact. The sharpness is, for want of a better word, perfect.'

Iwata mused on this.

'Sophisticated for such a primitive culture, wouldn't you say?'

Igarashi darkened for a split second, his eyes flickering like a bad signal.

'Mesoamerican cultures were *not* primitive, Inspector.' He cleared his throat and regained his lightness. 'In fact they were highly advanced in many aspects. Metallurgy, however, was not one of them. This is mostly due to the abundance of obsidian throughout Mexico and Guatemala. It was used in a whole range of life aspects: tools, warfare, decoration –'

'And for ripping out hearts.'

Igarashi grinned.

'And that.'

They paused at the marble stairs of the main entrance.

'Professor, do you think the killer could have fashioned himself an obsidian knife? Would that be possible?'

The professor turned up his bottom lip and started down the stairs, his large moccasins singing out.

'I suppose so. But the type of obsidian you'd need for working into a blade is restricted to deposits in Mexico, Guatemala, Armenia . . .'

They stepped out into rain. On the main road, the coaches spilled their contents, a tide of polo shirts, cameras and fat. Igarashi waved at his taxi and it pulled up on to the kerb, its back door opening automatically. The professor paused before getting in.

'Inspector, I have to say, I find it hard to believe there's a psychopath running around the streets of Tokyo, ripping people's hearts out with an obsidian blade.'

One side of Iwata's mouth curled up.

'Safe journey, Professor.'

Igarashi offered a large hand and they shook warmly. As the taxi dwindled into the red blur of rear lights, Iwata glanced up at the sooty sky. He felt something strange on his hand. He looked down. In the middle of Iwata's palm was a large, black smudge.

14. Stacks of Paper

La Fleur was a large, high-end coffee house in Nishi-Azabu popular with wealthy housewives and gaijin. The crowd would usually be much thicker by 5 p.m. but the heavy rain had seen to that. Old French love songs played quietly in the background. Iwata and Sakai sat in the corner by the steamy window. He sipped his first cappuccino, she smoked her second cigarette.

'I don't get his logic.' She took a deep drag. 'Why be so helpful to you if he's the killer? To deflect suspicion?'

'He knows we have nothing on him. Maybe he did it for fun.' Iwata sighed. 'I don't think I gave anything away but it felt like he was trying to read me too.'

'I wonder.' She looked out of the window. 'Well, the surveillance boys confirm he flew to Beijing. I'm still looking into his background but he's clean so far.'

'Why am I not surprised?'

'You're not the easily surprised type, Iwata.'

'Really. You know my type?'

'You don't want me reading you.'

'No, go on. I'm curious.'

'All right. Well, you're divorced, right? You have to be, you've practically got it written on your forehead. What was it, another woman? No, another man, I bet. She left you, did she? Long hours, blood specks, emotional brick walls. And you obviously didn't get the kids. You've isolated yourself even more by moving to Tokyo and it's not like you're in an industry where you're taking your bosses out for drinks and karaoke. No, I'd say you're completely alone. Dating is out of the question, too. You have nothing to offer, nothing to give. I think you're the type of person who will disappoint yourself before you let life disappoint you. And it's not like you could just leave it all behind and work in an office, could you? You're hardly the dull but dutiful type. No, you hate your job but then you need it like the air you breathe. If I had to guess, I'd say whoever Iwata was before Homicide? He's long gone now.'

Iwata downed his cappuccino and nodded.

'You see a lot with those eyes, don't you?'

'You asked.'

'I asked. Are you always this nice to your partners?'

'No.' She laughed. 'I'm not usually so gregarious.'

'I had a partner a long time ago, she was a bit like you. A great cop. Just a little more . . . I don't know.'

'No, go on. A little more what?'

'Gregarious, I guess.'

They smiled until the love song ended and Sakai stubbed out her cigarette.

'So.' She changed the subject with a curt puff of smoke. 'What do you want to do about Professor Igarashi?'

'I want to get his whereabouts for both murders. He had the ability to do it, as well as some kind of connection to the ritualistic side of it.'

'All right.'

'And if I get a single shred of evidence, even just a vague link, I'm bringing him in.'

Sakai opened her green leather handbag and took out her notebook.

'Speaking of shreds, Kanagawa PD got back to me with financial disclosure. Turns out Mrs Ohba was rich, more or less. She could have lived to 300 on those takeout dinners. But unlike the Kaneshiros, no cash injections in her account. In terms of outgoings, nothing significant either.'

'Hm. Perhaps the Black Sun knew that money wouldn't interest Mrs Ohba like it might have interested the Kaneshiros.'

'One of life's little mysteries, I guess. Iwata, why don't you go home? You look like shit.'

'Everyone looks like shit to you.'

'I've got a good eye, remember?'

Iwata noticed that Sakai was wearing a different perfume today – a floral, honeysuckle smell. Her lips were red for the first time that he had seen and there was a purple shadow about her eyes. She wore jeans, faded and tight, and a loose black jumper that hung from one shoulder. A leather jacket was folded over the armrest of her chair.

'I think I will go home, actually. What about you, Sakai?'

'Just meeting a friend.'

'Then get going if you want. I'll get this.'

Sakai wiggled her fingers goodbye and marched out of the café. Iwata watched her shake open an umbrella then stride out of view. He pushed his empty coffee mug away and took out his cigarettes before seeing the no smoking sign. He put them back in his pocket and felt a deep nothingness. Iwata wished Sakai had stayed, though he could not unravel what he felt for her – vague lust, curiosity, wariness perhaps. When considering Sakai, these impulses would surface in him, yet none of it would adhere reliably.

Iwata's inability to pinpoint his feelings for Sakai did not concern him. But the realization that he did not want to be alone shocked him. He thought of the people he had known in his life and searched for a name that he could reach for now, someone for whom he held the most minimal significance. He could think of no one.

He paid and left.

On Waseda-Dori, running just behind Iidabashi Station, Sakai skirted the bare birch trees. She stopped outside a brown, multipurpose building. Above a FamilyMart, an old sign read:

OSHINO BOXING GYM

Climbing the stairs, Sakai could already hear the percussion of the heavy bags, a constant pounding on leather and nylon mesh. The gym was bright and there was a faint trace of ammonia in the air. Younger boys off to the left were skipping and stretching. In the centre, the ring was occupied by two men sparring. Nobody paid Sakai much attention. There was a large, framed quote in English on the wall above the ring:

NEVER QUIT. SUFFER NOW. LIVE THE REST OF YOUR LIFE AS A CHAMPION.

At the back of the room, a door opened and a tall, muscular man with closely cropped hair and butterfly tattoos on his arms emerged. He greeted a few people warmly until he saw Sakai. He stopped dead in his tracks. Then a pure grin broke across his scarred lips.

'Noriko?'

One corner of her mouth turned up.

'Oshino!' she shouted. 'The champ is here!'

Some of the younger boys laughed and applauded, others wolf-whistled. Oshino blushed and motioned for her to follow. Sakai admired his powerful frame from behind as he walked. Resisting the temptation to grasp his buttocks, she followed him into a small, neat office. Oshino had a view of Koraku Park to the east and the Kanda River to the south. They sat at his desk and smiled at each other for a while, fascinated by the compound of changes and constants – the passing of time in flesh. What was lost, what was gained.

'Long time,' he said quietly, his voice deep.

'You've done well for yourself, Oshino.'

He looked away shyly. 'Thank you.'

'With your experience I bet you can charge whatever fee you like.'

'I rarely charge these days. I have enough to get by.'

'You never were one for money.'

'And you? You graduated from the academy?'

Sakai took out her police ID and handed it to him. Oshino took it respectfully, trying not to touch her skin.

'*Homicide?*' He raised his eyebrows proudly.

She laughed. 'You're surprised?'

'No.'

'You look it.'

'Well, not by this. I knew you would go far.'

'So surprised by what?'

His smile faded. 'I just . . . didn't think I'd ever see you again.'

Sakai immediately stood and faced away. She inspected the photographs of him hanging on the wall – young, slick with sweat, battered, but victorious. She wasn't in the photos but she had been there on those nights. She remembered the fights, its smells and music, the warm spray of sweat in the front row. She remembered the swelling pride she felt.

'*National champion,*' she said with awe.

'National youth champion,' he corrected. 'And half the kids out there are better than I ever was.'

'You've gone modest in your old age.'

'No, just honest. Anyway, the past is the past.'

Sakai smiled sadly with her back to him.

'The past *is* the past,' she murmured.

'So what brings you here?'

'I need your help, Oshino.'

'Then I'm glad you thought of me. Anything you need. You know that.'

'Are you still in contact with your friends?'

'Ah. I haven't had dealings with those people for years . . .' He looked at her gravely. 'But you tell me what you need and I'll do my best.'

'I'm searching for someone. I need her birth certificate, school records, that kind of thing. She'd probably be my age by now.'

Sakai wrote down a name on his blotting pad in neat characters.

'Wouldn't it be easier for you to look it up through police records?'

'Those searches leave traces. Traces lead to questions. Plus, I doubt there'll be anything criminal attached to that name anyway.'

'Is this work or pleasure?' Oshino asked.

'What's the difference?'

They shared a smile. Then Sakai took out a small wad of notes and her business card.

'Will this be enough for your friends?'

'That's more than enough. I'll call you when they come through.'

'And what about you, Oshino? What do you want?'

He licked his lips and looked down at the floor. 'What are you asking me?'

'I meant *money.*'

'You said it yourself, I never was one for money.'

Sakai laughed. 'You were punching above your weight even back then, champ.'

'With you, anyone would be.'

'Here. That should be enough.' She unfolded another few bills and passed them across.

'For what?'

'What else?'

He laughed as she stood. 'But there's no other woman like you.'

'Ass is ass, Oshino.' She opened the door and winked at him. 'Just make sure you find me what I want.'

He looked down at the blotting pad.

Midori Anzai

As Oshino rubbed his finger across the characters, the ink bled across the page.

Several uneventful days passed. Iwata spoke to distant acquaintances of the Kaneshiros and the Ohbas, hoping for some missed detail or angle, but was met with nothing more than pleasantries or sympathy – both currencies he could not convert. When Iwata turned his attention to Professor Igarashi, he could find nothing out of place, nor any connection to the victims. For her part, Sakai exhausted every public record and possible source of information but the search for a connection between victims proved absolutely fruitless.

Looking over his shoulder, Iwata called her from a temporary desk in Division One.

'There has to be something, Sakai. I refuse to believe the Black Sun Killer just chanced upon these people. Everything we know about him says he's meticulous.'

Sakai sounded tired.

'The *little* we know about him, yes. But you've put me in a library and asked me to look for a pair of full stops of matching size, Iwata.'

'Keep searching.' He slammed the receiver down and rubbed his eyes. When Iwata looked up, across the room he saw Moroto smirking.

'Aw, Mickey Mouse looks sad,' he jeered. 'Somebody get him a hotdog.'

Sniggers broke out around Division One.

On the morning of 2 March, two weeks after the first murders, Iwata drove to the garden city of Den-en-chōfu, thirty minutes south of Shibuya. He had nothing else to do and nowhere else to go. The tree-lined streets were quiet and the houses were large, in varying styles. Besides the bog-standard rich, the area was populated by ex-pats, baseball stars, singers, manga artists and politicians.

The address the surveillance team had given Iwata was a quiet backstreet near Tamagawadai Park. He put on a baseball cap and sunglasses and bought himself a black coffee with agave syrup from a stall. In the car across from Igarashi's house, Iwata immediately spotted two plain-clothes cops in a grey saloon car – one reading the sports page, the other dozing. Under the merest scrutiny the set-up would immediately seem suspicious, but Iwata was hoping Igarashi was not the observant type.

He strolled past the house, sipping coffee casually, and glanced up. It was clearly empty. Sports Page looked at him for a moment, but registered nothing and went back to his paper.

Iwata gave the house another few passes before returning to his car. Though he was not in mint condition, his ankle at least no longer throbbed. He glanced at the grey saloon and felt a vague affection for the two surveillance cops. They were part of a system that he commanded. Limited but loyal, they were his dogs – he just had to say *fetch*.

Iwata took off the hat and sunglasses before dialling Igarashi's number on a whim.

'Yes?' It was the same impatient tone he had opened his office door with.

'Professor, it's Inspector Iwata.'

'Ah, good timing. I've just passed through passport control at Narita.'

It was strangely exhilarating to hear Igarashi's low, calm voice again.

'How was your trip?'

'Not as productive as I would have liked. Made any progress?'

'About that. If you're back at the museum tomorrow, could I come by and ask you a few more questions?'

'I'll be in after twelve.'

'Until then, Professor.'

'I'll have some coffee ready this time.'

Iwata jabbed the call out like a match burning too close to the finger. He looked at his phone.

Coffee.

'Until then, you smug bastard.'

He looked up and saw something was wrong. Sports Page and Dozy were taking out their earpieces and packing up their cameras. The latter got out of the car with a bag of rubbish. Before he could reach the litter bin, Iwata was grabbing at his collar from behind.

'Hey! Where do you think you're going?'

The cop wheeled round with a snarl.

'You *watch* how you talk to –'

Iwata thrust his credentials in Dozy's face.

'I gave you no orders! *No orders!* You get back in that car and you watch him, you hear me?'

The cop was frowning at Iwata's ID while trying to shake off the hobbling, pale man it belonged to.

'What do you –'

'*Watch him.*'

Dozy blinked. The words on the police ID and the authority it carried surely could not apply to this frantic, sick man in front of him.

'Calm down, sir.'

'I'll be calm when you do your fucking *job*.'

'Division chief just called. The papers . . . Haven't you seen?'

Iwata blinked and a nearby sprinkler stifled its laughter.

'What papers?'

Sports Page, who was now halfway out of the car, tossed across his newspaper. It landed with a splat of reality at Iwata's feet:

MURDER FRENZY DESCENDS ON TOKYO: FIRST THE SUPERSTAR, NOW THE WIDOW

The intro spoke of crazed killers stalking the city streets and TMPD incompetence. The new justice minister was considering police budget cuts and streamlining. The main photograph was Mina Fong's smiling face, full of love and warmth for her public. Below it there was a grainy picture of Iwata entering Mrs Ohba's house.

'I better go,' Dozy said.

Iwata pointed to Igarashi's house.

'This man will kill again.'

'They point and I follow. You know how it is.'

The cop straightened his jacket and smoothed over his hair as he returned to the car.

'He's not finished!' Iwata called.

The saloon started up and quietly sailed out of its space, leaving a small cloud of exhaust behind. Iwata's voice was drained of anger.

'Even if we are.'

A clutch of pigeons cooed in the branches above him. Neighbours spied at him through expensive curtains and double-glazing. Iwata got back into his car, breathing hard through his nose. He closed his eyes tightly and bit his lip hard, willing the fury to pass quickly. He needed silence but instead his phone began to buzz.

'Iwata.' Shindo's voice was slow and emotionless. 'Are you there?'

'Yes.'

'You know why I'm calling.'

Iwata pinched the bridge of his nose, trying to control his voice.

'You promised me time.'

'Nobody can promise that. I need you here in thirty minutes. Everything has been pulled.'

Iwata hung up and tried to settle himself.

You ever wonder if maybe some of those cities are good and some of them are bad?

He pictured little Hana Kaneshiro's colourless face.

Snarling back his tears, Iwata punched the steering wheel repeatedly. The car horn bleated in the isolated grey of the peaceful backstreet. The cold morning drifted silently by.

Shindo's office had the same sour stink but the world outside had shifted since then. He entered the room, stressed and sweating, and immediately held up his hand.

'Not a fucking word, Iwata.'

The door clattered shut and Shindo dropped himself behind his desk, his swivel chair creaking loudly. He held up the various newspapers, one after another. Homicide, hysteria and horror in bold.

'The Fong murder was never going to stay a secret for long but the widow should have been contained. Honestly, I don't know how that got out. Kanagawa PD swears it wasn't from their end. Either way, it doesn't matter.'

Shindo pointed to the pile of newspapers as if indicating dog excrement to be avoided.

'After a couple of weeks of those, Satsuki Eda called Superintendent Fujimura this morning. That's Satsuki. Fucking. Eda. Minister of fucking *Justice*. Iwata, do you know what that means?'

'Heat.' Iwata covered his eyes with a palm.

'Correct. *Heat.* Which means problems. Which means people's jobs.' Shindo licked his teeth, searching for the right words. He came up empty-handed. 'Look, Iwata, it doesn't make any difference, but against my better judgement I asked for you to be given another chance on this case. I tried. But Fujimura –'

'Spare me the Samaritan routine. Why did you call me here?'

'All right. Here it is. There is an official complaint against you. This is a problem, Iwata. You're still well within your probation period and your position is going to be reviewed very soon. In the meantime, you're on holiday pay. Just so we're clear, it's your conduct that's under review, not your case management. If you come through this, you'd still be clear to lead investigations.'

'Shindo, what about my case?'

'The Kaneshiro case has been solved and closed. Now,

look, this review isn't a one-way street, you are within your rights to –'

'What?'

Shindo exhaled and looked away. 'Iwata, I can't defend you. Not like this. There were already questions hanging over you when you came in. Your absence. Your background. You need to think about –'

'What do you mean, *solved*?' Iwata's heart was hammering.

'That lame kid, Masaharu Ezawa . . . he's been charged with the Kaneshiro murders.'

'I don't understand, how can we charge him for something he didn't do?'

'Iwata, you really need to focus on your own problems.'

'On what fucking *evidence* has he been charged?'

'The search of his domicile turned up various artefacts belonging to the victim. He also had recorded footage of her.'

Iwata slapped that away.

'He admitted to all that under recorded interview. That is incidental.'

Shindo held up his hand.

'Iwata, the kid *confessed*.'

'. . . Bullshit.'

'Yesterday morning. He confessed.'

Iwata put his head between his legs as though his plane were falling from the sky. He closed his eyes and bunched his fists, the scabs on his knuckles reopening.

'This is a sham. Shindo, he's not even physically capable.'

'It is what it is.'

Iwata slammed his fist down on the bureau. Several silhouettes outside looked in their direction.

'Kid, you're not helping yourself.'

'How do you explain Ezawa murdering Mrs Ohba if he was in a Setagaya PD cell this whole time, then?'

'That case has been severed from the Kaneshiro investigation. Inquiries are still pending.'

'Who has it?'

'Iwata –'

'Who has that case?'

'Horibe has it.'

Iwata stuffed his fists in his eye sockets and pushed till it hurt. He was shaking his head. He was losing control. He needed a bar. He needed the warmth. It had always been there and now there was no pretending otherwise.

'Listen to me, Inspector, you should focus on yourself.'

'No. I'll speak to Ezawa. He can still retract that statement.'

'You can't.'

'Watch me. You fucking know it wasn't Ezawa. You *know* it.'

'Knowing a thing makes no difference here, son. As far as Fujimura is concerned, you had your shot and you hit nothing.'

'So the kid gets the noose? No, fuck you, Shindo. He might be crazy but he's not going to admit to something he didn't do. Not in his right mind.'

Shindo looked away.

'Ezawa is dead. He hung himself in his apartment after being released on bail.'

Iwata stood automatically, feeling winded. The truth flooded in. Ezawa was now the perfect perpetrator – a dead one. The system worked perfectly, crime followed by justice. The wind blew and the grass bent.

Shaking his head, Iwata tore open the door and the sound of Division One flooded in.

'Who interrogated him?'

'You're already hanging on a thread, kid. You need to let this go.'

'*Who?*'

Shindo sighed. 'It was Moroto. Under Fujimura's orders.'

'And what did you do about it?' Iwata spat.

'About what?'

'Any of it.'

'What could I do?'

'Stacks of paper.' Iwata shook his head in disgust. 'That's all you are, Shindo. You're just stacks of paper.'

He left without looking back. As Iwata marched across Division One to the elevators, he glanced over at Fujimura's office. Through a gap in the blinds, he saw old, watery eyes following him.

15. Games

Iwata screeched to a halt outside the Medical Examiner's Office. He marched through reception, not bothering to identify himself despite the protests of the man behind the counter. He descended to the basement, his fury simple and silent – an electrified wire, absolutely still.

The doors slid open and he saw Doctor Eguchi leaning over some papers in the office off to the right. Glancing up at him, she held up a finger – *one moment please*. Iwata ignored her and ploughed through the doors to the left, into the disinfected gloom. The entire wall was lined with large metal drawers – filing cabinets for the dead. Iwata began to slide them open. He ignored the bodies that did not belong to him.

'Inspector!'

'What?'

'What the hell are you doing?'

Ezawa's small, childlike face appeared in the blue-green dark.

'Tell me what happened to him.' Iwata's voice was thick.

'Inspector, this is unacceptable, you can't just come in here and –'

He grabbed her by the shoulders, his teeth bared.

'Fucking tell me!'

Eguchi gasped and Iwata let go. He blinked.

'I'm sorry. I'm sorry. I'll be gone in two minutes if you just tell me.'

Eguchi looked down at Ezawa's pallid face and sighed. She left the room and returned a few seconds later wearing a scrub suit, face shield, surgical mask and shoe covers. She flicked on the lights and slid out the metal tray. The full extent of Ezawa's small frame was revealed.

With her little finger she pointed to the dark furrows around his throat and the burst capillaries.

'Auto-asphyxiation, clearly. You see the rope signatures? But there's also this.'

She pulled back the sheet, revealing Ezawa's body to the waist. The small chest was badly discoloured. Two of the fingers on his left hand were broken. Both wrists showed deep cuts from where he had squirmed in his bonds.

'Not what killed him, but he was severely beaten. He was definitely in a bad way before he hanged himself.'

Eguchi shuffled around the body and pointed with her little finger again.

'Obviously, the ligature marks explain the lack of defensive injuries that would typically be found here . . . and here. Oh, and he came in with these in his mouth.'

Eguchi pointed to a large, clear plastic bag containing female underwear stiff with dried spittle. Iwata was already out of the room.

'Inspector?'

There was only the silence of the dead. Eguchi waited for a moment, then carefully covered Ezawa and slid him back into his darkness, never to be seen again.

Two blocks south of Shibuya TMPD headquarters, an old five-storey arcade stood between a sex shop and a knock-off handbag stall. A neon sign above proclaimed a single word:

GAMES

The automatic doors slid open and Iwata scanned the room. He saw office workers, couples on dates and teenagers with school bags at their feet. All of them were completely hooked in, devout worshippers at their chosen altars. A layer of cigarette smoke clung to the blue ceiling and the pink carpet was a filthy expanse that stank of lost hours.

Iwata stalked through the arcade, electronic jingles and frantic mashing of plastic ringing in his ears. On the top floor, lamps hung low over pool tables and salary men reached to make their shots, chewing gum exposed on the soles of their shoes. Over the smacking of balls and the shrill electronic bleating, Iwata heard a group of men laughing. He saw Horibe, Yoshida and Tatsuno clustered around an electronic dartboard. Stressed waiters in pink uniforms and yellow caps hurried over with snacks and beer. Other men sat with them, dressed in gaudy satin suits and unbuttoned silk shirts. A small pile of ¥10,000 notes had been collected on a table between them. Moroto, in the centre, was about to take his shot.

'Hey, look who it is! Iwata, come join us.'

'I need to talk to you.'

'One thing at a time.' Moroto threw his darts.

20.

20.

19.

This drew ecstatic cheering from half of the men and swearing from Tatsuno and Yoshida. They threw down more money on the table.

'Iwata, we're playing Yamanote Killer.' Moroto winked. 'Are you a betting man? Course you are.'

Iwata was now at the edge of the group, smiles all fixed on him.

'I need to talk to you.'

'Let your hair down, Inspector. How about it? It's fifty thousand to enter. What do you think? Think I'll make it?'

Before Iwata could reply, an arm was around his neck and he was being dragged down to the sofa by a powerful choke-hold. The grunts sounded like Tatsuno. One of the yakuza soldiers, wearing cat-eye sunglasses and a half-open leather shirt, grinned as he flicked out a knife and pressed it to Iwata's femoral vein. The vivid tattoo across his chest showed four dragons, open mouthed, converging on a woman about to be devoured. She was sitting cross-legged, eyes closed, smiling.

Moroto turned back to the dartboard.

'The rules are very simple, Iwata. Three rounds, three shots. Each round, I have to get a higher score than the last and my final score has to be superior to that of my opponent. Yoshida here hit an impressive 174.'

Double 11.

Double 11.

20.

More cheering and cursing.

'But I can't deny it. I'm in a good run of form.'

20.

18.

Triple 11.

The group broke out into celebration and he bowed. Horibe divvied up the bets and Moroto sat down on the dirty vinyl chair across from Iwata. He smiled in the neon gloom.

'Let go.'

Tatsuno reluctantly obliged. Air flooded back into Iwata's lungs and black spots appeared over his vision. Cat Eyes kept his blade at Iwata's thigh. Nobody from the other end of the arcade looked in their direction. Moroto drank half of his beer in two gulps, then slowly licked the foam from his lips like a kid messy with ice cream. His neck was a telephone pole and his eyes were curses.

'Maybe this sounds a little strange but I have to say, it's nice to see you again. You've been on my mind, Inspector Iwata.'

Darts thudded into the board and there was more whooping behind them. Moroto waved his black and orange tie in Iwata's direction like a dirty tabby's tail.

'Do you like it? I'm thinking of wearing it next week. I want to look good for your disciplinary hearing.'

'You're the one that should be out of this job.' Iwata's voice was a painful croak.

Moroto's large lips twisted into a smile. 'You know you were right not to bet on Killer, Iwata. I don't think it's your game. You'd throw too high on your first round and then? Well, then you'd be stuck. Just like you are now.'

'Ezawa didn't kill anybody. But you knew he would kill himself, didn't you? Or did you tell him to do it?'

Cat Eyes tutted like a disapproving grandmother. Moroto touched his hand to his lips in mock offence.

'*Inspector!*'

'You're a sickness, Moroto.'

'And what's so unfair about sickness? Is sunshine unfair? Any more than cholera? Maybe I *am* a sickness. But I'm not a god. I don't create the Ezawas of this world. I just destroy them.'

'You're going to jail.'

Moroto belly laughed.

'Who do you think keeps the jail in fucking business? And anyway, I don't like what you're implying. Mr Ezawa was resisting arrest and certain action had to be taken. He resisted arrest with you too, did he not? This violent perpetrator had form. We couldn't afford to take any chances.'

'Is that what you call beating a disabled kid with his hands handcuffed behind his back?'

Moroto popped open another beer and drank with deep satisfaction. He looked at Tatsuno and rolled his eyes, as if taking an annoying phone call from a nagging wife.

'You're a real stickler for detail, you know that?'

'Put your complaints against me – I don't care. But I will *ensure* that you don't get away with this.'

'Will you, now?'

'I swear it.'

Moroto smiled again and ran a hand through his black buzz cut.

'I don't get you, Iwata. You're just a few days away from being a civilian. What's the point in fighting the battles of the dead?'

'Because that's what we do. That's police. Have you forgotten?'

Tatsuno chuckled. Moroto and Cat Eyes shared a smile.

'Very sweet. Unfortunately for you, buddy, the TMPD needs a spring clean. Change is needed.'

The lights of the city are so pretty.

Something deep and distant clicked for Iwata.

'. . . It was you, wasn't it? You leaked the Ohba story.'

Moroto clapped and Tatsuno leant forward and ruffled Iwata's hair.

'You know what I like about you, Iwata? You never let me finish before. What I like about you is that you're too fucking stupid to realize you should fear me. And not because I can end your career. But because I *know* you, Iwata. I looked under your fucking rock. I know about you and about your fucking crazy American wife and your fucking dead half-breed kid. I know about your little sabbatical in rehab. And it wasn't just the one monkey on your back, was it? What was your vintage? Drink and prescription pills? You seem the vanilla breakdown type.'

Moroto leant forward and tapped him on the kneecap gently, as if he were considering a purchase.

'I know you, Iwata. And you know what will happen next week at the disciplinary? Your suitability will be discussed. You'll be put in front of a psych evaluation. The doctor will say, "Hmm . . . maybe the pressure has been getting to you. Understandable after what you've been through." Perhaps your history with alcohol will be discussed. Perhaps a link with your violent outbursts will be made. Such a shame, considering the talent of the investigator, but risk management is paramount. It's all very unfortunate.'

Iwata struggled but Tatsuno grabbed him again and Cat Eyes lifted the blade to his ear. Moroto's smile was almost sad.

'Do you know what I want from you, Iwata? I just want you to be honest with me. That's it. Tell me the truth. You're not a cop. You're only here to fill a hole. To fill a void. To keep you off the drink. You're not here to make a living, like us. I *know* you, Iwata. I know you have nothing else to live for. And do you know what I'm going to do? I'm going to take it all away from you. Your little girlfriend Sakai included.' Moroto walked his fingers like a small pair of legs up Iwata's chest and pulled on his bottom lip. 'Ah, don't feel too bad, this would have happened sooner or later. Whatever the opposite of love at first sight is, that's us. Your class and my class? We hate each other without needing a reason. Always have. It's in the blood, I guess.'

Moroto waved off his men and Iwata backed away from them. His balance was wavering, his vision swimming with bright colours.

'You're a long way from Disneyland now, Mickey Mouse. Tokyo is mine.'

Iwata staggered away, swerving to avoid pool players. Moroto was standing on his chair now, his face pink with jubilation.

'Hey, Inspector!' He raised his beer. 'You have a *real* productive day!'

Iwata descended the stairs into a glum basement bar. At the back was the only real draw: five dirty penguins huddling on a small concrete shelf above a tank of murky water. Iwata had come here years ago – another lifetime – though he didn't want to remember why. Disappointed American tourists avoided looking at the penguins as the waiter explained today's specials in broken English. Iwata doubted today's were any more special than yesterday's.

He sat at the bar and ordered a vodka tonic. At the other end, a young white-collar worker laughed desperately at his client's jokes, though the flush in his face conveyed embarrassment. Iwata drank three vodka tonics in a row, enjoying the warmth spreading through his head and chest. But the warmth scared him. Though it was an empty life, Iwata had at least attempted to start again – like a man walking away from a car crash, trying to thumb a ride with bloodied hands. But there was an angry addict inside him who did not want to start again. An angry drunk who could not be reasoned with. Like a great tide, the warmth would drag him under and toss him back somewhere else, far, far away, flotsam on the surface of an unwanted life.

Iwata drank another three vodkas. His earlobes burnt and his stomach knotted. He knew the drink would lighten him, would deaden him to consequences. It would make him look over the precipice, down into the smiling eye of his own world. He wanted to be engulfed by a cold so all-encompassing that it would obliterate all sensation.

Iwata drank until floating was the same as sinking, all the while trying to drown out Cleo. Somewhere beyond or beneath, the black sun murmured at him.

Hello?

Are you there, Iwata?

You can't sleep here.

Iwata opened his eyes and the neon around the ceiling was a blur.

'Go home, pal. You can't sleep here.' The barman said the phrase with fluency.

The penguins had woken. A plastic bucket had been over-turned, spilling shiny fish across the ledge. Silver and pink bodies slithered away from the beaks but the penguins languidly pecked at the guts. One of the penguins ignored the fish, climbed up to the highest point on the ledge and dived into the murky water instead, only to waddle out and repeat the process a few seconds later.

Peck, peck, guzzle, splash. Peck, peck, guzzle, splash.

Their black faces and white breasts were stained with filth and fish blood. A dog kennel painted with a smiling penguin's face on its side stood empty and unused in the corner.

Like a nightmare emerging, Iwata suddenly remembered why he knew this place. He had been here with Cleo, years ago, in his previous incarnation. They had come here for coffee and toast after a night drinking with friends.

Who had those friends been?

Iwata couldn't remember. He just remembered Cleo had laughed at this stupid little place. She loved Tokyo's gaudy details – cartoon silliness everywhere, despite the grey, expressionless reality of the city.

Iwata was off his stool now, his money missing the bar-top – he had to get out, even though there was no such thing. He took one last look at the diving penguin, stuck on a loop, forever hoping to surface somewhere else.

In the backstreets of Ikebukuro, Iwata staggered away from his vomit puddle using the moss-covered walls for balance. He ambled south. Though his apartment was ten kilometres away, Iwata was beyond sensing distance or hours.

He passed Gakushuin University, its old trees weeping over the road parallel to the subway. Blocking out a child-hood memory of riding the Yamanote Line, he passed the huddle of smokers outside Takadanobaba Hospital. The vastness of Shinjuku Station came into view, almost done swallowing its daily diet of 3.5 million passengers.

Iwata headed west and skyscrapers shot upwards, tapering monuments to order and profit. Logos took on strange sig-nificance – two cats representing a courier company, an eagle advertising car tyres, a red flower selling probiotic yoghurt. Outside a luxury hotel, a row of beige-and-yellow taxis con-tained sleeping drivers, hoping to be woken by guests hungry for Tokyo's flesh. Iwata walked south beneath the large ven-tricle of Metropolitan Expressway No. 4, traffic intermittently shushing over him. Looking up, he tried to see the stars but there were only skyscrapers and grey murk.

Iwata arrived home at 1.30 a.m., vomited and blacked out trying to picture Sakai naked.

Stars hang over Chōshi like a sheen of silver sweat. The ocean is timid and quiet tonight.

Cleo is in the kitchen, waiting for Kosuke to come home. She doesn't ask about the scuffed knuckles. She doesn't ask about the stains. She does not answer the phone, even though it will only ever be her mother calling. If not her mother, it will be the silent one. Cleo hardly leaves the house now. She doesn't think about what has become of her life. She prefers to think about the early days. In the distance, she hears the faint yearning of foghorns. She looks out of the window. The lighthouse blinks weakly. When he had first shown her the lighthouse, they had looked at it for a long time, a lonely quirk against the mulberry twilight. *They make me feel sad*, she had said. *They care about you but all they do is tell you to stay away.* Kosuke hadn't replied.

He is late again, and though it is a ridiculous time to prepare a dinner, she takes out vegetables from the refrigerator. She rolls up her sleeves, washes her hands and begins to chop carrots. She does this slowly, to feel like his routine is something that she can be part of too.

Thunk.

Thunk.

Thunk.

Cleo stops and looks at the knife. She can hear Nina's peaceful breathing over the baby monitor. Yet the sound of her child provokes nothing in Cleo. Nothing at all. That absence might have worried her but at least it was better than the bad thoughts. The thoughts that could not be spoken about.

Cleo closes her eyes and thinks about the past.

She thinks about the time when she and Kosuke lived naked in their nest, drunk on the warm glory of youth and love. They kissed hesitantly at first, nervous guests serving themselves at an unfamiliar table. They slept in snatches. Cleo spoke of the pastry shop windows she had looked through as a little girl. Of riding on the shoulders of her father like a king on an elephant. Kosuke liked those stories. They spoke as though everything before had existed only to transport them to this bed. The windows of Cleo's old apartment would frost over with their breath and she would trace hearts on the glass. The apartment was near a church whose bells rang for saints' days and other irrelevancies. They smiled at the clangour – as you would at a drunk telling jokes. She would look down at the streets below, sand from the nearby beach blowing along them. They would shed clothes for days at a time and eat like survivors in an abandoned city. Cleo's body was a skein of geese rising up, silently bound for winter sun.

They lived from each other, they nourished and shared each other. They went to all the places where true feelings hide – dark minerals cloistered under moss. Kosuke kissed her navel while she phoned in sick. Cleo kissed his knees while he recited poetry.

Memories.

Mourning.

Motes.

The door opens and Kosuke tosses his keys on the table.

'Sorry,' he says, scratching his face.

Cleo has stopped asking for reasons. She wonders if he knows what he's apologizing for.

'Are you hungry?'

'Don't go to much trouble.'

Thunk.

Thunk.

Thunk.

'How was your day?' he says, smelling his own armpits.

Thunk.

Thunk.

Thunk.

'Fine.' Cleo smiles.

Thunk.

Thunk.

Thunk.

'How is Nina?' he asks without interest.

'Fine.' She smiles. 'She's sleeping.'

'Good.'

'How is the case going?'

Thunk.

Thunk.

Thunk.

'Same.' He exhales. 'You know how things are here.'

Cleo does know.

A lonely island populated by lonely people, obsessed with mountains and things that die.

'Oh,' she says, washing the knife under the tap.

Kosuke opens the fridge and seems to realize something. 'Cleo?'

Her heart is breaking with love and the truth and everything in her that ever was. She knows Kosuke is no longer who he was, she knows that what they had is dead but even so, she still needs him. Needs him to tell her he loves her. Needs some small souvenir of human feeling.

Even if it's a lie.

'Y-yes?'

'How do these green peppers look to you?'

Iwata jolted awake, screaming, surrounded by his own vomit. For a moment of horror, he was in the shadow of the lighthouse, the waves breaking around him, sounding like the *rip rip rip* of a child's backpack. He ran to the kitchen, tearing open cabinets.

No. No. No.

He struggled into his shoes, threw on his raincoat and rushed down to street level. Heavy rain soaked him instantly and he realized he was wearing no trousers under his coat. It didn't matter to him. He ran towards the corner, and squinted as the automatic doors of FamilyMart gasped open for him. The clock read 3.04 a.m. The shop was empty. So was the soft ballad playing.

Iwata kept his eyes low and snatched up a litre bottle of vodka. At the counter, the cashier bagged the purchase, saying nothing. The price appeared on the register. Iwata fumbled for money. He would run for it if he had to but in the inside pocket of his coat he found an old credit card. The cashier swiped it and Iwata trembled as the card machine processed his credit.

'Thank you, sir.'

Before she could bow, Iwata was out of the store. He was ripping off the cap and swallowing as though he had dragged himself through a desert for it. A ripple of fire through his guts, and then an unnatural twisting, but Iwata at last felt the calm.

He crossed the road into a children's playground. He lay back against the metal slide, which soaked his back. He drank more and looked up at the sky, rain pattering his face. He stayed there until dawn dribbled through the grey clouds.

A woman was walking her dog at the other end of the park, trying not to look at him. There was dried vomit on his chest and his back hurt from the slide. Iwata pulled his raincoat around his body and walked. He found himself by Yoyogi-kōen Station, which was swallowing a steady stream of commuters now. It was 6.20 a.m. Iwata passed the level crossing, zig-zagging through the cyclists waiting for the trains to clear. He passed under the gloomy overpass and ignored the usual left turn. Instead, he carried on down the narrow path that skirted the fenced-off train tracks. A few hundred metres along, hidden by bamboo, was a doorway. The sign above it read:

SOAP

Iwata descended stairs lit by bare bulbs and stood in a small waiting room. The carpet was marked with cigarette burns and the walls were cheap slats of plywood. An elderly woman with rosacea and a blanket around her shoulders opened the door. She smiled a fox's smile. Iwata wanted to run.

Four young women appeared behind her, all staring at the floor, smiling demurely.

Iwata shook his head.

'I'm very hungry,' he said.

Unperturbed, the old woman picked up a phone and whispered something. The women left and Iwata was asked to sit down. He was brought a tray of cold soba and green tea. He hardly paused to chew, though it all tasted of nothing. When he was done he wanted to leave but the old lady appeared again.

'Better?'

'Yes. I should go. Please tell me how much I owe.'

'Oh no, you need to be taken care of.'

Iwata said nothing but felt himself nodding. A young Mongolian man stood behind the old lady now. She turned to speak to him slowly.

'Please take this gentleman downstairs, he needs a bath.'

The young Mongolian smiled and ushered Iwata down another set of stairs. He was led into a bathing room of old green tiles. Iwata smelled chlorine. There was a plastic stool and an old tub in the corner.

'Long night for you,' the man said in gentle, broken Japanese.

'I'm a policeman,' Iwata replied, without knowing why.

'Not first to visit.'

The man took Iwata's coat and hung it up carefully. He

bent down and took Iwata's shoes, seeming not to care that he wore no trousers. He unbuttoned Iwata's shirt, not looking into his eyes. He folded the clothes and placed them on a rack outside. The man returned and slid shut the frosted glass door, trapping the warmth. He pulled down Iwata's boxers and his erection jutted free. The young man showed no reaction and led Iwata to the plastic stool.

'Sit.'

Iwata sat and closed his eyes as he heard a shower hiss on. Then hot water was cascading down his spine. Iwata shivered as it ran down his buttocks and flowed over his chest. The young man soaked Iwata for a long time, scrubbing him with a soapy flannel. Iwata's penis bobbed like a fish gasping. The young man clutched it now.

'You need?'

'Wait.'

Iwata walked over to the wall. He rested his forehead against the hot pipes, breathing in the steam. The tiles were cold against his chest. The Mongolian stood behind him. Iwata felt a face between his shoulder blades, kisses at his spine.

A hand slipped around his waist and began to masturbate him.

I walk and walk, swaying, like a small boat in your arms.

Iwata came on the tiles.

The Mongolian showered them off, watching the semen curl into the drain.

Iwata stood there shivering, needing to vomit, needing to sleep.

'Do you need me to go?' he said.

The younger man shook his head.

He came up behind Iwata again and held him in the clouds of heat.

Iwata began to cry.

'I'm sorry. I'm sorry. I'm sorry.'

I am as one who is left alone at the banquet, the lights dead, the flowers faded.

16. Other Places

By 9 a.m., Iwata was back at home, looking at his reflection in the mirror. He had never looked older. This was, of course, a biological given for all living things. But today, it was a truth that clung to every crack of skin and every shining pore. He showered and shaved carefully, before combing his hair back and taking out a clean suit. He dressed, his head the silence after a quake.

Iwata made coffee, put on Glenn Gould's *Goldberg Variations* and looked out of his window. He listened only to Aria da Capo, allowing himself precisely two minutes and eight seconds of music. When it was over, he washed out his cup and left his apartment.

Outside, the sky was stainless steel but there was no rain. Iwata took the Chiyoda Line to Meiji-jingumae Station, where he switched on to the Fukutoshin Line. He sat between a teenager hunching over equations and a man deliberating over the wording of a covering letter to a medical devices company. Iwata thought of what Sakai had said in the car.

Tokyo is a million cities. You ever wonder if maybe some of those cities are good and some of them are bad?

Iwata pictured little Hana Kaneshiro's grey face once again, her body lying on the metal slab. He closed his eyes and clutched his forehead, waiting for the images to pass.

Beyond dull pain and a hangover, Iwata felt nothing today. He got off the train at Ikebukuro and walked the ten minutes to the small lot beneath the apartment block where he had left his car. Iwata called Sakai twice but got no answer. He started the engine and kept the radio off.

Seagulls circled over the dark teal of Sagami Bay. On the surface of the inlet, a single wooden plank floated. Dead leaves had gathered around it as though lonely. Mrs Ohba's road was still cordoned off, a single policeman guarding the house. Iwata parked in a sandy lay-by and showed his badge.

Inside, he searched each room devoutly, hoping for some new angle. He had come here instead of the Kaneshiros' house because he knew the likelihood of the killer becoming complacent was higher on the second occasion than the first. After all, an old widow cut off from the world would require less concentration than an entire family. Iwata knew this was true statistically, but he also knew deep down that complacency from the Black Sun Killer was a long shot. Then again, those were the only shots he had left.

The first time Iwata had entered this house he'd sensed *something* from the killer – like the last few moments of a dream before it untangled. But whatever he had felt back then was long gone now.

Upstairs, the only sound was the distant breathing of the waves and the tiny ticking of the gold watch by the bed. Iwata went back out to the corridor and peered at the holiday photographs on the wall, the Ohbas' faces ageing, their postures sagging – a chronicling of decline. Under each framed photograph, a small white card carried a location and date.

Paris 1988.
Guam 1994.
Italy 1979.
London 2000.
Okinawa 1973.
Egypt 1992.

Every single holiday commemorated, stretching back into the early 1970s – one for each year. Strangers from all over the world had been asked to take these pictures, asked to record these smiles in front of landmarks and sunsets. They were all that was left of the Ohbas now. Iwata took out his notebook and wrote down the dates and locations.

He went back downstairs, this time looking for any possible way the killer might have spied on Mrs Ohba. Serial killers were likely to watch their victims before a kill but there would have been no easy way in these conditions. It was clear the widow hardly used the lower level of the house except for the Butsudan, which was in a room with no windows. All windows downstairs were covered. Upstairs, there were large windows, but the house was tall and there were no vantage points behind it. In front, there was only ocean. The killer would have needed a boat and some kind of telescopic lens to see her.

Remote possibility?

Iwata shook his head.

'He knew you were here, he came for you specifically. But why?'

Iwata sat down on the floor and shut his eyes, a wave of fatigue filling him. He pictured Mrs Ohba's chubby, brutalized body which had lain within arm's reach. It had been taken away, like an unpopular fairground attraction finally removed.

Kei flicks ash in the girl's direction.

'Look at the fat on that. It's what I've been trying to tell you. There's no class in this town.'

Kosuke gazes after the girl. He sees the movement of her buttocks under her skirt and the black sheen of her hair in the autumn sun. He feels an instant rush of desire.

185

The schoolgirl hurries past them, wondering how two boys her age can sit out sipping Cokes and smoking cigarettes on a Tuesday morning.

They're sitting outside the less pathetic of the two cafés in town. Kei is still only fifteen but he has grown into his features already – a boisterous pair of lips, a darkening chin and a stubborn crop of black hair. Kosuke is not yet there, the undecided softness of turning adolescence still about his face. He returns to the table as the jukebox plays the opening bars of Billie Holiday's 'Gloomy Sunday'. Kei rolls his eyes and snaps his fingers at the waiter.

'Another Coke for my friend here.'

'Kei, have you actually got the money this time? I'm not running.'

Kei sits back and puffs smoke between them, squinting one eye.

'You know what your problem is, Kosuke?'

'My choice in friends?'

'You have no faith.'

Kei leans back on his chair and lifts up his shirt, revealing an alarming amount of hair creeping up from his navel and a small wedge of bills in his waistband.

'Let's get out of here. This joint bores me.'

Kei raises his voice at these last words just as the waiter returns with the Coke. Kei drops the money contemptuously.

'Take that with you, come on.'

They set off down the road, Kei bobbing on his heels. Kosuke follows him, Coke bubbles spilling down his knuckles. He checks over his shoulder.

'Kei, where did you find that money?'

'I didn't steal it, if that's what you're asking me.'

'I'm asking you where you found it, I didn't say anything about stealing.'

'That's your downfall. You never say what you mean.'

'And that's yours. You find fault in everything.'

Kei laughs.

'Am I ever wrong?'

Kosuke drains the last of his Coke and slings away the bottle. It rolls down a ridge and is swallowed by the long, dead grass. They walk on for a time and cross the concrete bridge. Kei spits into a stream flowing underneath. This place is just two listless hamlets that merged for want of anything better to do. A dog raises its head above the grass-line but doesn't bother barking.

'Where are we going, then?' Kosuke asks.

Kei shrugs.

'Somewhere, man, I don't know. Where *is* there to go in this fucking place?'

Kosuke checks his watch and Kei laughs bitterly.

'You got somewhere better to be?'

'Class. Uesugi will shit if we cut again.'

'Will he now?'

The mountain on the horizon is a pale blue pyramid. Farms spread out on either side of the road into the distance, a patchwork of boring colours. In any part of this town you can see its end.

'You know something I won't find fault in?' Kei had regained his smile now.

'What?'

'The yakitori at The Foxhole. How about it, Kosuke-kun? I'll even let you play your goddamn American love songs.'

'Kei –'

'No, fuck that, man. Fuck "Kei". We'll sit outside The Foxhole with yakitori and beers and watch the ugly bitches of this town go by like fucking kings. Don't hold out on me, man.'

'Uesugi –'

'Uesugi nothing. What's he going to do, kick you out? Best thing that has ever happened to you, if he did.'

Kosuke looks up at the sky scornfully and tries to imagine other places.

The Foxhole is empty at this time of day and they have prime seats to watch the flow of schoolgirls returning home. Kosuke tosses another skewer away and licks his fingers clean.

'I tell you.' Kei pats his belly. 'This goddamn chicken is the only worthwhile thing on this fucking mountain.'

'So leave.'

'Watch me. Just a couple more years and I'm cutting loose for Tokyo. Then it'll be city living and all the mod cons.' Kei juts his chin towards the street. 'Hey, look at the tits on that one. Shame about the eel face.'

Kosuke looks at the girl, who is easily beautiful, and wonders how his friend can see things so differently from him.

'And what if Tokyo turns out to be a heap of shit as well?'

Kei waltzes his beer bottle between his thumb and forefinger, then drains the last of it.

'I'll go somewhere else. But at least it won't be the same shit every day, man.'

'Hey, what about her?'

'Buck teeth?'

'No, the shorter one.'

Kei scoffs as he picks his teeth clean with a skewer.

'I'm beginning to think you have a thing for fat chicks, Kosuke.'

'There's no fucking way that you could call her fat.'

'I'm sure she's a nice girl and I'm sure your parents, if you had any, would love her. But she's *clearly* a fucking fat pig.'

'Kei, I can't remember one single time you ever pointed to a girl in this town and said, "She's OK".'

'That's because I haven't. Look, I'm not saying I'm too good for everybody. I'm just saying that I'm not interested in living in these mountains all my life with some fucking dim peasant girl, waiting about for me to make her pregnant again.'

'In this whole valley. Not *one*?'

'Not a single fucking one. Show me one fucking chick in this backwater worth my time.'

Kosuke shakes his head.

'Go on, *one*.'

Kosuke finishes his beer, wipes his fingers on his thighs and beckons. They cross empty, half-flooded paddy fields, towards the caramel and copper of the treeline. The forest is dense and twisted beneath the shadow of the mountain, never having seen enough of the sun. They pick their way through brambles and duck through exposed roots. They come to a path marked mostly by deer tracks.

After a silent mile, a brick enclosure, about head-high, comes into view. Kosuke leads them off to one side around it. There is a house in the middle of the enclosure and the garden surrounding it is a sight to behold. Water trickles, pebbles are brushed into place and the plants and rocks sit in harmony.

They hear a small cracking sound. Kosuke first, then Kei, peek over the wall. A thin wisp of smoke drifts up from a foliage fire, which is surrounded by chestnuts in their spiky casings. A small pile of bare Spanish chestnuts sits by the fire, while a linen sack has been fixed above the flames. The smoke wafts through the bag.

But Kosuke does not notice any of that. He is mesmerized by the girl. She sits by her pile, reading her book, occasionally fanning the fire. Her hair is swept up in a bandana to keep the smell of the smoke out, Kosuke presumes. She is very beautiful and the weak golden light only makes her more surreal. Her lips are two slices of red apple skin and Kosuke aches to know why she paints them like that. He aches to know why – and for whom.

'*There*,' Kosuke whispers. 'There's one.'

Kei glances down and sees that Kosuke's penis is pushing against the bricks. Kei sees his quivering bottom lip and unblinking eyes.

'All right,' he whispers back, returning his eyes to the girl. 'There's one.'

She closes her book and shuts her eyes to look up at the sun, unaware of her two observers.

17. Favours

Iwata walked the illuminated streets of Roppongi, passing foreign embassies, international schools, designer boutiques and modern art galleries. The luxurious Park Residences rose up in the distance. He cut through the rock gardens and cypress trees of Hinokicho Park. The cherry trees surrounding the artificial lake were bare.

Iwata forced his way through the media scrum outside the Park Residences building and identified himself to the officers at the doors. The plush lobby was empty except for the immaculately dressed concierge at his desk. Iwata walked down the sleek corridor, its pink marble floor gleaming. On either side there were modern chairs and tables holding expensive lamps.

A large reproduction of Henry Moore's *Pink and Green Sleepers* hung on the wall.

Iwata took the elevator to the penthouse suites. The doors slid open to a tastefully lit corridor, the air smelling faintly of wood and lemon, the carpet pure wool. There were strange oil paintings of lakes and dancers on dark beaches. Iwata passed the first suite, which belonged to a famous variety show host. At the other end of the corridor, the door to Mina Fong's apartment was open.

Inside it was a spacious mix of dark greens and champagne yellows, the furniture and surfaces all complementary. The apartment would have been a tranquil space but for the twenty-strong police forensics team.

At the far end of the apartment, curtains billowed out of the open terrace doors. Iwata saw Sakai.

She stood alone, looking out over Tokyo. She hugged herself against the cold, her short hair wild in the wind.

'Sakai.'

'Iwata.'

'You heard what happened?'

Sakai nodded.

'And you know Ezawa killed himself?'

'I spoke to Shindo this morning.' She looked over her shoulder. 'You shouldn't be here, Iwata. If Moroto comes back . . .'

Below them, traffic ran along straight lines, trains ran along curves. Millions of Tokyoites poured through all available space. Innumerable existences. Aphids skating on a grey lake.

'What's the deal here, Sakai?'

She puffed out her cheeks.

'Different killer, same sinking feeling. Mina Fong was beaten to death. No real evidence left behind. They're ramping up the investigation. Not that there's much else they can throw at it.'

'There must be CCTV in a place like this.'

'Oh, there is. In the car park, elevator, lobby – pretty much everywhere except the residents' corridors and apartments. And we did pick up footage of an unidentified male on the night of her murder. He spends twenty minutes up here, then he's back in the elevator. No angle on the face.'

Sakai went back inside, pouring herself coffee from a thermos.

'What does the concierge say?' Iwata said.

'Guy came in through the car park; the concierge never saw him.'

'So he must have access.'

Sakai winced as she sipped the coffee and motioned for

them to move away from the forensics team, which was buzzing around a bloodstained wall. They sat at a long, black lacquer dining table – a perverse honeymoon breakfast scene.

'Telemetry shows nothing. The security company has no records of access or egress by anyone other than residents. Last telemetry activity is her key card access from the *outside* – meaning Fong coming home.'

'What about visitors?'

'All logged by the concierge. She didn't get many. Last visitor was Inspector Akashi.'

'Akashi? He knew her?'

'He was investigating death threats sent to her by a stalker.'

She nodded to the small mountain of brightly coloured fan mail on the table.

'Fun week ahead.' She blew her fringe out of her face.

Iwata shook his head.

'So let me get this straight. The angle is: deranged fan somehow got her to open the door then killed her?'

Sakai held up a series of colourful death threats.

'Yes, Iwata. That's the angle.' She then held up CCTV stills of a man in a black hooded jacket. 'Not everybody hears hooves outside their windows and thinks zebras.'

'Have you got any copies of those?'

'No. Now look, on the fourteenth of February at 02:12 we see him arriving by bicycle –'

'The fourteenth? Within a day of the Kaneshiro murders.'

'Must have been a full moon. Now listen, he arrives by bicycle in the car park, though he leaves it in a blind spot. He takes the elevator up to the top floor. By 02:31 he's back in the car park, then he's gone. He never looks to camera, seems to know where they are. And even so, quality is very grainy.'

'What about the bicycle?'

'Dark blue or black in colour. But there are seventy-two million bicycles in this country.'

Iwata chewed his lips in thought.

'What's the name of the security company?'

'Hawk Security.'

'No signs of forced entry at all?'

Sakai rolled her eyes.

'Funnily enough, that was already considered. And your next question will be, if Mina Fong was getting death threats, why did she open the door of her own free will?'

'To which you'd say . . . ?'

'Maybe she'd had enough and she snapped. Maybe she'd ordered a pizza. Maybe the barbiturates messed her up enough to open the door.'

'She was a user?'

'Oh, she was a fucking junkie; her assistant told us that the studios were threatening to fire her if she didn't get her shit together.'

'Beaten to death, you said?' Iwata asked.

Sakai fished out the crime scene photographs. Mina Fong lay face up, naked and covered in blood. She had bunched her fists and closed her eyes tightly, like a baby screaming. Where her skin wasn't covered in blood, it was purple and discoloured. Her face was swollen, both her eyes closed by bruises. Her nose was a shiny red mushroom, her lips were thick and her eyelids were blackened as if burnt.

'Time of death?' Iwata passed back the photographs.

'Coroner was actually pretty vague about it, 4 p.m. through to 8 a.m. But the unidentified male is captured on CCTV in the early hours of the fourteenth, so we're working to that timeframe.'

'Tell me about the stalker complaint.'

'Fong contacted the local police some weeks back but she

couldn't say anything for sure. Maybe I'm being followed, maybe this, maybe that. Couldn't give us any specifics until her dog was snatched. The assistant was walking it down in the park. Said a man just came up, punched her in the face and snatched the dog – walked away before she knew what hit her. Couldn't give a description.'

Sakai handed Iwata another photograph. A decapitated dog had been draped over Fong's face.

As she sipped her coffee, Sakai wiggled her eyebrows.

'At least the missing dog turned up, huh?'

Iwata put down the photographs and rubbed his eyes. He felt a frustrating mix of déjà vu and helplessness.

'Something doesn't sit right here, Sakai.'

'This murder is too boring for you?'

'Just the opposite. It's crazy. Textbook crazy.'

'Get the fuck out of here, Iwata.'

'Pathological attachment follows a fairly common road map. There are several stalker typologies that could apply here – a love-obsessional stalker idealizing Fong from afar. It could be a domestic stalker – a man she had some kind of sexual contact with in the past who refuses to let go. Statistically, that's the most likely. Or we could be talking about a simple case of erotomania. But *this* . . .'

Sakai drained her coffee and brought the cup down to the table a little too loudly.

'Iwata, nobody gives a shit about your FBI encyclopaedia here. You're not even police any more.'

'Maybe so, but tell me this isn't all a little too neatly packaged.'

'You're going to tell me there's no link between getting a death threat and being beaten to death a week later?'

Iwata shook his head.

'That's the problem. Of course there is a link. But it's too perfect. The guy who writes letters, decapitates dogs and carves names into his arm? That guy leaves behind traces, Sakai.'

He tapped the hooded figure in the grainy photograph.

'Yet *this* guy has left behind nothing. You've an entire forensic unit who can't find a crumb. That's a disconnect right there.'

Sakai rubbed her temples.

'So we haven't found anything yet. But a pair of gloves and a hood doesn't make him a genius. We'll get him.'

Iwata turned down his lips.

'Fair enough.'

'But you didn't come here to give me tips. What are you doing here?'

He chewed his bottom lip absently and shook his head.

'Look, Iwata, whatever it is, you better just say it.'

He spread his hands on the table.

'Ezawa is dead and Fujimura closed our case.'

'*Your* case.'

'As far as TMPD is concerned, the Black Sun is dead and they've got me with one foot out of the door. But we both know he's still out there.'

'What do you want?'

'I need your help.'

She snorted.

'*Help?*'

'We worked well together.'

'No, Iwata. I ran errands for you – that's different. Anyway, what can I help you with now? It's already over.'

Iwata swept back his fine, messy hair and traced his upper lip with his thumb and forefinger.

'You know Moroto has lodged an official complaint against me? The disciplinary meeting is next week.'

'I know.'

'Well, I'm asking you to put in a counter-claim against him. You don't have to make anything up, just tell the truth. That would at least show that there was a reason for my hitting him.'

Sakai smiled bitterly.

'You never fully trusted me, Iwata. And now you're asking me to go out on a limb for you. Why would I do that? Have you even asked yourself? What, because I appreciate what you did to Moroto? For the old times? Or because that's what women do?'

Iwata pinched the bridge of his nose.

'I'm just asking you to tell the truth. That's all.'

She glared at him and went over to the makeshift coffee station. Iwata glanced down at the Mina Fong case file and then followed her.

'Sakai, without your help, the case is fucked.'

'No, *you're* fucked.'

'And when the Black Sun kills again, so will you be.'

Sakai took her coffee out to the corridor and stood in the many gazes of Mina Fong.

'All right, look, I don't think Ezawa committed those murders either. But fuck, it wasn't like we were getting anywhere with that case. What's done is done.'

'And the killer? You think *he's* done?'

'What you're asking isn't simple. You're asking me to stand against Moroto. What about my career?'

'Is this about your career? Or is it about Moroto?'

Sakai stabbed a finger into his chest.

'*Fuck you.*'

'Look, I'm sorry, I just –'

'You think calling me chicken will get you anywhere? Stop acting like you did me a favour. You wanted to swing dicks with him and you did. That was never for me.'

'We work well together, you know it's true. I've never had that before, I'm betting you haven't either. We *can* get him.'

'You and I were there for the Black Sun murders. Nothing else held us together.'

'Please, Sakai. I need your help.'

She bit her tongue and then lowered her voice.

'Fujimura won't live for ever. Who do you think the crown will fall to once he's gone? You think it will be Shindo just because he's the oldest? Wake up. OK, Moroto is a prick. But show me three guys in the TMPD that aren't.' She shook her head, breathing hard through her nose. 'I saw him this morning talking to the public prosecutor. I know I don't have to spell it out for you, Iwata. He has friends both in the staff room and out in the playground.'

'You're saying no to me, then.'

'What's my word worth, anyway? Your outcome was fixed the moment you stepped through the doors of Division One. But this is *my* path, Iwata. This is *my* career. I won't risk it. Not for anyone. And not for you. Take some responsibility for your actions.'

Iwata leant forward and spoke quietly in Sakai's ear.

'I'm the only one who can find the Black Sun Killer. You know that, don't you?'

She shunted past him.

'All the best, Iwata.'

He was left staring at Mina Fong's ten-year-old face, grinning with an almost identical girl as they both blew out birthday candles. She was looking to camera, ensuring the joy of the day was conveyed. The other girl, probably her older sister, was looking at the photographer. Iwata puffed out his cheeks and headed towards the front door. But something stopped him opening it.

Another photograph, hanging at a crooked angle, as if

recently replaced. It was of Mina Fong's sister receiving a school diploma, a little shy but clearly proud, beaming at the camera.

She was the less pretty of the pair, taller, plumper. Her smile was less polished, though it carried more warmth. Iwata glanced up the corridor. This was the only photograph that was off-kilter. He thought it was unlikely the forensics team had left it like this.

Who, then?

Iwata ran a finger along the top of the photo frame. His distal phalanx came back lightly coated in dark, sooty powder. He sniffed at it gently and registered a distant burnt smell.

'Strange.'

He checked the frames of all the other photographs but found only dust. On a whim, he returned to the dining table, made sure nobody was looking and picked up the Mina Fong case file. As he left the apartment, he also took the disturbed photograph from the wall.

Back inside his car, Iwata dialled the number for the Park Residences security company.

'Hawk Security.'

'This is Inspector Iwata from the Tokyo Metropolitan Police –'

'This about the actress?'

'That's right.'

'One second.'

There was a click and a woman with a gruff voice answered.

'Yeah?'

'My name is Inspector Iwata and –'

'Just tell me what you need.'

'The Park Residences CCTV footage across a forty-eight-hour period – starting on the morning of the thirteenth and ending on the evening of the fourteenth of February. I need

Mina Fong's floor, all access and egress points and I want printed stills, too. How long will that take?'

'If you're collecting, I could have it ready in an hour.'

'Then I'm on my way.'

Hanging up, Iwata picked up the Mina Fong case file he had stolen from the dining table. He leafed through until he found the right page.

MINA FONG – NEXT OF KIN

Father – Shoei Nakashino. Japanese national. Deceased – natural causes.

Mother – Mary Fong. Resident at Green Peak Psychiatric Hospital (Hong Kong).

Siblings – Jennifer Fong. Deceased – suicide/misadventure – Cathay Pacific Medical Office (Hong Kong).

Iwata looked down at the photograph of Jennifer Fong that he had taken from the apartment. He peered into her happy eyes.

'What happened to you?'

Rain began to patter on the windscreen. It took him a few moments to decide. Then Iwata scrolled through his address book until he stopped at a name:

TABA

Iwata rocked the phone in his hand, as if testing its weight. 'No choice.'

He exhaled and dialled. After five rings a familiar voice answered.

'Chōshi PD.'

'Taba?'

'Yeah, who is this?'

'It's me.'

'. . . Iwata?'

'Yeah.'

A strange silence passed before Taba spoke again. Iwata wondered if he would hang up.

'What do you want?'

'I need to ask you a favour.'

Taba laughed loudly.

'After what *you've* done? You're actually asking me for favours?'

'I'm sorry but I have to. I know I have no right. I also have no choice.'

He heard Taba take a drag and exhale incredulously.

'Nobody has balls like Kosuke Iwata.'

'Look, Taba, I'm sorry to call you. I am. But this isn't about you and me. I'm working a serial killer. Nothing like this has ever been seen before. So I'm asking for your help this one last time. After this, you'll never hear from me again.'

There was another drag and another puff of smoke. Iwata pictured Taba at his desk. If he were to swivel around, from his window he would be able to see the sun setting over the ocean.

The lights of the city are so pretty.

'A serial killer?'

'The worst I've seen.'

Taba sighed.

'Whatever help you gave me when I was coming through is squared after this. You understand that? I don't want to hear from you again. You leave me and my wife the fuck alone.'

'Of course.'

'What do you want?'

'Is your brother-in-law still in Hong Kong police?'

18. Found at Sea

The 6.20 a.m. Hong Kong Express out of Tokyo Haneda took the better part of five hours to reach its destination.

Iwata spent the flight studying the Mina Fong case file and the still images he had picked up from Hawk Security. By the time he landed at Hong Kong International Airport, Iwata had also picked up a cold. In the arrivals hall, he sat down with a tasteless coffee and waited. Half an hour passed before a slim man with prominent eyebrows approached, hands in his pockets.

'You?' he asked in English. 'Iwata?'

'That's me.'

'The day after tomorrow at 8 a.m., the Cathay Pacific Medical Office. Doctor Wai will be waiting for you.'

'Thank you.'

'I don't know what you're doing here. I don't know why Taba would want to help you. But I do know what you did to him and my sister. If I were you, I wouldn't cross paths with me again.'

Then the man was gone. Iwata swallowed a couple of decongestants and approached the taxi kiosk.

The taxi worked its way through the misty roads of Lantau Island, and then over the bridges towards Tuen Mun. Pulling up outside Green Peak Psychiatric Hospital at 2 p.m., Iwata stepped into the drizzle clutching his bag. He looked up at the old building. It was set high up on the green hills overlooking Butterfly Beach, an old British structure built in a time when peace and an ocean view were the only real remedies available to the mentally troubled.

A portly man in a cream linen suit was waiting on the hospital steps. His round, neat face peeked out from beneath an expensive umbrella.

'Mr Iwata? I'm Mr Lee, the Fong family lawyer.'

'Mr Lee. Thank you for seeing me.'

'Welcome to Hong Kong.' He gave a cold, soft handshake. 'I must say your English is excellent. For a Japanese, I mean.'

His laughter was a high-pitched crest. Iwata followed him into the reception and the nurse behind the counter smiled and waved them through.

'Mrs Fong doesn't get visitors any more. I'm sure she'll be glad. Even if she doesn't say much, she's listening.'

Lee led Iwata into a large room with French windows. Elderly patients read newspapers or dozed. The TV news was almost deafening. At the open doors to the garden, Lee stopped.

'Mr Iwata, I think it best if you see her alone. If she sees me coming, she'll only think I'm bringing more bad news. She's had such an awful few years, as you know.'

Iwata thanked the portly lawyer and stepped out on to the long stretch of lawn overlooking Hong Kong's skyscrapers. Mary Fong was sitting beneath a white canvas parasol, wrapped in a blanket, her face expressionless beneath sunglasses. He saw Cleo as a withered old woman, drooling in silence, eyes still fixed on that same, never-changing horizon.

I'm happy with you.

Fighting the feeling he had been here before, Iwata crouched down by the old woman.

'Hello, Mrs Fong. I'm Kosuke.'

She turned her head to glance at him but said nothing. Mrs Fong went back to her view.

'I know you've spoken to police many times about your daughters, but I was just wondering if I could trouble you for a few minutes. I've come from Tokyo.'

I'm happy with you. Please let me hear.

'Tokyo? Ohh.'

'That's right. Mrs Fong, you know that nobody has yet been apprehended for Mina's murder . . . I hope that will only be a matter of time. But that's not why I'm here.'

In the distance, seagulls hung suspended in the grey. They looked no different from those that flew over Sagami Bay. Above them, planes made their final glum approaches. Iwata took out the photograph he had taken from Mina's apartment. He held it up in front of Mary Fong, who quivered for a moment, then looked away.

'Mrs Fong, I need you to help me.'

'Of course.' Her English carried a subtle accent. 'You've come all this way.'

'From what I gather, Jennifer died some years ago in a boating accident of some sort?'

She laughed defensively.

'You have the wrong person, dear. Jennifer is alive and well, thank you. You must have just missed her, in fact.'

'She came to visit?'

'Just now.'

'Mrs Fong, from what I can gather, Jennifer's body was found at sea. Quite far out, in fact. Did she know anybody who owned a boat? A boyfriend, perhaps?'

Please let me hear. Those words of love from you.

Mary Fong chuckled and looked at him over her sunglasses. Her eyes were pink and watery.

'Jennifer is a good girl. She wouldn't have anything to do with that.'

'As far as I know, the authorities labelled it as death by

misadventure, possible suicide. Was she acting any differently at the time of her death? Were you ever worried? Did she seem unhappy?'

Mary Fong looked away and pulled the blankets tighter around her frail body.

'Jennifer is a good girl.'

'I'm sorry to ask you, Mrs Fong, but I really need to be sure about what happened.'

She frowned slightly.

'I'm sorry you've come such a long way. But I think you have the wrong person. I'm really very tired, my memory isn't . . .'

Iwata stood up and straightened his legs. He took a chair from a nearby garden table.

'Do you mind if I smoke, Mrs Fong?'

'That's fine. Tell me, have the cherry blossoms arrived in Beppu?'

Iwata puffed out smoke.

'Beppu?' The cigarette bounced on his lips.

'Such a wonderful place for a honeymoon. How is the weather there at the moment?'

'I don't know. But it's too early in Tokyo for cherry blossoms.'

'Ah, *Tokyo*.' She inhaled with pleasure as though she were walking through Yoyogi Park at this very moment, sniffing the blossom-rich air.

'You know Tokyo, don't you? Did you visit Mina there?'

'She's such a beautiful child. She wants to become an actress when she leaves school, can you imagine?'

Iwata smoked in silence for a while, then stubbed out his cigarette. The clouds were darkening as they settled over Hong Kong. He checked his watch.

'I worry for that girl sometimes.' The old woman sighed. 'She never visits me, you know.'

'Do the names Yuko and Terai Ohba mean anything to you?'

'I've never heard those names.'

'What about a family by the name of Kaneshiro?'

'I'm afraid not.'

'Thank you for talking to me, Mrs Fong.'

'Goodbye, darling. Tell Jennifer that I need my hair cut, if you would.'

Iwata stood and left Mary Fong to her memories.

Outside the hospital, Mr Lee was waiting on the steps, watching the rain.

'Was she any help?'

'Unfortunately not.'

The lawyer reached into his inside pocket and produced a pair of keys.

'The address is on the tag.'

'Thank you for your help, Mr Lee.'

'I hope you find what you're looking for, Inspector.'

Iwata started down the hill, heading for the seafront.

As the ferry chugged across the bay, Iwata ate rice balls and watched the waves. He could tell his cold would get worse before it got better.

After docking, he explored Discovery Bay – an upmarket, seahorse-shaped residential development built at the foot of the green hills that rose out of the ocean. He walked past modern apartment complexes, luxury villas, expensive restaurants and various social clubs, all of them requiring membership. At this hour, the only pedestrians were new mothers pushing two-month-salary prams and elderly couples dressed for tennis.

After the better part of an hour, Iwata finally found Mrs Fong's apartment building. It was a concrete afterthought at the end of the bay. He took the elevator to the top floor, unlocked number 912 and was immediately hit with the smell of dead flowers. He took in gold mirrors, motionless wind chimes and faded ink drawings of birds. To the right, he saw Mrs Fong's room and the bathroom – to the left, the girls' rooms.

Mina's room was spacious, the orange walls adorned with stickers, sea shells spelling out her name. The window looked out to the sea. A white vanity unit stood beneath it. Her walls were a patchwork of magazine cuttings and teenage torsos. Iwata spent the next hour searching her room but he could turn up nothing more than the components of a life that Mina had left behind. Her hiding places contained nothing of interest, the wardrobe contained only clothes. There was nothing in this room that Iwata could match to her new life in Japan.

At her desk, he read through good grades that had steadily declined and report cards that spoke of a natural intelligence marred by a waspish attitude. He pictured her sitting before her teacher on parents' evening, her mother next to her, exhausted from working long-haul flights, solemnly nodding at the teacher's words.

If Mina applied herself, she could study anywhere in the world – it's all ahead of her.

But Iwata knew how the story had ended. At eighteen, she would drop out from the London School of Economics to pursue modelling work in Tokyo. Celebrity and wealth would find her. As would loneliness and barbiturates. Finally, she would be murdered in her own apartment.

Aching and tired, Iwata took another decongestant and swallowed it with tap water from the bathroom. He opened the door to Jennifer's room, a much smaller space with lilac walls. The colour was either Jennifer's favourite, or a stand against the tyranny of the younger sister's bright orange. There was a single Bon Iver poster. An almost life-sized stuffed toy dog had been dry-cleaned and shoved in a clear plastic bag in the corner. He pictured Jennifer and the dog together, her tears and secrets fed into the dog's neck down the years, its eyes glassy, its smile permanent.

Iwata sat on Jennifer's bed and took out his ferry schedule. He calculated that Mina and Jennifer would have had to have woken up at 5.30 a.m. each day to catch the ferry in time for the school bus. He already knew that their father had kept up regular payments. But Mrs Fong's salary from Cathay Pacific had always been meagre and after school fees and rent, life would have rarely been anything other than tough down the years.

Iwata started to search the room – rifling through drawers, looking under the bed and unfolding folded clothes. He found nothing. Her mattress concealed only a forgotten receipt for an inexpensive summer dress. Inside the speakers of her music player were only wires. Her books contained only pages. He felt behind the mirror but touched only glass.

Then he opened her underwear drawer and there, under folded socks, he saw diaries. Jennifer Fong had filled out five large, thick journals through her short life, all of them kept together. The entries were not dated but were all in English. Iwata spent the next two hours ingesting the dead girl's hopes and fears. Her confessions of lust and hatred.

As a child, everyone had said how pretty Jennifer was. As she grew taller and larger, the compliments passed down to Mina. Jennifer frequently worried about her figure. She was taller than all her friends and had a thick waist and large breasts. Her clothes no longer fitted her and she concluded she must be fat. Her relationship with her friends was a complicated one. Occasionally, she would pour out her love for them on the page, hoping that their bond would be a lifelong one. But she regarded them, more frequently, as an ancillary commitment in her life, an inconvenience that she did not particularly care for. She was, however, very close to her sister and her mother, though they often argued.

As Jennifer got older, most of her friends started relationships, but whenever she met a boy she liked, she felt too unattractive to initiate one. At sixteen, on a school trip, an English boy named Neil began talking to her. He repeatedly told her how beautiful she was. He was skinny, shorter than her, with braces and clumsy facial expressions. But nobody had ever shown an interest before. When he asked to meet her the next day, she agreed.

He walked her around the city aimlessly for three hours before eventually taking her to the beach. The sky was battleship grey, and in the distance a storm was building. Sitting in the damp sand, they shared a can of Coke without saying anything. When it was gone, Neil kissed her. As she tasted the metallic sugar of his saliva, she knew this wasn't what she wanted.

On the way home, she cried without knowing why. When Jennifer told her friends, they made such a fuss over her that she began to feel her life was, at the least, becoming more interesting. She began to feel important things were going to happen to her soon. She stopped wearing glasses and went on the pill. She did not speak to Neil again for several years, though they seemed to rekindle a strong friendship later on.

Teachers always liked Jennifer, perhaps because her younger sister had been prone to tantrums. In contrast, while Jennifer did not display the same academic potential, she was friendly and likeable. In fact, the only detectable animosity in any of her journals was towards her Japanese father – Shoei Nakashino.

Mina and her father would often tease Jennifer. They

would call her 'Baby Elephant' in Japanese, then stomp around the room with imaginary trunks, knocking things over. It was one of the few 'games' he seemed to enjoy with them. Jennifer would never let her tears spill until later.

If he took his girls to the beach, he would watch from a distance, dressed in a full suit, tie slightly loosened, the only casual thing about him being a baseball cap to protect his balding scalp. Jennifer would call for him to join them in the water but he would pretend not to notice over his news-paper.

Iwata flipped ahead in her life, well into adolescence.

Father has been in touch. He'll be visiting for two days and he wants me to book a table for our 'usual' meal for three. He uses the word 'usual', though this actually means annual. I suggested inviting Mum, but of course he found this ridiculous. I really don't see the point any more. His dinners require two or three cancellations beforehand, and when they finally do come around, he just half-listens and checks his watch the whole time. Not that he looks me in the eye any more. The second I sprouted breasts, he stopped looking me in the eye. Maybe he thinks I'm no longer a little girl and his work as a father is done?

Shoei Nakashino died two weeks shy of his fifty-sixth birthday, a perfunctory heart attack in the London office of a nappy conglomerate. Jennifer, Mina and Mary Fong had attended the funeral and were summarily ignored by Naka-shino's second family.

In her diary, Jennifer's musings on death were short and sad. It was hard for her to see how she could wait a full year until university began. She was desperate for something or someone to come along.

And as the diary entries came to an end, it seemed as if someone had.

Between the pages, she had kept cinema tickets and a dried Chinese hibiscus petal. Beneath it, the simple words: *I've never met anyone like him.*

No introduction, no explanation, no outpouring of first love. Just that statement. Iwata went back to the start and read through a second time but could find no other mention of *him*.

Checking his watch, Iwata returned the journals to their nest and squinted at the photographs around the frame of the mirror. Most were of Mary and Mina, who were both naturally photogenic. There was only a single photograph of Jennifer, sitting on the beach, shielding her eyes from the sunset. Her hair was wet from the ocean and the muscles in her arm were captured clearly in the orange light.

Iwata knew Jennifer was a good swimmer – she had letters from the beach authority thanking her for her lifeguard volunteering.

I love the ocean. It's the only thing I'll miss next year.

Next year had come and gone.

Iwata sat at her desk and opened her school yearbook. He scanned the faces and names, wondering who might have known Jennifer, who might have hated her, or loved her from afar.

Cross-referencing with Jennifer's journal, he recognized only three names in the yearbook:

Kelly Ho

Susan Cheung

Neil Markham

Shutting the yearbook, Iwata ran his finger across the gold-leaf address.

19. If There Is a Him

In the taxi, Iwata accepted roaming charges and looked up the school website. North Point International School was approaching its thirtieth year with a 1,500-strong student body and a teacher-to-student ratio of 1:9. Annual fees for reception students were $15,500, while years 7–11 ran at $24,000. The headmaster was a Swiss national with a PhD in economics and extensive experience in educational management across Europe, the US and Asia.

The street leading up to the school was lined with eucalyptus trees. Chauffeurs clustered together under umbrellas, smoking and laughing. When their designated child emerged, they hastily stubbed out their cigarettes and fixed their smiles.

The taxi pulled up at the bottom of the road and Iwata watched the last of the day's students drain out of the doors. There were no rebellious haircuts, facial piercings, or kissing couples.

Closing his eyes, Iwata saw a big building with tall windows in the middle of an empty field.

You must be very tired, Kosuke.

Feeling a nauseous twist in his gut, he shook off the memory. He paid the driver, climbed the steps and showed his TMPD credentials to the security guard.

Inside, the empty corridors smelled faintly of feet and linoleum. The school looked nothing like Sakuza Orphanage but the smell was a perfect echo. Iwata consulted the floor plan and took the elevator to the top floor. At the end of the corridor, he knocked on a door with a brass plaque:

A doughy, balding man wearing rimless spectacles opened the door. He wore a tan suit with a red silk handkerchief in his breast pocket and a single gold ring. He had freckles over his nose and a curious look on his face. Iwata held up his ID once again.

'Doctor Rossetti? I'm Inspector Iwata, Tokyo Metropolitan Police. I was wondering if I could take a moment of your time.'

'Oh. Come in.'

The floor-to-ceiling window framed Hong Kong and its jade waters like a canvas. Iwata sat in an expensive brown leather chair before a Murano glass bureau.

'Well, you *have* come a long way. I presume you're not here to make inquiries about enrolment?'

His chuckle was a cloying peal.

'I'm here about two former students. Mina and Jennifer Fong.'

'Ah, of course.' Rossetti's smile faded. 'We were very sorry to learn of what happened. What a terrible episode. You're investigating?'

Iwata nodded noncommittally.

'Doctor Rossetti, do you know if Jennifer was having a relationship of any kind while she was a student here?'

'*Jennifer?* No, I never heard of anything like that.'

Rossetti plucked delicately at his chin as if it were a small fruit.

'Was there anything that stood out about her?'

'To be honest, Inspector . . .'

'Iwata.'

'*Iwata*, what does that mean by the way?'

'Stony rice paddy. You were saying . . .'

'To be honest, Jennifer always seemed the timid type. I wouldn't put her with that sort of thing.'

'Doctor Rossetti, I'm going to need the contact details for three former students.'

'That wouldn't be a problem but I was actually just on the way out. Would it be possible to send you the information tomorrow or –'

'I won't be here for long, sir. I'd appreciate those details right away. The first name is Susan Cheung.'

Rossetti exhaled and went over to a large grey cabinet. 'You may be in luck. We try and keep our records up to date as we host various reunions and fundraising events with old students. Now, let me see. Susan Cheung. Bit of a handful, if I remember correctly. Here she is . . . no, all I have is an address for her, but our last mailing was returned undelivered, I'm afraid. Looks like she moved.'

'And what about Kelly Ho?'

'Ah yes, Kelly. Now that's a name I know well. She worked here for a year.'

'She's a teacher?'

'That's right. Well, for a time.'

'Why did she leave?'

Rossetti shifted with mild embarrassment.

'Ms Ho was a perfectly good teacher. But she met her husband and then, well, you know how these things are. Now what was that last name?'

'Neil Markham.'

Rossetti looked up from the files.

'Is this to do with what's been in the papers?'

'I don't know anything about Neil Markham and the papers.'

'If you say so.'

Rossetti sat back down, wrote two addresses on his notepad and ripped off the page like a prescription.

'That first one is for Kelly Ho. The second is for Neil Markham. When you see them, please extend my regards.'

Iwata stood and gave a lacklustre bow.

The taxi stopped outside a handsome gated community with high white walls and metal railings. Iwata sneezed and dabbed at his streaming eyes with a tissue as he passed palm trees and perfectly green lawns. It was as though a small, wealthy village had been constructed on top of a golf range. Kidney-shaped pools were still and dark. Statues of lions made from faux marble stood guard outside doors. Except for the distant droning of aircraft and a yapping dog, the community was silent.

Iwata glanced at his watch as he walked past identical houses; it was 7 p.m. He stopped outside number 14 and pressed the bell. A short woman with a soft but tired face answered the door. Kelly Ho was halfway through adjusting an earring and her make-up looked hastily applied. Her lips glistened and her hair was expensively styled but there was a pink rawness beneath her eyes and the smell of baby milk about her.

'Please come in, Inspector.'

'Sorry I couldn't give much warning.'

'Not at all. Come through.'

The dark wood floors gleamed and practically every surface held fresh flowers. Lamps cast a mellow light. She gestured for Iwata to sit on the large white sofa laden with cushions. Donna Tartt's *The Secret History* lay open on the coffee table. A baby monitor blinked in the corner.

Iwata looked away.

'Would you like some coffee?'

'That would be much appreciated.'

She returned a few moments later with a pot of coffee,

two glasses and a small jar of honey. She poured Iwata a glass and looped in a spoonful of honey.

Honey for my honey bee.

'Are you all right, Inspector?'

'Fine,' he said through gritted teeth. 'Flying doesn't agree with me, that's all.'

She sat on the seat across from Iwata and curled her bare feet underneath her, hugging the cardigan around her slight frame.

'My husband is constantly flying. He's the same.'

'What does he do?'

She gestured around the large house with her hands.

'Investment banker.'

Iwata laughed, then coughed.

'He's visiting his mother in Denmark at the moment. She's not very well.'

'I'm sorry to hear that. He's Danish?'

She nodded.

'And you, Inspector? Married?'

Iwata swallowed hot coffee but tasted nothing.

'Yes.' His smile was weak. 'What is it that you do, Mrs Ho?'

'*Lund.* It's Kelly Lund now. It's been a couple of years and I'm still getting used to it myself. And as for what I do?' She nodded over her shoulder. 'I look after the baby. Read books. Answer the door to strange detectives.'

They shared a polite smile and she quietly set her glass down.

'Inspector, on the phone you said you were investigating Mina Fong's murder. But I have to ask, why would a policeman from Tokyo come all this way to talk to me? I never really knew her.'

Iwata finished his coffee and set down his glass beside hers.

'But you knew Jennifer.'

Sadness washed over Kelly Lund's face and she involuntarily glanced towards the baby monitor, her sleeping child still so innocent of the world that awaited.

'Why do you want to talk about Jennifer?'

'Because I want to find out whether her death was an accident, a suicide, or something else.'

She met Iwata's eyes for a second.

'I don't believe she killed herself.'

'Why do you say that?'

'Because I *knew* Jennifer. The idea of Jennifer killing herself is ridiculous. It just never sat right with me, I can't explain it.'

'She wouldn't do that?'

'No, absolutely not. The idea of her dying of a drugs overdose on some stranger's boat is just as stupid. None of that *feels* like Jen.'

Iwata held up the print-off from the Park Residences CCTV footage of the unidentified man in the hooded jacket.

'I don't suppose you recognize this man. Even just his clothes?'

'No, who could recognize that?'

'These images were taken from Mina's apartment complex the day of her murder.'

Lund looked at the man in the image and then back at Iwata.

'You think whoever killed her was also responsible for Jennifer's death?'

'It's a possibility I can't yet rule out.'

Iwata put the photograph back in his bag and held up a newspaper clipping of the new Mesoamerican exhibition opening at the Tokyo National Museum.

'How about him? Doctor Igarashi.'

Kelly Lund squinted at it, then shook her head. Iwata changed tack.

'Was Jennifer seeing anyone in the year before she died?'

'No, I don't think so. We'd speak on the phone sometimes, go for the occasional coffee. She never mentioned anything like that.'

'Would she have told you, do you think?'

'Absolutely. I mean she was a happier listener than a talker, sure, but there's no reason for her to keep that kind of thing a secret from me.'

'Did she have any friends with access to a boat?'

'Several. We went to school with very wealthy people. But I couldn't tell you one person who'd let her drown like that. Or go that far out on the open sea. It doesn't make sense.'

Iwata thought about this and then looked at the paper Rossetti had given him.

'What can you tell me about Neil Markham?'

'Sweet guy. He and Jennifer had a thing briefly as kids, but I really can't imagine him having anything to do with this.'

'Did he have a boat?'

'Not that I knew of. But he made a fortune with some sort of car exports website a few years ago, so it's quite possible he has one now.'

A wave of exhaustion washed over Iwata and he leant back on the sofa for a moment. Above him was an oil painting of a beautiful pink dawn. The cliffs were awash with orange, the rocks below were like a broken jaw.

I'm happy with you.

'Are you all right?'

'Yes I'm . . . just a bit run down.'

Please let me hear. Those words of love from you.

'Let me get you some cold water.'

I walk and walk, swaying, like a small boat in your arms.

Iwata shook his head.

'No, really. I should get going.'

He stood now, coughing. He was freezing inside, sweat streaming down his neck, forehead and thighs.

'Thank you for your time. And the coffee.'

Kelly Lund shrugged.

'I don't think I was much help. If there's anything else you think of, I'll be here.'

Lund opened the front door and the sound of rain hissed in.

'Actually, there is something. Do you have Susan Cheung's address?'

Lund hesitated before nodding and returning with a piece of paper.

'She probably won't be home until morning. And you should be careful around there.'

'You're no longer friends?'

'We . . . move in different circles.'

'Thank you again for all your help, Mrs Lund.'

'I hope you catch him, Inspector Iwata. If there is a *him*.'

20. A Lonely Bluff

Iwata parked his rented Volkswagen Golf outside a luxury apartment complex on a quiet bend of South Bay Road. He killed the engine, crossed the road and pressed Neil Markham's buzzer.

A weary female voice answered.

'Yes?'

'I'm looking for Mr Markham, I need to speak to him about –'

'Christ, it's past ten. Don't you people ever sleep?'

Iwata heard a muffled male voice in the background before the woman returned.

'You're wasting your time, my husband won't speak to you.'

'But –'

'Just piss off.'

The line went dead and Iwata became aware of a presence to the left.

'Haven't seen you before.'

A man with a smoker's voice was sitting cross-legged in the shadow by the main door. He was wearing a windbreaker, listening to a portable radio and drinking coffee from a thermos.

'I'm sorry?'

'Which paper are you from?'

'No paper. I'm a police inspector from Japan.'

The man pursed his lips.

'*Japan?* What's this guy to the Japanese police?'

'I'm afraid I can't say.'

'Well, he is having a bad week, then.'

'Why?'

'You *are* from out of town. Neil Markham was something of a VIP in the local business scene – "Forty Most Influential Under-forties", that sort of thing. He started up a luxury car export business a few years ago and it really took off. But in the last few days, it's come to light that the IRD are after him.'

'The tax authority?'

'Yes. And my editor's favourite thing in the world is a fallen star. Thus my picnic.' The journalist nodded to his thermos and Tupperware container.

'Thanks.' Iwata returned to his car and spent the next two hours sneezing and shivering.

Just after 11 p.m., the shutters to the car park opened and a lime green sports car emerged. Iwata immediately recognized the driver from Jennifer's yearbook. Neil Markham was picking up speed, heading north. Iwata started his engine.

The narrow roads wound between slivers of forest and walls of sheer rock. Markham hugged the coastal road, easily doubling the speed limit.

Finally, he stopped at a red light.

Iwata pulled up alongside him and glanced over. In the blue gloom of his car, Markham looked up impatiently at the light. Iwata could see now that he had grown into a plain-looking man, his soft face winnowed by years of stress. Though he was balding, he was in need of a haircut. There was pale flab about his neck and cheeks.

The lights turned green and Markham shot forward, arcs of amber street light sweeping over his windscreen. He ripped on to Island Road, horns blaring at him. Markham took the turning for Route 1 now. Cranes in the distance slept like flamingos. Beyond them, silver skyscrapers hiding jagged black mountains. The road narrowed, now flanked by roadworks and flashing cones as the city streets built up around them, and Markham reduced his speed.

On Lyndhurst Terrace, he abruptly pulled into a narrow alleyway. Iwata stopped in a pay space a few hundred metres down the road, then hurried back to the alleyway. Turning the corner, he passed fire exits, mounds of rubbish and air billowing out of vents. Markham's sports car was parked in front of a stairway. Above it, red neon letters glowered:

THE GREEN CARNATION

Iwata descended into a cramped, smoky bar. Six narrow booths ran along the right. Black-and-white photographs of old Hong Kong lined the walls, pink fairy lights twinkling above them. A wartime ballad was playing. Markham was sitting at the furthest booth by himself, swigging from a bottle of beer as he scanned the room.

Iwata sat at the bar, ordered a drink and watched Markham until it was clear he wasn't waiting for anyone. Instead, Markham glanced up hopefully each time a man passed his table.

Iwata made his move and slid into the booth.

'Hello,' Neil said with a smile.

Iwata returned the smile.

'No ice.' Markham nodded at Iwata's whisky. 'A man that appreciates flavour.'

'My name is Kosuke Iwata and –'

'Relax.' Markham took a seductive swig of beer. 'But if

you really want to do this the old-fashioned way, I'm Neil.'

'Yes I know who you are, Mr Markham. I'm an investigator with the Tokyo Metropolitan Police Department.'

Markham looked around the room. His smile was casual but his tone rigid.

'Why are you here?'

'You were friends with Jennifer Fong. I need to ask you some questions.'

Markham traced his lips with his thumb and forefinger.

'All right. But not here.'

'Then where?'

It was after midnight when Iwata and Markham parked their cars on a lonely bluff, high up near Victoria Peak. Markham got out of his sports car and faced away from the wind to light a cigarette. Iwata stood next to him by the precipice, his eyes tearing up as he surveyed the cityscape. Between the sloping shoulders of the black hills, Hong Kong looked like a glittering diamond.

Markham offered a cigarette but Iwata shook his head. Instead, he bent down and picked up a pebble. It was cold and smooth in his hand.

'Neil, I spoke to a journalist outside your apartment building.'

'Just the one? That's something, I suppose. It was a pack of them before. They've been out there all week.'

'Does your wife know you go to gay bars?'

'Probably. Or if she doesn't it's because she doesn't want to know.'

'I see.' Iwata tossed the pebble into the black. 'I can't judge anyone, but is that really something you should be doing right now? Given the press attention?'

'In for a penny, in for a pound.' Markham remembered his

cigarette and took a nervous drag. 'You said you wanted to talk about Jennifer.'

Iwata nodded.

'You were school sweethearts?'

'Not really.' He smiled distantly. 'We were just friends.'

'Close friends?'

'Yeah, close. We lost touch somewhat in the year before her death, but yeah. Best friends, more or less.'

'So how did you lose touch?'

'I was flat out getting the business on its feet, getting married; she was preparing for university. It wasn't a conscious thing.'

'Did you ever know her to have boyfriends?'

'Not really, she didn't do all that much socializing outside of her little circle. Jen wasn't what you'd call a particularly confident girl.'

'Think, Neil. Anyone. Anyone at all. If not boyfriends, male friends perhaps? Anyone that stood out, anyone who could have been special for her?'

'Well, I suppose there was one man who might fall into that category. I don't know about boyfriend, but I saw them together a few times. Come to think of it, I'm pretty sure he was Japanese.'

Iwata looked up.

'Do you know his name?'

'No, sorry.'

'Describe him.'

'Tall. Well built. Much older than her.'

Iwata delved into his bag and pulled out the newspaper cutting of Igarashi. He fumbled with the interior light.

'Him?'

'It's not a great picture but I'm pretty sure it's not him.'

'Tell me about this man.'

'I bumped into Jen in a nightclub and I remember that it surprised me – that wasn't her scene at all. I asked her what she was doing there. She just said she was with a friend.'

'How did she seem?'

'She looked different, actually. She'd lost weight and was all dressed up but, I don't know, she also looked spaced out. Anyway, we spoke for a few minutes, she said she'd call me soon and then she disappeared. I didn't think much of it but two minutes later, I'm in the bathroom when this man corners me. I thought he was going to mug me at first.'

'What did he do?'

'He got me in the corner. And then he just whispered in my ear. Told me if I went near the girl again, he'd slash my face.'

'*The girl. Slash your face.* He used these exact words? Are you sure?'

Markham smiled wryly and stubbed out his cigarette.

'It's the sort of phrase that sticks in the mind.'

The rain picked up and they got into Iwata's rented car.

'He spoke in English?'

'Broken English, but clear enough.'

'You definitely never heard a name?'

'I never thought to ask. I just remember thinking this man would probably be the sort of arsehole that Jen would have to learn about the hard way.'

Iwata considered the raindrops on the windscreen, turned mercury by the headlights.

'You said "spaced out". What did you mean?'

'I don't know. I wouldn't say coke. She sort of seemed . . . I don't know, floaty. Like she was tripping? I mean, it didn't *seem* like Jen. But that's what was in front of me.'

'Did you see her again after that?'

'Yeah, a few weeks later, I think. I managed to persuade

her to have a coffee with me. But she was distracted. She was due to go to university but she admitted she didn't have anything sorted out. I mean funding, accommodation, I'm not even sure she'd had formal acceptance. I was shocked. That didn't seem like her either. I mean, that really was an alarm bell.'

'Did you talk about the man at all?'

'Yeah, she was still seeing him. I raised the issue. I said that I was concerned that whoever he was, he was distracting her from her future. Come to think of it, he *was* Japanese. Yes, I'm certain. I was shocked, I'd never seen her speak so sharply to anyone. Let alone to me.'

'And then?'

'I said that I knew what men were like. I asked her to be honest with herself – what was he getting out of it? All right, so he was important to her, but how did she know the same held true for him? Then she got pissed off and left. That was the last time I saw her.'

Iwata rubbed his eyes and, after a while, nodded slightly.

'All right, Neil. I might call you if anything else crops up.'

Markham nodded and got out of the car.

'I loved Jennifer. Let me know if there's anything I can do. Good luck, Inspector.'

Iwata started the engine and headed back towards Discovery Bay, arriving at Mary Fong's apartment after 3 a.m. Collapsing on the sofa, Iwata fell asleep watching the ocean.

21 Work Work Work

Iwata is roused by the sound of life. The apartment is small, but through the open window he can hear the Pacific Ocean exhale. Iwata rolls to Cleo's side of the bed and it is still warm. He hears the clatter of washing up and unselfconscious singing. When she's finished, she waters all the plants, chatting to them as she does so.

Iwata sees the trinkets on Cleo's dresser, her clothes on the floor and the morning sunlight streaming through her blinds. He realizes that this is what it is like to be in love.

The door opens and the smell of coffee wafts in.

'Wake up, lazy head.'

The voice is wrong. As if heard from a great distance.

The footsteps are wrong.

The cups clatter to the floor and blackness seeps into the carpet.

Iwata sees why.

She has no balance. She can't walk. Her legs are badly broken, shinbones piercing through skin.

'No cream, or sugar. Just a dollop of honey for my honey bee.'

Her words gurgle into one another. There is water in her lungs.

Iwata screams.

Though Iwata woke after midday, he felt exhausted, as though he'd barely slept. He had eaten very little in the last two days but he had no appetite. Instead, he breakfasted on decongestants and tap water. Iwata looked up the address Kelly Lund had given him and ordered a taxi – he couldn't face driving in circles on his weary bones today.

While he waited, he plugged in the television and slid in the duplicate videotape of the Park Residences CCTV from Hawk Security.

Grainy footage appeared on screen, split into eight boxes like a comic strip. Except for the concierge in the lobby reading his newspaper, each of the different angles showed stillness throughout the building.

The tape started at 23:59 on 12 February 2011, running as far as 23:59 on the 14th.

As Iwata fast-forwarded through the tape, a flurry of life began to swarm around the building over the course of the day. When the timer read 02:11 on the 14th, Iwata pressed play. The building was still again, the concierge was at his desk.

One minute later, in the bottom right-hand box, the car park gate opened. A figure on a bicycle glided in, head down – without hesitation. He left the bike in a blind spot, then calmly walked to the elevator and got in, pressing the button for the top floor. His arms hung at his side, his head was lowered. He did not move as the elevator made its ascent. The doors slid open and the man stepped out. Then nothing.

Iwata jumped ahead to 02:31 – the elevator doors opened at the top floor and the man stepped back inside. His demeanour had not changed. His posture was the same. He seemed calm. When the elevator reached the car park, he walked unhurriedly back to the bicycle. Then he was gone. There was nothing after that until three hours later, when the first few residents started to leave the building.

The tape cut out.

Iwata frowned at the black screen and rubbed his lips with

a closed fist. He rewound the tape to the start and watched the morning before Mina's death unfold. He watched it several times and made notes of each of the movements of the residents up until Inspector Akashi's arrival at 08:06. Nothing seemed out of place. On the fourth viewing, Iwata let it play out.

Akashi arrived on foot. He was tall but with a stooped gait. He walked languidly. It was the first time Iwata had seen him. Akashi's head was completely shaven but he had the face of a seasoned leading man – Ahn Sung-ki, perhaps. Masculine, well-built features, pleasing to the eye. It was the sort of face that could endorse quality whisky or expensive Swiss watches.

Akashi shook out his umbrella and gave a winsome smile as he showed his badge to the concierge. He entered the elevator and leafed through some papers as he ascended. Iwata watched with fascination. He had followed this man's footprints for so long now it was hard to remember anything else. What an odd thing, then, to be able to see those footprints being made.

At 08:07, Hideo Akashi got out on Mina Fong's floor and disappeared out of frame.

Iwata pressed fast-forward. The timer showed 08:50 when Akashi appeared again in the elevator. He was talking on his phone this time. On the ground floor, he thanked the concierge and left by the main entrance, pausing to glance up at the sky. He was saying something to himself, cursing the rain perhaps.

Iwata again hit fast-forward, stopping at 16:22 of that same day when Akashi returned. The night concierge waved him through. Akashi thanked him cheerfully as he adjusted his bag, which was clearly very heavy. He had no umbrella now. He took the elevator back up to Mina Fong's floor, getting out at 16:24.

Iwata jumped ahead. At 17:11, the elevator doors slid open

and Akashi stepped in. He stopped the doors from closing several times with his foot as he carried on a conversation, though Iwata could not see Mina Fong in shot. He was smiling, nodding and squinting in the last, desperate rays of sun – blindingly bright. Iwata could not hear what Akashi was saying but it was evident that he spoke well. After less than a minute, Akashi bowed and the doors slid shut.

The last time anyone had seen Mina Fong alive.

'What the hell were you discussing with her, Inspector?' Iwata asked.

Akashi checked his nails on the way down, the smile slowly fading from his face. In the lobby, he waved goodbye to the concierge and was gone for ever too.

Iwata closed his eyes, trying to get his timelines straight.

'Three hours later, you killed yourself,' he whispered.

Iwata rewound the scene several times and shook his head. The absurd thought that the video had somehow been doctored crossed his mind. That was next to impossible, but Iwata also knew something wasn't right here.

Half an hour later, Iwata's taxi was winding through the Sham Shui Po district. This was another Hong Kong – dirty metallic shutters and folded businesses. The further in they went, the more run-down it got. Ripped awnings were filthy with grime. Trucks unloaded carcasses and blue crates to pitiable restaurants. Above them, broken neon signs were green and brown with rust. Steam hissed out of windows carrying the thick warmth of laundry.

Iwata got out of the taxi in front of a crumbling apartment block. The walls were criss-crossed with long-dead air conditioning units. TVs blared, cooking hissed, residents argued. The lobby stank of urine. In the half-dark, cockroaches scuttled away from Iwata's footsteps.

Cockroaches. Cockroaches. Kill the cockroaches.

Iwata thought about the dead family. He thought about Ezawa, limping away. Iwata had found him. And now he too was dead. All of them trodden underfoot.

The wind blew, the grass bent.

By the time Iwata reached the sixteenth floor his legs were shaking and he was finding it hard to breathe. Knocking on Susan Cheung's door, he heard crying inside. A thin, pale woman in an oversized vest opened the door. It was hard to tell her age. It was not hard to read her expression.

She held a cigarette between her fingers and a half-eaten apple in the other hand. She regarded Iwata without fear, only weariness.

'Police?'

'No.'

'No?'

'Well, yes but –'

'I've paid up this month.'

She shut the door sharply.

'This is about Jennifer,' he shouted.

At least ten seconds passed and the door opened a crack. An eye blinked.

'Jennifer who?'

'Jennifer Fong.'

Cheung chewed her lips.

'Talk.'

'My name is Kosuke Iwata and I'm from Tokyo Metropolitan Police. I know Jennifer was your friend.'

'So?'

'I believe there's a possibility that whoever killed Mina Fong was also involved in Jennifer's death.'

Cheung bit deeply into her apple, then opened the door a little wider.

'Jennifer Fong killed herself.' She spoke with her mouth full.

'And if she didn't?'

Cheung took a drag and shrugged.

'OK, Mr Tokyo. I'll give you ten minutes. I'm tired.'

Iwata followed her into a shabby studio apartment. A little boy was crying on the floor. An elderly woman sat motionless in her chair, making soothing noises while looking out of the window.

The boy stopped crying to look at Iwata in amazement. His upper lip was crusted over with snot and he had deep red rings around his eyes. Piles of dirty clothes had built up and jagged towers of dishes filled the small sink. Red and black dresses hung in a plastic wardrobe next to a mattress on the floor.

Cheung placed a stool by the mattress for Iwata and she sat down cross-legged. She smoked and ate her apple slowly.

'Ask your questions, policeman. You're on the clock.'

'You were close to Jennifer?'

'I loved Jen. She loved me.'

'Around 2005, was she seeing anyone?'

'Yes.'

The little boy lost interest in Iwata and climbed into his grandmother's lap. He began to curl his own hair.

'Who?'

'I don't know specifics. I just saw her once or twice with an older guy. She introduced him but we never really spoke about it or anything like that.'

'He was Japanese?'

'That's right.'

'What was his name?'

'Ikuo. I only remember it because I thought it was a weird name. Didn't suit the guy.'

Iwata's face didn't flinch but his chest contracted and his heart began to soar. He recalled the note in Tsunemasa Kaneshiro's calendar: *Meet I.*

'Why weird? You think it was fake?'

'It didn't suit him. He was so intimidating. He only ever spoke to me once, when Jen introduced him, but I don't know . . . it's like he just looked *through* me. Doing what I do, I meet a lot of assholes or lonely guys putting up a front. But he was something else.'

'He was a big man?'

'Sure, huge, but it was more than that. He just had this hardness to him. Jen either didn't mind it, or didn't see it.'

'Can you describe him?'

Cheung clucked her tongue as though she had just been told by her mother to pick up her clothes from the floor.

'Tall, like I say. Prominent eyebrows. Not much hair. Big eyes, like he hadn't slept in a long time. It's hard to remember him clearly. It sounds strange, but it's more the expression that I recall. Just so absent.'

Iwata took out the clipping of Igarashi and, trying not to hope, held it up.

'No. Definitely not him. He looks too bookish, too nice.'

'Susan, did you see much of Jen in the months before her death? Both Kelly Lund and Neil Markham said she fell off the map during that time.'

Cheung's phone bleeped. She snapped it open, immediately scowled and snapped it shut.

'I didn't see her much around that time, no. That was probably down to me as much as her. But Kelly Lund? Look, honestly, I don't think she ever really knew Jen. Or at least, Jen would never have opened up to her.'

'Why?'

'Just my opinion. Kelly is too much of a good girl. Always was. You can't trust purity. I wouldn't listen to what she has to say about this.'

Iwata raised his eyebrows.

'Kelly was of the opinion that Jen didn't have a boy-friend.'

Cheung stubbed out her cigarette on a plastic baby plate.

'Like I said, she's full of shit.'

'When did you last see Jen, do you remember?'

'She was talking to Charlie Choi – big-time dealer on the night scene here.'

'Where?'

'I can't remember exactly but he supplies a few of the hotels on Portland Street and the Wan Chai area. It'd be somewhere around there. Anyway, it struck me as strange that Jen would be talking to a man like that. But then she was with that Japanese guy, Ikuo, so I didn't think too much of it. I assumed he knew Charlie and just wanted to pick up a little blow.'

'How did she seem at that time? Scared? Anxious?'

'Happy. Like she was having fun.'

Cheung's phone bleeped again. Swearing, she stood and went through her wardrobe. She sniffed a pink cocktail dress and then took it out.

'You gotta get going, Mr Tokyo. Work, work, work.'

'Where can I find Charlie Choi?'

'Five thousand is a fair price.'

'You said you loved Jen.'

'And I did. But she's dead and I'm not. Five thousand. You think those things are free?' Susan Cheung pointed to the sleeping child in her mother's lap.

'I don't have that much on me.'

'I'll walk you to the ATM. I need to pick up cigarettes any-way.'

'How will I recognize him?'

'Charlie? Trust me, you'll know it's him.'

22. Misadventure

Iwata walked between expats, street hawkers and club promoters until he cut into the main artery of Lan Kwai Fong. It was 11 p.m. The grubby, narrow streets were clad in scaffolding that glowed with pink neon. Puddles were grey with stray cement. Bags of rubbish were piled high, glimmering like giant blackberries. Adverts for beer and cigarettes filled all the available space between the construction and bars.

Wet footsteps rang out behind Iwata. He turned to see a man in a leather jacket, no taller than one metre twenty, approaching with his hand outstretched.

'Speak English?'

Iwata nodded.

'Charlie Choi?'

The man held his arms out – *the one and only*. Choi had a winning smile. His features were even and well taken care of. His hair was carefully tousled. His clothes bore no labels but their expense was clear.

He led them to a corner bar called Jaguar and the bouncer nodded respectfully. Inside, the walls were faux black fur and the décor was tacky night safari. Choi took them to the VIP booth at the back. The table was a wooden Maasai shield and the seats were made of zebra skin. Photographs of Choi posing with various celebrities hung on the wall in marula wood frames.

A waitress in a Tarzan-style loincloth appeared and greeted them as though it were a pleasure for her.

'Charlie! What'll it be?'

'Whisky?' Choi offered.

Iwata nodded.

'Whisky for the gentleman and just San Pellegrino for me. I'm working.'

Tarzanette winked and left them to it.

Charlie Choi held his smile, though Iwata could tell he was uncomfortable.

'So. You're Japanese?'

'That's right.'

'And Susie is a friend of yours?'

'Well, I was a friend of Jennifer. That's how I knew Susie.'

Choi nodded at the mention of Jennifer, though Iwata could tell it meant nothing to him.

'First time in Lan Kwai Fong?'

'First time.'

'Well, then.' He gestured around him. 'Welcome to my office. Hawkers, hookers, ravers, dealers, gangsters – they're all here, man. The *shitterati*.'

The drinks arrived and Choi watched Iwata as he downed his whisky in one.

'So what are you after? Up? Down?'

Iwata took out the photograph from Jennifer's yearbook and pointed to her young, smiling face.

'Fuck,' Choi hissed, looking over his shoulder. 'You police?'

'This is personal. I'll pay you.'

'I don't sell that.'

'Look at her face.' Iwata leant forward, his jaw hardening. 'You've seen that face.'

Choi glanced down for a moment.

'Maybe, yeah. I dunno, man. I meet a lot of people.'

Iwata put HK$10,000 on the bill Tarzanette had left.

'I'd prefer it if you just accepted the money, Charlie. But there are other options.'

'All right, relax.' Choi glanced down at the money. 'I think I saw her once or twice. But I can't tell you shit. I don't even know her name.'

'But you do know the name *Ikuo*.'

Choi nodded, suddenly interested.

'That was her guy? Yeah, I remember him, he was fucking weird. You know, I was wondering if anyone would ever come asking after him. And here you are.'

Iwata took out the clipping with Igarashi's photo.

'Him?'

Choi shook his head.

'Similar build, but that's definitely not him. He said he was a businessman. I didn't believe him, though. He looked more like a gangster. Big, mean-looking bastard. I figured he was yakuza, maybe on the run. Anyway, you could see it in his fucking face, man. Like he'd seen a world of shit. He wore straight clothes – suits and loafers and all. But it was obvious that there was no way a guy like that sits at a desk and draws a steady salary.'

'Anything else?'

'Now that I think about it, he did have some kind of a scar on the palm of his hand. His left, I think. It felt weird to the touch.'

'What kind?'

'I don't know, man. A scar. Maybe it looked like a burn.'

Iwata thought about this.

'When was the last time you saw him?'

'Fucked if I know. We're talking five years ago. But the last time I saw him, he was alone. That I do remember.'

'And he was buying?'

'LSD. He was only ever in the market for tripping. Never interested in anything more family friendly.'

'How did you meet? He just approached you?'

Choi snorted.

'Fuck that, man. That's not how I do business. A guy like me stands out from the others, you dig? No, no, no. To dance with Charlie Choi, you gotta have a dance card.'

Iwata called Tarzanette over and ordered another whisky.

'So, how did he get your dance card?'

'I don't know, man. I never usually do. Just like you're sitting here now. My guess would be that he knew my guy in Tokyo.'

'Who's your guy in Tokyo?'

'Listen to my words, pal. I don't fucking know this kind of stuff. That's the *point*.'

The whisky arrived and Iwata tried not to sink it in one.

'How would I find him?'

Charlie Choi sipped his water to disguise his irritation.

'Yeah, sure. Let me just get my address book. You think I'm stupid?'

'Charlie, listen to me, I have no interest in your set-up.'

'So what's your beef?'

'My beef is my beef. I'm just looking for Ikuo. You can help me.'

'I don't sell that, I told you.'

Iwata leant forward and spoke through gritted teeth.

'Do you want to see photographs of dead children? Because that's what I'm working with here, Charlie. Or maybe you want me to resort to threats? One way or another, you're going to tell me what you know. I'm not going away.'

Choi mulled over these words and nibbled a small thumbnail.

'Kids?'

'I can't talk details with you. But if there's a chance your guy in Tokyo might know where Ikuo is, you need to tell me.'

240

'If that's even his real name.'

'If that's even his real name,' Iwata echoed.

A group of young women walked in and called Choi's name. His reflex grin was empty. When they were gone, he spoke.

'All right, look. You'll find my Tokyo associate on 2Chan. It's a text board. User name is *Coco La Croix*. Leave a post and he'll either get back to you, or he won't. That's the best I can do.'

Choi reached across and slipped the ten-thousand into his inside pocket.

'Drinks are on the house.' Choi grinned, transaction complete. 'Enjoy Hong Kong.'

Iwata left. The street was thicker with bodies now and he had to shunt his way back to the car. Inside, he checked the dashboard clock. It was a little after midnight – 1 a.m. in Tokyo. He scrolled through his phone book and stopped at Hatanaka, the young cop who had found Asako Ozaki.

Iwata dialled.

'Who is this?'

'Up late jerking off?'

'Who –?'

'Iwata. Inspector Iwata.'

Hatanaka sighed.

'What do you need?'

'Hey, look at that. You're a fast learner. You got a pen?'

'Go on.'

'Write down this name: Ikuo. First thing tomorrow morning, you look that name up. Any kind of TMPD record, I'm interested. I'm looking for red flags here, kid.'

'Just that name? You haven't got anything else?'

'Just that name. Second thing. I want you to get in touch with the Hong Kong Tourism Board –'

'Hong Kong?'

'You get them to go through records for all hotels and rental apartments since 2005 looking for a Japanese national –'

'Let me guess. Somebody by the name of Ikuo.'

'Good boy.'

Iwata hung up and started the car.

On the second floor of the Cathay Pacific Medical Office, the beige lobby was empty except for wilting pot plants and an old vending machine. On one side, the windows looked on to the airport. On the other, Iwata could see the road leading to Discovery Bay – Jennifer's childhood home.

At precisely 8.30 a.m., the swing doors swooshed open and a young pathologist holding a slim green folder greeted Iwata. Doctor Wai wasn't yet thirty, with a slim build, an anxious face and spectacles far too small for his face.

'Inspector? I'm Wai. We spoke on the phone.'

'Yes, thank you so much for seeing me at such short notice, and on a Saturday.'

Wai leafed through pages as he led Iwata into a small office that smelled of pine cones.

'Excuse the mess, Inspector. I recently took over and I'm still trying to get things in order. Some tea?'

'No, thank you.'

Wai took off his glasses and laid the pages out in front of him like puzzle pieces.

'Before we begin I just want to state this isn't my area of expertise. Ninety per cent of what I do is mid-flight cardiac arrest. But this . . .'

Wai glanced down at the pages.

'Well, like I say, this isn't my area of expertise.'

'All right.'

242

The pathologist put his spectacles back on.

'First off, you should probably just read the basic autopsy notes recorded by my predecessor, Doctor Pang.'

Wai took out a single sheet and passed it over.

FONG, JENNIFER

Subject: well-nourished female stated to be 18 to 19 years old. 73 kilograms. Eyes: normal, irises dark brown, pupils fixed and dilated. Sclera and conjunctive: unremarkable, no evidence of petechial haemorrhages. Upper and lower teeth: natural. No injury to gums, cheeks or lips. No deformities, scarring or amputations are present. Head is normocephalic. Nose and mouth: unremarkable. Neck and upper chest show no injury. Abdominal injury is described below. Genitalia: healthy with no evidence of injury. Sharp force injury is located 30cm below chin. Pathway found through skin, subcutaneous tissue, just below fifth rib. Wound seems that of a clean cut with parallel edges. Possible striking of propeller. Cause of death almost certainly consistent with drowning, probably by misadventure.

Iwata looked up.

'Misadventure –'

'We'll get there. Autopsy diagnosis of drowning can be tricky as findings are often minimal, or obscure. There are a few reliable signs of drowning but Jennifer had only one – waterlogged lungs. That, to me, suggests death from syncope. An unconscious state.'

Iwata nodded.

'You think she was dead before she even hit the water?'

Wai made an inconvenienced face.

'Well, yes. In cases of syncopal death, signs will be slight. Now, the report does make it clear that high levels of lysergic acid diethylamide were found in her system, almost two hundred milligrams, which is about twice the amount in a standard LSD tab. But that's nowhere near fatal – certainly not what killed her.'

'So, if she didn't drown and she didn't overdose, she died from the wound?'

Wai hesitated for a moment. It seemed as if he were searching for something to say before passing the file across his desk.

'You'd better see for yourself.'

Iwata took out two photographs from the file. The first was a close-up of Jennifer Fong's torso, which had been destroyed. It was a canvas of savage tears and welts. The second photograph was taken from further away. The bottom half of her pale face was visible. Her skin was pale and waxy. There was a massive, gaping wound to the ribs below her left breast.

'There's no decomposition?'

'None whatsoever. The body was found by fishermen only one day after death. Two max. Only a few oval lesions from aquatic life. Nothing major.'

'A propeller injury.' Iwata tapped the second photograph. 'Doctor, is that what we're looking at here?'

Wai took off his glasses and rubbed his naked eyes.

'Propeller-related injuries don't look . . . like this.'

Iwata opened up his bag and frantically rifled through his documents until he found the right photographs: the destroyed corpses of Tsunemasa Kaneshiro and Yuko Ohba. The craters across their abdomens were almost identical. Iwata felt the rush of a hunch confirmed. He felt it before even asking.

'Jennifer Fong, her body was missing the heart, yes?'

Wai nodded.

'It's nowhere on the report. It never came into this office. All of her other organs did, but not the heart.'

Iwata's own heart began to pound. He stared at Jennifer's

body next to those of the other victims. The ages were all different, the genders inconsistent, and there was no easily conceivable way any of them could have met in life. But lying next to each other in death, they seemed like one broken family. Somehow, the Black Sun Killer had chosen them. The Kaneshiro family. The Widow. And now Jennifer Fong.

'She was murdered,' Iwata whispered. 'She was the first.'

Wai shook his head and pointed to Jennifer's wound.

'Look, this *isn't* a propeller strike. And this isn't from aquatic life. This type of sharp force injury should automatically go to the city coroner and a police investigation should have then followed.'

'So why did it come here?'

Wai took off his spectacles again and rubbed his eyes.

'I don't know. Everything about this is off. Doctor Pang, who conducted the autopsy, would have known that it would be unlikely for a propeller boat to be that far out to sea, for one thing.'

'Go on,' Iwata pushed.

'Look, finding bodies on the open water isn't unheard of. But the victim was a few hours south of Xidan Dao, Inspector – that's almost forty kilometres. We're not talking about some leisurely cruise on the water.'

'Any idea how long that would take by boat from here?'

'Depends on the vessel of course. But let's say an average sailing speed of 5.5 knots on the open water? Most likely four or five hours' sailing.'

'So, whoever took her out there is experienced on the water?'

Wai shrugged.

'To a point. A day skipper would have the necessary proficiency to do that in fair weather and daylight. And to reach that level, you'd just be looking at a couple of five-day courses. Not necessarily what you'd call an expert.'

'Doctor, the coroner in Tokyo suggested some kind of sword or machete was used in my murders. Looking at the similarities in these photographs, what do you think?'

Wai sighed.

'I'm not sure what inflicted that wound. Sure as hell not any knife I've seen. But I can tell you with certainty that it was applied by a person – not a propeller.'

Iwata nodded.

'So let me turn to the elephant in the room. Why wasn't this treated as a murder? Doctor Pang refused to follow protocol?'

Wai looked away, his gaze fixing on a photograph of his wife and young child.

'I'm . . . really not sure. Doctor Pang was a good man who was respected in his field. He's only recently passed away. I don't know.'

'So let me ask you this – what do you think happened to Jennifer Fong?'

'I would invoke Occam's razor, Inspector. I don't know how she got there, why she got there, nor who would do this to her. But I do know that someone took her aboard their boat, plied her with LSD, ripped out her heart, then pushed her overboard. The explanation should make no more assumptions than necessary.'

'Did you know Doctor Pang personally?'

Wai stood up and gripped the frame of his window. It wasn't much of a view.

'He was my mentor.'

'Why might he make a misleading report?'

'I know he had some money problems. But to file this as a normal death . . . it's just so hard to imagine. It makes no sense to me. Who benefits?'

'The killer.'

Wai shook his head, clearly out of his depth. Iwata returned the photographs to his bag and, with Wai's back turned, he took Jennifer Fong's autopsy report too. If the pathologist noticed, he gave no sign. Iwata stood.

'I've taken quite enough of your time, Doctor Wai. I should be going.'

Wai turned and they shook hands. Iwata felt the cool, smooth palm in his own and it triggered another question.

'Doctor, how common is a hand injury in sailing?'

'Very. One of the most common, actually. Often resulting from accidents with winches or cleats. The scars are usually clean diagonals. Why?'

'Around the time of her death, Jennifer was seeing a man who had some type of scar on his hand. A burn, perhaps.'

'That kind of injury rarely heals well, Inspector. Something to keep an eye out for.'

He bowed to the pathologist and left him with his view of the foggy skyline.

As Iwata got into the rental car, he tried to picture the man calling himself Ikuo. The name – it meant 'Fragrant Man' – was so ill-fitting it was almost ridiculous.

Who are you?

Iwata went over what he knew. It wasn't much.

He knew he was looking for someone tall and physically imposing.

Someone Japanese, though most likely using a false name.

Someone with a taste for acid trips.

Someone who could sail.

Beyond that, he might as well have been hunting for a ghost.

Whoever you are, you're my killer.

23. Playing Chess in the Dark

On Tsing Ma Bridge, Iwata stopped his rental car and signed up to 2Chan using his phone's web browser. After a tedious period searching through dining and nightlife pages, he finally found a post from Coco La Croix:

The unbelievable talent of DJ Mothra playing @ secret venue 07/03/11
  – set begins at 00:00. See you there! C

Iwata wrote the following:

My friend Charlie can't say enough good things about Mothra! Can I get a
  head's up on that venue? Flying over from Hong Kong especially!

He got out of the car and stood on the hard shoulder, looking out over the ocean. Inchoate clouds moved quickly, their dark shadows blanketing the green hills below. Small lobster boats chugged out to sea.

On a whim, he took out his phone and dialled Sakai's number.

'Iwata?'

'Hello, Sakai.'

'I didn't think I'd be hearing from you again.'

'I have to tell you something.'

'Iwata, if it's about the case file you stole from me, I don't even –'

'The Black Sun Killer murdered Mina Fong.'

She fell silent.

'Now I know what you'll say: the Black Sun's trademarks

aren't there. But I'm sure of it, Sakai. He also killed Fong's sister, Jennifer. I have her autopsy report. He took the heart.'

'But why risk that? Mina is so high profile, it would bring so much attention and –'

'*Exactly!* Don't you see? The stalker, the dog, the movie star. It all makes one hell of a diversion.'

Logic fought with the truth. A beat. Then a moment of realization.

'. . . Oh my God.' Her voice was soft. 'He murdered the Kaneshiros less than twenty-four hours later.'

'Meanwhile, half the TMPD are on the other side of Tokyo, rummaging through Mina Fong's underwear drawer.'

'Holy shit, Mina Fong is a diversion.'

Iwata checked his watch.

'I've got to go, Sakai. My time here is running out.'

'Time where? Hang on –'

'Forget it. Everything you said about me was right. I just thought you should know.'

Iwata hung up and dialled Hatanaka's number.

'Iwata?'

'How's my favourite Boy Scout?' He found himself smiling.

'I found your man, Inspector. *Ikuo Uno*. Strange name. It's the only one that flags up on our system.'

Iwata gripped the railing of the bridge and breathed deeply before asking.

'So, where do I find him?'

'You don't. He's dead. Gas leak in his apartment some years back. After that, his bank accounts were cleared and his credit cards were used abroad – South America, Hong Kong, all over Japan . . . It has to be your guy, right? Using a dead man's ID?'

Iwata mulled this over, shaking his head. He was playing chess in the dark.

'Hatanaka, I'm going to be landing at Haneda in twenty-four hours. Meet me in the car park with Ikuo Uno's file.'

'Uh, OK. Should I wear a hat or something?'

'Funny. Now which hotel did Ikuo Uno stay in?'

'He didn't. The tourism board were kind enough to go through records for the entire city and found zip. But they did make it clear that their records didn't include boat rental accommodation.'

'Boat rentals . . .' Iwata slapped his forehead. 'Of course.'

'I made a list and got through to all but three of the rental companies listed on the tourism board's database. None of them had ever heard the name Ikuo Uno. The three I couldn't get through to were Seahorse Charters, HK Fun Yachting and Ruby Rentals. You got that?'

'Hatanaka, you're a damn hero.'

South of Silverstrand, on a green limb facing Shelter Island, Iwata stopped outside Ruby Rentals Ltd. Seven boats of varying size were moored to a rotting jetty. The office was a single concrete cube with a broken window and missing letters.

'Can I help you?' The accent was American; Kentucky, Iwata guessed.

A tall white man with red stubble and sunburnt skin stood outside the office. His Hawaiian shirt was open and rivulets of sweat snaked down his large, freckled belly. Iwata held up his police ID but didn't bother pointing out that it carried the legal authority of a video rental card in this city.

'Maybe you can. I'm investigating a homicide and I have a few questions. Could I trouble you for a minute, sir?'

The man spat out a mouthful of chewing tobacco and

pointed towards the office. Inside, it was dim and stank of sweat. Maps and charts covered all available wall space. A laptop was transmitting an American football game while a tin of tobacco lay open on the desk.

'I'm Inspector Iwata.'

'Boyd Botner.'

The man grunted towards one of the plastic chairs across from his bureau and stuffed another pinch of tobacco inside his cheek.

'I'm looking for a customer who may have rented a boat of yours a few years ago. Do you do long-term rental here?'

'One of the few in town that does.'

'What's your limit?'

'Seven-day limit. Practically all the other joints just do twenty-four hours.'

'Can the customer then renew?'

'Officially, no.'

'I need you to search your records for a man called Ikuo Uno. Japanese.'

Botner sighed and went into a back room. He returned several minutes later holding a crinkled sheet of paper.

'This is him. Spent three weeks on the *Midnight Viv* and paid in cash. Last person to rent her, back in '05.' She's not exactly a popular model. That's his signature right there.'

The Ruby Rentals letterhead was red and cheap. The signature at the bottom of the page was a large, spiralling sprawl in black.

'This man, did he ask specifically for the *Midnight Viv*?'

'Don't recall, friend. But I did tell him she was a bit of a handful – sixty-nine feet of temperamental. He didn't seem to give a shit.'

'What did he look like?'

'Big guy, shaved head, built like a minder.'

'Did he take anyone on board with him?'

'I didn't see anyone. We don't keep passenger logs here. So long as the boat ain't broke when it gets here, I don't ask questions.'

'Did you notice anything strange about the vessel after he returned it?'

'Yeah, actually. I remember thinking how squeaky clean it was. Most rentals come back looking like they've sailed through a shit storm. But your guy had washed every nook. I guess that makes sense now – you're Homicide, huh?'

His grin was missing a tooth.

'Mind if I take a look?'

'*Mi casa es su casa*. She's the Bermuda-rigged ketch, the fat one on the end. Just do me a favour, don't take too long? I want to head off soon and there's one coming in off the books.'

'One what?'

'A typhoon. Just my fucking luck – cops and storms on the same day.'

Outside, the sea was sullen. Foamy waves smashed against the jetty leaving blinking eyes on the dead wood. In the distance, loons dive-bombed for prey. Iwata smelled the sour air as he walked to the end of the jetty. It was a warm day but he shivered with sickness.

The *Midnight Viv* came into view. Iwata could tell, despite her graceful lines, she was no spring chicken. She swayed alone, almost imperceptibly, in the soft wind.

'Fishing?'

Iwata turned to see an old, sea-weathered man crouching between crates and old rope. He held a fishing rod between his legs and a roll-up between his grey lips. His eyes did not leave the waves.

'I'm a police inspector,' Iwata replied. 'Do you live here?'

'Nobody live here.'

The old man said nothing more. Iwata climbed the narrow steps to the *Midnight Viv* and pictured Jennifer Fong doing the same. He saw her, wearing a summer dress, excited for her adventure.

I love the ocean. It's the only thing I'll miss next year.

Feeling nauseous, Iwata went below deck. It was clean, if a little dusty, and unremarkable: a banquette, a sink, a fixed table, a kitchenette, a toilet compartment, a small television, maps on the walls, and old shelves crammed with even older romance novels.

Did you tell her the boat was yours? Feed her a line about the open sea?

Iwata pictured Jennifer floating alone on the darkness of the ocean, human flotsam.

Did she wear a summer dress? Did she wear a summer dress for you?

Iwata sat on a small berth and it creaked under his weight.

She was your first. Why did you want her? Why was she special? Did she lie here with you? Did you want her? Did she want you back?

Iwata pulled back the blankets and found only a musty mattress beneath. He smelled nothing on it. The autopsy, if it could be believed, listed no genital injury.

You weren't there for her body – just her heart.

Iwata peered at the wall around the mattress and looked for stains but found nothing.

It was too cramped in here, wasn't it?

He climbed back on deck and looked up at the sun. It shone in snatches then hid behind clouds.

Of course, you did it up here. Out in the open. With no possibility of a witness.

Did you lay her down on this deck? Was the promise a picnic?

You brought food and drink – laced with LSD.

Did she think you were going to kiss her?

Where did you hide the knife?

Did she close her eyes for it?

Yes, she closed her eyes for your kiss.

And you pushed off the straps of her dress.

And she lay beneath you.

Shivering in the warmth, on the vast nothing of the sea.

You kissed her.

And as you kissed her, you cut her.

You cut her very deeply to open her.

You severed her major arteries in one swipe.

And you pushed your hand inside her.

And before she realized that this was not a kiss, you were reaching up for her heart.

And you felt it at your fingertips like a creature in its hole.

And you ripped it out to the light.

You held it over her, raining her own blood down on her.

Did she look? Did she see her own heart as it beat out, alone and uncovered?

Did she have time to realize, then, that you were not a man at all?

And when you threw her into the void, did you stay to watch her sink?

Iwata vomited over the side of the boat.

When he finished, he fell back against the mast. The wind shifted and dappled shadow fell across him. Iwata looked up and noticed it: a chink of sun streaming through the sail.

High up.

Strange.

With great difficulty, he began climbing the aft mast, his limbs trembling. He paused several times on the rungs to catch his breath. Ten metres up, Iwata reached what he had seen. It was level with his face, an arm's length away – a tear in the sailcloth.

'What . . . ?'

The wind shushed him, as if he were saying too much.

Iwata reached as far as he could, the rip in the fabric tickling his fingertips.

He forced himself another centimetre.

Another.

The wind picked up.

Iwata's balance was gone.

His grip was gone.

A desperate clutch and Iwata was falling, his hand full of ripping sail cloth.

The impact was painful and it took Iwata a minute to regain full consciousness, but the destroyed Dacron sailcloth had taken most of the momentum out of the fall. Wheezing, he forced himself to stand and looked up at the torn sail.

Backlit by the sunset, fluttering in the wind, was a huge, jagged sun.

Beyond it, a storm was coming in.

It was 10 p.m. Iwata had a blanket draped around his shoulders and a takeout box of half-eaten dry noodles on the coffee table. Outside, the storm was raging. There was nothing else to do and nowhere else to go, so he played the CCTV video once more. He watched Akashi talking to Mina Fong from the elevator again. The conversation lasted less than thirty seconds.

Iwata watched it again.

And again.

He watched the silent sequence play out over and over as he sipped cold almond tea.

What the hell is wrong here, Akashi?

Iwata stood up with the blanket around his shoulders and from the home bar poured himself a whisky, which he drank with decongestants. The burn made him cough but he felt better for it.

On the coffee table, his phone buzzed.

There was a reply on 2Chan from Coco La Croix.

Hong Kong Fan, you won't be disappointed! Venue = highest point in Dogenzaka. See you on the dance floor. Look for the top hat. CLC.

Iwata raised a toast.

'To new friends.'

He closed his eyes and drank. Warmth unfurled in his chest like a waking bird. Outside, the sea churned. Only the faintest city lights twinkled in the black.

Iwata, you ever think that some of those cities are good and some are bad?

In Iwata's dream he was walking down the jetty, a sense of dread deep within him. The jetty stretched out interminably, over a calm, grey sea. The *Midnight Viv* was too small. On the deck, a figure was standing with its back to Iwata. Its skin was very dark, billowing in the wind as if it were stitched. The figure's neck was very thin – funnel-like. Its belly was grotesquely huge. It seemed to be panting.

The old fisherman called out.

'Don't get on boat, Inspector.'

'I need to talk to that man.'

The fisherman looked up from the waves, his eyes milky.

'It not man.'

'What are you talking about?'

'Ngo gwai.' Hungry ghost. The fisherman shook his head. 'You should leave this place. Go before it see you.'

'But I can't. I know who it is.'

Iwata started up the stairs to the boat and drew his gun.

The dark figure began to turn round.

24. A Nice Metaphor

It was a gloomy dawn over Discovery Bay. The storm had blown itself out in the night and a foggy hush enveloped the island. Iwata forced himself up from the couch and looked out of the window.

A fisherman repaired his net. An old lady walked her dog. A man scrubbed bird droppings from the parasols of the terrace restaurant – all of them at the mercy of animal rhythms.

The room was bathed in a flickering blue light and shadow.

The video of Akashi in the elevator was on pause. A smile was frozen on to his face. He was mid-bow. Sunlight streamed through the hallway. His shadow was plastered on to the wall inside the elevator.

Beauty lies not in objects, but in the interaction between their shadow and light.

'Your shadow. In the sunlight,' Iwata whispered. 'But Mina's shadow . . .'

Iwata rushed over to the television and pressed his face to the screen.

'Where is her shadow, Akashi?'

Laughing, he punched the wall victoriously. There was no mistaking it. Mina Fong was *not there*.

Akashi was alone in the elevator and he was simulating a conversation.

'Was this for show? Or had you just lost your mind?'

Iwata recalled Akashi's burnt-out shack in Chiba.

Did the fog seep through your thin walls?

Did it soak through your house and absorb your mind in the days before death?

Did you go through the motions, saying what you were required to say?

The phone began to ring, mewling like a newborn. Iwata answered absently, his eyes still glued to Akashi's false smile.

'Yes?'

'. . . Mr Iwata? It's Mr Lee, Mrs Fong's lawyer. I just had a visit from the police.'

Iwata instinctively looked out of the window.

'So?'

'They were asking about you and what you're doing here. I explained our reason for meeting was quite legitimate but they made it clear that you have been breaking the law here, making official inquiries for which you have no authorization. They were talking about a diplomatic incident.'

'I'm not here in an official capacity. I spoke to people of their own free will.'

'Mr Iwata, I'm telling you this as I believe whatever it is that you're doing is in the interest of this family. So you should know they asked me where you're staying and I had to tell them. This wasn't more than ten minutes ago.'

The clock showed 5.50 a.m. Less than ninety minutes before Iwata's plane left.

'Thank you for the warning, Mr Lee.'

'Good luck, Inspector. I wouldn't come back, if I were you.'

Iwata hung up, snatched out the videotape and frantically started packing his bag – files, photographs and clothes. He did a last sweep of the rooms, leaving Jennifer's until last. There, he looked at the dusty objects that would never be used again. The silence pulsed, desperate to reign once more. Feeling sick and breathless, Iwata turned to leave.

He almost missed it.

A photograph lodged in the frame of the mirror of Jennifer as a young girl.

He'd seen it before but he hadn't *seen* it. The timestamp showed 1996. Jennifer's father's arms were awkwardly slung around her. They posed against a skyline – *somewhere*. Behind them, a glorious sunset. They were in some sort of small room with big windows. But there was something else.

Something Iwata had seen before.

Behind Jennifer and her father, the unframed limbs and unposed expressions of other tourists had been captured. And in among that, a hand clutching on to a handrail.

And on the wrist, a gold watch.

A gold watch with a sapphire face.

Iwata snatched up the photo, left the apartment and hailed a taxi for the airport. As it pulled away, he watched old men along the marina setting up their fishing rods for the day.

Iwata closed his eyes.

The lake looks like a prehistoric crater filled with copper-green water. Kei and Kosuke are fishing in their underwear as they smoke cheap cigarettes. Their pale torsos are a brilliant white in the sun. Empty beer cans are strewn around their small, shabby camp.

Kosuke puffs out his cheeks.

'Shit, it's hot.'

'You know what?' Kei speaks out of one side of his mouth to keep the cigarette in his lips. 'I think I'm actually going to fucking miss this. Crazy, huh?'

Kosuke casts his line again.

'You stuck it out to the end. I never thought you would.'

'Someone had to look after your sorry ass.'

The line twangs.

Kei bounds into the water, reeling furiously.

He turns, grinning, holding up a thrashing silver fish. He nods at its impaled face.

'A nice metaphor for the last ten years.'

'Looks like you, too.'

Kei kisses the fish on the mouth and tosses it into the gutting bucket.

'So, where will you go after?'

'Tokyo, probably.' Kei shrugs. 'We don't all have rich American stepfathers.'

'I'm not sure how rich he is.'

'Somehow I doubt your mother would marry a pauper.'

Iwata shrugs. A dragonfly buzzes between them. 'Maybe. You know her as well as I do.'

'So why come back for you?'

'Who knows?'

'But I mean why now, why is she back *now*? You've seen what I've seen. Parents only come back for puppies.'

'Kei –'

'New husband, new house, new Cadillac. I guess she thinks she might as well throw in the long-lost kid, too?'

'You know something? I don't care.'

'Come on, Iwata-kun. You don't *care* why she's back?'

'I'm leaving this place. That's all I know and all I need to know.'

'Oh, I get it. I get it. What you really want to know is why she *left*.'

'Kei –'

'No, I'm right. You know I'm right. You want to know why she left you. You want to know, just like every other fuckin' kid in Sakuza. You wanted to know the first day you were dragged in. You wanted to know when I put my arm around your shoulder. And you still want to know now.'

'Not this shit again.' Kosuke throws his rod into the water and wades away.

'Iwata!' Kei calls after him.

'You know everything, don't you?'

Kei bounds after him and grabs his shoulders with wet hands.

'All right, come on! You don't care, OK. And you're right, I *don't* know shit, I don't even have any fuckin' parents – what could I know?'

'I'm sick of fishing.'

'Come on, man. Have a beer with me.'

Droplets scurry down their tanned backs. The mud between their toes is warm jelly. Crickets chirp for the ending summer.

'Come *on*, Iwata. You gonna drown yourself?'

'You're a sanctimonious asshole.' Kosuke squints up at the sun. 'But I'm thirsty.'

Kei claps him on the back. They return to the sandy bank and open their last beers. Kosuke lets the foam drip down his chin and land on his knees.

'You know,' – Kei scratches his navel – 'this was fun. In parts.'

'What, today?'

'And the rest of them.'

They look at each other uncertainly.

'In parts,' Kosuke says, his smile wry. 'Yeah.'

The distant roar of the dam can't take away the birdsong behind them.

'So, America, huh?'

'The land of the free.' Iwata raises his can.

'Maybe I'll get some money together in a year or two, come visit you. We'll do the whole thing. Drive-in cinemas, cheeseburgers, big tits – the *whole* fucking thing.'

'The American dream.'

Kei crushes his can and ekes out the last drops of beer on to his tongue.

'You think they have yakitori in California?'

Kei asks this distantly, the silver of the water illuminating his face.

'I don't know,' Kosuke says. 'But they don't have The Fox-hole.'

Kei laughs at the smallness of their world – they became kings without knowing it.

Kosuke's line twangs now and he frantically reels it in. This fish is much smaller, almost not worth keeping at all, but he tosses it in the bucket anyway.

'Hey, Iwata-kun.' Kei smiles sheepishly. 'I got you something.'

'What are you talking about?'

Kei parks his fishing rod and goes into his bag. He takes out a portable record player and sets it on top of a log between them.

'Doesn't that belong to the orphanage?'

'Play it, you prick.'

Kosuke eyes him suspiciously and lowers the needle. He hears brass – blue but brave – now strings – sorrowful but spirited – and feels the rush of a favourite song.

> The lights of the city are so pretty.
> I'm happy with you.
> Please let me hear.
> Yokohama, Blue Light Yokohama.
> Those words of love from you.

Kosuke turns to Kei.

'Shit, I love this song. How did you get this?'

'In Kyoto. Don't be a sap about it. No big deal.'

'The day Uesugi took you to the doctor?'

Kei's face darkens for a moment at the memory but he shakes it off and leaps towards Kosuke.

He grabs him by the waist and waltzes him around the muddy bank. It is a silly waltz and he begins to imitate Uesugi in that way that he does, placing his hand on Kosuke's head and quoting him, quoting someone else – Plato, or Christ, or Chekhov.

Uesugi becomes the chestnut girl now and the waltz becomes less rough.

'I got an idea,' Kei says.

He dips his fingers into the gutting bucket and paints his lips glistening red with fish blood. He paints his eyebrows with mud and wets his eyelashes into black spikes with water.

Kosuke isn't laughing any more.

Kei steps into his shadow. His lips part. His breath smells of blood.

Kosuke turns away, towards the glittering water. Kei's fingers encircle his torso, almost fitting between ribs like piano keys.

He kisses Kosuke on the nape of the neck.

'What are you doing?' Kosuke asks, closing his eyes and shuddering.

Another kiss on the shoulder.

Droplets of water slide down Kosuke's spine.

I walk and walk, swaying,
like a small boat in your arms.
I hear your footsteps coming.
Give me one more tender kiss.
The scent of your favourite cigarettes.
Yokohama, Blue Light Yokohama.
This will always be our world.

263

Kei slips his hand into Kosuke's pants and he grips his penis. He clamps his arm across Kosuke's chest like a harness on a roller coaster and he begins to masturbate him.

'No.' Kosuke's voice is thick and hoarse. 'Kei.'

Kei sings along with 'Blue Light Yokohama'.

'Give me one more tender kiss. I walk and walk, swaying, like a small boat in your arms.'

He quickens the strokes now and Kosuke can't say any more, he can only close his eyes. He is a boy standing over the precipice of the whirlpool below. He is a boy spying on nuns as they bathe in the lake. He is a boy looking at the chestnut girl through her window as she dresses.

'Nobody loves us,' Kei whispers. 'Except for me. I love us. I love you.'

Kosuke's breath catches in his throat and his semen curls into the water. The sun illuminates it in pearlescent snatches, quick as fish scales.

Shaking, Kosuke opens his eyes and sees Kei's dirty fingers gripping him. He sees the purple juice of the dead fish in the bucket. He feels a wave of fear and anger rush over him and he is a little boy again, sitting on a bench, alone in the bus station. He snaps around.

Kei, with a scared smile, does not expect the punch in the mouth. He drops to one knee, tears forming in his eyes. He grips his jaw, blood seeping through his fingers.

'Coward.' He slurs the words, watching Kosuke run away. It hurts to speak but he says it anyway.

'Our glories float between earth and heaven like clouds which seem pavilions of the sun!'

He laughs, his mouth dripping thick blood.

'You're a fucking coward, Iwata!'

Kei picks up the record and launches it at Kosuke's distant figure.

'You won't ever outrun that!'

This will always be our world.

25. A Hundred Hearts Would Be Too Few

Iwata stepped off the plane and looked up. Japan was warmer than he had left it last week but the sky was still grey and uneasy. Passing through the airport, he half expected to feel a hand on his shoulder but he cleared immigration without incident.

Hatanaka was waiting in the parking lot, arms folded. He had dyed his hair black. Out of uniform he just looked like an impatient kid waiting for his father.

'You have the file?'

Hatanaka handed over a folded newspaper, the file inside.

'Good man, walk with me.'

'Am I going to lose my job by helping you, Inspector?'

'You're young, you'll bounce back. Now the file, give me the upshot.'

'So Ikuo Uno was mostly low level – gambling in the main, though he had tentative links to yakuza. His file runs for over five years but he never came close to an arrest.'

'Who was his handler?'

'Akashi, senior homicide. The dead guy. You know him?'

Iwata shook his head, his smile cynical.

'Yes and no.'

'Well, I looked into him. There's not much on his suicide online, nothing particularly expansive. Just the one news article. The honourable Inspector Akashi jumps to his death from Rainbow Bridge – a man who fought for justice all his life but who was sadly overcome by depression after his divorce blah, blah, blah. I printed the article, it's in the file.'

Iwata got into his car, tossed the file on the dashboard and wound down the window.

'Hatanaka, I need something else from you.'

'Look, about that. My CO is starting to notice the amount of time I'm spending off from my caseload. This is beginning to be a problem for me.'

Iwata waved this away.

'Do you want to be standing outside doors for the next ten years or do you want to do police work? Listen, you take my laundry from time to time and I'll help you out with a recommendation. A recommendation from a lead homicide investigator is worth something in this world. Now, note this down.'

Hatanaka sighed and took out his phone.

'Go on.'

'Coco La Croix — that's the 2Chan username of a drug dealer.'

'Coco . . . ?'

'*La Croix.* I need you to find out who he is and where he is. What time do you finish your shift tonight?'

'Nine.'

'All right, when you finish up, I need you to get eyes on him and tell me where he goes. He'll be heading to a club in Dogenzaka tonight. Got that?'

Iwata started up the engine.

'Now *that's* how a car should sound.'

Iwata parked the car behind 6082 Misakimachi Moroiso and got out. The sound of waves and changing winds conspired with the ugly cries of cormorants. The sky was slate over Sagami Bay.

Crooked trees hung over the black bluffs.

It was early afternoon but there was no one in sight. The

police tape crossing the door was gone. It looked like any other empty house. The door was boarded up but Iwata forced it open without difficulty. He flicked the light switch but there was no longer any need for power in this house. He took out his flashlight and criss-crossed the gloomy hallway. Nothing moved but thick motes. Upstairs, the bedroom had been cleaned, though there was still a faint darkness in the carpet from where Mrs Ohba's life had been ripped from her.

Iwata heard soft ticking and looked to the bedside table. Turning the gold watch over, he found an engraving on the bottom of the case cover:

> A hundred hearts would be too few
> To carry all my love for you

Iwata took out the photograph he'd taken from Jennifer Fong's bedroom and held it next to Mr Ohba's gold watch. The gold watch in the image had an identical sapphire face. It was unmistakably the same as the one in the palm of his hand.

'I've got you,' Iwata whispered.

He looked again at the timestamp in the photo – 1996.

Fumbling out his notebook, Iwata rushed into the hallway. With a shaking hand he re-examined the holiday snaps on the wall. None of the dates matched the timestamp in the photograph of Jennifer, her father and Mr Ohba's gold watch.

'Come on, come on, come on.'

He scanned through the dates he'd written down in his notebook. The first Ohba holiday was Okinawa in 1973. The last was Hawaii in 2008. Iwata had recorded them as they appeared on the wall, in no particular order. Now he rewrote the dates, this time in chronological order.

'One year is missing.'

1996.

He hurried back into the bedroom and bulldozed his way through cabinets and boxes. He found only dust and orphaned mementos. He moved on to the little office where he'd argued with Shindo. He began to rip open drawers, thrashing through papers.

'Come on!'

Under the desk, he found storage boxes marked with date cards. He shunted the others out of the way and tore off the lid to the box marked *1995 – 2000.* It was full of dark green photo albums. Iwata pulled out 1996 and sat cross-legged like a frenzied birthday boy. The label read:

NAGASAKI / GOTO ISLANDS

Iwata breathlessly flipped it open. Each photograph was carefully marked by location:
 – The Nagasaki Peace Park
 – The Dutch Slope
 – The Atomic Bomb Museum
 – Spectacles Bridge
 – The Nagasaki Prefectural Art Museum
 – The Oura Catholic Church
 – The Kurosaki Catholic Church
 – The Michimori Shrine
And there, the album ended.

At the back, there was a small brown envelope. Inside, more photographs. They had no locations marked on them.

Mr and Mrs Ohba boarding a small aircraft.

Mrs Ohba giving a thumbs-up as she looked through the window.

Mr Ohba asleep, his mouth open.

Some kind of national park with high cliffs and volcanic cinder-cone formations.

Mr and Mrs Ohba boarding a ropeway.

The Ohbas posing outside the cable car itself, both of them slightly tanned.

The next photo was almost identical to the one he had taken from Jennifer's room. This one instead framed Mr Ohba and some of Jennifer's hair.

Iwata saw now that they were not in any room, but aboard a cable car – a cable car somewhere in the Nagasaki Prefecture. He flipped on to the next photograph and his breath caught.

'Oh my God.'

They were all there. The Ohbas. Jennifer and her father. A younger Tsunemasa Kaneshiro. Hideo Akashi in his late twenties. The dead, all standing together.

'I've got you.' Iwata whispered it. 'You son of a bitch, I've got you.'

Now Iwata saw others in the photographs he did not recognize. Akashi's girlfriend, or maybe wife.

A little girl around ten years old.

And a woman by herself – she was sitting down, alone, wearing filthy, unseasonal clothes and staring down at the floor. The last photograph was just a beautiful panorama of the islands, the ocean glittering pink in a sunset.

Iwata bundled together the photos and ran for the door.

Outside, a storm had picked up, its mind finally made up.

He tossed the brown envelope on to the passenger seat, took out the detachable turret light from the boot and fixed it to the roof. The Isuzu picked up speed as the siren screamed louder. He took out his phone and dialled.

'Come on, come on, come on.'

Shindo finally answered.

'Iwata?'

'Hideo Akashi, was he married?'

'What?'

'There's no time, Shindo. Was he married or not?'

'Yeah. Once. I mean she left him, remarried, guy by the name of Tachibana I think, but –'

'Did she have freckles? About five-three?'

'Yes, what's this –'

'Shindo, I need you to listen to me and answer my questions. If you don't, more people will die. Now, Akashi's wife – is she alive?'

'Yumi? She's alive. But you need to tell me what this is about.'

'Shindo, I know how he's choosing them. And I know where he's going to strike next.'

Iwata shot through a red light, hurtling on to the expressway, streaking blue in his wake.

'How?'

'For some reason this all comes down to a ropeway in 1996 somewhere in Nagasaki. I don't know why yet but you need to get round-the-clock police protection on that woman and it needs to be now. If you don't, he's going to tear her apart and anyone else around her. There are also two other people in danger, though I've yet to identify them.'

Shindo sighed shakily.

'Iwata –'

'I know what you're going to say, but I also know I'm right.'

'And if you're wrong?'

'I'll have my resignation letter delivered to you with roses.'

There was a long silence.

'If I do this, you're going to have to tell me what you know.'

'Mina Fong's sister, Jennifer, was murdered by the Black Sun Killer. Her death predates any of our victims. Not only that, I'm certain that Black Sun killed Mina as well.'

'Mina Fong . . . ?'

'It was nothing more than a diversion, Shindo. A smoke-screen.'

'Kid, you don't have a case any more. You can't keep on interfering –'

'Actually' – Iwata smashed the horn as he overtook an SUV – 'I do. As of ten minutes ago.'

'What are you talking about?'

'If Mina Fong is another Black Sun victim, it means the investigation into her murder is erroneous and it also happens to exculpate Masaharu Ezawa in my case – you just have to see the CCTV footage from her apartment for that to be obvious.'

'Fuck me, Iwata –'

'As you said yourself, it's my conduct that's under review, not my case management. Until my disciplinary, procedure dictates my case should be reopened and that I should re-assume its command. Procedure dictates, Shindo.'

Iwata pictured the old cop staring out of his viewless window as he mulled it over.

'Your disciplinary is under a week away, you realize?'

'I realize.'

Shindo laughed.

'Fucking Geronimo, right, kid?'

'Shindo, there's no time for this.'

'OK. OK. I'll get the protection over at Akashi's ex-wife's place. I'll send you her address now. But look, I can't give you manpower – you're stained here, Iwata. Nobody will work with you. You'll just have to do what you can in the time you have and do it by yourself.'

'That's all anyone ever can do, boss.'

'All right, you're back online.'

Iwata hung up and accelerated harder.

Out of the corner of his eye, he saw the Ikuo Uno file Hatanaka had given him. There was a faded sticker on the front:

LEAD INVESTIGATOR – HIDEO AKASHI

Iwata chewed his lips in thought.

You were Homicide – why handle such a low-level grunt?

And if Ikuo Uno was your informant, you must have known someone was using his money after his death. Yet you didn't stop it . . .

He remembered Akashi smiling in the elevator, an empty charade.

Iwata was thinking too fast. He was driving too fast. But none of it was fast enough.

The lights of the city are so pretty.

He swerved hard to overtake a truck, and the file on the dashboard fell open. The article on Hideo Akashi's suicide peeped out. The photograph was an old one – perhaps from his police graduation. His hair was cropped short, his smile a half-curl, his skin tanned.

You're hiding something. Did the Black Sun Killer have something on you?

Akashi smiled up at Iwata.

The siren wailed and wailed.

Looking into the dead man's eyes, a cold realization stabbed Iwata deep in the gut.

North of Haneda Airport, sitting opposite central Tokyo, lay the island of Odaiba. It was home to Yumi Tachibana and her husband Yoshi. In the summer, they had picnics on the beach. In the winter, they would sit in coffee shops overlooking the bay and they would read – Yoshi usually went for Scandinavian crime while Yumi preferred short stories. On Monday mornings they would complain about having to commute to the 'mainland'. They loved the island's wide, tree-lined streets. Odaiba had a sparseness that did not feel like Tokyo. Parking spaces could be found without great difficulty, kindergartens had reasonable waiting lists and dog walkers greeted each other on corners. The baby was due in a few short weeks. The names were picked out long ago. Yumi and Yoshi Tachibana were happy.

Kosuke Iwata's blue turret light was streaking over Rainbow Bridge, towards Odaiba. It was after 6 p.m. and the sun had already set. The yakatabune boats were out as usual, dyeing the bin-liner black water neon pink. Iwata saw Daikanransha Ferris wheel change colours in the distance, wedged between warehouse-sized arcades. The Yurikamome Line monorail shuttled past in the opposite direction on the lower deck of the bridge. He looked back at the city, its red lights warning off low-flying aircraft. Tokyo was incapable of darkness.

Two minutes clear of Rainbow Bridge, Iwata saw the police line. A troop of TMPD officers were covering the entrance to Green Gardens Community. A wave of elation filled him.

'Shindo, you old bastard, you did it!'

Iwata parked up and scanned the scene. A huddle of residents talked among themselves, excited and irritated in equal measure. He saw a prohibitively high fence, CCTV cameras and on-site security. It wasn't an easy breach before the police, let alone now.

Would the Black Sun Killer still come?

Iwata knew the answer.

He looked up and down the street, hoping for tall men. There were one or two. Iwata searched their faces, looking for anger. He registered only curiosity. In this street light, it was hard to tell.

Iwata began to wonder if this had been a mistake.

What if the killer had been driven underground? He would resurface, almost certainly, but when?

A month? A year? A decade?

Iwata's phone began to ring.

'Yeah?'

'It's Hatanaka.'

'Hit me.'

'Coco La Croix's real name is Masanao Maeda. He's a chemistry student, among other things. Organizes underground parties, sells acid, ecstasy, some legal highs. Oh, and he runs his own fashion website, too.'

'Well done, kid. Where are you?'

'University of Tokyo, following him now. He's going for the subway, I think. I'll call you when I get out.'

Iwata hung up and got out of his car. Approaching the gates, he showed his ID to the officers, drawing looks from the crowd as he passed through. Yumi Tachibana's house was a few hundred metres away. It was an angular structure with cream walls, brown shutters and a small garage. More policemen guarded the front door. Iwata held up his ID again and it was checked off a short list.

He stepped into a long hallway with modern art lining the walls.

He is happiest, be he king or peasant, who finds peace in his home.

Iwata followed quiet voices upstairs into an open-plan living room and kitchen with dark slate floors and clean, geometric lines. There was an L-shaped sofa and a glass dining table. In the corners of the room, there were large pots of bamboo and palm. Yumi and Yoshi Tachibana sat at the table drinking tea. They were sitting next to each other, looking into space. It reminded Iwata of the couple in Hopper's *Nighthawks*.

They stood as Iwata appeared at the top of the stairs.

Yumi was heavily pregnant. She was older than in the photograph, of course, but Iwata knew her frame and the freckles at once. Yoshi was a tall man with a slim face, a beard to disguise it, and a nervous smile.

Iwata bowed.

'Inspector Iwata, I'm handling this case.'

Yumi's face was pale, her exhaustion obvious.

'Shindo told us you're one of his best.' Yumi gestured for him to sit.

'I see. Well, I hope I can live up to his kind words.'

'What is this about exactly, Inspector? Nobody has explained a thing.'

'It's my job to stop this . . . individual getting to you.'

'*Individual*. And what does the individual want with us?'

'We're still trying to establish that.'

Yumi snorted.

'You must have some idea.'

'Yes. It seems there may be some kind of grudge against you.'

Yoshi cleared his throat. He too was pale, his eyes fearful.

'Inspector, we don't understand. We're good people, we don't get involved in . . . whatever this is meant to be.'

Iwata nodded.

'I can imagine this is a horrible shock for you both. But I'm afraid you're going to have to be patient. I can't reveal too much. Many things aren't yet clear.'

Yumi sipped her tea and smiled bitterly.

'That much is obvious.'

Noting the tension, Yoshi Tachibana pointed towards the kitchen area.

'Would you like some tea, Inspector?'

'Please.'

He went over to the sleek kitchen and boiled the water. He gripped the counter as he waited. Iwata imagined it must have been a preposterous situation for this simple man. The idea that someone would want to come into this space, a space he had worked for all his life, with the intention of destroying his family. Tachibana returned with an expensive stone cup and Iwata thanked him.

'Inspector, you say this person has an issue with us. So what is it we're supposed to have done? Any idea?'

Yumi rolled her eyes.

'Of course he knows.'

Iwata held up his hand.

'I'm going to get to that. First, I need you to answer my questions and then I'm going to need to talk to your wife. In private.'

'I'll be on the balcony.' Yumi stood. 'I need some air anyway.'

She left the two men alone.

'Inspector, you can imagine how it looks to my employers for me to be mixed up in this kind of thing. And all this stress isn't doing Yumi any good.'

'I understand, sir. But I'm afraid I can only ask you to be patient. You're safe here.'

'But this can't last for ever. I mean, what if this is all just a misunderstanding?'

'Mr Tachibana, if that were the case, I'd be delighted.'

He slapped the tabletop.

'Then how long? You could take months to find him!'

Iwata leant forward, his tone now caustic.

'Listen to me. This man is capable of doing things to you and your wife that you can't even begin to understand. I want you to trust me here because this is what I *do*. If I were you, I'd just hope that I find him before he finds you.'

Tachibana blinked.

'I'm sorry. I'm just . . .'

'Don't apologize. Let's get started. Have you noticed anything out of the ordinary lately?'

'I've been wondering about that myself. But no. Nothing.'

'Think carefully, sir. Anything at all.'

Tachibana shook his head.

'I really can't think of anything, I'm sorry.'

'No one following you or your wife? No phone calls or strange communications?'

'No.'

'What about at work? Even if it seems very minor, it could be relevant.'

'I'm afraid not.'

'What is it you do?'

'Residential design – I'm an architect.'

Iwata took out a photograph of the black sun symbol.

'Have you ever seen this before?'

Tachibana shook his head. No tangible flicker of recognition at all.

'You're certain?'

'No, I would remember seeing that.'

'All right, Mr Tachibana. I may have more questions after.'

Iwata stood. Outside, Yumi was sitting at the table, looking out over Rainbow Bridge. It twinkled in the cold night.

'Take a seat.'

Iwata sat and she searched his eyes.

'He wants to kill us, doesn't he? That's why you're here.'

'Yumi, believe me. It's not going to happen.'

'Has he killed others?'

'Yes. But *before* we knew what to look for. You have nothing to worry about now.'

Yumi looked away with a sad smile.

'You know I used to be married to a cop? You sort of remind me of him.'

Iwata smiled and he wondered if it looked like Akashi's smile.

'All right, Inspector.' She sighed. 'Ask your questions.'

Iwata held up the photograph of the black sun symbol.

'Ever seen that before?'

Yumi shook her head.

'What about this?'

Iwata took out the photographs from the Ohbas' 1996 holiday album. He spread them out on the table. She flinched and looked away.

'Yumi?'

'Yes.'

'You need to tell me everything you can.'

26. Just Moving Flesh

Yumi spread out the photographs like a tarot reading, moving them around the table as she studied them. She peered at the different faces for a long time.

'It was so long ago,' she said quietly.

'This is a ropeway, yes?' Iwata asked.

She nodded.

'Where?'

'It's not there any more. It was a small attraction, about an hour from Nagasaki. It went from one of the little islands, across the water, on to the mainland, past the Michimori Shrine and up to . . . Mount Yahazudake. Yes, that was it.'

'You were there with your ex-husband. Akashi. Why?'

'We just stopped on a whim. It was such a beautiful day. I actually didn't want to but Hideo was adamant. Absolutely adamant we had to go.'

Iwata shifted in his seat. He had a floating feeling in his chest.

'Something happened? Something out of the ordinary?'

'There was a . . . disturbed woman. She stabbed the cable car attendant, then jumped out and killed herself.'

Iwata pointed to the woman in unseasonal clothes in the background and Yumi nodded.

'Nineteen ninety-six was a *bad memory*,' he said.

'Excuse me?'

'That's why they hid the photos away.'

'Who?'

'Nothing, please go on. What happened?'

'Hideo . . . my ex-husband, he tried to save her but he couldn't. You can't save someone who doesn't want to be saved. I told him that over and over. Poor man. It was awful, truly.'

'Tell me about him.'

She looked at Iwata curiously.

'It really affected him. He was like a different person over-night. It's like the person who went up on that ropeway wasn't the one who came down.'

'How?' Iwata's heart was thudding. 'Akashi was different?'

'He . . . just shut down. He was angry, sometimes violent. Sometimes he didn't come home for days at a time. When he did, it seemed like he hated me. He would just *stare* at me, his mouth hanging open. I thought that maybe he was just look-ing in my direction, maybe he was deep in thought. But his eyes were tracking me.'

Iwata sipped his tea to pace himself.

'Did he talk about the ropeway?'

'We never spoke about these things. He just wasn't that sort of person. He wouldn't discuss his childhood. He wouldn't discuss the ropeway. He would never discuss *us*. He was a wall. After that day on the ropeway our marriage was as good as over.'

'When did you divorce?'

'In the spring of 1998.'

'Did he react badly?'

Yumi looked at the floor.

'He seemed sad, but I think he understood. He apologized and he said he loved me very much. I never saw him again. But what has the ropeway got to do with our situation now? You clearly think there's a link.'

'Mrs Tachibana, for some reason, somebody is killing the people who were on the cable car that day.'

She blinked.

'Why?'

'I don't know. But there are only two people in these photographs left alive today. You' – Iwata pointed to the little girl in the background – 'and *her*.'

Yumi peered closely at her face.

'My God, there *was* a little girl.'

'Do you know her name?'

'I'm afraid not. Maybe I heard it . . . it's just so long ago.'

'Did Mr Akashi ever discuss suicide with you?'

'No.'

'Never? He never talked about having nothing to live for? Or being a burden to you or others? Did he ever mention feeling trapped or unbearable pain?'

She shook her head. 'I don't think so.'

'Did you ever hear him say goodbye to those close to him? Did he give away prized possessions?'

'No. He seemed empty at times. He seemed full of rage at others. He would swing from ignoring me absolutely to then seemingly hating me. Like I say, I think the incident on the ropeway affected him very badly. But suicidal? No, he never seemed suicidal.'

'Mrs Tachibana, what do you think about Mr Akashi killing himself?'

'What kind of a question is that? Obviously, I think it's awful. What does that have to do with anything?'

'Let me rephrase. Does jumping off Rainbow Bridge seem like something you could ever have imagined him doing?'

Yumi chewed her lips.

'. . . I hadn't seen Hideo in a long time.'

She exhaled shakily and raised her cup to her lips before realizing it was empty.

Iwata's phone rang.

'Excuse me.'

He went over to the end of the balcony to take the call. A cold breeze lashed up from the bay below. Distant clouds lit up with silent lightning, luminous cocoons about to split open.

'Hatanaka?'

'Coco La Croix has just gone into a club called Eclipse. Shall I follow him in?'

'No. Stay by the exit and make sure he doesn't leave. I'll be there in fifteen.'

A storm had enveloped Dogenzaka. Iwata hurried past love hotels and shot bars. There were shabby Chinese palaces, Parisian bordellos and Babylonian harems. Red lanterns bobbed in the wind. Graffiti criss-crossed grimy walls. A neon sign blinked at him:

ENJOY YOURSELF – REST ¥4000 – STAY
¥6000

Overhead, a canopy of slick black cables. Empty blue crates had been stacked in all available gaps. Dying potted plants had become ashtrays. The buildings grew taller and the streets wider now.

It was 11 p.m. and the crowd was beginning to thicken. Dogenzaka had no routine beyond light and darkness.

Iwata saw the club's entrance.

A long queue had formed already and young women huddled under umbrellas, clouds of breath floating out. The doormen pressed their fingers to their earpieces as though guarding the prime minister. Hatanaka was standing across the street, holding his jacket over his head. Iwata tapped him on the shoulder.

'Fucking hell, Iwata. You scared me.'

'Is he still in there?'

'Yes. I've been sneezing my ass off for the past half-hour.'

'Is the club on only one floor?'

'Yes. The doormen are aware of the situation. It's up on the twenty-third level.'

Iwata looked up at the skyscraper, its peak shrouded by dark clouds.

The lights of the city are so pretty.

'Give me the number for your department head. As of tomorrow morning, you're on my team. One-week secondment. He won't say no to me.'

'. . . You're fucking with me.'

'Would you rather be playing pachinko?'

A smile spread across Hatanaka's fried egg of a face.

'Thank you, Iwata. I mean I just want to, uh, say that –'

'You can rub my shoulders later. Right now I need you to do something for me. The Akashi suicide article gave me an idea. You find out where his body was taken after jumping off Rainbow Bridge. I need you to get on this first thing tomorrow.'

Hatanaka cocked his head.

'Iwata, are you thinking this wasn't suicide?'

'Just find out where he was taken.'

He looked up at the silver skyscraper arrowing up into the purple and ash. His head swam.

'Iwata?'

'Huh?'

'I said, do you need me to come up there with you?'

'No. You go home. You'll need the rest. Tomorrow I'm going to work you hard.'

Iwata showed his ID to the doormen and took the elevator to the twenty-third floor. The doors opened to a short stainless-steel staircase. Purple neon lit the way down. Techno music throbbed through the walls. An odd fear surged through his stomach as he looked across the dance floor. In the strobe lights, it was hard to make out the contours of the room. The entire back wall was a glazed view of Tokyo's nightscape, blocked by bodies. Above, an enormous screen played a surgical close-up of the DJ's decks. Black vinyl spun like a whirlpool's gullet. The strings of an orchestra rose as electronic beats thudded through them. A human mass of dancing was a tentacle changing colours – red to electric blue and then green. Nobody was here for meaningful contact. There was nothing beyond the flailing boots and tightly shut eyelids – hands thrown up in praise of nothing.

Look for the top hat.

Iwata moved into the mass like stepping into a wave – just moving flesh. Ravers thrashed, their bodies covered in luminous paint. Bass crackled like artillery. A robotic voice bellowed words:

MOTHRA – MOTHRA – MOTHRA

The entire room screamed and surged harder, a feeding frenzy in a pigpen.

Iwata saw a top hat.

Coco La Croix was a slender man with long, platinum hair and tattoos. He was dancing freely with two companions, one male, the other female. They passed round a bottle of champagne.

Iwata began to force his way through the bodies but, instinctively, stopped by a pillar for cover. The top hat was turning.

Coco La Croix was facing someone behind him now.

A tall figure with elaborate face paint.

I hear your footsteps coming.

But the eyes were too wide – perfect circles with deep black pupils like Felix the Cat – it was all wrong somehow.

The Lord is my light and my salvation. Whom shall I fear?

Iwata realized it wasn't face paint. It was a mask – a cobalt blue and jet black skull.

This masked man leant in low to speak. Coco nodded and took off his top hat. He passed something over and the man snatched it, turning away. As he did so, he waved at Coco. The neon illuminated the gesture, less than a full second, but Iwata had seen it – a clear, diagonal scar on the palm.

Before Iwata could stop himself, he raised his finger and pointed.

He pointed at this masked man.

I found you.

The man stopped dead still in the sea of movement and stood there, statue-like.

The Lord is my light and my salvation. Whom shall I fear?

He turned.

He looked at Iwata.

Then he pointed to himself.

Cartoon-like innocence: *Who, me?*

Iwata fumbled for his gun but it was too late. The man had already cut Coco's throat and was pushing his way through the dance floor. The strobe lights caught arterial spray in neon green. Gun held high, Iwata fought his way through the ravers.

'Oh, God. Oh, God. Oh, God.'

He could hardly breathe – a diver at the bottom of the ocean, his tank almost empty. Every fibre told him to run away but he was chasing. The masked man was going for the fire exit at the back of the club. Iwata lost him from view for a second. When he caught sight of him again, the man had an arm locked around a woman's throat, dragging her backwards. She flailed wildly, a seal dragged under by a shark. Nobody noticed.

Iwata saw the mask properly now – it made no sense. Black and turquoise stripes on a skull face. Human teeth about the open mouth. Huge and glassy black eyes.

A stray elbow caught him in the face and he dropped the gun.

Iwata fell to his knees, feeling between feet and plastic cups for his weapon. He found it quickly but the fire escape doors were already swinging closed. Iwata burst through them into a dank fire exit. Six flights up, another door slammed shut. Trembling, he took out his phone and dialled Shindo's number. He began to climb the stairs, his footsteps echoing in time with the dialling tone.

'Shindo! I'm at Club Eclipse in Dogenzaka. He's here.'

'Slow down. Who?'

'Who do you think?'

'*Him?*'

'He's already killed one, he's taken a hostage. He's heading for the roof. I'm going for him.'

'Wait, Iwata –'

Iwata hung up and took the stairs three at a time. At the roof access door, he regained his breath then stepped out into the rain.

He saw gravel, pipes and vents. Clouds of steam hissed out. A cold wind shrieked. Bolts of lightning were hidden in strangely formed clouds all around him. Tokyo's roofscape glittered through the rain. Iwata cleared his sight-lines, taking short, sharp breaths. He gasped around corners. He wiped sweat from his eyes with his sleeves and scanned the ledges above him.

Too many places to hide.

He heard a moan and found the hostage on the floor, by the edge of the roof. Iwata crouched over her and felt for a pulse. Her nose and jaw were badly broken but she was alive.

'Stay calm,' he whispered.

Her eyelids lolled open and focused somewhere over Iwata's shoulder. He snapped his fingers in front of her face but she wouldn't look at him. She just gurgled.

'You're going to be fine, just hold on.'

She gurgled louder and Iwata realized it had been a warning.

Give me one more tender kiss.

Before he could turn, a massive boot hacked the gun out of his hand. Iwata thought he heard a snap but there was no time to consider this – a knee shattered into his temple and everything lost its certainty.

I hear your footsteps coming.

Iwata heard wet gravel crunching under heavy footsteps. He blinked as raindrops fell into his eyes.

He hadn't registered the fall but he now realized he was lying on the floor.

I walk and walk, swaying, like a small boat in your arms.

Far above him, the masked man came into view, just another skyscraper in the night sky. Iwata reached for his gun like a child grasping for an escaped balloon. The man kicked the gun away and stepped over him, one foot on either side of Iwata's head. Iwata couldn't focus on the face, or whatever the man was wearing for a face. He knew he was going to die.

This is what death would be.

The Lord is my light and my salvation. Whom shall I fear?

The man gripped Iwata by his coat lapels and hauled him up to eye level. Iwata heard his seams rip. The wind flapped at his trousers and he vaguely thought that he was being held over the edge of the building. Between his shoes, he saw atoms in flux. Tokyo spun.

The lights of the city are so pretty.

And now the man spoke with a deep, outlandish voice.

'*Eek.*'

He leant in like a curious dog. His breath smelled of earth and meat.

'*Hach k'as. Eek.*'

'. . . But I found you,' Iwata whispered, struggling to retain consciousness.

The masked man began to make noises, guttural and rasping.

Iwata realized it was laughing.

A dark, cavernous laugh.

This will always be our world.

27. Next World Makes Up for This One

Kosuke wakes up, cold. Kei's bed is empty. They have not spoken since the lake. Kosuke wants to speak with him but the right words are fish he has no line for. He knows he should go back to sleep but he doesn't. He gets up, led by a curious fear that he had forgotten about years ago. He opens the old door and pads down the icy corridor. He passes the dormitory for the younger boys but hears nothing. At the end of the corridor, he passes Sister Mary Josephine's room. She has a keen ear so Kosuke takes extra care as he passes.

The atrium is a freezing, moonless cavern. The wood is so cold, he can no longer feel his feet. He makes his way up the creaking stairs and turns left, towards the infirmary. Double doors give out to a glass skyway, overlooking the forest and mountains on one side and the courtyard on the other. The courtyard has a broken fountain in its centre, which is surrounded by plants.

Kosuke hears muffled voices and ducks down.

'*No*, you know the rules. Now give me what you owe.'

He peeks down and sees that it is Kei. He's facing away from Uesugi, who is naked, his clothes in a heap on the ground. Uesugi is sweating, his hair drenched, his breath visible on the cold. His penis is jutting up and he is trembling.

'Come on, boy –' He places a hand on Kei's shoulder but it's slapped away.

'Not until next month. Now give me my fucking money.'

Uesugi slumps back on to the fountain's rim and takes out an envelope from his jacket. Kei snatches it out of his hand

and stuffs it in his back pocket. The older man reluctantly puts on his trousers, completely defeated. He watches Kei buttoning his shirt unselfconsciously and a wave of anger scrunches up his face now.

'Such a rush to get away.'

'It's cold.'

'You used to like talking afterwards.'

Kei smiles politely, as though he has just been told a bad joke. Outraged, Uesugi grips Kei by the arm but the boy is expecting it. He knees Uesugi hard in the stomach and the director crumples to the floor, wheezing. Kei carries on dressing as Uesugi begins to cry.

'You know I love you, boy. You know that, don't you?'

'No, Uesugi. You love nothing.'

'I cared for you more than *anyone*.'

'Yes, I'm such a special boy.'

'You don't treat me like a human being.'

Kei laughs a disdainful laugh, one that Kosuke knows well.

'That's because you're less than that.' He pats Uesugi's balding head. 'This was the last time. Next time, I want my money for zero. Hold out on me and I'll go to the papers. Do you understand, old man?'

Kei slips away, into the amorphous blue of the shadows and the plants.

Kosuke feels like he has been kicked in the stomach. He feels a deep revulsion and loss. He looks down at Uesugi, who is alone, his face desolate.

Uesugi looks up at the skylight, his eyes glimmering like cold waterfronts. He speaks quietly.

'I am as one who is left alone at the banquet, the lights dead, the flowers faded.'

*

Iwata woke wrapped in soaked sheets. He was in a drab studio apartment. Sakai was curled up in the window seat, smoking, looking out at the drizzle. The dawn was duck-egg blue. She wore an old grey cardigan and socks. Her legs were bare.

'Bad dream?' she asked without looking over her shoulder.

Iwata sat up and raised his hand to the back of his head, wincing as he realized how much pain he was in.

'Don't touch the bandage. He got you pretty bad.'

He groaned, seeing his heavily strapped right hand. It felt like it had been run over by a train.

'Where am I?'

'Not dead.'

'What time is it?'

'Almost five.'

'What are you doing here, Sakai?'

'This is my place, asshole.'

'So what am *I* doing here?'

'Bleeding everywhere. Oh, and talking to yourself in your sleep. You say more to your dreams than you do to the living.'

'What?'

She laughed.

'Don't worry, you didn't say anything incriminating. Just kept talking about lighthouses.'

Iwata looked around. It could have been anybody's room. Messy. Unloved. Built for solitude.

The fan stirred warm air around the dark bedsit. What furniture there was, was mismatched. She had one foldable table, which held insurance reminders, tapes, a dictaphone and junk mail. She had no pictures or trinkets on display. Her bedside table was a mound of case files and interview transcripts. The clothes hanging in her wardrobe seemed expensive, yet her underwear, mostly strewn on the floor, was a collection of cheap, supermarket brands.

'Nice place.'

'Home sweet home.' She puffed out smoke.

They regarded each other for a moment and Iwata tried to grasp what he felt for her. He hadn't been sure of that from the start. He imagined the same was probably true for her.

Without her eyeliner, she looked much younger. He tried to imagine her growing up, but he couldn't picture it. It was impossible to think of her as a little girl. Iwata's thoughts drifted into a stark, bright room and then to Hana Kaneshiro, alone on the stainless steel. Looming above her, the skull of the Black Sun Killer.

'Iwata?'

'Huh?'

'I'm talking to you. What's wrong?'

'Nothing.'

'Nothing?'

'I'm just in pain. But that's not important. What's important is that I found him.'

'Right. What I want to know is *how*.'

Sakai stubbed out her cigarette and went over to her disordered kitchenette. She poured two glasses of whisky and dropped headache tablets into both. She set about popping out ice cubes.

'Go on, I'm listening.'

'The Black Sun Killer posed as a TMPD informant named Ikuo Uno in Hong Kong. He was there to kill Mina's sister, Jennifer. He bought LSD from a local dealer and through him I was able to track down Coco La Croix. It was pure chance that the guy we're after was there last night.'

'Fuck me, your first lucky break.'

'Lucky. Sure. That's how I feel.'

'Well, he got away clean.' Sakai shrugged. 'You were the only one who saw him and you gave no description when you called it in. They surrounded the place anyway but nothing turned up. No useful CCTV and nobody saw anything. Fujimura is spitting blood.'

She handed Iwata his glass and put the whisky bottle on the floor. She sat on the edge of the bed, facing away from him.

'What about the hostage?' Iwata asked.

'Needs reconstructive surgery. She never managed to get a proper look at him but she thinks he was wearing a mask anyway.'

'He was. It was like a fucking nightmare. He could have killed me. He *should* have.'

'Killing cops draws heat. Maybe he figured he has enough as it is.'

'Well, it bothers me, Sakai.'

'Only you could be pissed off that you *weren't* murdered on a roof.'

'We know he's not scared of us and we know he doesn't hesitate to kill. He killed La Croix, why not me? It just doesn't make sense.'

'Well. Despite your best efforts, you're still alive.' She smiled. 'Kampai.'

They drank in silence. Iwata's whole body hurt, his lips swollen, his head throbbing. Focusing on different limbs uncovered new pain, as if only just occurring to his body.

'So.' Sakai downed her whisky and bared her teeth. 'What now?'

'I don't know.'

'Iwata, the whole of Division One is in a cloud. In the space of a few hours, you managed to unsolve one case, discredit another and shut down half the city. The press have their knives out and the justice minister has a hard-on the size of Tokyo Tower. You have a week left before they fire you, maybe even prosecute.'

'But I found him, Sakai. I *found* the Black Sun Killer.'

'I know. So let me ask you again. What now, Iwata?'

He stuck out his bottom lip.

'Yumi Tachibana's house is under police protection but I doubt that will last after my disciplinary hearing. I think that's where the killer will strike next. But as for what now? I don't know.'

He rattled his empty glass and Sakai clambered up the bed to refill it. As she leant forward, he tried not to look at her buttocks.

'Well, I'll give you some credit,' she said softly. 'I didn't think you would be able to do it. Find him, I mean.'

Iwata nodded.

'I know.'

They sat next to each other, thoughts apart, watching the rain snake down the window. A long time passed until Sakai spoke again.

'They've asked me to speak against you. At your hearing.'

Iwata looked up at her, then out of the window again. He sucked on an ice cube in thought.

'Well?' She looked at him.

'You should do it. It will be good for your career.'

'I've already agreed. I suppose that won't surprise you. You never did trust me.'

'I don't trust anyone, Noriko.'

She stared at him, taken aback by the use of her first name. Iwata finished his drink and laid his head on the pillow. He could feel her looking at him, her eyes on the back of his head. He heard soft sirens far below. The windows were washed a gentle pink and blue.

'Iwata, tell me something.'

'Mm.'

'You ever wonder why they gave you this job?'

He had no reply. He was already asleep.

Hirofumi Taba taps his feet irritably and looks up at the calendar: 2009 is almost over. He is too big for most chairs but this one is particularly uncomfortable. The man sits to one side of him, wearing a chunky-knit jumper and a gentle smile. Though his words are kind and hushed, it is an odd angle at which to address someone. Taba presumes he is trying to be an unobtrusive voice so that his 'client' may instead consider the painting of the beautiful mountain landscape. Taba juts his chin towards it.

'That supposed to relax me?'

'It's just a painting that I like,' the man responds with a delicate smile.

The landscape doesn't look Japanese, probably American or European. The room is small and intimate, lined with books and flourishing plants. But it is far too warm.

'Mr Taba, when relationships end, it's perfectly natural for there to be traumatic feelings . . . confusion . . . many contradictory emotions.' The counsellor looks out of the window in thought, as if this were the first time he'd had to grapple with these concepts. 'But what I want you to take away from today's session is that *all of these* responses you're having are perfectly in line with your situation. Perfectly normal.'

Taba stands.

'Do you mind?'

'Pardon?'

'If I open the window.'

'I tend to keep it shut so that clients don't have to hear the outside world and feel –'

'Well, this client doesn't mind the sound of car horns. So. Do you?'

'Please go ahead.'

Taba breathes in chilly air and looks down at the street. He wonders if his mini-tantrum has been noted and interpreted. Below, he sees a busy crossroads, the lights commanding thinning traffic. Across the street, a small huddle of protestors stand outside a government building, their placards bouncing against, or in favour of, something or other. The trees along the street are bare. It is a brisk morning.

'Mr Taba, I know this might be an unpleasant experience for you.' The counsellor has regained his gentle smile. 'But what I would like to do is to try and normalize your experiences during this life stage that you're going through. I want you to know that *all* of what you're feeling is perfectly typical. Whether you're feeling relief, distance, resentment, guilt –'

Taba drops back into his seat.

'Why would I feel guilty?'

'I didn't mean to imply that you should be feeling anything in particular. I'm just trying to convey that the breaking-up process, while it naturally does have crucial triggers or points of disagreement, is rarely the result of *one* moment or incident. It is rarely caused by *one* party. These situations often extend over many years and it's important to know that, ultimately, it's a perfectly natural thing for people to be at different stages in their lives.'

'Different stages? Was it natural for my wife to be at the fucking-my-partner stage, then?'

The counsellor chews his lips for a moment. Taba knows nothing about his world but he can tell a rookie when he sees one.

'Mr Taba, I'm only trying to underpin the point that none of this is your fault –'

'I just fucking told you, I know that.'

The counsellor forces a smile and clicks his pen a few times.

'Do you resent having to be here?'

'My division chief specifically ordered me to attend.'

Taba takes out a cigarette. He offers one across but doesn't give the counsellor a chance to explain smoking is not permitted here.

'How do you like that? My partner fucks my wife, I get upset and now I'm the one sitting in front of a shrink. You can't say life doesn't have a sense of humour.'

The counsellor pushes across an empty glass for the ash. Taba spends a long time staring at the burning tip, occasionally shaking his head. The counsellor waits in silence.

'So,' Taba finally asks. 'How long will this take?'

'Sessions are one hour.'

'I meant in total.'

'I know what you meant. Healing takes time.'

As the man begins to speak about creating distance and the folly of fault-finding, Taba zones out. His thoughts again rest on his daughter. He is already reading a book on the effects of divorce on children. He knows the probable outcome – he remembers words such as denial, abandonment, anger, acting out, triangulation, projection. Most of them mean little to him, but he realizes separation from Hoshiko will crush the girl. Taba wishes he could spare her from all this but there is no getting away from what has happened. What Hoshiko and Iwata have done.

Iwata.

The name triggers a taste in his mouth now. Had Iwata ever stopped to wonder how this would affect his child? And that was to mention nothing of Cleo and Nina. Taba had always thought their family so beautiful and perfect. Why had Iwata destroyed all that? How could a woman such as Cleo not be enough for him? She was a sight to behold. Once, during a dinner party, he had asked himself if he loved her. But the idea of propositioning Cleo, let alone *touching* her, well, that was something preposterously alien. How could that even be considered?

Taba wipes his brow with a shaky hand. Even though cold air seeps into the room, he is sweating. The counsellor is still talking, nodding to punctuate points as per his expensive training.

What a fucking situation to be in.

Taba stubs out his cigarette. He is wallowing, he knows it – overthinking, pointlessly retracing. Iwata would never do that. Was that something Hoshiko liked about him? Taba cannot stop asking himself questions for which there can be no answers. He cannot stop thinking about Iwata. It is as if Iwata has been reborn overnight, no longer made of wiry muscle, hair and blood but now a man built from carnival mirrors – reflecting every flaw in Taba.

Every character trait and physical detail belonging to Iwata is a strength he holds over Taba. Every quirk is a precious commodity that Taba can never hope to provide. He has seen Iwata many times in the changing room at Chōshi PD but never given him a second thought as a *male form*.

He was just police – the same as the blue binders on the shelves, the logging of evidence, the taste of the bad coffee from the dispenser. But Hoshiko's actions have forced him to think of Iwata as a man. Iwata is smaller, lissom, with a quick, determined step. He is more intelligent. Elegant even. Taba is a tall man, particularly burly for a Japanese, and there have always been family jokes about secreted Mongolian heritage. What had Hoshiko seen in Iwata that he lacked? Perhaps Taba was too oafish, too rough. Perhaps he was not warm enough. Perhaps he gave his wife too little affection.

Taba knows, if he chooses to face facts, that it is simply the case that his wife no longer loves him. More than that, he knows she probably has hatred for him. As an act of sabotage, he can almost understand why Hoshiko would do this. But *his partner*?

He supposes that Iwata has not been himself for a long time. Now that he thinks of it, Iwata has been withdrawn, angry and distant ever since his paternity leave. Almost a year now. He never answers the routine questions colleagues ask about home life, the baby, the future. He never shares jokes about nagging wives any more. But despite this, Taba has never stopped to question what Iwata *was to him* – his partner. It was a given. True, they had never shared secrets or dodged bullets together. They were not what either would call friends. But they shared more than social engagements and secret complaints. Iwata had covered for him. Iwata had punched faces for him. Iwata had cracked jokes with him when faced with some perfunctory horror. Though they disagreed about everything, the two men shared a deep intimacy – their daily routine. The car, the desks, the interrogation room. Every contour of their world expected them together, like batteries in a toy.

Until this. Almost instantly, Iwata had ceased to be his partner.

Taba thinks about his wife.

He does not know if he is still in love with Hoshiko, he has stopped pondering this a long time ago. But he cannot imagine that Iwata loves her either – after all, he married a beautiful American woman with blue eyes. What could he have seen in a skinny, sullen woman from a backwater?

Yet Taba is surprised, he feels little jealousy. No, the thing that really nauseates him is that Iwata has destroyed his day-to-day life. The jocular dialogue of the office. The occasional thrill of interrogation. The sense of satisfaction when a case was closed. The rhythms in which he existed.

Now one of them will have to be reassigned, clearly. As the better detective, it is unlikely to be Iwata. Not to mention Taba confronted him in the office and caused a scene. He even threw a punch, though it contained no real conviction.

'So really, what I'm hoping you will share with me is –'

'I suppose' – Taba interrupts the man mid-sentence – 'the main thing I'm feeling . . . is a desire for revenge. You can write that down. But don't worry, I won't do anything to him. My partner, I mean. Or to her. What has happened, happened. I just mean that I hope something fucking horrendous happens to him, you know? And I'll be there to drink it in when it does. That's all I have to say to you.'

There is a swampy silence until Taba's phone begins to buzz. The counsellor tries to protest but Taba silences him with a finger.

'Yeah, chief?'

'Taba, where are you?'

'I'm in my *session*.'

'You haven't heard?'

'Heard what?'

'It's Iwata. I need you to get down to the lighthouse right now.'

At the mention of Iwata's name, anger buzzes in Taba like a bare lightbulb. Perhaps because Chief Morimoto *knows* about his shame. Perhaps because Morimoto expects him to continue as if nothing has happened. Or that he expects him to share his concern. Taba pinches the bridge of his nose. He wants to say, *Iwata can fuck himself.* He wants to say, *I hope Iwata is dead on those rocks.* He wants to say, *Fuck Iwata, fuck Chōshi PD, fuck therapy and fuck you.*

301

But Taba takes a breath.

'The lighthouse. I'm on my way.'

A little over an hour later, he pulls up in the parking lot near Inubōsaki Lighthouse. Police tape surrounds the area and uniforms are keeping reporters at bay. Even a camera crew from Tokyo has turned up. Chief Morimoto is off to one side, looking down at the crashing waves. He calls Taba over solemnly.

'Chief.'

'Taba.'

'What have we got?'

'It's Iwata. You're going to have to speak with him.'

'About what? You know the situation between us. There is no speaking.'

Morimoto points to the ambulance at the cliff's edge. Iwata, mouth open, expressionless, is wrapped in a blanket. Taba has seen many people in shock and many people in the back of ambulances. But never one of his own. It is as if Iwata has dressed up in a silly disguise.

Realization hits Taba hard.

'Where's Cleo? The baby?'

'Told him she was going for a walk.' Morimoto shakes his head and spits on the floor.

'A walk. So?'

'Looks like she snapped. The baby was with her.'

Taba's stomach lurches. He already sees the full picture but it can't be that way. He was never the brightest, maybe he has this wrong.

'W-what are you saying?'

The wind blows. They taste salt and hear seagulls screaming. The hacks behind the police tape are straining to see details, scribbling down notes. Tomorrow morning, thousands and thousands of people will buy words that tell the same story: *just one of those things*.

Morimoto points at the cliff beneath the lighthouse.

'Two types of people come here, Taba. You know this. And Cleo was not here for tourism.'

'Oh fuck.'

'Talk to him. You were friends once.'

'I should . . . I should follow procedure.' He looks over at Iwata, pink and then blue in the light of the ambulance.

'Procedure? What procedure is there? The kid was fucking ten months old.' Morimoto closes his eyes. 'Let's just hope the next world makes up for this one.'

When Iwata opened his eyes, it took him a long time to realize where he was. Long hair was splayed out on the pillow next to him.

Cleo?

But the hair was black. Sakai was sleeping on her side, facing away from him. She made no sound. She was completely still. Without thinking, Iwata reached out and touched her naked shoulder. Her skin hardened, the goosebumps soft and grainy as an ocean bed. He retracted his hand. It had been a mistake to touch her.

As if sensing it, Sakai turned around to face him. Her eyes flicked from one side to another, searching his pupils.

'I'm sorry,' he mumbled.

She looked at his mouth for a moment then she swept off the duvet from their bodies. Her eyes were dumb with need. Iwata gritted his teeth as Sakai used his battered shoulders for balance, hooking one leg over to straddle him.

'Sakai.' His voice was hoarse.

She thrust her small breasts into his face to silence him and reached behind to grip his penis.

'Stop this.'

She slid down on to him, making no sound as she took

303

him all the way in. Iwata looked up at her, shocked. He saw no expression on her face. With her body revealed in this light, he saw that she was covered in bruises like a thumbed Plasticine figurine. Her legs were covered, though fading into sickly greens, golds and indigos. Sakai looked down at him with nothing in her eyes as she began to jerk her body at the rhythm she needed.

It didn't take her long. Iwata felt her constrict and then she coughed once.

She clambered off him, his penis glistening and slightly bloody. Sakai covered herself with the duvet again and turned away from him. They stayed like that for a long time.

28. Irregularities

Iwata woke in an empty apartment. Sakai was nowhere to be seen. His phone was ringing. Head pounding, he struggled to his feet and answered.

'Hatanaka?'

'I've called you, like, fifty times. Are you OK?'

'I'm standing.'

'Well, the boss hasn't heard from you yet and he's pretty pissed off –'

'Forget that. Now, did you find out where that body was taken?'

'I got what you need. Hideo Akashi jumped from Rainbow Bridge on the seventeenth of February at 1 a.m. First, he was taken to Saiseikai Central Hospital, where he was pronounced dead, then on to Chiba University Hospital for identification where a . . . Doctor Taniguchi signed for him.'

'Good. Where are you?'

'Setagaya PD.'

'I'm on my way.'

A few minutes north of Minowabashi Station, between a barber's and a second-hand electronics store, Sakai stopped outside a small apartment block. She made her way up narrow stairs and heard soap operas and vacuum cleaners through thin doors. She stopped outside Oshino's door and knocked three times.

'Who is it?'

'Open up, police.'

Oshino opened the door, rubbing his face off with a towel. His neck and cheeks were raw pink from a recent shave, his vest bright white and the brawn in his bare arms clearly defined.

'Noriko, come in.'

She smelled cloves and soap as she passed.

'Morning, champ. Sorry I'm early.'

She held up a bag of pastries and two polystyrene coffee cups. Smiling, Oshino led her into a sparse apartment. She tossed her jacket on his bed, sat cross-legged at the low table and laid out the pastries on paper plates.

'You used to have a sweet tooth,' she said. 'Hopefully, you haven't grown out of it.'

Oshino sat across from her and ate half a croissant in one bite.

'Nobody grows out of sweetness.'

'How infantile.' She poured two sachets of sugar into her coffee, sipped it and looked at Oshino. He had grown into his features seamlessly, his scars beautiful. She liked the way the muscles in his face rippled when he changed expression. And she liked being able to say a few words to make that happen.

'Never married?'

Oshino shook his head gently. He didn't return the question.

'No girlfriend?'

'Intermittently.'

'Boyfriend?'

He laughed, looked down at the cup and stirred his coffee.

'You never used to be able to take your eyes off me,' Sakai said. 'Have I aged that badly?'

'Come on, my entire gym dropped what they were doing to look at you.'

'But not you. You can't look at me.'

He glanced up. Sakai was smiling but he couldn't register humour in her words.

'Noriko, it's not easy.'

'What isn't?'

'Looking at you . . . it's like looking at the past.'

'But the past holds good things too. Sweet memories.'

'Bittersweet.' Oshino looked down at his coffee and resumed stirring. 'For me.'

'You're right. I'm sorry. I was the one that walked out. And now I walk back in and give you a hard time.'

He shook his head.

'It's good to see you, Noriko. I'm just bad with words.'

They shared homesick smiles for a moment until Sakai cleared her throat. Oshino went into his bedroom and returned with a small plastic folder which he placed carefully on the table.

'This is her, the girl that you're looking for. But there's hardly anything. No birth certificate, no school records, no nothing until the age of twelve. She's a ghost.'

'What happens at twelve?'

'Open it.'

Sakai opened the folder and took out a microfiche print-out of a newspaper article from the *Nagasaki Shimbun*.

12 JULY 1996

A thirty-year-old woman stabbed a man to death on the Michi-mori Shrine Ropeway yesterday evening. Keiko Shimizu, an unemployed mother of one, of no fixed abode, jumped from the cable car to her death after committing the crime. The victim, Hirokazu Ina, was a nineteen-year-old student who worked part-time for the ropeway. It is understood that Mr Ina was stabbed while attempting to dissuade the woman from opening the cable

car door. Local police have ruled out any kind of personal rela-
tionship or vendetta between the two as the aggressor was
hitherto unknown to the victim.

Hideo Akashi, an off-duty police officer from Tokyo, happened
to be on the cable car at the time of the attack. 'I attempted to
stop the young woman from jumping but she was very disturbed,'
he said, adding, 'I'm just glad that more people weren't hurt.'

The incident is the latest in a series of setbacks to affect the
newly opened ropeway. Owned by a local energy magnate, the
Michimori Shrine Ropeway has been dogged by poor ticket sales
and technical difficulties since its opening early last year.

The woman's twelve-year-old daughter, Midori Anzai, has
been taken into state care.

Keiko Shimizu's father, Yukitoshi, a Nagasaki resident, declined
to comment.

Sakai put down the article.

'That's her.' Oshino tapped the bottom of the clipping. 'It has to be.'

'What happens to her after the ropeway?'

'It's a puzzle. Orphanages, foster families all over Japan and then nothing. Maybe she died. Maybe something else. Could be a name change. Could have moved to Botswana. Whatever happened, the trail runs out.'

Sakai looked out of the window.

'Who is she?' Oshino swallowed his coffee in one. 'Midori Anzai?'

'Someone you don't ask me about.'

'All right, understood.'

From the back of the folder, she took out an address written on a Post-it note.

'What's this?'

'The girl's grandfather from the article,' Oshino said. 'He's still in Nagasaki.'

Sakai closed the folder and stood up.

'Thank you for this. I mean it, Oshino.'

Sakai kissed him on the cheek and picked up her jacket.

'See you around, champ.'

Oshino jumped up and followed her to the door.

'But I won't see you, will I?'

Sakai smiled and wiped sugar grains from his lip with her little finger.

'I don't think so.'

A knock came at the door of Doctor Ken Taniguchi's Chiba University Hospital office. Iwata and Hatanaka entered, the latter now wearing a new but ill-fitting grey suit. Iwata had on his usual intent expression.

'Doctor Taniguchi? I'm Inspector Iwata of Shibuya Division One.' He took out his police credentials. 'This is Assistant Inspector Hatanaka.'

Taniguchi gestured at the seats opposite, somewhat alarmed at the curt tone with which he was being addressed.

'You signed for the body of Inspector Hideo Akashi last month, yes?'

'That's right.'

'We have some questions. Could we see the file?'

Taniguchi nodded, turned to his computer and peered at the monitor over his spectacles. It took him a few moments to find the right file.

'Here we are. Hideo Akashi. Suicide.'

'Could you print that for me?'

Taniguchi complied, then passed across a single page. Iwata and Hatanaka peered at it.

'Doctor, you signed off on this body, is that correct?' Iwata said.

'That's right.'

'But Doctor,' Hatanaka interjected, 'this says that the medical examination wasn't carried out by you.'

'That's right.'

Iwata took back the baton.

'You're the chief pathologist here, correct?'

'Yes. But this procedure was carried out by my assistant at the time. It was perfectly normal for her to carry out the examination.'

'Name?'

'Ayako Wakatsuki. She was a very promising student.'

'Was?'

'Is.'

'I'd like to speak with her.'

Taniguchi shifted in his seat, looking up from Iwata to Hatanaka and back again.

'Inspector, do you mind me asking what this is about?'

'Frankly, I do.' He pointed to the file. 'Are there are no photographs of the body?'

'No, why would there be?'

'There was nothing strange about Akashi's death, then?'

Taniguchi sat back.

'Not to my knowledge.'

Iwata looked over his shoulder at Hatanaka, who said nothing. Iwata turned back. Taniguchi was clearly unsettled but his face was too uninterested, an inexperienced poker player laying down a weak hand.

'Doctor, you're lying.'

Taniguchi laughed incredulously.

'I have nothing to lie about.'

There was a moment of silence and Iwata smiled venomously.

'Doctor, if I ask Assistant Inspector Hatanaka to lock this

door, he will. But I would rather not have to ask him. Do you understand what I'm saying?'

Taniguchi exhaled, his resistance gone.

'I don't want to have anything to do with this once we're done, is that understood?'

'Talk first, Doctor. Then we'll see.'

Taniguchi ran a hand through grey hair.

'OK. It was Wakatsuki. She found some . . . *irregularities* with Akashi's examination.'

Iwata could hardly breathe.

'Go on.'

'You should really speak with Wakatsuki herself, I'm not quite sure. Superintendent Fujimura made it clear that this matter should not be discussed.'

Iwata and Hatanaka shared a look.

'Fujimura,' Iwata spat. 'You spoke to *Fujimura*?'

'Directly. I called him to tell him there could possibly be a basis for an autopsy and the public prosecutor would have to be contacted. He became . . . very angry. He made it clear that it was unacceptable to create such a stink over such a sad event. He was very clear – he did not believe this matter to be anything other than a tragedy.'

'And then?'

'He found out Wakatsuki had carried out the examination. The next morning, she requested a transfer to a different faculty. She was a very promising student, so it's a real shame, as I say.'

'All right.' Iwata folded Akashi's examination page away. 'So where is Ayako Wakatsuki?'

29. Ketchup

At the back of Chiba University library, Ayako Wakatsuki was hunched over textbooks. She was cute and plump with a short bob and large hoop earrings. As Iwata and Hatanaka approached her, she looked up. Curiosity first. Then anxiety.

Iwata held up his police ID.

'Are you Ayako Wakatsuki?'

Her eyes flicked from cop to cop.

'Why?'

'You're in no trouble. You remember Hideo Akashi?'

She looked around.

'I'd rather talk elsewhere.'

Ayako Wakatsuki led them clear of the university grounds to a half-empty Freshness Burger a few blocks away. Despite the early hour, Hatanaka and Wakatsuki ordered cheeseburgers and lemonade, while Iwata stuck to coffee. Blushing, Hatanaka insisted on paying. They sat down in a corner booth.

'We just have a few questions,' Iwata said. 'You have nothing to worry about, Ayako.'

Wakatsuki dabbed at her mouth with a napkin.

'Really?'

'Absolutely.'

'Within an *hour* of examining that policeman's body I was receiving threats. I was told that things could happen to me. Things could be arranged. I was followed. From my apartment, to class, even to my mother's house – day and night. All of this by policemen and all of this just because

I did my job. So you'll forgive me if I hold on to my worries for now.'

Iwata held up his hands.

'I know the way they operate. I do. But I need you to trust us now because we're not the same as them.'

'So what are you, then? The good ones?'

'We're investigating a series of murders and we believe Akashi's death may be linked. That's all. If you talk to us, nobody will find out. You can rest assured. But we do need your help. People's lives depend on this. On you, Ayako.'

'Great, so no pressure, then.' Wakatsuki sighed gently. 'I mean, I figured you weren't the same as them the second you asked about Akashi. Those other cops had no questions whatsoever.'

'They're assholes,' Hatanaka blurted. 'We don't have any kind of agenda. We won't force you to do anything.'

She looked at Hatanaka for a moment, then back at Iwata.

'Series of murders, huh? So you're talking, like, a serial killer?'

He nodded and Wakatsuki wrinkled her nose.

'All right. OK. I mean I can't really say no to that.'

Iwata produced Akashi's death certificate.

'Doctor Taniguchi said you found irregularities.' He unfolded the page. 'But I can't see anything irregular here.'

Wakatsuki took a sip of lemonade.

'Unsurprising.' She took out a scrapbook from her bag. 'These are my original notes. I would always jot them down here first before writing them up officially. Whatever you were given was what Taniguchi filed after I left.'

Looking around the restaurant, she passed over her notes. Iwata and Hatanaka peered closely at her small, scrawled text.

Severe maxillofacial injuries.

Iwata looked up.

'How severe?'

'*Extensive* trauma. Completely smashed in.'

'So he . . . had no face?'

'Correct.'

Hatanaka frowned.

'So Akashi was dead before he even hit the water?'

Wakatsuki nodded.

'Not particularly common in this type of death, but the damage could well have been on contact with one of the support struts or the iron outcroppings from the bridge.'

'But how? There's only open space from the bridge to the water.'

'No, he jumped from the tower – the very top of the bridge – not road-level. That's over one hundred metres.'

'So to clarify,' Iwata said, 'Akashi was unrecognizable?'

Wakatsuki took a pen from her bag and sketched a cartoon face on a napkin. Then she took the bottle of ketchup and squeezed it until the face was covered completely.

'Like this.'

She tossed the pen into her bag, and, noticing a dollop of ketchup on her finger, sucked it clean.

Hatanaka blushed as Iwata carried on reading.

Small lacerations present on top of subject's head.

'What are these lacerations?' Iwata asked. 'From aquatic life?'

'Unlikely. He wasn't in the water for long at all. If I had to guess, I'd say he had recently shaved his head. Just not very carefully.'

'To play devil's advocate,' Iwata said, 'just how "irregular" might all this be?'

Wakatsuki slurped her drink through her straw before nodding to her notes.

'Finish reading.'

Ring finger on left hand badly broken. Small but clear ligature marks on wrist.

'. . . He was restrained.'

'And, from the shape of the marks, I'd say handcuffs,' Wakatsuki chirped.

'But wait, why just the one wrist?' Hatanaka said. 'Akashi was a big guy, if you were going to restrain him —'

Iwata interrupted.

'Because someone handcuffed Akashi *to* something.'

They fell quiet for a moment as a family passed by with their breakfast specials.

'Then you were right, Iwata. Akashi didn't kill himself. He had help.'

'Who identified the body?' Iwata asked her.

'It was a cop called . . .' Wakatsuki closed one eye to recall. 'Suzuki? Yes, Suzuki I think.'

Iwata frowned.

'Suzuki? A cop?'

'Pretty certain. They were talking like he was Akashi's partner. *Tough break about your partner*, that type of thing. But he didn't look like a cop.'

'Why?'

'He was so drunk he could hardly stand. Honestly, he looked like he was homeless. In any case, Doctor Taniguchi would have his address.'

Wakatsuki checked her watch.

'Look, you can keep those notes. But I have class in forty minutes.'

'One last question, Ayako. What do *you* think happened here?'

She smirked darkly.

'The broken finger, the smashed face, the ligature marks . . . Inspector, if you're asking me if Hideo Akashi was murdered, then my answer is yes. There's no doubt in my mind that the injuries on his body were consistent with being restrained, assaulted and then, most likely, thrown off Rainbow Bridge *after* death to simulate suicide.'

She chewed her lips for a second, then carried on.

'And not that I'm trying to do your job here, boys. But I'd have to wonder why your fellow policemen were so intent on ruling this out as murder.'

'Thank you for your time, Ms Wakatsuki.'

'Good luck with this mess,' she said before turning to Hatanaka. 'And thanks for lunch.'

When she was out of the door, Iwata turned to Hatanaka, who was still staring in her direction. Iwata snapped his fingers.

'Listen up, Romeo. I want you to go to Rainbow Bridge and get in touch with the Bureau of Port and Harbour. I want CCTV footage from the day of Akashi's death. Get as much as possible on either side of the date, too.'

'Got it.'

They left the restaurant and headed back towards the Chiba Hospital car park.

'Hey Iwata, answer me something. If the Black Sun Killer murdered Akashi, why did he go to the trouble of making it look like a suicide? I mean, he didn't bother going to those lengths with the others, right?'

Iwata smiled and pinched Hatanaka's cheek.

'Now *that's* the question, isn't it?'

Hatanaka shrugged him off, trying not to laugh.

'Have you considered this probably had nothing to do with the Black Sun case?'

Iwata smiled conspiratorially.

'What you really want to ask is: *What if it was someone in the TMPD?*

'No.' Hatanaka kicked a pebble into a bush. 'I don't want to ask that question.'

'Then you're not as stupid as you look. Now *you* answer me something, kid. Why don't you ask Wakatsuki out?'

Hatanaka glared at him.

'Yeah, sure. I'll wait outside her classroom if you'll give me the afternoon off.'

'I'm serious.'

The younger man snorted.

'Iwata, I don't . . .'

'You don't what? Like women?'

'I like women, I just don't . . .'

'What?'

'Women don't like *me*, all right?'

Iwata grinned up at the sky.

'Oh yeah, thanks for finding it so fucking hilarious, Iwata. I might suck with women but at least I have such a cool, understanding boss.'

Iwata held up his hand.

'I'm not laughing at you, kid. But I'm going to tell you something. The only reason women don't like you is because *you* don't like you. So bite the bullet. Ask this girl out. If she says yes, who knows? If she says no, what does that change?'

'Look, I can't ask her out. "Hey, I'm investigating a murder, actually you're cute, shall we go to the movies?" Forget it. What have we even got in common?'

'Dead bodies, for one thing. She answered our questions and she had *fun*. Fuck, Hatanaka, you've already bought her a burger. Ask her out for a beer as well.'

They had reached the car.

'Under that quiet, brooding shit, you're actually a nosy bastard, you realize that, Iwata?'

'That's why I'm good at what I do.'

'Yeah, sure. Where are you headed?'

'To find this Suzuki. Now remember, Bureau of Port and Harbour.'

'Yeah, *I got it.*'

Iwata started the engine and pulled away. Hatanaka followed the black Isuzu with his eyes and pictured Wakatsuki sucking her finger.

Despite the frantic banging at the door, Ryozo Suzuki did not open his eyes. He prayed for it to stop but he knew it wouldn't. Swearing, he saddled his usual collection of agonies and lifted his frail body out of bed. It wasn't actually a bed, there was no futon or mattress, merely a corner in which he bundled his clothes to sleep on. The room was a squalid chaos. It stank so badly of cigarette smoke and sweat that it was hard not to cough when walking in. The single window had long been broken and the masking tape did nothing to stop the cold.

Suzuki spat on the floor and grimaced as he forced his boots on.

'All right, all right!'

He collected the last of his things and opened the door. An emaciated shrew of a man wearing blackened clothes pushed past him. He slung his bags of tin cans and plastic bottles on the floor and kicked off his shoes.

'I should charge you the extra hour,' the man growled. 'I've been standing out there like a damn snowman.'

From the doorway, Suzuki looked across the street at the car park. Above it, an old advertising board for car oil showed the time.

'More like ten minutes, you old fuck.'

'They were *my* ten minutes!'

The old man was still screeching but Suzuki had already

closed the door on him. He shifted his grubby pack but there was no position that wouldn't hurt his back. He walked past an open kitchen window and caught a snatch of local radio.

'It's just coming up to eleven in the morning and what a beautiful morning it is in Taitō. Your top stories again. Police descended on Uguisudani early this morning following the suicide of a forty-four-year-old unemployed man at Uguisudani Station. It's the second suicide in a month at this station and questions are already being asked in the local area about the cost of the anti-suicide blue lights on the Yamanote Line. A spokesperson from Japan Rail was unavailable for comment . . .'

Suzuki gripped on to the railing of the narrow balcony and looked down at the street below. People sat in the café over the road, eating French tarts. A repairman worked on telephone wires. A delivery of water tanks for a small office had just arrived. Cherry trees had started to sprout their first tentative white petals. This slice of city had once been home to undertakers, butchers and prostitutes. Now Taitō was like most other parts of Tokyo – being prepared for something else.

Suzuki's breath shortened. He gripped on to the railing waiting for it to come and there, right on cue, the coughing started. It was like inhaling glass and hot water at the same time. Recently, it ended in blood. Suzuki knew he was dying. His had not been a particularly fulfilling existence. Even so, he didn't have too many complaints. At least the weather couldn't hurt him today.

Thirty minutes later, Suzuki was setting up his blue tarp in the usual place.

It was late morning and only joggers and dog-walkers came to the park at this time. Most of the regulars hadn't turned up to pitch today and Suzuki figured the good weather had given them high hopes. A shining sun made people more generous, Suzuki knew that, but he couldn't face the crowds today. The blood was too thick in his throat, the pain in his limbs too sharp, the accumulated cold in his bones too burrowed.

Suzuki felt a rare twist of hunger deep in his belly and he tried to remember when he had last eaten. He took out a can of lentils, cut it open with his knife and drank the salty water. He allowed himself to swallow a few mouthfuls before he closed the tin and hid it in his bag. He closed his eyes to savour the juice, clasping fingers over his lips in pleasure. That's when he felt a shadow fall across him.

'Ryozo Suzuki?'

A slender man in a crumpled raincoat stood over him. Though he clearly hadn't slept in a while, his eyes were sharp.

'Who are you?'

He held up his police ID – Kosuke Iwata, TMPD.

'Figures. I had you pegged for a cop.'

'I need to ask you some questions.' His voice was tired.

Suzuki took out a flimsy wallet from his coat pocket and held it open in reply. It was empty.

30. The Devil Himself

Suzuki slurped down three full bowls of udon noodles and four cups of coffee. Iwata handed over cigarettes and ¥10,000 in cash. Suzuki lit up and savoured the nicotine as the smoke curled up past his grubby face.

'God damn, that is the genuine article.'

'Now you talk, Suzuki.'

'Beauty is truth. Fire away.'

'Why did they ask you to identify Akashi's body?'

'I was his partner for years. I assumed you knew that.'

'So why not a family member?'

'He had no family.'

'And you didn't find it strange?'

'Find what strange, pal?'

Suzuki inspected the glowering tip of his cigarette as it burnt.

'That the TMPD would go find a man living in a park, out of the force for almost ten years, to formally identify a body?'

'Thought never crossed my mind.'

'They paid you?'

'More than *you* did. Look, strange or not, you saw how I'm living. You don't like it? Well, I got news for you. Neither do I.'

'I didn't come here to pass judgement. I just want to know what happened to Akashi.'

Suzuki finished the last of his broth before wiping his mouth with a dirty sleeve.

'Then you're wasting your time, Iwata. You already know

he jumped off Rainbow Bridge. What are you asking me for? All I did was look at a corpse.'

'How did you know it was him?'

'In the morgue? Of course it was him. I knew right away.'

'How could you know? He had no face.'

'He had the same frame, the same shitty clothes, the wedding ring. Look, it was him all right. No two ways about it.'

'Ring?'

'His ex-wife gave it back to him when they separated.'

'Yumi.'

Suzuki smiled yellow teeth and let a memory wash over him.

'What a woman.'

'What if it were possible that Akashi didn't kill himself after all?'

An amused smile played on Suzuki's lips.

'Then I'd say full speed ahead, Captain Ahab.'

'Why?'

'OK, look, I never thought Akashi would be the sort to top himself. But then I haven't seen him in years. People change. Look at me.'

'Can you think of anyone that might want him dead? Was there anyone he feared?'

Suzuki chortled.

'I'm sure there were a lot of people that wanted him dead. Akashi did a lot of bad things. But he wasn't the sort to fear anyone.'

'Why not?'

Suzuki shrugged.

'It wasn't just that he had no fear. It was more that he always knew the angle. Look, Akashi was the smartest bastard I ever knew.'

'Start from the beginning. I want to know what you know.'

Suzuki sighed – *a deal is a deal.*

'We were first put together in Nerima PD, a long time ago. Let's just say that Akashi hit the ground running. The guy was a machine, best clearing record I'd ever seen. Within a few years, he transferred to Shibuya's Division One and got to pick his own team.'

'I'm guessing you got lucky.'

'Yeah, along with this dumb fuck, Nomura. Honestly, that choice confused me at first. He was a good guy but any little simple task took him twice as long. He was constantly stuck between overthinking something pointlessly, to not thinking it through at all. He was completely dependent on Akashi, like a fucking retarded little brother or something. We grew to love him, though.'

Suzuki suddenly hacked up blood on the counter, his eyes streaming. When he was breathing normally again, he non-chalantly wiped away the stain with napkins.

'You should see a doctor.'

'I'm uninsured, they won't see me. Just finish your questions.'

'All right. You were saying. Akashi transferred.'

'And how.' Suzuki ordered a bottle of beer and lit another cigarette. 'So there followed a golden age of police work. In a relatively short amount of time, Akashi and his two trusted henchmen became the tip of the spear. We fucking *owned* Shibuya. The commissioner loved us. The other cops envied us. They called us the Three Little Pigs. To be honest, I always kind of liked the name.'

'So how did you end up . . .'

'What? Here?'

'Yeah.'

Suzuki's expression soured for a moment and he looked at a speck of blood in the ashtray.

'What happens to all streaks? Our luck ran out.'

'Go on.'

'In 1994, Akashi was tasked with heading up an infiltration unit – completely off the books, well-funded, full operational discretion.'

'Infiltrating what, organized crime?'

Suzuki shook his head.

'*Cults.*'

'Why?'

'Japan was shit scared back then. Aum Shinrikyo had hit Matsumoto and Tokyo with sarin gas attacks and the TMPD realized it had no real rulebook for dealing with them. I didn't see Akashi for a couple of years after that. I'm not sure what happened to the infiltration unit but there were one or two cult groups that got swallowed up and prosecutions did follow.'

'And then?'

'Akashi was reassigned to our old unit. We were given a case nobody wanted. This guy murders three children and then just falls off the map. We never worked a case harder than that and, in the end, we did manage to discover his identity – a guy called Matsuu.'

Something fell away in Iwata's chest. He thought back to his first time in Shindo's office and what Sakai had asked.

What about the Takara Matsuu case, sir?

'Matsuu?' Iwata repeated.

'That's what I said. Anyway, so we dug up every fucking rat in Japan and paid any asshole to whisper to us. In the end, we managed to corner Matsuu in some fucking field in Chiba. He was hiding out in this shack. Akashi tells us to stay outside while he goes in. Ten minutes later, he walks out, empty-handed. *Not here*, he says. After that, Akashi was never the same. You could tell it was eating him up. It was around that time our clearing rate dropped. We started accepting "gifts". Got involved in black-market casinos. We started to owe the wrong people money. The sort of people that don't give a fuck whether you have a badge or not. One thing led to another, as they say.'

'Hold on, go back. *Takara* Matsuu?'

'That's right. Big fucker.'

Iwata shook his head.

'But they *did* find him. Or at least, until he went missing several weeks ago.'

Suzuki shrugged.

'Well . . . I guess they must have caught him. I'm not really one for current affairs, you know?'

'But if he murdered three children, how did he get out at all? He would've hanged.'

'Fucked if I know. Must have had a pretty hot defence lawyer.' Suzuki downed his beer. 'Not that they exist in this country. Matsuu probably served his time and then became an informant after he got out. Makes sense, if he's missing. Nobody likes snitches.'

'But informing on who? On *what*?'

'You work it out, man. Anyway, you want to know what happened or not?'

'I want to know.'

'Our bribes got bigger. The risks got even bigger. Our feuds got out of hand. And we got fucking rich. We weren't staging photo-op drug busts any more. I'm talking vote-rigging, fixed public bids, *entire projects*. We were so far inside the yakuza, we'd go weeks without turning up at HQ. We didn't have the tattoos but we knew what we had become.'

'And then?'

'Nomura, the poor bastard. One day he comes to Akashi and tells him that he can't do it any more, he wants to leave.

Can't face killing or being killed. Akashi embraces him, says something in his ear and leads him to the door. When Nomura turns his back on him, he cuts his throat.'

Suzuki looked upwards at the fan, the slow blades chopping the oily air.

'That was when I knew, I guess. But Akashi rationalized it, as he always could. He said that it would only be a matter of time before an ethics review would identify Nomura and they'd work him and we'd all be fucked. I swore never to tell anyone and we tried to keep things subtle for a few months. Funny thing is, Akashi was right. TMPD did clean house. One morning I wake up with a torch in my face and my own colleagues arresting me.'

Suzuki ordered another beer.

'You wanna know my story, Inspector? First it was the jail, then it was the car plant, then it was the park.'

Iwata shook his head.

'So you're telling me that Hideo Akashi was, among many other things, a murderer. You're sure of this?'

'I came up with Nomura in the academy. Seeing him killed in cold blood isn't exactly something I could misinterpret, you know what I mean?'

'How did Akashi get away with that?'

'Staged it as a yakuza hit. Found some patsy to hang and we both testified. That was that. As for the rest of it, Akashi put everything on me. Probably called the ethics review himself.'

Suzuki ran a dirty finger through a clump of ash and exhaled. Iwata glanced up at the clock and stood.

'I've got to go. Thanks for your time. Take care of yourself, Suzuki.'

The door trilled as he opened it.

'Inspector,' Suzuki called. 'You think he jumped to get away from someone, don't you?'

Iwata nodded.

'Then I'm telling you it must have been the devil himself.'

'Why?'

'Because in this world, the only thing that Akashi feared was Akashi.'

Speeding through Tokyo's grey arteries, Iwata glanced at the dashboard clock. Time was running out. His phone rang.

'Hatanaka?'

'Iwata, I'm at Rainbow Bridge but the office is closed. Don't worry, I'm not going until I get the CCTV.'

'Good job, kid. You wake up anyone that you have to.'

'Did you find Suzuki?'

'Yes, and all it really did was confirm what we already suspected – somehow Akashi is key to all of this.'

'Where are you headed now?'

'TMPD Central Records. I'm looking for a guy called Takara Matsuu. Before Sakai was put on the Black Sun case she was investigating him as a misper.'

'You're not going to call her?'

'No. I'm betting the Matsuu case was being led by Akashi before his death. Every time I've mentioned him, she's clammed up. Something isn't right.'

'OK, boss. I'll be in the Shibuya TMPD video suite as soon as I have the footage.'

'I'll meet you there.'

A quarter of an hour later, Iwata was driving through Chiyoda. To the north, he could see the twinkling lights of the Imperial Palace. Around him, the Ministry of Foreign Affairs, the National Diet Building and Hibiya Park to the east.

Iwata skipped up the steps to the Tokyo Metropolitan Police Department headquarters. It took him several minutes to clear security. He punched in the temporary code he had been given to the elevator and descended to Level −4. The doors opened on a huge, windowless office and a young man in an immaculate suit greeted Iwata.

'Good evening, Inspector. You need Central Records access?'

'That's right. Active case. Missing person. Takara Matsuu.'

'Please follow me.'

Iwata was led to a plush break-out area where he was offered mineral water. The young man promptly returned with a tablet computer.

'Here we are, Inspector. Takara Matsuu. Convicted of the murders of three children aged between five and eight – under Article 199, Part Two of the Penal Code.'

'Sentence?'

'He was sent to a psychiatric unit where he spent five years. On his release in 2004, he took a role as an informant for the TMPD.'

'That's it? He got five years?'

'That's what it says here.' The man frowned. 'Though I don't understand why he'd get such a lenient sentence after killing three children.'

'I think I might have an idea.' Iwata stood. 'Thanks for your help.'

31. Elephant Clouds

Yukitoshi Shimizu lived in a cheap cut of Nagasaki – low-level office workers, factory workers and hard-luck families. The billboard above his apartment building was being offered for advertising but nobody was interested.

At dawn, Sakai knocked lightly on the door. A small, elderly man opened. Heart beating, she held up her ID.

'Are you here about my daughter?' His voice was a soft croak.

'That's right.'

The tiny apartment, while neat, was tellingly sparse – it had the damp smell of long-standing grief. The old man made tea, returning with a trembling tray. They sat at a cheap table and drank in silence for a while. Shimizu's face was like that of a faded statue, a man familiar with nothingness.

'It's been a long time since I've had a visitor.'

'I'm sorry for imposing on you, Mr Shimizu.'

'Not at all. Please ask your questions.'

'Thank you. I don't have many. Let me begin by asking you, when was the last time you saw Keiko?'

'Fifteenth of May 1982. She was going away with friends for the weekend on a camping trip but she never came back.'

'Did you ever find out where she went?'

'No. She sent me a letter a few months after her disappearance. It just said that she was happy. She talked about nature, the mountains, finding herself. A year or two later, she sent another. This time there was a photograph.'

'Mr Shimizu, apart from these letters, she never got in contact with you?'

'Oh she called me once or twice but never said anything coherent. She wouldn't tell me where she was. I begged her to come back, of course, but she told me she was happy with her new life and that was that.'

'She used those words? "New life"?'

'Yes.'

'So the next you heard was after the incident at the ropeway?'

'That's right. The police questioned me.'

Sakai sat back. She considered the old man before her. Could she picture him hurting Keiko? Abusing her? She searched for old lies in this man but could find only grief. She considered his small head, the thatch of white hair in his ears, the papery lips wet from tea, the ancient folds of his eyelids. It was clear to Sakai that Yukitoshi Shimizu would live out the rest of his days in a bubble of painful irresolution.

'Sir, I have to ask. Why do you think she did what she did up on that ropeway?'

'I don't know. But . . . I must blame myself. What alternative is there? Her mother died when she was young. I was not a good father to her.'

Shimizu's eyes were pink. His voice had furrowed deep in his chest.

He sipped tea to steady himself and breathed deeply.

'I met Keiko's mother at university. It was a period of change for Japan and I suppose back then I stood for something. I think that's what appealed to her. At first, I thought it was some joke, or some kind of trick – a woman like that loving me. But she did. We used to wake up early and plan out our days carefully. *At ten we'll do this, at eleven we'll get custard buns.* But we never did any of it. We just stayed in our little room. Japan was tearing itself apart but we just slept straight through.'

Shimizu ran out of words as he lost his smile. He peered into his tea.

'Are you married, Inspector?'

Sakai shook her head.

'Perhaps it's better that way. At night, I always felt this dread. This looming sadness. The inescapable reality of the ending night – somehow it would get to 1.30 a.m. and we would have to face our dreams alone. The next day of classes alone. I realized that we could only ever be together in snatches. That the dread would never go away, it would always win out in the end. Turning off that bedside lamp each night wasn't just darkness, it was separation . . .'

Shimizu remembered to blink.

'They say meeting someone is the first step to losing them. Have you heard that saying?'

Sakai nodded.

'Well, that's how it felt each night. And it felt no different in the hospital at the end. Turning off my wife's life support was the same as turning off the bedside lamp after a long day. I don't know why I thought of this at such a time . . . perhaps the mind focuses on the small details to stop one from contemplating the enormity of one's loss.'

He folded his hands in his lap.

'She was so young. I suppose I just had nothing left for Keiko after that.'

Sakai nodded once, fingering away a tear.

'I'm sorry,' she said thickly.

'No, it's me who should apologize. You didn't come here to listen to my past.'

She cleared her throat.

'Did Keiko have any problems in her life that you knew of? Any enemies, for example?'

The old man looked up at the ceiling.

'Honestly, I don't know. I was never close to her. So much time has gone by now . . .'

'Mr Shimizu, why do you think she left?'

'I don't know. I think I loved my wife too strongly to give my child that same devotion. It's hard to tell you, but it's the truth. When she was born, in among all my anxiety, there was . . . something else. Like a voice trying to warn me that I would fail this child. And then she was born and she cried whenever I held her. Even later, she would never take to my games. The only one she liked to play was the cloud game. You know the one? You look up to the sky and find animals or princesses in the clouds. She liked that one. For some reason, we always found elephants. "*Elephant clouds*," she would say.'

Another painful smile faded from his lips.

'Could I see that photograph she sent you, sir?'

Yukitoshi Shimizu nodded. For several minutes, Sakai heard the room next door in motion. The old man had buried it deep.

When he finally returned, he didn't look at the photograph as he handed it over. Sakai glanced down and saw the picture of his daughter.

Her breath caught.

Keiko was beautiful and familiar. She was standing in a forest, holding a baby, looking down at it lovingly. With one hand she was brushing back the hair from her face. Golden sunlight, faded by time, slanted around them.

'I don't even know if that's my granddaughter,' he said quietly.

Sakai searched the image for any kind of useful detail but it gave nothing away other than a date stamp: *June 1984*.

Sakai was about to hand it back when she saw Keiko's wrist. Squinting, she made out a tattoo.

'Could I use your magnifying glass, Mr Shimizu?'

Shimizu took it from the top of a bundle of old newspapers and handed it over. Sakai enlarged Keiko's wrist and blinked.

She was looking at a black sun tattoo.

Kosuke is dreaming of his new life in America. He is just a few weeks away from leaving the orphanage. Leaving Japan. His mother is coming for him with a new father – an American.

A car door slams and Kosuke opens his eyes.

It is a moonless summer night but light is filling his room. Blue light. Then pink. He wraps the quilt around his shoulders and pads over to the window. Outside, he recognizes the policeman who brought him here. He looks much older now, smaller in his uniform. He is talking to Mr Uesugi while behind them, policemen are passing around flashlights. Kosuke sees that Mr Uesugi is gesticulating wildly, occasionally clutching his head in his hands. In the pink and blue light, it looks like a terrible dance. The night is warm and a red fringe of dawn has surfaced at the horizon.

Kosuke gets into his shorts and tennis shoes and hurries downstairs as quietly as he can. In the foyer, the main door is ajar and he can hear the voices.

'How can I be *calm*, Tamura? The very reputation of this facility depends on the safety of these children.'

'I appreciate that, but Mr Uesugi –'

'It's just a bear, sergeant. One solitary bear! How hard can it be to find?'

'That's a story, sir. It's more likely the boy wandered off by himself.'

'Then you get out there and you find him!'

Kosuke hears footsteps and he hides in a lagoon of

shadow. Uesugi shuts the door behind him and sags against it. Christ looks down on him. Fallen saints watch on. Black-and-white photographs of former pupils, Uesugi at the front of each class, smiling broadly.

We are together and we are joyous. For whosoever is delighted in solitude is a wild beast or a god.

With a trembling hand, Uesugi wipes sweat from his fore-head. He looks at his wet palm and, for some reason, he shakes his head at it. He takes out a handkerchief and wipes the back of his neck and under his armpits. He is having trouble breathing.

Kosuke steps out of the shadow.

'Why are they here?'

Uesugi gasps and flinches.

'Iwata.' He chuckles. 'You gave me a fright.'

'Why are they here?'

'Don't worry yourself. It's very late, you must go back to bed.'

Kosuke can only make out Uesugi's teeth in the dark blue gloom. Old wood creaks. The grandfather clock ticks. Then he realizes.

'Where is Kei?'

The question rings out in the hall. Uesugi's mouth becomes a tight line.

'Get back to bed, boy.'

Above them, Sister Mary Josephine appears on the land-ing. Uesugi glances up at her, seems to change his mind about something, then walks away, his footsteps echoing in the darkness.

Kosuke looks up at the nun and her gaze falls to the floor.

He runs out of the orphanage, as fast as he can go. He runs through the field, a sea of gossamer webs lit up silver by the rising sun. He runs for the forest, its treetops lambent in the warm light. He runs for the whirlpool, forgotten by the world. But Kosuke knows, deep down, he will not find Kei.

Nobody will.

32. People Seeking the Truth

Fifteen hours after she had spoken with Yukitoshi Shimizu in Nagasaki, Sakai was deep in the guts of TMPD Shibuya. She walked down a dim corridor and stopped outside the door with the plaque above it:

YOJI YAMADA – CULTS & RELIGIOUS GROUPS DIVISION

Someone had drawn a cartoon shit on the name. Though it was past midnight, the lights were on inside. Sakai knocked and opened the door to a large, messy office with a futon in the corner. Yamada, covered in a blanket, his feet up on the desk, was sipping coffee. He was a short, portly man in his late thirties. Despite greying hair and early balding, his face was youthful. A thin moustache gave him the look of a man out of sync with his time.

Seeing her, Yamada almost fell off his chair.

'Night owl, huh?' Sakai folded her arms.

'I don't sleep very well.'

'You know who I am?'

'Everyone knows who you are.' He smoothed over long-vanished hair. 'Can I help you?'

She held up the Kaneshiro crime scene photograph showing the black sun symbol.

'I hope so. Recognize this?'

Yamada nodded.

'The Black Sun murders. Well, I already offered to help with that. I was ignored.'

'Look, Iwata is a stubborn son of a bitch. But he needs your help.'

'I'm sure he does. Way I heard it, he's on the way out. Word gets round, even down here.'

'It's true, he's toast. But he still has a few days left. And I have a lead.'

Yamada sipped his coffee and regarded Sakai in the lamp light. She was used to that.

'Sit down,' he said.

She took a dusty swivel chair across from him.

'So, then, what did the infamous Inspector Iwata actually do?'

'It's less what he did and more what he won't do.'

'Which is?'

'Come on, Yamada. You work here too. You know what they want. And they know Iwata won't toe any lines. That he'll call them out when they falsify clearances and run their usual little games. Oh, and he punched Moroto. Allegedly.'

Yamada shook his head, trying not to smile. He considered Sakai – sallow, beautiful, resolute. He wondered how she had ended up here, in this world.

'Will you inherit the case after Iwata?'

'No, I've already been reassigned.'

One half of Yamada's moustache curled up.

'So you found your lead by extracurricular means. Is this something either of us should be getting involved with?'

Sakai pointed to the door.

'There's a serial killer out there, Yamada. He's ripping out people's hearts. That's all I have to offer you.'

'So why are you trusting me?'

'Three reasons. One, nobody else in the TMPD trusts *you*. You're nothing here. Which puts you in the same boat as Iwata. Two, I believe there may be a cult angle in this case. Your knowledge could bolster the investigation. Now for better or for worse, Inspector Iwata has command of it for the next few days. I can't say it'll be good for your career but there again, you're in a basement reading books.'

Yamada mulled this over, his expression that of a man who had just sipped a scalding drink.

'What was the third reason?'

'Like I said, I have a lead.'

Sakai went into her coat pocket and passed across a photograph. Yamada looked down at Keiko Shimizu and her black sun tattoo.

'You ever seen anything like this on a person?'

Yamada looked closely and nodded.

'That's the symbol of the Children of the Black Sun.' He looked up her. 'Jesus, this is basically the same symbol the killer is leaving behind.'

'Tell me about the cult.'

'A pretty nasty one, but long defunct. It was active mostly through the sixties, seventies and eighties. Died a death in the nineties. Though it had resources, it was relatively mediocre in scale, no more than a couple of thousand members at its peak. It was a pretty typical model – hidden meaning, charismatic guru, controlled truth and so on.'

'Which was?'

'A combination of quasi-Buddhist teachings mixed with apocalypse narrative taken from ancient South American beliefs. Actually, pretty niche. Of course, those elements would only be revealed once you were part of the inner circle. But self-marking and self-harming were common in this particular sect.'

'Well,' – Sakai tapped the tattoo – 'I for one don't believe in fairy tales. There *is* a connection between that cult and these murders. Trust me, I know it.'

She took out some papers from her handbag and handed them over.

'This is her background and how it ties into the case. Read this.'

Yamada looked up at the ceiling.

'Say I agree. What would you need from me?'

'Firstly, I need to know where this cult would have been based.'

'Easy enough. They had rep offices in Tokyo, Sapporo and Osaka, I believe. But its HQ was a large compound up in the mountains near Gero. What else?'

Sakai closed her eyes and suppressed a wave of nausea.

'Gero?' she echoed softly.

'Yeah, why?'

'. . . Nothing.'

Yamada eyed her until she rubbed her eyes and regained her composure.

'You OK, Sakai?'

'Fine.'

'What else do you need?'

'I need you to meet Iwata at Yoyogi-kōen Station in three hours. Are you in?'

'Will you be there?'

'No. I can't do this any more. I can't.'

Yamada nodded without really knowing why. But he found it hard to see pain across Sakai's face.

'So why Iwata?'

Sakai looked down at the black suns, side by side.

'Because he's the only one who can stop this now.'

'All right.' Yamada shook his head. 'I'll do it.'

'Thank you.' She smiled at him. Though it was artificial, it still thrilled him. 'Oh, one more thing?'

She took out a small yellow envelope from her jacket and placed it on the desk. There was a single word scrawled across it:

IWATA

'What's that?' Yamada asked.

'Just a tape. When you get back from Gero, give it to him. Not before, OK?'

'OK.'

She stood and bowed. Yamada rushed after her. At the door they shared a look.

'Where will you go?' he asked.

'To prepare.'

'For what?'

'Whatever is coming.'

She bit her lip and nodded for no particular reason.

'Hey, Yamada?'

'What?'

'I don't sleep well, either.'

Sakai smiled sadly and patted the door frame goodbye.

At 3.30 a.m., Yamada hurried across the slick road to the waiting Isuzu. Night trains slowly screeched past, the warning bells from the level crossing clanging in panic. Wet slushing sounds from the highway could be heard in the distance. Yamada sat in the passenger seat and set down a plastic bag between his feet.

'Who the fuck are you?'

Iwata reached for his gun but Yamada held out a hand.

'Yoji Yamada, Cults and Religious Groups. Remember me?'

'Where's Sakai?'

'She's not coming. She sent me.'

Yamada held up the photograph of Keiko Shimizu's tattoo.

'She gave this to me to show you, Iwata. She asked me to work with you. She has a lead.'

There was an uneasy silence.

'Speak,' Iwata said.

'In 1982, a woman called Keiko Shimizu left her home in Nagasaki on a camping trip and never came back. She sent letters and called home a few times speaking about her "new life" and "finding herself". In 1996, she ended up on a ropeway where she murdered a man before killing herself.'

'That symbol, Inspector Yamada, is the same symbol the killer is leaving behind in my crime scenes.'

'It's also the symbol of a doomsday cult. So fill me in. Come on, Iwata. I know you're not the buddy-buddy type, but you also know that I could be able to help you here. I have expertise. Sakai gave me the basics but I need to know the lay of the land.'

Iwata tapped the wheel and nodded reluctantly.

'If I tell you, you tell no one. Understand?'

Yamada spread his hands.

'Nobody listens to me anyway. You included, remember?'

'All right. I believe the Black Sun Killer was one of the passengers on that same cable car.'

Yamada pursed his lips.

'Shit.'

'For whatever reason, he's killing everyone onboard that day. Now we know that Keiko Shimizu is dead. That just leaves Yumi Tachibana – she's already under police guard – and a little girl who was about ten years old at the time.'

'You think the baby in the photo is the girl on the cable car?'

'Could be, it would make sense. Tell me about this cult.'

'Your symbol is almost a carbon copy of that belonging to a dead cult called the Children of the Black Sun. A few thousand strong. Doomsday narrative, apocalypse not arriving soon enough, let's provoke it ourselves through mass murder, biological weapons, that kind of thing. Their compound was up in the mountains near Gero. Our killer was almost certainly a member.'

Iwata looked at him.

'Now I understand why Sakai called me and told me to bring all my case notes.' He pointed to the sports bag in the back seat.

'Like I said, she wants us to work together. So. What do we have?'

'Not much. A shaky MO. No solid suspects to speak of, no real evidence and a boatload of question marks.'

They sat in silence for a while, both of them watching the traffic lights change colour.

'Well.' Yamada grinned. 'At least I'm out of the office.'

'Where did Sakai say she was going?'

'She didn't. Just that she was going to prepare.'

'For what?'

Yamada shrugged and looked at the sports bag.

'I suppose I'd better read while you drive.'

Iwata started the engine and pulled away. Yamada took out a thermos from his plastic bag and poured coffee.

'Iwata, drink this. It's a long way, and from the looks of you, you're going to fall asleep at the wheel.'

Iwata took a sip and sputtered.

'What the hell is that?'

'It's a little Yoji special blend. Proper coffee.' Yamada winked.

'Stick to cults.'

Muttering, Yamada snatched the cup back.

They left Tokyo behind, heading north at speed. The roads were empty except for delivery trucks heading for the city and waste trucks going the other way. Tomatoes, crayons, sex toys.

Tokyo wanted it all.

Tokyo was always hungry.

Yamada splayed out a map and gave occasional directions. With the overhead light switched on, he went over Iwata's mountain of notes and photographs.

After a few hours, he turned out the light.

'Well?' Iwata asked.

'I get the picture, yeah.'

'And?'

'And I think we're fucked. For one thing, your take on this case doesn't look good for various people in positions of power. You must realize that?'

'I realize that.'

Yamada tugged on his moustache in thought.

'Listen, Iwata. I know a guy. He works for a big newspaper. Why don't you talk to him? Ridiculous as it sounds, something could conceivably . . . happen to us and it'd be nice to have a little insurance –'

Iwata shook his head.

'I've got no time for that. This time next week, speak to whoever you want. For now, I just want you to give me your thoughts on the case.'

Yamada sighed.

'All right. Well, first off I'm going on the assumption that Keiko Shimizu is part of the Black Sun cult. I'm also thinking that the little girl is her child. If she's around ten or twelve in the cable car, then the dates would more or less match up.

343

Now Keiko would have been very young to be a mother but rape is common in many cult environments.'

'Wait, didn't you say there were a few thousand people in this group? Wouldn't someone have objected to young girls getting raped?'

'Often those that are indoctrinated might *sense* that what is happening is wrong, but you have to realize that they might well have lost their ability to make their own decisions. "There is no good and bad."'

Iwata shot him a doubtful glance.

'Brainwashing. You're for real?'

'You're sceptical?'

'No, not at all. I just think you already have to be crazy to fall for crazy.'

'Iwata, I'm not talking *Star Trek*-style mind control but people are less sophisticated than they think they are. You would not believe how quickly and effectively a healthily pragmatic mind can be completely invaded. We're designed to conform. These people are told, "You are God in your own universe – a universe that you caused. We love you." We call that love-bombing, and for many it's massively addictive.'

'Flattery.'

Yamada rolled his eyes.

'We're wired to seek the approval and love of others. We're social creatures. When you walk around as a god among men for two weeks and you're showered with love and attention, that's something you can get used to. And when it's taken away, you want it back. People will go out of their way to get it back.'

Iwata shook his head as he overtook a night bus.

'I'm sorry, but being nice to people for a few days isn't enough for them to throw away their entire lives and all their money. How is that even possible?'

Yamada took out some bread rolls, passed one to Iwata and answered with a full mouth.

'Sometimes it can be as simple as depriving the individual of protein, or giving them only three or four hours of sleep a night over a period of time. Compliance is a relatively easy thing to achieve. Your scepticism is natural, Iwata. But trust me, it snares people.'

Iwata stuffed half a roll in his mouth.

'*How* then?'

'There are any number of ways in. A common one is via workshops and seminars. They can go on for several days. Or say a university drop-out walks into a bookstore, gets talking to an attractive older woman. They have a common interest, say yoga, and she invites him to her class. There, he starts speaking with others – older, wiser people who show him interest. They get to encouraging his mistrust of society, even a little conspiracy is thrown in. By the time he realizes they are part of Cult X, he thinks, "Mm, this is a little crazy but hey, *these people* are definitely not crazy – they seem nice enough, how mad can it be?" Of course, by that point, having invested so much time, effort and sometimes money, the young man is unlikely to want to see this as a cult. What I'm saying is, the kid who walks into that bookshop is unlikely to be the same one who walks out. As for the seminars and classes, they are well advertised. Dressed up as ordinary.'

'So who goes to them?'

'The lonely, the curious, the lost, the empty – there's no typical profile. In more extreme cases, once at these seminars, they are insulted, demoralized and repeatedly told, "There is nothing to strive for." This can trigger hysteria. Then they're brought up on stage and insulted. They're slapped. Sick bags are provided. Then they're told that they'll soon "wake up". A taste of elation and fulfilment is experienced. Things somehow begin to make sense to them and now they're hooked. "Join us," they're told. "Join us and be free." Who doesn't want to be free? So they can end up leaving their jobs, their marriages, their kids – entire lives abandoned for this new way. And they come willingly.'

Iwata looked at Yamada.

'People seeking the truth?'

'Hasn't that always been man's most common preoccupation? But you have to remember – Iwata, do you have to chew like that? – that in among all of these schemes, sooner or later the unquestionable leader is revealed. Charismatic, beguiling, funny, aggressive – it doesn't matter, the point is they are the ultimate authority. The new member quickly realizes that the leader's approval is the most powerful thing of all. And they begin to exist only for that.'

The Chūō Expressway was quiet. To the north-east, the black fringe of Lake Suwa glimmered.

'So this cult – the Children of the Black Sun. What was it, exactly?'

Yamada passed Iwata another cup of coffee. Instead of sputtering, this time he just winced.

'It was based on a pretty typical mix of mysticism and self-help psychobabble. I forget the exact premise, but its central pillar was the "end sun", along with certain pre-Colombian creation myths. But instead of a purely religious angle, it also took in astrological and therapeutic aspects.'

'I can't believe I'm still drinking this coffee.' Iwata grimaced. 'So, why therapy?'

'Why not? After all, therapy is to be *encouraged*. Trusted. It was a smart angle for them to take. The members would work their way up, progress through the ranks and sooner or later, the *real truth* would be revealed.'

'Which was?'

'Some sort of imminent apocalyptic narrative. In this case it was the death of the sun and the ascendancy of a darkness in its place. The Black Sun.'

Iwata smiled.

'Nothing ups the stakes like the end of the world, right?'

'It's a common narrative in most major religions. And, of course, by following the guru, all the *children* are now safe and everyone else is fucked.'

'So who was this guru?'

'Takashi Anzai. Born to a Japanese oil magnate. Grew up in the Central American jungles. Returned to Japan as an adolescent. First ping on the radar is yoga classes in Osaka. His classes grew, as did his fees. Then he moved on to seminars. Somewhere in the early seventies, he obviously decided to dream a little bigger and started his own spirituality group. His cult emerged out of his growing hatred of traditional Buddhism. He incorporated ancient pre-Colombian folklore into his own version and threw in some psychic-development techniques for good measure. He went from twenty or thirty members to some two hundred and fifty or so by 1977. By the time of his arrest, the group had over two thousand members and Anzai had purchased land in the Philippines, East Africa and Mexico.'

'Go on.'

'Well, not much more is known. After his arrest, he barely said a word. It didn't really get the coverage it might have done because Aum Shinrikyo had just been destroyed and the media were having a field day – indictments, bankruptcy and death sentences. By then, the Children of the Black Sun were seen as just another fad. But they too were crushed in time. As for Anzai, by the time of his execution, he had fathered over thirty children. Mass graves were found at the compound.'

Iwata mulled this over. They drove past a garden centre, its parking lot empty. A roadside Mr Donut had just turned on its lights for the day's business. A neon cow above a closed steakhouse was blinking red. Yamada rubbed his eyes.

'Iwata, you know what I think? We cops tend to find a detail – in some natural, organic way we find the detail. And it confirms a suspicion. It makes sense. It *feels* right. It becomes our North Star. It's what we build the rest around.'

'Yeah, so?'

'Well, your North Star is that black sun symbol. Along with the taken hearts, it's the only consistent element in this case.'

'It's not present at Mina Fong's apartment.'

'Which you think was a distraction anyway. Mina Fong aside, we've got a black sun at every step of the way – leading all the way back to that cable car in 1996.'

'OK, so?'

'So what if we're wrong? What if there is no link between Keiko, the cult and your killer? What if they're just two symbols that happen to be similar?'

Iwata glanced at Yamada.

'Then we've got nothing.'

Yamada shrugged.

'Well, too late to turn back now anyway.'

They shot past a sign – GERO 170KM.

33. God Is Never in a Hurry

A weak sun had risen over Mount Ontake. The only sound in the forest came from snow falling from branches with soft thuds. Rocky bluffs to the east glistened in the dawn. Moss-strangled trees cowered below them, their branches withered in death. Pale scrub hunkered over the hills in supplication. Mist pressed low over the land. It was too cold for colour here.

Yamada led the way, following his compass. Iwata checked over his shoulder frequently. Both men trembled and wiped their streaming noses. They blew into their hands as they crossed black, dead fields. Seen from a distance, their clouds of breath formed a small train, huffing slowly across the land.

They had been trekking for the better part of two hours when they found the road they were looking for. The tarmac was brittle and cracked by weeds as tall as a man. Between the bush and snow, it was barely visible. The road wound through the deep forest, wide enough for just a single vehicle.

Yamada consulted an old map and held his compass over it while Iwata leant against a tree to catch his breath. He could still hear a ringing from the blow he took to the head from the Black Sun Killer on the roof of the nightclub. The cold painted his breath on the air, smiling faces forming in the white. His broken fingers creaked with pain.

'You OK?' Yamada asked, folding the map back into his pack.

Iwata nodded and they set off down the road. They followed it for another twenty minutes until it dipped through a cluster of pine trees.

They saw a concrete wall. It was around five metres high and looked like a prison perimeter. Though it was old and crumbling, there was no way over without a ladder. With nowhere to blow through, the snow had collected around the compound in large drifts. The main entrance was blocked by two thick doors, splayed in police tape.

Iwata and Yamada followed the boundary, stopping at a side entrance – a tall heavy-mesh gate secured with chains and padlocks. Yamada started climbing. Reaching the top, he swore and sucked blood from his thumb.

'Watch yourself here, Iwata.' He carefully swept clumps of snow from the top of the gate to reveal broken glass. Iwata grimaced as he grasped the frozen metal links. Able to use only one hand, he struggled up the gate. He made sure to heft himself over the top without touching the glass. Iwata couldn't afford any more injuries.

Hopping off the fence, he saw that he was standing at the back of a long, squat building. Double doors stood open, rusted and weathered, beyond which was a canteen. Melting snow poured through holes in the roof. Shards of sunlight pierced the walls. Chairs were upturned and tables lay on their sides. Iwata saw empty chicken coops and long-dead herb patches. A broken bucket rolled from side to side in the wind.

Yamada led the way through the canteen, wrapping his thumb in a handkerchief.

'You hurt yourself?'

'Almost fourteen years on the force.' He laughed. 'It's my first field injury.'

They left the canteen and saw the full size of the area now, a small theme park. More than two dozen buildings sat across from each other leading all the way up to the end of the compound, where a church-like building loomed.

Without a word, they separated, Yamada took the right-hand side, Iwata the left.

Brushing his way through an overgrown baseball diamond, Iwata came to a locked door. The padlock was rusted and flimsy and he broke it easily with his torch. Shunting the door open, he spread a beam of light across the room and saw that it had once been a classroom. Slime and moss had claimed the chalkboard, its lessons long forgotten. Children's drawings of suns and moons curled away from the wall. Detritus carpeted the floor where puddles hadn't collected. Clusters of small desks had formed.

At the far end, a desk larger than the others lay on its side. Above it, a framed photograph of what Iwata presumed to be Takashi Anzai hung on the wall. He was old with a patchy beard and large, tinted sunglasses. His mouth was too long and thin for such a narrow face. His eyes looked off to some distant concept, which had caused a slight smile.

The desk contained nothing of interest. Iwata left and headed for the next building. Passing through the tall weeds of the baseball diamond, he heard a loud noise and dropped out of sight.

Realizing he'd been spooked by Yamada breaking a lock, he swore and carried on to the next building. It was much larger than the first. Inside, rusted empty bunks lined the walls. A small mountain of rubble had formed from a collapsed roof.

The wind howled through but there was no movement. Iwata searched through boxes and small cabinets but found nothing other than abandoned personal effects – the objects deemed unnecessary, articles not remembered in the rush.

Iwata could make out families in these forgotten things –
children, single men, widows. They had all gone, never to
return.

Each box he found contained a thick copy of the same
book: *The Black Sun's Ultimate Truth*, by Takashi Anzai.

Iwata prised open wet pages to scan through the introduction. It spoke of a brave and exciting first step the first-time
reader was taking. By opening the book, readers were also
opening themselves up to a realization – that they were, like
anything else in this world, subject to the sun's pull. Not just
gravitationally, but also spiritually and universally. Unlike
conventional gods reliant on fantastical theological architec-
ture, Anzai was simply pointing up to the sun that would
watch over the reader for all the days of his or her life and
saying, '*There* is our divinity.' His message was simple: that
God would soon die and the 'real world' would be revealed.

*You, my dear friend, are holding a most precious opportunity in your
hands that should not be passed up.*

Iwata tossed the book away and climbed over the mound
of rubble, causing a small avalanche of concrete and dirty
snow. There was nothing at the far end of the room. The
next building Iwata came to was set some distance from the
others and much smaller. It had been erected sloppily, with
hasty brickwork. The door had been torn off at the hinges.
Evidently, the police had had some trouble gaining access.

Inside, there was no fitting for a bulb overhead. This space
had not been constructed for light. Along one wall, ten
refrigerators stood side by side, all of them old and rusting.
A slat for passing through food and removing waste had
been carved into their doors. Broken padlocks lay in coils of
rusted chains beneath them.

'A jail,' Iwata whispered.

He went on to search each building in turn, finding nothing more than the ruins of Anzai's lost civilization. Countless traces of the sect and its followers. But of Keiko Shimizu, he found nothing.

It was early afternoon by the time Iwata had cleared his half of the compound. He sat on the broken steps leading up to the church and, with ruined fingers, smoked his last cigarette.

Yamada emerged from his last building, his palms held out – *no luck*. He sat down next to Iwata and they shared the cigarette, each blowing into his hands while the other smoked. Yamada swept snow from his shoes.

'Next time we'll dress for the occasion, huh?'

Iwata chuckled out smoke, wincing at the pain in his skull.

'For a guy who's spent fourteen years in a basement reading up on lunatics, you have a sunny disposition.'

'That's what an endless supply of job satisfaction will do for you.'

Yamada handed back the cigarette. Iwata took a final drag and stubbed it out.

'Well. I found nothing on my side.'

'Nor I.' Yamada held up his sliced thumb to the sun. 'Shall we finish this?'

The two policemen stood and approached the doors of the church, which were secured by a thick chain with a heavy padlock. They made their way to the side of the building and found the fire exit propped open. It was chained from the inside, but there was enough space to squeeze through. They came up a sodden carpeted stairway leading into a gloomy expanse. The stench of urine and broken bottles that covered the floor made it clear that this place was used for shelter by the local homeless in warmer months. Corners were laced with cobwebs. The walls were decorated with graffiti and burn marks. Iwata spread his torchlight across the filthy pews and pigeons corkscrewed into panicked flight, making both men jump. Water dripped through cracks in the ceilings and lost snowflakes swirled in the air, illuminated by stray sunbeams. A gutted piano had been smashed up for firewood and burnt. They split up, taking one side of the church each. Halfway down the pews, Yamada called out.

'Iwata, look at this.'

He held up a handful of empty bullet casings and pointed to polka dot holes on the wall behind him.

'Looks like they didn't leave quietly.'

A few paces ahead, Iwata came to a portable generator hooked up to the mains. He pulled the starter cord three times until a loud sputtering resounded and the bare bulbs above lit up. At his feet, Iwata found a tape recorder. Picking it up, he dusted it off and set it on the small plinth it had fallen from. A framed picture of Anzai hung above it, its glass cracked. On a whim, he pressed play and the tape crackled into life at surprising volume. It was like no voice Iwata had heard before. It was loud and strong but not strained, musical but droning too.

'*Brothers and sisters, there is HARDLY ANYTHING that can be done properly that is done in a HURRY. A glass of wine, a stroll, a chat, a view, a fuck – ALL GOOD THINGS are done with time. Our GOD is NEVER in a hurry. He takes his time to make a baby, or a flower, or a dolphin. He is NEVER in a hurry.*' There was a long, hissing pause. '*Unless he is angry.*'

Now came terrified but excited applause.

'*I have heard rumours – RUMOURS – in this happy kingdom. I have heard that I am too old to lead my brothers and sisters any longer. I have heard that our days are NUMBERED. I have heard that you believe that the ignorant COME FOR US.*'

Iwata left the tape on and made his way towards a closed side door. Kicking a mound of dirt out of the way, he forced the handle.

'Well, my children, I must tell you . . . these rumours are true.'

Audible gasps.

Iwata was now standing in a small side office, the carpet almost completely covered in sodden paperwork. The room stank of pigeon shit. Two filing cabinets lay on their side. One half of the room was blackened from fire damage. A mound of files had been burnt in the corner.

'But FEAR NOT. Fear FORSAKES all that I have taught you. Have I not told you of this time? Have we not always known that these days would end? Yes, it is true, the ignorant COME for us. As sure as you hear my voice now, they COME FOR US. But come as they may, they will NEVER tarnish our TRUTH. No, children. The truth cannot be taken from us. FATHER will NOT allow it. Will HE allow it?'

The crowd screeched in disgust.

'Will HE allow it?'

A whole chorus of screaming NOs erupted. Anzai giggled now.

'Speak his name!'

The crowd screamed as one.

'TEZCATLIPOCA!'

'Speak his name!'

'TEZCATLIPOCA!'

'That's right, children. Lord of the Night, Lord of the Far. Lord of the Wind, Lord of the Darkness. His time looms. LOOMS. And no man can take what he has BESTOWED upon me. In turn, no man can take from you what I have GIVEN YOU. Remember always, soon the sun will turn black and die and will be replaced by his TRUE FORM. The Black Sun Tezcatlipoca will REIGN over this night world and the ignorant all around us will be ENGULFED. Their hearts RIPPED OUT leaving them BLIND.'

Squeals.

'But not you, my children. For YOU have followed me, your humble *father, in the ways of the LIGHT TO COME. You have followed me towards the ONLY salvation from the DARKNESS.'*

There was loud applause.

'In the years to come, long after me, this message will be clear and strong and a new people will rise up from our flesh. A new people and a new faith, with new tenets and new missions. I have given you many brothers and sisters and my essence will live on through them. I will always be there to lead you, now, and in the new world. But remember, my children . . .'

There was a long, painful silence. Those that couldn't bear it cried: *'Tell us! Tell us!'*

'Our god is NEVER in a hurry. And you ARE his creations. So, do not hurry about your tasks. LET the ignorant come. Remember that the time of the BLACK SUN draws close. Remember that the ignorant and their puppet systems can only touch you outwardly. Do not FEAR them. Accept them. For the DARKNESS will see to them. The darkness will ENVELOP them. And you will all walk FREE in the revelation.'

Yamada appeared in the doorway.

'You know, I'd never heard Anzai's voice before. It has a certain compelling quality about it, eh?'

'Why did he record that?'

'Probably to ensure there'd be enough people here to keep the cops busy when they showed up. Anzai fled long before the police raided this place. He ordered his men to fight to the death and the women and the children to poison themselves. Over fifty of them did.'

'He got away?'

'Anzai was found in Vietnam working as a church minister a year later.'

Yamada nodded to the scorch marks.

'Looks like they tried to destroy as much as they could.'

'But they used the wrong accelerant.' Iwata sniffed the

walls. 'See the burn marks? That fire took a long time to get going, which tells you they didn't use gasoline. Whatever they used would have been relatively easy to put out.'

'Let's just hope there's still some trace of Keiko Shimizu or her girl left here.'

They started on the filing cabinets, scanning personnel records. Though many were destroyed, there were still hundreds of files left. The information contained within ranged from basic data to extreme detail. Bank balances. Penis length. Criminal records. Secret fears, admissions and perversions were all recorded. Each file had a small Polaroid portrait. Young, old, male, female. Each face compliant, submissive, hopeful.

Iwata opened a file and read aloud.

'"Mr Junichi Ando, 206:F – during group session he admits to sexual contact with sister." Why would they record that?'

'Leverage. It would be framed as therapy through honesty, but with this kind of information, they could strong-arm sect members for huge "donations". They could also ensure members would never leave for fear of recriminations.'

Iwata tossed his file away and picked up another. They stretched their limbs and tried to keep warm as they worked through the afternoon.

It was almost dark when Yamada spoke.

'Iwata.' He looked up, his eyes wide. 'I think this is it.'

'You're sure?'

'Number 1137:H, Ms Keiko Shimizu. This is her.' He met Iwata's eyes. 'She *did* have a baby . . . Oh shit.'

'What is it?'

'The name of the little girl is Midori *Anzai*. I think she was the child of the cult leader, Iwata. They weren't married according to this file. She was probably a sex slave of some sort. Doesn't say why but it looks like she absconded from the camp and was then excommunicated. Keiko then returns for Midori and takes her from the compound several months later. "Kidnaps" her, it says here.'

'But if Anzai has banished Keiko, why let the child live here?'

'As the cult leader, I'm not sure how much contact Anzai would have had with the child. Children were everywhere in these camps. They were often separated from their mothers early on, forced on to other women, names changed – it would get so that nobody could remember whose child was whose. Perhaps Midori simply blended in this way. Either way, clearly Keiko loved her. She came back for her despite the severe risk.'

Iwata looked up through the ceiling at the cold purple sky. He remembered gazing at the road, waiting for his mother to come. *She'll come*, Kei had called.

'Iwata?'

'Yeah.'

'I was saying that after the abduction, Keiko and Midori now had to make it on their own. The outside world would have likely been a terrifying place for them. The compound might have been dangerous, but it was at least familiar. The outside world offered no protection, no friendly faces, no familiar infrastructure. By that stage, it's likely Keiko would have been assaulted often enough to have become desensitized to it. Perhaps she survived outside the cult by prostituting herself – possibly even the child too. It would have been an itinerant lifestyle, hand to mouth, until Keiko reached breaking point.'

'Couldn't she have gone back to her father in Nagasaki?'

'Estrangement from family is very common. Many of those affected by cults never really recover. Once you've had your mind rearranged, it's not a question of simply snapping back to normality. Plus who knows what kind of relationship they had.'

Iwata looked at the picture of Anzai on the wall. Beneath it, the symbol of the black sun was displayed.

'Pass me that.'

Yamada reached up and handed Iwata the framed photograph. It was half-burnt but the left side was clear enough. Takashi Anzai in black ceremonial robes. Next to him, a young man with a similar face and less ornate robes.

'That was his eldest son,' Yamada said. 'By all accounts the favourite – Akira Anzai.'

A muscular arm, from a third person, was draped around Akira's shoulder. The face had been obliterated by scorch marks but it was clear enough – a mask hung from this unseen person's hand. A mask Iwata had seen before. Iwata closed his eyes and recalled the words.

Hach k'as. Eek.

'Son of a bitch.' Iwata tapped the photograph. 'That's him. Whoever attacked me in Dogenzaka was wearing this mask. This is the killer.'

'This would have been Anzai's personal shaman. Not everything is known, but from what I've studied, we're essentially talking about somewhere between a personal bodyguard and most trusted ally. This man would have died for him.'

Iwata was reeling.

'I should have opened the door to you.'

'Focus.' Yamada put his hand on his shoulder. 'What do you want to do now?'

Iwata slapped himself in the face and nodded.

'Midori Anzai. We have to find her. She's in immense danger.'

'Then we need to go now.'

Iwata and Yamada left the church and returned to the wall. Crows had gathered at the top of the fence where Yamada had cut himself. They pecked at the bloody snow and broke the frozen silence with their caws.

34. On the Brink

The Isuzu Coupé was speeding through Tokyo's outskirts like a black pinball. Skyscrapers mushroomed. A dark limbo of thundery cloud pressed down on the skyline. Iwata's ankle throbbed from mashing the pedal but the car couldn't give him any more.

His phone rang.

'Hatanaka, be quick, my battery is low.'

'I've got him.'

'What do you mean, "him"?'

'I mean you need to get here *right now*. Video suite four. Ninth floor, Shibuya.'

'I'll be there soon. Don't let anybody else in that room. Do you understand?'

'Got it.'

'Hatanaka, you're really sure you have him?'

'I'm looking at his face right now.'

In the dank gloom of the TMPD Shibuya car park, Iwata switched off the engine. He took a breath. The dashboard clock showed 9.37 p.m.

'Yamada, do you have access codes for the central system?'

'I've hardly ever used them, but theoretically they should work.' He pulled at his moustache. '*Should*.'

'Can you access the system from your office?'

'No, I'll have to use one of the hot desks in Division One. Hopefully, nobody asks me what I'm doing up there.'

'Go now. You need to find Midori Anzai. Tonight. Find her, and bring her here.'

'I'll try my best.' Yamada nodded solemnly.

'Yoji, if you fail, she will die.'

They saw a group of uniformed cops enter the car park, laughing as they walked. When they had passed, Yamada got out of the car, head down, and made for the main stairs. Iwata waited a few seconds before heading in the other direction. At the elevator, he jabbed at the call button and checked over his shoulder. The cops were looking in his direction, talking among themselves.

The doors slid open and he stepped in. The posters hadn't changed since Iwata first entered this elevator, over two weeks ago.

1. STATE WHAT HAPPENED.
   – 'THERE IS A ROBBER.' = 'DOROBO DESU.'
   – 'THERE WAS A TRAFFIC ACCIDENT.' = 'KOTSU JIKO DESU.'
2. STATE YOUR LOCATION.
3. STATE YOUR NAME & ADDRESS.

Iwata closed his eyes. He knew he was close. But he also knew time was running out.

The doors opened. The ninth floor was a warehouse of tall racks holding endless bags of evidence. Large blue plastic trays contained items yet to be processed – bloodstained chairs, bedsheets blackened from fire and underwear to be swabbed for semen and pubic hair. All of it was to be bagged and tagged, a collection of criminal curios. The corridor narrowed, with large climate-controlled laboratories on both sides. Toxicologists and forensic investigators looked through microscopes and jotted down numbers dispassionately. It was a production line of case-building.

At the back of the floor was Electronic Evidence. Video suite four was a soundproofed cubicle hidden by a vending machine. Hatanaka was anxiously peering through the blinds. Seeing Iwata, he opened the door, relief spreading across his face. He let his superior in and locked the door. Then he sat down in front of a large computer monitor and cracked his knuckles as Iwata pulled over a spare chair.

'You ready, boss?'

'Play.'

The footage had been paused. It showed the pedestrian walkway on Rainbow Bridge. Hatanaka pointed to the corner of the screen. The timestamp showed 17 February at 00:35.

'So?'

Hatanaka hit the space bar on the keyboard and the CCTV footage began to play. A vehicle, dark in colour, stopped on the hard shoulder of the bridge. The footage wasn't crystal clear but there was no mistaking Hideo Akashi as he got out of the car. He hopped over the barrier and walked along the footpath. He passed nobody as he made his way, unhurried, along the path. After eleven minutes, he reached the first support tower. Inside, there were two doors. One for the elevator, the other a maintenance door. Akashi looked around. He picked up a fire extinguisher and broke the door down.

'After that,' Hatanaka said, 'he's not seen again.'

He pressed fast forward. The tape sped up, showing a security guard discovering the broken door. This sparked a flurry of activity, until finally the police arrived. The tape ended around twenty-four hours after Akashi jumped. Iwata looked at Hatanaka impatiently.

'We know all this. Hatanaka, you said you had him.'

Hatanaka held up a finger and then pressed fast rewind. The tape shot back to 14 February at 03:00.

'OK, we're now about seventy hours *before* Akashi jumped. Keep watching.'

The same vehicle appeared on the bridge. Again, Hideo Akashi got out of the car.

This time, he was not alone.

Another man got out of the car.

He was a wearing a black hood.

He was tall.

'Iwata, it's him. *This* is the Black Sun Killer.'

'How . . . ?'

'Just watch. He tries to keep his face hidden but I'll zoom.'

'Who –'

'*Watch.*'

When the man in the hood looked up to screen for a split second, Hatanaka hit pause.

And there it was, clear as day.

Ten minutes later, there came a violent knocking on the door of video suite four. Iwata was still sitting in his seat, stunned. But he had seen what he needed to see. The knocking at the door grew more intense.

'Who is it?' Hatanaka whispered.

'Kid, whatever happens, you keep hold of this tape, you understand? I have to go but I'll be calling you as soon as I can. Are you with me?'

'I'm with you, boss.'

Iwata opened the blinds. Horibe's angry face came into view.

'What do you want?'

Horibe glanced at Hatanaka, then back to Iwata.

'What the fuck is going on in here?'

Iwata opened the door and stood in front of Horibe, blocking his view.

'You already know I don't enjoy repeating myself, Horibe. What do you want?'

'*You*, actually. Fujimura wants a little chat. I'm headed that way. Shall we go together?'

'Lead the way.'

Iwata heard the door lock behind him and he followed Horibe towards the elevator. As the doors slid shut, Iwata braced himself but Horibe kept his hands in his pockets and said nothing. They ascended to the twelfth floor in total silence.

The doors opened and the usual hubbub of Division One washed in. Iwata got out alone, Horibe grinning at him as the doors slid shut. Yamada was sitting in the corner, cradling a telephone, face glued to a terminal. They made no eye contact. Heading for Fujimura's office at the end of the floor, Iwata ignored the curious looks.

Without knocking, he entered and sat across from the elderly superintendent. Fujimura linked his twig-like fingers together and smiled. He was a small, enfeebled man, well into his seventies. Dark purple splotches had hardened on his cranium like fossils and his grey moustache quivered involuntarily as he regarded his subordinate.

'Kosuke *Iwata*.' He smiled. 'Finally, we meet. Sit, please.'

'Sir.'

'Tell me something, Inspector. How are you doing?'

'Fine. Horibe said you wanted to talk to me.'

'You want to cut to the heart of the matter – I appreciate that.' Fujimura indicated the clock behind him. 'Time is of the essence, after all.'

Iwata said nothing.

'How do you find working with Assistant Inspector Sakai?'

'We're not currently working together.'

'She's assigned to assist Inspector Moroto, I realize. But what's she up to?'

'I don't follow.'

'Where is she *going*, Inspector Iwata? She's not clocking in. She's not doing her paperwork. She's not doing her job. She's doing something *else* with her time. So. What do you know?'

Iwata shifted in his seat.

'I'm not sure what I'm being asked, sir. But it seems to me that *all* Sakai does is her job. Whether that's in this building or not is irrelevant.'

'Then tell me, what do you think of her?'

'I respect her very much. She's a talented investigator.'

'Quite. And outside of work? You're friends?'

A quivering smile hid itself in Fujimura's little moustache. Iwata began to tap his foot.

'Why do you ask, sir?'

'There's been a lot of talk in this department surrounding you, Sakai and your case. I'm sure that's no surprise.'

'Nor is it a concern.'

'Mm, that's good. Gossip doesn't concern me, either.'

Fujimura regarded Iwata in silence. Behind him the city glimmered in the rain.

'Forgive me, sir. Why did you summon me here?'

'For your opinion.'

'On?'

'Yourself. Inspector Moroto regards you as a rogue officer. He tells me that you are unfit for duty. Of course, your forthcoming disciplinary hearing attests to that. What is your view?'

'With respect, Moroto can tell you whatever he pleases. I'm not the cop that charged an innocent man with murder for the sake of convenience.'

'That was unfortunate. But off-topic . . .'

Fujimura stood up, with some difficulty, and looked out of the window at the city. Iwata wondered if he saw order down there. He could see only shadow these days.

Too many places to hide.

'My problem, Inspector, is not what Moroto says about you. My problem is receiving complaints from Setagaya PD about misappropriation of resources. Notification from the Chinese authorities about illegal investigations in Hong Kong coming out of Division One. Less than favourable headlines in national newspapers regarding the work of my department. My problem, Inspector, is knowing that precious funds are being thrown at thirty men on overtime to guard a housewife just because, if I understand this correctly, she once appeared in a photograph.'

Fujimura dropped the blinds and turned to face Iwata's back.

'You asked me why I called you here. I called you here because I want to know why I should bother with a hearing at all. I want to know why I shouldn't just take the case away from you this instant, inexplicably open as it still is, and have you immediately investigated. What is your view?'

Iwata laughed and answered over his shoulder without looking at the old man.

'I'm not interested in bravado, Fujimura. You would have done this already if you were going to do it. Either way, I'm on the brink of finding the killer. Something your entire Division One cannot do.'

Fujimura wheezed out laughter and dropped himself back into his chair.

'I can see why Shindo has a soft spot for you, son. Honestly, I can. Unfortunately, I don't share your confidence.'

'I know a dead Masaharu Ezawa is the perfect patsy for

the Kaneshiro case. But there are too many other bodies left to explain. Sooner or later, the press will get a hold of that fact. They're riding us hard enough as it is. Imagine what will happen if the Black Sun Killer strikes again. The papers will have a field day, whether I've been sacked or not.'

'Inspector, are you making threats?'

'I'm talking in realistic terms.'

Fujimura chuckled, almost admiringly.

'On the brink, eh? What evidence do you have?'

'With respect, I'll divulge that information after my disciplinary review.'

'You're refusing me?'

'I'm absolutely refusing you.'

Fujimura's moustache quivered and his small face turned pink.

'Iwata, the only reason your transfer was approved is because we were a man down after Inspector Akashi's death. You're a chimp in a raincoat, boy. Now, I'm going to let you have your forty-eight hours because it would take just as long to effect your dismissal. But understand me. You will not survive your disciplinary. This is the end of any kind of career for you in law enforcement. And once you're out, I'm going to look at criminal proceedings, either here, or in Hong Kong.'

'Is that why you summoned me?'

'I just wanted to tell you personally. Man to man.'

Iwata stood.

'Then you wasted my time.'

At the door, he turned back to look at the superintendent, the highest power in Division One. Fujimura held life and death in his frail hands. He could click his fingers and Tokyo would fall in line. But he was, in the end, just another old man sitting behind a big desk.

Iwata could find no words to change that.

The door slammed shut and Chief Superintendent Fujimura was left alone. The old man glanced at the clock and gave a shuddering sigh.

'Time to go.'

Beneath Rainbow Bridge, in the rotten yellow light of the Shibaura docks, Fujimura looked over his shoulder again. He had been waiting a long time. He stood in the usual place, behind the warehouse farthest from the street. Spring was due but the night still held a bitter chill. The old man stared at the restless black waters until an angry wind made him blink away tears.

From the shadows between rusting sea containers, a figure emerged. Fujimura knew at once who it was. He tried not to cower as the man stood before him – almost twice his height. The man wore a black hood over his head, his face covered by a mask. His bright eyes swept over the docks for a long time. Then he spoke.

'*Why . . . are you . . . here?*'

'It's this fucking Iwata. He's looking into things he shouldn't be.'

'*Things . . .*'

The man repeated the word as though it were a novel discovery. The voice unsettled Fujimura so deeply, he struggled not to tremble visibly.

'Yes. Things like Takara Matsuu. And not only that. He says he's close to finding you.'

'*Close.*' The man looked up at the bridge, glowing green across the bay. '*Yes . . . close.*'

'I just thought I should warn you.'

The tall man turned his back on Fujimura.

'There's something else. Iwata and Sakai aren't working

369

together any more . . . I think she's alone. I think she's conducting her own investigation. It could be to do with you.'

'*Sakai*,' he whispered, no longer speaking to Fujimura.

The man unhurriedly slipped out of sight. Fujimura, wheezing in the cold, waited a long time to make sure that he was no longer needed before he left.

For the second time in twenty-four hours, Iwata was speeding on the expressway. His whole body pulsed and fear rose up his throat like bile. Within a few minutes of returning to the video suite, Iwata had called Shindo down to the ninth floor and played him the footage from Rainbow Bridge. Blinking away his shock, Shindo had said he would contact a judge he trusted to put together the arrest warrant for the man they now believed to be the Black Sun Killer.

This is when Iwata's phone had rung.

Seeing the dialling code had come from rural Nagano, he had started to apologize for the lateness of his payments to the Nakamura Institute.

No, sir. It's about your wife. She's gone.

It was 2.45 a.m. when Iwata reached the outskirts of town. He screeched around corners, shooting past the derelict factories and abandoned shops, then up into the Nojiri Hills. At the gates of the institute, two nurses were already waiting for him.

'What happened?'

'Mr Iwata, it's all right. We've found her.'

He pushed past the nurses, through the disinfected corridors once again, out into the darkened garden. The papier-mâché flamingos stared on with their yellow eyes, the elephants' trunks thrown back in delight.

The lights of the city are so pretty.

'Cleo!'

She was slumped on a sun bed, her gown undone. Her nightshirt beneath was soaked red. Iwata ripped the gown open and thrust up the nightshirt to see the wound.

I'm happy with you. Please let me hear.

'Mr Iwata.' One nurse tried to restrain him, the other went for help.

'Mr Iwata, she's fine!'

Those words of love from you.

There was no wound. Just Cleo's pale, shrunken breasts, her small ribs and a message. In red marker pen, someone had written words across her chest:

SEE YOU SOON INSPECTOR

Iwata wheeled around and bellowed at the nurse.

'*Who did this?*'

Flinching, she took a step back.

'W-we don't know. Her door was open and she was gone. We found her here shortly after we called you.'

Iwata clasped his skull with his hands, his crooked fingers screaming at him again. He looked down at his broken wife. Her eyes were half open and she was drooling from one side of her mouth. He saw her C-section scar and looked away, needing to vomit, needing to drink.

The nurse put a tentative hand on his shoulder.

'Are you all right?'

'Did anyone come to visit her today?'

'Yes. A tall man. He didn't give his name. He had a badge, he said he was your friend.'

Iwata looked up at the sky and understood now.

'It was them.' His voice was quiet. 'They did it to waste my time.'

Iwata sat down on the damp grass next to Cleo. He reached

up and took her small, limp hand and ordered himself not to cry. Exhaustion, pain and helplessness again. For Iwata, pain would never be new, it would always be there, waiting to be reborn.

He looked at Cleo, her body slowly shrinking and dying, but her mind already dead to the fact – dead to everything. He envied her and resented her. Not just for what she had done to him, but for her perfect abandonment. For Cleo, there was only the bliss of nothingness. The ecstasy of surrender. The perfection of the abyss. No more suffering. No more sacrifice. No more reasons.

Iwata's head was swimming, the feeling of a falling dream. He pressed his eyes shut hard, realizing that even this hurt. He floundered, grasping desperately for a reason to stand. A reason to defy them. A reason to not take out his SIG and end it all there, on that very lawn. And then an image took Iwata like a small hand grasping his. He saw little Hana Kaneshiro and slipped his hand into his shirt to feel the wound between his ribs. He needed that pain. He needed it all.

Because that's what we do. That's police . . .

Iwata stood and wiped away a tear with a sleeve.

'Please, take my wife back to her room.'

Iwata left, trying not to look back at Cleo as the nurses prepared her to be moved. He got back into the Isuzu and saw that the tank was almost empty. He drove well clear of the town before he stopped to fill up. Iwata tried to steady his breathing. He listened to the pumps hum as his old car greedily swallowed down its juice. It was a warm, familiar noise. He closed his eyes and felt himself falling asleep. In just a few seconds he would be gone.

Iwata hurried over to the vending machine and drank two energy drinks in a row. Slapping himself in the face, he started the car, shouting to himself as loudly as he could.

'He is happiest, be he king or peasant, who finds peace in his home!'

He flicked on the turret light and was about to floor the accelerator when he looked down. His phone was ringing.

'Yeah?' Iwata shouted over the siren. 'Shindo, I can't hear you.'

'It's Sakai,' he said, his voice breaking. 'It's about Sakai.'

35. Introductions

At 5.50 a.m., a bone-weary Iwata clambered out of the Isuzu and entered the Medical Examiner's Office in Bunkyō. Doctor Eguchi was standing at the entrance, smoking a lonely cigarette, looking up at the branches above her. She nodded to Iwata but said nothing.

I'm happy with you.

Inside the building, Iwata paused to get his breath back several times. His balance was fragile as he stepped out of the elevator.

It's Sakai.

Iwata shook his head, unable to accept it. He had already relented so many times to cobble his theory together. He had bled for it. He couldn't be wrong again.

Please let me hear. Those words of love from you.

The elevator doors slid open on the long corridor leading to the morgue. Only one of the autopsy rooms had its lights on. Iwata breathed in then exhaled before entering.

The Lord is my light and my salvation.

Whom shall I fear?

Sakai's dead body occupied one of the four autopsy tables. Shindo was on his knees, sobbing. Seeing Iwata, he clambered to his feet and left the room.

In death, Sakai's face had lost none of its cold beauty. If anything, it was sharper, free of the distortion of expression. Cuts and bruises around her face and neck showed that she had died fighting. Iwata closed his eyes and felt the echo of the Black Sun Killer's blows, the raw power he had wielded over him. Sakai wouldn't have stood a chance. Numbly, Iwata pulled back the sheet to see her ravaged body. The cavity beneath her ribcage gaped open. He knew the heart was gone.

'Why you?'

He brushed the hair out of her face and was about to cover her when he saw that she gripped something in her left hand. Iwata snapped on a rubber glove and eased her fingers open. It was a small black wallet. He knew what it contained because he had one too. He opened it carefully.

SAKAI, NORIKO – ASSISTANT INSPECTOR, DIVISION ONE

In the photo, a young Sakai, not quite smiling, but brimming with defiant hope. Blood had leaked around the edges of the photo. He had seen her flash it dozens of times. But he had never noticed the seal on the corner of her photo. The seal of the issuing police station was from Nagasaki.

Iwata thought back to their first day in the car. She had said Kanazawa.

That's where you're from?

I got my badge there.

Sakai had lied to him reflexively.

He put the wallet back carefully and, as he closed her fingers, it all fell into place.

He sagged against the counter, shaking his head.

Looking at Sakai's pale face, he felt a wave of sad relief.

'So that's who you are,' Iwata whispered. He finally understood. But too late. 'Forgive me, Noriko.'

He bowed deeply before her, forty-five degrees, and held it for a long time. Then he left the room. As he stepped into the corridor, Shindo spun him by the shoulder and punched him hard in the face. Slumping back against the wall, Iwata spat out blood.

'You hit hard.'

Shindo stepped over him, his eyes red, his voice uncertain.

'Was it you?'

'What?'

'*Was it you?*'

'Shindo, you can hit me, but you're not making any sense.'

'They're saying you're a suspect.'

'What?'

'Your DNA was found at Sakai's apartment. You were seen leaving.'

Iwata thought back to Fujimura's office.

And outside of work? You're friends, are you not?

'Son of a bitch.'

'Were you there?'

'I was there, but this is ridiculous. That must be obvious. Come on, you know it.'

Shindo began to pace.

'Fuck, I shouldn't be telling you this . . . Fujimura is pushing to arrest you as a suspect in Sakai's murder. You don't have long.' He punched the wall, a loud, whooshing echo down the corridor. 'You should have looked after her!'

'Shindo, you know as well as I do, there was no looking after Sakai.'

The older man slumped back against the wall next to Iwata, his anger drained. There were tears in his eyes.

'I feel old,' he said.

Iwata clutched his numb jaw and felt it hardening. 'It was the Black Sun Killer.'

'Yeah, I know.' He sighed. 'Which is why I spoke to my judge. Your arrest warrant for Yoshi Tachibana will be issued tomorrow at midday. But we're going to have to get this right or we won't catch him.'

Iwata nodded.

'You're a good man, Shindo.'

'No. I'm not. Neither are you.'

Iwata struggled to his feet. He patted the shoulder of his superior, who looked at the floor with lost eyes. There was nothing else to say.

As Kosuke Iwata left the building, he stepped into sunlight. Eguchi flicked ash in his direction, still whistling 'Greensleeves'.

'You should get some rest, Inspector. I don't want to see you back here in a bag.'

Iwata was too tired to respond. He drove to his apartment slowly, almost falling asleep at the wheel several times. When he finally arrived home, he collapsed on his futon. He was gone before his head hit the pillow.

Iwata opened the curtains to an unremarkable, chilly dawn. The sky was grey with a pale yellow fringe where it met the horizon. He made coffee and put on Glenn Gould's *Goldberg Variations*, listening only to Aria da capo. When it was over, he washed out his cup and left his apartment.

At a few minutes past 1 p.m., two squad cars stopped outside the Green Gardens Community. Iwata, Hatanaka and Yamada, along with three uniformed police officers, approached the Tachibanas' home. There were few neighbours in sight. A weary Yoshi Tachibana opened the door. He was accustomed to police by this stage but something was different this time. He saw that now.

'What is this?'

One of the uniformed cops applied an arm lock, slamming him into the door. Another snapped cuffs on him and gripped him by the nape of the neck.

'W-what are you doing?'

Iwata held up the warrant and spoke in a slow, loud voice.

'Yoshi Tachibana, I'm arresting you, under Article 199 of the Penal Code, on the charge of multiple homicide. You are not obliged to speak at this point, but anything you do say may be used in court against you, thus I urge you to exercise caution. Do you understand?'

Tachibana's face blanched.

'What is this, Iwata? What the *fuck* are you doing?'

With a wave of his hand, Iwata gestured for Tachibana to be taken away to the waiting car.

Yumi was now at the front door.

'Where's my husband?'

Before she could become hysterical, Yamada led her back inside and closed the door.

Hatanaka handed Iwata a cigarette and turned away from the wind to light up. 'How do you think she'll take it?'

'Not very well,' Iwata replied.

They watched the squad car pull away. Tachibana was in shock in the back seat.

'So what now? What do you need?'

Iwata shook his head. 'Today's my last day, Hatanaka. Time's up. I'm finished. Go home.'

The younger man looked down at the floor, disappointed.

Iwata slapped him on the back.

'Come on, kid. You did good work, I mean that. I'm going to ask Shindo to put in a word for you. Hopefully my name won't smear yours.'

Hatanaka shook his head.

'It was an honour to work with you, Inspector.'

They shook hands and Iwata turned away.

After a few paces, Hatanaka called after him.

'Boss!'

'What?'

'Your mandate doesn't expire until midnight, right?'

'So?'

'There's a café across the street from Odaiba-kaihinkōen Station. I'll wait there if you need me. You know, just in case.'

'Hatanaka —'

'Just *call me* if anything comes up. Life takes turns.'

Iwata nodded and the younger man smiled.

There were no uniformed cops in sight and life in Green Gardens had, on the surface, returned to normal. As Iwata walked back to the Isuzu, he tried not to glance up at the nearby rooftops. Though there was no sign of it, he knew the sniper squad of the Tokushu Sakusen Gun Unit would be in place. He got into the car and adjusted his rear-view mirror to see if there was any movement on the rooftops, anything that might spook the killer.

He saw nothing.

Your move.

Shindo was in the back seat, chewing his nails, trying to act naturally.

'How many are up there?' he asked.

'Eleven, I think. They have every angle of approach covered. Six is the designated shooter.'

'I don't see shit.'

'That's the point, Shindo.'

'If we're wrong about this then I hope you've got some special talent to fall back on cos police work is out.'

Iwata laughed.

'What did you tell your judge?'

'Exactly what we agreed. That Yoshi Tachibana killed the Kaneshiro family to facilitate the Vivus project in Setagaya.

379

As a freelance architect in financial turmoil, his career and the well-being of his wife and unborn child depended on it. The family was his only obstacle. After killing them, he gave the killings a ritualistic slant to lead suspicion away from him.'

Iwata nodded.

'That's good, go on.'

'Next, he needed Ohba's wife dead. Mr Ohba had originally signed off on the project until Kaneshiro's lawyer managed to secure a ruling against it. When Ohba died, the green light was left in the limbo of Mrs Ohba's study. Yoshi couldn't afford for there to be any witnesses, so he killed her too. With the family gone and the Ohba permit magically recovered, Yoshi's contracts with Vivus were renewed.'

Iwata chewed his lips.

'It won't take long for this to melt, Shindo.'

'No, it won't. My judge did, however, ask about Akashi's connection to the case. He seemed concerned about his original handling before it was given over to you.'

Iwata glanced at Shindo.

'What did you say?'

'I said that Akashi was battling with depression and stress. The only good thing in his life was Yumi, even though she was now his ex-wife. I told the judge that it seemed clear to me that a man like Hideo Akashi, who had nothing to lose anyway, would have rather died than have to investigate her current husband. After all, he would have ruined her life by arresting Yoshi. Not to mention, there's a baby on the way.'

Iwata started the engine.

'This sounds like total bullshit.'

'My judge signed it today. Whether we go to jail for it tomorrow is another matter.'

Iwata kept his eyes on the Tachibanas' door. There was no

movement, no change, nothing out of the ordinary. Shindo scanned the windows above. The Black Sun Killer could have been behind any one of them. Or he could be half a world away.

'You think he saw our little charade?'

'I think he's watching,' Iwata replied.

'And you're sure about leaving Yamada there?'

'Yamada's idea. He made a good point about it looking more natural this way if we follow standard procedure. The killer might become suspicious otherwise.'

'All right. We better head back to HQ and make sure Yoshi hasn't shat his pants.'

'I'll explain it to him, you handle the lawyer.'

Iwata pulled away from the kerb, towards TMPD Shibuya. He took one last look at the front door.

Please God, let him take the bait.

A tall, hooded figure was crouching down in the filth of the sewer, one hand holding a flaming torch out in front of his body. He spoke to himself as he searched the dark tunnels. Tied around his shoulders, a squirming sack – terrified screeching came from inside.

'*O Master, O Lord, O Lord of the New, of Night, of Darkness – in what manner shall I act for thee?*'

The flame quivered in the darkness, a river of discharge at his feet. His left hand gripped the obsidian blade. His tongue flicked in and out of the ancient, yellowed teeth of the shaman's mask. His penis jutted up hard against the filthy rags that he wore.

'*I'm sorry, I'm sorry, ma'taali'teeni', ma'taali'teeni'. Soon, soon, soon, soon, soon.*'

The shaman was shaking with anticipation, quaking with terror.

'*There you are. Yes, yes, yes.*'

He held the flame close to the slimy bricks. There was the chalk marking on the wall. Looking up, he saw the rusted rungs. He began to climb.

'*For I am blind, I am deaf, I am an imbecile, and in excrement, in filth hath my lifetime been . . . perhaps thou mistaketh me for another; perhaps thou seekest another in my stead.*'

The shaman had reached the top of the ladder. He paused for breath, as though he were about to dive into deep water. He tossed away the torch, took out a key from his rags, then stabbed it into the manhole cover. In seconds, he had the cover free.

'*Titlacauan – we are his slaves. Ipalnemani – he by whom we live. Necoc Yaotl – enemy of both sides. You are the Lord of the Darkness. The Lord of the Night. Tezcatlipoca, O my Lord, I will nourish you. O Lord, I will nourish you. Allow me to serve you, allow me to nourish you. Allow me to cleanse this earth for your return. I beg of you, do not darken the skies. I will pay you, Lord.*'

The shaman clambered into the daylight and stood directly beneath the Tachibanas' balcony.

Two hundred metres away, on the rooftop of a self-storage warehouse, Sniper No. 6 immediately reported the movement. He described the appearance, the weapon and the location of the shaman as he emerged from the sewer. As he began to climb the drainpipe, No. 6's radio flickered into life.

'Six, copy?'

'Copy.'

'Target endorsed. You are clear for the shot.'

Sniper No. 6 checked his watch, as he always did.

Time of death will be 2.46 p.m.

He swallowed the shaman with the crosshairs of his M24 rifle and winked at death. With expert steadiness, he froze over the head. In the next second, it would be pierced by a 175-grain round and the target would be dead. No. 6 began to squeeze his trigger, anticipating the bullet's crack, but it was a different sound he heard.

A metal churning.

Then a monumental convulsion threw him off his feet and the earth bellowed into life.

Radio traffic began roaring on every channel.

'Earthquake! Earthquake!'

No. 6 tried to get to his feet but it was impossible – this quake was like nothing he had ever known before. Metal scaffolding above began to come loose. The sniper glanced across the street.

The target was gone.

There was only a large bullet hole in the concrete a metre away from the drainpipe. Fumbling with his radio, No. 6 tried to get the message across.

'Negative kill,' he gasped. 'Repeat, negative kill.'

Nobody was listening to him any more. Wood was ripping. Metal was screaming. The floor was collapsing. The scaffolding was crashing down on them. He looked up and saw it come free.

Time of death.

After the longest six minutes anyone could remember, the Tōhoku earthquake finally ended. From beneath a desk, Iwata crawled out. The lights were off and back-up power had failed. The TMPD office was a bedlam of papers and overturned furniture.

Iwata, one of the few people to not be open-mouthed in shock, picked up the nearest phone and dialled Yamada's number. The network was blocked. He dialled for the Tachibanas with the same result.

'Fuck!'

He ran towards Shindo's office, hurdling fallen chairs and pushing people out of the way. He kicked the door open.

'Shindo! The plan is fucked! The sniper missed his shot, he's *there*!'

From beneath a fallen filing cabinet, Shindo groaned.

'I think my arm is broken.'

Iwata swore and raced for the emergency exit stairway. He was heading for the car park.

36. Alone Together

Iwata screeched out of the car park and up on to street level but immediately killed the engine.

It was as though he had just driven into a news report from a war zone. The road was ripped in half. The air was thick with white dust and carried the smell of far-off burning. The sky above was billowing black. Loose chunks of concrete, the size of family refrigerators, fell from above. Telephone poles had collapsed. Windows had shattered.

Iwata got out of the car, his foot sinking in the liquefied tarmac. He clambered up on the bonnet and squinted into the distance. All the traffic lights had died. No vehicles were moving. Fearing aftershocks, many were abandoning their cars in the rush to get away from tall buildings.

Chaos had flooded through Tokyo.

Iwata was ten kilometres from the Tachibanas' house. Ordinarily, it would have been a fifteen-minute drive in good traffic, but driving was now an impossibility. Even running would be difficult, in his condition. He figured it for a two-hour walk. Taking out his phone, he tried to dial Yumi's number but the mobile network was jammed.

'Fuck!'

He had chosen to explain the ruse to Yoshi Tachibana in person, never doubting the sniper unit's ability to protect Yumi and her unborn child. But he hadn't factored in an act of God. Now the Black Sun Killer would slaughter them all and there was nothing he could do.

No man was smart enough to account for dumb luck.

Iwata put his hands on his head and bellowed.

When he had nothing left, he slumped down on the floor.

A man in greasy overalls ran past. Iwata saw the embroidered logo on the back as he ran towards the shop across the street. It was a snake's head over a chequered flag, beneath which were the words: RATTLESNAKE MOTORCYCLES.

Iwata pulled himself up from the floor and ran after the man. At the entrance to the shop, he caught him by the shoulder and thrust his police ID into his face.

'Need a bike.'

The man blinked and Iwata shook him hard.

'A bike! *Now!*'

'W-we just do parts, some repairs . . .'

Iwata pointed to the vintage motorbike in the window. The sign below it read: 1980 TRIUMPH BONNEVILLE – ¥800,000.

'Is the tank full?'

'Full enough for test rides but –'

Iwata was already marching the bike off the stand, out on to the road. He flipped the kill switch into position, turned the key and hit the start button. He gave the throttle two slight twists to get fuel into the cylinders and the bike lurched forward, picking up speed fast. In seconds, Iwata was hurtling through quake-shocked Tokyo. The Triumph weighed just a few hundred kilograms yet the power it generated was incredible. He smelled the road, the exhaust and the thick dust in the air. No window frame obscured his view of the broken city.

Iwata, sailing through fire and destruction, was completely connected to it all. A numb silence reigned over Tokyo, a child cowering before its furious parent. And Iwata was racing towards the Black Sun Killer, towards death itself, feeling nothing but a quiet relief. Perhaps it was this understanding of the end that sharpened his senses. As Rainbow Bridge loomed into view, Iwata felt a clear readiness.

By the time Iwata had reached Green Gardens Community, the Triumph had begun to sputter, it didn't have much left. All around him, Odaiba was ablaze. A thick canopy of black smoke pressed down low. Metal creaked. People in the street crouched down, faces blank. Car alarms blared in the distance.

Iwata approached the main gate and drew his gun. It was 3.05 p.m., some twenty minutes since the sniper had missed his shot. He scanned the rooftops. Across the street, the warehouse where the sniper unit had been positioned was simply no longer there. It took Iwata a moment to realize that it was now just rubble, dust and smoke. Nothing moved. Only Yamada and one uniformed cop were inside the house.

Iwata reached the front door. To his surprise it was still shut. He closed his eyes for a moment and tried to clear his mind.

'The Lord is the strength of my life. Of whom shall I be afraid?'

He turned the door handle and it quietly relented. Stepping into the gloom, Iwata instantly smelled copal. His stomach lurched and his knees became weak.

You're a fucking coward, Iwata. You won't ever outrun that.

'When my father and my mother forsake me, then the Lord will take me up . . .'

Iwata forced himself up the stairs.

'Teach me Thy way O Lord, and lead me in a plain path because of mine enemies. Deliver me not over unto the will of mine enemies for false witnesses are risen up against me, and such as breathe out cruelty.'

Iwata heard a scream. He quickened his pace. The SIG

weighed him down as though he were holding an anvil out in front.

'I had fainted unless I had believed to see the goodness of the Lord in the land of the living.'

Iwata wiped sweat out of one eye and squinted through the dusty darkness. He leant down against the stairs and crawled the rest of the way up. On the last stair, he poked his head over.

Another scream and a blur.

But no impact.

Opening his eyes, Iwata saw a large turkey strutting around the carpet. Two other birds had been slaughtered. Their black eyes shone like valueless stones. Blood and black feathers were strewn around the room.

Trembling, Iwata got to his feet and wondered if he had shouted out. He listened for any sounds but the apartment was silent again. Through the copal, he could smell gun smoke now.

Iwata followed the smell and found Yamada lying on the floor of the kitchenette, his eyes closed. Blood oozed from a gash to the back of the head. Iwata felt around his body but found no other injuries. He put his fingers under Yamada's nose and felt faint breathing but there was no time for relief. Looking across the room, Iwata saw that the uniformed cop had been eviscerated, his entrails pink snakes trying to slither out of his stomach. The eyes were blank, the expression slightly concerned. Next to the body, the balcony door was wide open.

Iwata started up the stairs, fear clouding everything now, his legs slick with sweat. Every one of his senses squealed with the purity of human fear – its stench, its rate, its vitality. Every muscle quivered with focus.

'Wait on the Lord. Be of good courage and He shall strengthen thine heart.'

Iwata reached the top of the stairs and heard hissing. The bathroom was empty though the shower was on. A stream of urine led from the bathroom, into the corridor, towards the bedroom.

Iwata began to creep towards it, whispering words without knowing why.

'The lights of the city are so pretty . . . I'm happy with you . . . Please let me hear . . . Those words of love from you . . .'

The bedroom door was closed. He wiped away tears as he stood before it now, his heart flapping like a dying bird.

Let us not fear the bear.

Iwata smashed the door open with his shoulder, immediately yelling out in pain and losing his balance. He saw movement on the left of the room – the skull mask and the glinting black blade raised overhead. Iwata fired twice – then realized that his shots had cracked the wall mirror opposite his target. The shaman was already bounding towards him. He was huge, naked and covered in soot.

The rattle of the decorative bones pronounced each movement, turkey feathers adorned his chest and blood dripped from his black blade.

Thud, thud, thud.

He moved in a terrible, unnatural way, like film that had been speeded up and then slowed down.

Iwata fired three times.

Miss.

Miss.

Hit.

The shaman roared and jerked sideways, losing all balance. He fell across the mattress, rolled and landed on the other side of the bed. Iwata aimed his gun over the mattress and fired blind.

Silence. Pounding. Gasping.

Yumi was spreadeagled on the floor, encircled by candles and feathers. She was not moving. Eyes fixed on the bed, Iwata crawled over to her. Her bare skin was covered in blood but she had no wounds that he could see. The black sun symbol had been drawn on her massive belly. Her eyes were closed and her face was expressionless.

'Yumi, it's me. Are you all right?'

He touched her shoulder and her face twisted. She began to sob. Iwata saw the small tablets strewn around her.

'You're tripping, Yumi. Don't worry. Just don't move.'

Iwata struggled up to his feet. Sweat poured down his face, stinging his eyes. His hand shook violently. He was struggling to breathe.

'Hideo Akashi,' Iwata shouted, grasping for authority. 'I'm arresting you for murder. The house is surrounded. Give up your weapon and you will not be harmed.'

Deep laughter bubbled up from behind the bed.

'*Akashi.*' The shaman spoke the word as if repeating a good joke.

Iwata hadn't kept count of his shots.

How many rounds did the SIG hold? Seven? Nine?

Quaking severely, Iwata forced himself to peer over the mattress.

'Akashi, come out.'

The obsidian blade whistled towards Iwata's face. Gasping, he fell backwards as the knife thudded into his solar plexus – handle first. Badly winded, he dropped the gun. Akashi stood now, another blade in his hand. He took a step forward but something stopped him.

A voice coming from downstairs.

'Iwata! Are you there?'

'Up here! He's here!'

390

Footsteps crashed up the stairs.

Hideo Akashi smashed the window with his elbow and hurled himself out. Iwata scrambled to his feet, picked up the gun and ran to the window. Akashi, unharmed by the fall, was running, head down, putting distance between himself and the house with long, powerful strides. Iwata staggered away from the window.

'Yumi, stay here. You're safe now.'

He opened the door and ran straight into Hatanaka. The younger man slumped against the wall and puffed out his cheeks.

'Fuck, Iwata. I almost shot you in the head.'

'Yumi is alive.' Iwata pushed past. 'Have you called an ambulance?'

'Already done, but there could be a delay – where are you going?'

'To finish this.'

Iwata mounted the Triumph and hit top speed in a few seconds. He knew where the Black Sun Killer would be heading.

Hideo Akashi ran on to the footpath leading into Rainbow Bridge. A hundred metres behind, Iwata hopped off the Triumph and began pursuit. They were now on the pedestrian walkway, a contained aisle with a waist-high railing, fifty-two metres above Tokyo Bay.

Iwata could just about see Akashi up ahead, head down, arms pumping, pouring on the speed. He seemed unaffected by the distance he had run. The walkway narrowed – not wider than two or three metres – and was now enclosed by metallic grilles on both sides. Occasional cars thundered by, close enough to touch. The grilles rattled deafeningly when they passed. Iwata could smell a faint sea breeze. Thick clouds of black smoke obfuscated the city. It was as if they were suspended in the sky.

Alone. Together.

The smoke dissipated now and Iwata squinted. He could no longer see Akashi.

'Are you there?'

He had to be, there was nowhere to go.

Iwata pressed on, but he could hear a strange sound getting louder now – a wet sound, like a thirsty giant swallowing too fast. A crashing sound with a murmuring underneath that.

Ug.

Ug.

Ug.

Feeling himself falter, Iwata grabbed the railing with one hand. He no longer felt any pain – he knew that was a bad sign. He could draw only short, spindly breaths. He realized now the blow to the solar plexus had done more than wind him. Iwata's consciousness ebbed and slackened, his gun was an impossible weight.

He was now in a small room. Familiar somehow. He'd seen this before.

Wanna see something?

'Kei?'

Well, do you, or not?

He closed his eyes and saw his friend. Kei pointed downwards.

The eye of the whirlpool was blinking up at them.

And Iwata realized where he was standing.

The first tower of the bridge.

The maintenance door swung open and there was Akashi, the shaman, the Black Sun Killer, skull mask grinning. Iwata fired.

He missed.

Click.

Click.

Click.

Akashi stepped forward, as if to embrace him. One hand on Iwata's shoulder, a dull thud, then the sound of ripping grass.

Before registering the ruin, Iwata smashed his gun into Akashi's face. It was all he had.

Then he was on the ground, coughing up blood.

He could hear only the sound of his own eyes.

Blink.

Blink.

Blink.

His eyes or distant explosions. Blinking or Cleo's chopping board.

Thunk.

Thunk.

Thunk.

Iwata sucked in breath in quick threes.

Then twos.

Then slow.

Far above him, Hideo Akashi circled into view like water going down a drain. His face was blackened. His eyes were so white. His movements were beautiful, like a predator around its prey.

Iwata realized his own lips were moving.

The lights of the city are so pretty. Give me one more tender kiss.

Akashi crouched down and cupped his ear to Iwata's mouth.

'What are you saying?'

I walk and walk, swaying, like a small boat in your arms.

'What are you saying to me?'

I hear your footsteps coming. Blue Light Yokohama.

Iwata hacked up blood and realized he was laughing. Akashi bared his gums, reached down and tore out the knife from Iwata's belly. There was no pain, no sensation. Just the sound of air being sucked in, or expelled. Akashi held a modern hunting knife over Iwata's face, dripping blood across his lips. Iwata tasted metal and salt. He knew why it tasted this way, he knew the copper was there to help transmit nerve signals. He knew it would take ninety minutes to cremate his body.

But he felt nothing.

Let us not fear the bear.

Akashi pushed the knife against Iwata's cheek.

'You laugh?'

With great effort, Iwata spoke. 'You're just crazy.' His voice was soft. 'That's all.'

Akashi's face scrunched up with anger.

'What a *recent* little invention you are, Inspector. What amusement you give the earth – passing judgement on its natural way of things, punishing the strong and protecting the weak.'

Akashi gestured wildly with the bloody knife.

'*Unworthy* man, you tread on that which you do not understand. This world is destined for darkness unless we nourish The Maker. And you would defy *Him*, for the sake of the insignificant?'

'They're people, Akashi. People.'

Akashi spat in disgust.

'The family. The old woman. The girl. All of them. They were all marked for death and *I am* that death. I *am* the nourishment.'

'Marked by you. Potential witnesses, Akashi. Nothing more.'

'*Disbeliever.*'

Akashi stood up on the railing now, smiling with wild reverence at the blackened skyline.

'Look at it. This thing they call "city". An *absurdity*. We are so near now. Soon it will die.'

You ever hear that saying about Tokyo being a million cities all at once? You wonder if maybe some of them are good and some of them are bad?

'*Witness* what happens when the living foundations grow angry. This world cracks open without nourishment – Tezcatlipoca *screams* for the blood of the indebted. You could not stop me feeding him, Iwata. You could not. And if you had strength enough to look inside yourself, you would feel the divinity of my work.'

'Is that what you call it? "Work"?'

Iwata closed his eyes. He knew he shouldn't but it didn't matter.

'Soon enough the world will witness the New Way. And perhaps one day what I have done will be recognized. The sacrifices I've made will be seen. Perhaps one day the name Hideo Akashi will be spoken of as *the one who cleared the path.*'

Akashi reached down for his shaman's mask, adjusted the leather straps and lodged it on his face. One half of it had broken off, revealing the left eye.

'But I have grown weary of your little footsteps.' Akashi lifted Iwata's chin, exposing the trembling Adam's apple beneath. '*Hach k'as. Eek.*'

Iwata saw Kei balancing, arms out, as he tightrope walked across the boundary wall.

Maybe I'll get some money together in a year or two, come visit you.

A tremendous convulsion tore through them.

Metal yearned. An aftershock roared into life, slamming

Akashi into the steel maintenance door. Rainbow Bridge was an animal struggling against its shackles.

Heavy footfalls grew closer.

'Iwata!'

Akashi, still off balance, snapped his head round. He saw Hatanaka too late.

The shoulder tackle was hard, crunching into Akashi's nose. He stumbled backwards into the metal railing, his weight carrying him over. Hatanaka threw out a hand and clutched a leg – Akashi's weight lifting him off his feet.

'Iwata! *Help me!*'

Hatanaka's voice was a long way off.

Iwata didn't want to hear it any longer.

He saw Kei, casting a line on a warm afternoon. He saw the chestnut girl in her lonely garden. He saw Hana Kaneshiro on the slab, lips white. He saw the policeman's granddaughter, blue in the glow of the screen. He saw Jennifer Fong, floating on the waves. He saw Cleo at her counter, shuffling through dust jackets.

And then he saw it.

The lighthouse.

The lighthouse.

The lighthouse.

He saw Cleo in the sunset, standing on the cliff.

He saw the baby broken on rocks below.

A little dollop of honey for my honey bee.

Bleeding badly, Iwata rolled on to his front. He crawled towards the feet of Hatanaka. Through the railings, he saw Akashi dangling above the abyss. His eyes were black and vacant as he screamed at the sky.

'*Ma'taali'teeni'! Ma'taali'teeni'!*'

Hatanaka kicked Iwata's shoulder hard.

'I can't *hold* him!'

Iwata reached out, snapping handcuffs around Akashi's ankle and the metal railing. Hatanaka let go and fell against the stairs with a thud. The two detectives stared at each other, panting.

'Oh shit,' he gasped, seeing Iwata's gushing stomach.

Iwata closed his eyes as Hatanaka called it in. First, he called for medical assistance – *officer down*. Then, taking a breath, he announced the capture of Hideo Akashi.

Much later, Iwata registered being carried into an ambulance. He looked up at the skyscrapers and felt rain on his face. All around him, Tokyoites tentatively returned to the streets. He didn't know what would happen now but he'd done his job. Kosuke Iwata was free to die.

High above his ambulance, the grey clouds looked like restless elephants.

37. A Deer Hears the Shot

On the fourth page of the *Mainichi Shimbun* newspaper, buried under the fallout from the Tōhoku earthquake, the following article was printed:

POLICE CORRUPTION EXPOSED AS TMPD FINALLY CATCHES 'BLACK SUN' KILLER

BY TETSUYA SUDA

Less than an hour after Friday's terrible earthquake, Tokyo Metropolitan Police Department homicide detectives sensationally arrested a former senior inspector for murder. Hideo Akashi, 48, who was thought to have killed himself last month, has been charged with multiple homicide, including the attempted murder of a heavily pregnant Daiba housewife. (See page 3.)

While the police should, of course, be praised for capturing the culprit in what has been dubbed the 'Black Sun Murders', these sick acts must not overshadow the depth and the scale of corruption in our city's noxious police force.

Following allegations of falsification of evidence, torture, misuse of funds and even collusion with yakuza groups, the National Police Agency has assumed immediate command of Shibuya's homicide department – Division One. TMPD's highest ranking police officer, Chief Superintendent Uwatoko Fujimura, 72, has been charged with a range of criminal offences. Fujimura was last seen on Friday afternoon by his wife, though rumours abound that he may have taken his own life. Several senior inspectors in Division One have also been charged, and a raft of more junior officers are now under investigation. While many details are yet to be established, from documents received from an anonymous source, it seems that entire cases have been fabricated in order to increase funding, bribes have been freely accepted by yakuza groups and even investigation expenses have been fraudulently inflated.

Recently appointed public prosecutor Mikine Murata is also keen to question several members of the Police Fund Auditing Board. While she refused to comment directly on ongoing cases, on Monday morning Murata issued the following statement:

'Through the valiant actions of a small number of police officers, a much-needed spotlight has been shone on Shibuya's TMPD. What has become clear to me, and will soon become clear to the public, is that radical change is needed in our capital's police force. Corruption is unacceptable in any facet of life, let alone in the very institution we rely on to protect us, fight crime on our behalf, and ultimately, to uphold our laws.'

We at the *Mainichi Shimbun* echo these sentiments and, unfortunately, must also strongly criticize the current police system. It is a system that seemingly allows men and women with little actual experience of real police work to assume positions of considerable responsibility in the TMPD. 'Career cops', often hand-picked by police executives straight out of university based on family wealth and prestige, can be elevated to positions of power without a single arrest or any investigative experience. If these young professionals, already recruited so whimsically, develop in a corrupt environment where the law does not apply – how can we expect future generations to break free of this avarice?

There seems to be little to distinguish the police career ladder from the hierarchies found in yakuza gangs – these being nothing more than differing orthodoxies. The evidence is clear and irrefutable: corruption was not a cancer in Shibuya TMPD. It was, in fact, the very glue that held it together.

The new Prime Minister has sworn to do whatever is necessary to ensure that Tokyo does not merely have the largest urban police force in the world, but also the cleanest and the best. We at the *Mainichi Shimbun* welcome that message, though we remain unconvinced that a handful of convictions can achieve such a sea change in institutional attitudes and cultures. The word Public Prosecutor Murata used was 'radical'. And we believe radical change must indeed sweep through every echelon of the police force.

Iwata let the newspaper fall to his lap as the TV caught his eye. Wincing, he sat up in his bed to watch. It was a feast on police corruption and bureaucratic incompetence. He turned up the volume and reached for an apple. The news footage showed Horibe, Tatsuno and Moroto, among others, being bundled into police vans. They all tried in vain to cover their faces from the snapping photographers. With a mouth full of apple flesh, Iwata waved at the screen.

'You have a *real* productive day now.'

The footage switched to the recently dismissed Public Prosecutor Shiratori. Journalists and cameramen swarmed around him as he tried to get to his car. Instead of tears or bowing, the old man was indignant.

'Mr Shiratori, do you have any comment?'

'None of the farcical charges against me have been proved, nor will they. Time will show this whole affair to be nothing more than a ridiculous witch hunt. And frankly, what a worrying and disgusting waste of resources in the face of our country's worst natural disaster in the modern age. But I'm an old man with a long career behind me. The ones who will really suffer are the young, valiant police officers who protect this city. Officers who are needed now more than ever. Yes, some are imperfect. But putting them all in jail is like smashing your window because you see a smudge.'

Iwata laughed, though pain gripped his stomach. His body

felt alien, stitched together with foreign elements and held in place only by painkillers.

This was his fifth day in JSDF Central Hospital, though he had stabilized within seventy-two hours of arriving. It would be a long road to healing but, according to the doctors, he was more or less out of the woods. Iwata wondered if that would ever be true.

On the screen, a makeshift Division One stood in front of the Kaneshiros' lonely, empty house. Surrounded by nothing, it had been unaffected by the quake. The policemen all performed the saikeirei bow, inclined at seventy degrees, their eyes locked regretfully on the mud at their feet. Flowers were placed outside the front door. He changed channels, but everything else was entirely dedicated to the earthquake and tsunami. The number of dead and missing grew with each passing day.

Iwata switched off the TV and looked out of his window. To the west, he could see the green of Setagaya Park. The rain would keep visitors away today but the trees and the flowers would be glad. Unhurried, scattered clouds drifted by. He glanced at the bouquet on the windowsill from Yumi Tachibana. The petals were beginning to wilt a little.

The bedside phone rang.

'Kos? It's Dave. How are you doing?'

'Yeah, OK.'

'Fucking typical monosyllabics there from Kosuke Iwata. How are you *doing*?'

'Doctors think I'm going to have some pretty good scars, but I'm doing OK, more or less. Don't sound too disappointed.'

'Well, I was going to send you a fruit basket but how the fuck do you find a fruit basket in this country?'

'In this country we tend to *visit* friends who are almost stabbed to death. Or have you been saving on the train fare?'

There was a smiling pause before Schultz changed tone.

'Listen, Kos, this whole fucking thing . . . it's crazy. I mean, I haven't seen your name in the press yet, the earthquake is obviously more . . . I guess what I'm saying is, if you, uh, need to go away for a while, my folks would love to have you.'

'Don't bother them, I'll be fine. I might not win any popularity prizes any time soon but no horses' heads in the bed yet.'

'When do you get out?'

Iwata ran his finger lightly along the apple core on the table next to him. It was already rusting.

'Couple of days. When I'm back on my feet, I'll come up and see you. It'd be good to get out of Tokyo for a while anyway.'

'You should do that. Hey, listen, you remember Emi? Emi Hayashi?'

'Yeah, I remember her. She's doing the psych evaluation for Hideo Akashi.'

'Her students are all doing that Hannibal Lecter impression with the tongue. Emi being Emi, she laughs it off. Anyway, she asked me how you were doing the other day. You should say hello to her when you're in town. I think she likes you. Must be crazy.'

'Coming from the fat divorcee.'

'Touché.'

Iwata wondered why they had stayed friends all these years. Perhaps it wasn't due to anything in particular. Perhaps it was simply both men accepting their friendship as an established fact after all the scars of change that they had accumulated down the years. After this long, perhaps it was nothing more than relying on each other not to change.

'Well, I better jet. You hang tough.'

'Take care, Dave.'

Iwata hung up and lay back in the bed.

He had been dozing a while when there was a knock at the door. A smiling nurse came in.

'You look better today, Mr Iwata.'

'Your nose gets longer and longer.'

The nurse laughed and held up a package.

'This just came for you. From an Inspector Yamada. He said he'd visit tomorrow. Seemed like he was in a big rush.'

Iwata chuckled.

'All of a sudden he's real police.'

The nurse shut the door and Iwata inspected the package. No marks, no details. He opened it and found an old Walkman, along with a small yellow envelope with his name written on it. He put the Walkman and the earphones to one side, then opened the envelope. A thin gold butterfly necklace and a cassette tape dropped into his lap. It had no label but there was an address on the back of it.

'Strange.'

Iwata gingerly reached for the earphones, slipped in the tape and pressed play.

'Iwata. It's me, Sakai. If you're listening to this, then I'm probably dead . . . I was going to call you but neither one of us is the sentimental type so . . . Look, I wanted to say sorry for lying to you. About who I am. You would have figured it out sooner or later anyway. I didn't want to lie but then that's what my whole life has been . . . And now I see that.'

A long, hissing silence passed.

'He's coming for me . . . Just as he came for my mother on the cable car. You should know, Iwata. He was coming to kill her. He wanted her heart. But she beat him to it. And so he stole me. He raised me. Fed me lies like they were greens. He loved me. Some days. Beat me others. Raped me when I got older. Paid for the best schools. The finest clothes.

403

Daddy's little girl to the devil himself. And the whole time it was like I was caught in a dream. I could barely look at him for the hate . . . yet I loved him. Wanted to make him proud. I don't quite understand my own version of it. I think I blocked out entire years. I spent so long soaking up his lies that they became my own, clouded what was real.'

Her voice faltered now.

'And then I met you. And together we walked into that house and I saw that symbol. Akashi's symbol. Their fucking symbol – the Children . . . I started to shake, I was worried you could tell. And that's when I knew, deep down. That I'd been so far down a well, I couldn't remember anything from before. My mother's own face. The compound. The cult. The road when we ran . . . I needed clarity. I asked a friend to help me. I knew, of course, who I really was. But I needed someone else to open the box, you know? And he led me to the truth. To my grandfather. To the answers I needed. I put the pieces together, I climbed out of that well . . .'

Iwata heard her lighting a cigarette and blowing out smoke.

'If you haven't already looked, you'll see that there are no real records for my mother – Keiko Shimizu. That's because they were protected, Iwata. She was going to be a witness for the state. Indictments were being written up. The Children of the Black Sun didn't want that to happen. So somewhere along the way, she ran. And now, like her, I'm running too. Because he's coming for me, just as he was sent by Takashi Anzai to find my mother . . . Akashi is coming and he won't stop until he finds me. I realize now he raised me like a pig for slaughter. Encouraged me to go into the force. Then he used me down the years. "Hide this for me. Say we were drinking in such a bar at such a time. Look the other way, Noriko." And I did. I did it all for him . . . And all the while my career progressed. What a lie. What a waste of a life.'

There was another long silence until Sakai stubbed out her cigarette.

'Iwata, I don't know if he's alone, or if he's still part of the Children. But you should know that this man won't stop until he's dead. If

you cross Akashi's path, don't try and bring him in. Just kill him. Believe me, it's the only thing you can do.'

Sakai exhaled, a butterfly in the wind.

'Hey, Iwata. If you manage to walk away from this, do me a favour. Do something else with your life. You're better than this. Get out of the TMPD. And what I said about you having nothing to offer? That was bullshit. You're a good man. You're not so ugly. You don't talk too much. So meet someone. Meet someone good. Have a kid . . . And remember something for me, Iwata. Something I could never put into practice. The whole 'fuck-you-world' thing? In the end, it won't get you anywhere. Especially not you.'

She laughed softly and then sniffed.

'OK. OK. I'm done. My grandfather's address is on the back of this tape. That's where my ashes should go. Funny thing is, I'm not afraid. Not yet, anyway. Oh, and Iwata? One more thing . . . Don't think about me after this, OK? No lilies or any of that shit. Take care of yourself, my friend. Stay out of trouble.'

Iwata looked out of the window as he cried. When he was done, he wiped his cheeks with a fist and kissed Sakai's butterfly. For the first time in as long as he could remember, he didn't dwell on anything in particular when he closed his eyes.

A long time had passed. It was dark. A silhouette stood in front of the window. Cold silver rivulets twined down the glass.

'Who's there?' Iwata's voice was weak.

Shindo stepped out of the darkness and sat down in the corner chair.

'You look terminal, son.'

'I'm fine, thanks for your concern. You?'

'Tired. The division is half empty now, as I'm sure you can imagine . . . I spoke to the Minister of Justice this morning.'

'Satsuki-fucking-Eda?'

Shindo smiled.

'He's very happy, despite everything. The budget cuts have been shelved. Apparently, we're no longer a problem.'

'What are we now?'

'A *platform*.' He laughed.

'You're good at what you do, Shindo. If they have any sense, you'll be heading up Division One now.'

Shindo looked out of the window, his faced embossed with the shadows of raindrops. They were much larger in shadow.

'You know they found Akashi's cave of wonders? Turns out he was living in a sea container on the Shibaura docks.'

'I imagine they turned up some interesting things.'

'Stolen evidence, for starters. But also dirt. *A lot* of dirt – yakuza players, Fujimura, Moroto and the others. This new Murata woman is all over it.'

Iwata nodded.

'I've seen the news. What about Akashi himself?'

'Oh a judge will find him insane, no doubt. But the bastard was meticulous. Yamada has been looking into it and it's clear he was planning this for years. He was extorting big money from everyone with pockets to fund his little crusade. All kinds of people have turned up on his payroll, from the bottom to the top. Even as far as Hong Kong. And, of course, stolen identities.'

'Ikuo Uno,' Iwata said.

'And another one – Idane – possibly your 'I' from Kaneshiro's calendar. Funny thing is, most of these identities line up with missing persons.'

Iwata almost laughed.

'Son of a bitch.'

'He created a win–win situation – killing Mina Fong didn't

just create a nationwide diversion, it also created money for Fujimura to skim, thereby keeping him in Akashi's pocket.'

'Fujimura and everyone else.'

Something passed over Shindo's face.

'Iwata, just in case it crossed your mind, I never –'

'It didn't cross my mind.'

They fell quiet for a time, unaccustomed to speaking with each other on matters beyond murder.

The rain tapped on the glass gently.

'All this time,' Shindo said. 'That's what gets me. All this time and I saw nothing.'

Both men stared at the rain, as if it could wash away the filth of the world.

Shindo looked away, his gaze falling to the floor.

'Sakai. Who was she?'

Iwata shrugged.

'Someone running from the past.'

'She knew?'

'See that tape on the table? Listen to it. It'll tell you what you need to know.'

The older man exhaled shakily.

'You think she knew what was coming?'

'I think she was ready. In the end, she fought him.'

Shindo shook his head.

'I knew her since she was twenty-two years old. She would never let anybody . . . see her. The real Sakai I mean.' His face reddened. 'I asked her once if, you know, she and I might . . . but she said she loved someone else. When I think of the way she looked at *him* now, the awe in her eyes, I don't know. And he just ignored her, Iwata. Never once looked in her direction. Fuck, I knew Akashi for *years* and –'

'It's over, Shindo. Don't dwell on ghosts. That's the only thing I can tell you.'

They sat in the warm, silent darkness of the hospital room. Both men considered what had been done and what had been lost. Iwata felt little more than fatigue.

Shindo noticed the watercolour painting on the wall depicting a forest. He pointed at the stag in the foreground, its head raised, nobly regarding the horizon.

'When I was a kid my father took me hunting for deer once. We hid in this bush for hours and hours until one eventually came along. My father took the shot but the deer bolted like the bullet just sailed straight past him. So I was crying and shouting, "You missed, you missed!" But my father shook his head and pointed to the bloodstains in the earth. We followed those bloodstains, I don't know how long for, but field after field. I didn't know how much an animal could bleed until that day. Eventually, we found the body and my old man explained: a deer hears the shot and he bolts – the last message from the brain being *run*. And the body obeys, even though it's already dead.'

Shindo looked at his gnarled, yellowed hands for a moment.

'I still think about that deer sometimes. Then I end up thinking that maybe we're not so different. People, I mean. Running across field after field, even though we're already dead. Unable to change.'

Shindo stood, embarrassed by his rumination.

'Well, anyway.' He laughed. 'Better let you get your rest, kid.'

He opened the door but Iwata called after him.

'Hey, Shindo. Do me a favour? That kid from Setagaya – Hatanaka. I owe him. Request him as a full-time Assistant Inspector for me. He'll work hard for you.'

'All right.'

'Another thing. I know that Yamada is filling in for me. I

want him to take over permanently. They both belong in Division One.'

'Done. But what about you? When are you back?'

'I'm not coming back. I resign.'

Shindo puffed out his cheeks and scratched the back of his head.

'Where will you go?'

'I don't know yet.'

'It's not my business but it's my business, you understand?'

Iwata laughed, then grimaced.

The older man stepped into the corridor. He paused to speak over his shoulder.

'You want to know something funny? Day before you started, Fujimura comes down to my office. Says we're hiring a no-mark to replace Akashi. Just a few years of experience in some backwater. I complained, of course. There were ten other better guys vying for your place. But Fujimura told me he wanted a bumpkin – low on salary and low on brainwaves. Now he's gone and things are going to change. Me included.'

'He was right about one thing,' Iwata croaked. 'The salary *is* lousy.'

Shindo laughed.

Then his smile faded. This was goodbye.

'I'm not going to thank you for doing your job, kid.'

'You trusted me. That's worth more.'

Shindo patted the door frame and left.

In the elevator, he wondered if they ought to have shaken hands.

38. The New Way

Tokyo's Supreme Court was a Dalí painting of white stone. Strange shapes cast long shadows on a beautiful spring morning. Inside Chamber Number One, Kosuke Iwata sat before three judges – One, Two, Three. Their togas were ink blue, their cravats a perfect white. Behind them, enormous paintings depicted gods and ancient history. Above the judges, an inscription ran in gold letters with the imperial chrysanthemum seal – *in the name of the emperor.*

In the rows behind Iwata, various officials from the National Police Agency, TMPD and Tokyo judiciary sat with concerned looks on their faces and mobile phones at the ready – evolving strategy and official lines to be taken.

The three judges were of differing age and gender, yet they all wore the same expression, the same expectation in their eyes as if all carved from the same beechwood wall panels.

Iwata cleared his throat and leant into the microphone.

'That's correct, Chief Justice. It was a case of Occam's razor.'

'Would you be good enough to clarify, Inspector Iwata?'

'Simply put, Hideo Akashi didn't add up from the beginning. He was leading all the relevant cases – Mina Fong's stalker, Ikuo Uno, the Takara Matsuu murders and the subsequent missing persons file. But so little made sense. Until the charade in the elevator –'

Judge Three held up her hand.

'You're referring to the CCTV footage from Mina Fong's apartment building.'

'That's correct, Chief Justice. I realized that Akashi was the last person to see her alive. But, of course, he was dead before she was killed, so how could he have anything to do with it? The answer was simply that *he was not dead*. Akashi killed Mina the *first* time he visited her apartment. The charade inside the lift confused the timeline and gave him a watertight alibi, not that he'd ever be suspected. But it also meant he was able to hide in plain sight. After all, who would come back to a crime scene in disguise *after* having killed someone? And, in any case, who would suspect the great Hideo Akashi?'

The three judges shared furtive glances. Behind Iwata, murmuring broke out.

Judge Two, the eldest, cleared his throat.

'So you focused your investigation on Senior Inspector Akashi at that point?'

'That's correct, Chief Justice. It later transpired that a homeless man – a former colleague of Senior Inspector Akashi, Ryozo Suzuki – had been asked to formally identify the body. A body without a face. A body that was the right size for Akashi, with a recently shaved head and broken fingers to accommodate his ring. A body that I believe belonged to Takara Matsuu, a child murderer whom nobody would miss.'

Judge One coughed and took off his spectacles.

'Inspector, throughout this entire . . . *situation*, at no point did you raise concerns with your superiors or seek any kind of assistance. Do you accept that, perhaps, this was not the wisest course of action to take?'

'Sir, with respect, it was the *only* course of action. I knew that the killer had someone inside the TMPD. The work was too perfect. Always one step ahead. And no surprise, considering the dirt Akashi had on everyone –'

Two held up his hand.

'Inspector, you are referring to the subject of ongoing investigations so I would ask you to avoid informality.'

Iwata smiled thinly.

'Forgive me, Chief Justice. My only point was that, given the levels of corruption – alleged corruption – in Division One, there was no safe place for me to turn. But by keeping these things back, I was also certain my . . . *improvisation* with Yoshi Tachibana would work.'

One clucked his tongue.

'That's an interesting choice of words, Inspector. Do you appreciate now, with benefit of hindsight, the damage that your little ruse may have done? Not just in financial terms to the TMPD but also to public confidence in Japanese law enforcement? Frankly, I fail to see how this "improvisation", as you so blithely call it, has not yet been considered as part of Public Prosecutor Murata's formal investigation.'

Iwata bowed.

'Forgive me, Chief Justice. I wholly accept responsibility for my actions. As such, I gave notice of my resignation to Superintendent Shindo last week.'

The judges looked at each other.

'That's not in these pages.'

Shindo, in the gallery, avoided eye contact.

'I believe the superintendent may have been hoping I might stay on. However, my decision is final.'

Judge Three accepted this with a nod.

'All right, Inspector. Let's proceed. At what point were you sure of Akashi's guilt?'

'The CCTV from Rainbow Bridge confirmed it – Akashi and Matsuu were at the bridge two days before the former's supposed suicide. He must have killed Matsuu, shaved his head and caused the severe facial injuries post-mortem. This gave Akashi a two-day period to carry out his plan. When he was ready, he swapped clothes with the body, tied it to his own and jumped.'

One interjected.

'Inspector, we appreciate that Hideo Akashi's mental state may have been somewhat altered. But this is also a man, according to you and the body of evidence before us, capable of meticulous planning. A man capable of eluding authorities for long periods of time, inside help or no. How then would you explain the contradiction? A meticulous strategist yet also an individual disturbed enough to take a hundred-metre-plus leap at the extreme risk of death?'

Iwata leafed through the pages before him.

'If I may read from Doctor Hayashi's psychiatric report, Chief Justice?'

One nodded.

'"The subject displays clear signs of personality disassociation, his principal persona being 'the shaman'. It is likely that he came to inhabit this 'main' persona after leaping from Rainbow Bridge, thereby ceasing to be Hideo Akashi. The subject sees himself as the living embodiment of the destruction of the 'old world', and that his entire raison d'être is to pave the way for a 'new reality'. The subject refuses, however, to discuss his views on this new world in any detail and shuts down whenever pressed. He does acknowledge his devout belief in, and criminal representation of, the cult known as the Children of the Black Sun. He sees himself as a warrior monk, a fervent apostle-assassin prepared to commit any act for the word of his guru – Takashi Anzai. The subject admits to an extremely close relationship to this man, a father–son dynamic as well as a leader and follower. While the subject frequently and seamlessly conflates reality and fantasy, I would strongly advise investigation into any such reanimation of

413

this criminal sect. Akashi's belief in a New Way should, in my view, be considered credible. If he is to be believed, The Black Sun will dawn.

"'As his signature at every one of his murder scenes, the significance of the black sun symbol also manifests itself in the passing of the old and the dawning of the new. Despite the subject's psychological framework, incredibly sophisticated though it is, there can be no doubt that Hideo Akashi is a fastidious and highly dangerous individual. After many hours of interviews, in my opinion, there should be no doubt whatsoever that the subject will kill again if released. Once his "crusade" is complete, I believe his mental framework is flexible enough to shift and latch on to a new apologia. Hideo Akashi presents, in my view, one of the most complex and dangerous criminals in Japanese history. My professional recommendation is that he remain incarcerated in a maximum security psychiatric facility indefinitely.'"

Iwata put down the pages and he continued.

'In answer to your original question, Chief Justice, there is clear antecedence of people falling from great heights without any kind of protection and surviving. Personally, I believe Akashi was fully aware that he was risking his life. But he also would have known that by doing this, he was completely free to act out his agenda. If we are to follow Doctor Hayashi's analysis, it's quite possible that he considered this a test of sorts. A baptism of fire, perhaps. To Akashi, climbing out of the bay could well have been confirmation of the divinity of his work.'

One fingered through some papers.

'And what of Assistant Inspector Sakai? Or Midori Anzai, to give her her real name.'

Iwata closed his eyes and imagined Sakai as a little girl, terrified, holding her mother's hand as they boarded the cable car. He pictured Keiko pointing the knife at the crowd, her eyes locking on to Akashi – *you stay away from me.* He pictured Akashi picking the girl up and leaving the cable car.

I'll be looking after you now.

Iwata sighed.

'Assistant Inspector Sakai was a talented and devoted investigator. Without her, Akashi would still be at large and it's quite possible that many more would have died. I was deeply gratified to learn that Superintendent Shindo has requested a promotion to the rank of Inspector and the very highest posthumous honours for her.'

Judge Two snorted and looked in Shindo's direction.

Shindo, chest puffed out, stared back.

'The Supreme Court does not convene to apperceive matters of gratification.'

'The question was open-ended, Chief Justice.'

'Well, let me put this in clearer terms: do you believe Noriko Sakai to be innocent of any connection to the Fujimura scandal?'

Iwata glared at him without reply for longer than the room was comfortable with.

'If we accept, sir, that by your question you mean *free of moral wrong*, then I absolutely believe Noriko Sakai to be innocent. In my own modest experience in law enforcement, I've never served with a more honourable police officer.'

Judge Three put her hand up. She'd heard enough. She shuffled through her papers and glanced up at the clock. She shot Two a look. Two shook his head. One shook his head.

She shrugged.

'Very well then, Inspector Iwata. You are dismissed.'

Hands in his pockets, Iwata walked along the corridor, his footsteps ringing out on the soapstone. He passed white marble sculptures of long-dead judges and prosecutors. He pictured Sakai sipping hot chocolate before shuffling through the case file.

Seems we're looking for a giant.

He imagined her calling it in – *suspect apprehended, case closed.* He imagined how it would have electrified that smile of hers, the real one she kept hidden away, the one no one would forget once they'd seen it.

Iwata sighed and closed his eyes in the warm sunlight. That's when he heard footsteps – high heels. He turned to see a tall, middle-aged woman in a mauve suit coming his way. She was wearing gold earrings and a broad grin.

'Iwata!'

When she caught up, they exchanged bows – Iwata's deeper than hers.

'You know who I am?' she asked.

'Our new public prosecutor.'

'And a very unfit one at that. I'll see you out, Inspector.'

'Sooner or later people are going to have to stop calling me that.'

Murata laughed warmly. She hadn't bothered to hide her crow's feet with make-up and her hair was up in a simple ponytail. There was something at once both very likeable and fearsome about her.

'Iwata, the importance of your work here can't be overstated. I wanted to thank you for your courage and your determination. Tokyo is a better place today because of it.'

'Ma'am –'

Murata stopped him with a hand on the shoulder.

'No, I won't accept humility. Not on a day like today. I just want you to know that you have my gratitude.'

'Thank you.'

She smiled and they carried on down the corridor.

'I understand Shindo accepted your resignation.'

'That's right.'

'And I understand that you're an intractable man.'

'Some say.'

They had reached the main entrance. Murata handed him her card.

'Well, Iwata, you know I want good people in this town. Tokyo could really use you.'

Smiling, he shook his head.

'She'll be fine.' Iwata skipped down the steps. 'She always is in the end.'

'Good luck, Inspector,' she called.

'And to you.'

Outside, Yoji Yamada, wearing a bright linen shirt and sunglasses, was leaning against the black Isuzu. He folded up his newspaper, the headline still visible – COLLUSION, CORRUPTION AND COP KILLINGS in bold.

'I see you're not in handcuffs. A rare thing in this town for a cop these days.'

'I'm the one leaving but you look like you're going on a cruise.'

Yamada's smile faded.

'Listen, Iwata, I've done some digging. You've heard of Theta?'

'They're always in the discussion pieces. "New religion or cult." That kind of thing?'

'Bet on the latter. Anyway, you remember Akira Anzai?'

'Yeah, Takashi Anzai's eldest.'

'Right. Well, I checked the financial services register – he's officially the new leader of Theta. Now outwardly, they're peaceful and happy clappy. They've even set up a disaster fund for earthquake victims. But I'm worried, Iwata. Look at their tax returns. They're *growing*. You saw the same photo in the compound that I did.'

'So?'

'So, I think we should move to place Theta under surveillance. We'll need a court ruling but I think we can get it. Now you said that Akashi specifically spoke of a "new way". The Children of the Black Sun believed in a new way, a new dawn, a new guise. What if those two things are linked?'

Iwata got into the car and wound down the window.

'Where are you going with this, Yamada?'

'Well, what if Akashi wasn't just a crazy lone wolf? What if he *was* clearing the path for whatever it is that Theta is underneath all the PR? What if Akashi isn't as crazy as he makes out?'

'Take it from me. He's crazy.'

'Look, I know he is, but answer me this – don't his murders seem an awful lot like tying up loose ends? Severing the past from the future? What if Akashi wanted to be part of this new way and was eliminating anyone who knew his past? What if –'

Iwata passed him Murata's card.

'I'm out, Yoji.' He patted him on the arm. 'Tokyo has you, now.'

39. Blue Light Yokohama

Sometime after dawn, Iwata began to pack up his things. It took less than a quarter of an hour to put everything he owned in the car. Shutting the boot, he looked up at his apartment window one last time. Motoyoyogicho had never really been home. Starting the engine, he felt nothing, as though leaving behind a mid-range business hotel.

Iwata drove towards Shibuya on quiet, hesitant streets. Tokyo was rebuilding again. It always did. Through his sunroof, he absorbed the news on the giant LED screen above a department store.

A famous young actress had announced her engagement to a member of an up-and-coming idol band. A popular comedian had apologized for tax irregularities. There was a new Number One record in Japan. The broadcast ended with an insurance company's slogan:

THIS IS WHAT JAPAN SHOULD BE.

At the southern entrance of Shibuya Station, the first few street vendors had assembled, smoking and sharing cups of coffee as they laughed.

Iwata drove on to Meguro, listening to the radio.

'Six months on from the installation of specially designed blue LED lights above the platforms of dozens of Yamanote Line stations, politicians and rail executives alike are branding the scheme a success. This despite 2011 being well on course to surpass 30,000 suicides. For Mr

Hiroshi Namba, director of a non-profit suicide prevention group, these figures are not surprising.'

A man with a soft voice could now be heard.

'The situation is very serious. Of course, I hope these blue lights are helping. But it's a bandage over a gunshot wound. Train suicides account for between four and six per cent of the annual total. Every positive measure is welcome but what is really needed is constant, ongoing support. In the streets, in the homes, in the workplace. People can often find themselves struggling with multiple issues. Unemployment leads to debt, debt leads to depression, depression leads to entrenched patterns of suicidal thinking. There are no easy solutions, but what is certain is that there needs to be far more support from society as a whole – not just some blue lights.'

The show cut back to the newsreader.

'It's four years ago to the day that the government released a counter-suicide white paper, setting aside 12.4 billion yen in suicide prevention assets. Positive results were expected by 2017, yet nearly halfway to the target date, Japan seems a long way off from this. As for the blue lights, it looks like they're here to stay. This is Sumiko Shimosaka reporting for –'

Iwata turned off the radio.

Outside Matsumoto's storage building, he slowly loaded up the car with his boxes. When he was finished, he went back to the hole in the wall and bought another plate of vegetable and shrimp dumplings.

'You came back.' The old cook grinned. 'A man that keeps his promises.'

Chewing, Iwata watched life flow along the main road. It was impossible to tell Japan had been brutalized a few months before. At the end of the street, a fragile row of cherry trees were in a shy bloom.

Just before lunchtime, Iwata paid Cleo's overdue Nakamura Institute bills, covering her in advance until the new year. He then asked if he might make a donation. Taken aback, the nurse agreed. But when Iwata led her out to the cardboard boxes stacked by his car, she turned to him.

'I'm not sure I understand.'

'My wife owned a record store in California. I want to give this music to the institute. I'd like it if she could hear her own music every once in a while.'

The nurse smiled uncertainly.

'Of course.'

Iwata filled out a form and borrowed one of the better wheelchairs. He found Cleo in the garden, in her usual place. He lowered her in, trying not to hurt her weak muscles. Getting her comfortable in the car was no easy task but Iwata managed it by moving the passenger seat all the way back and lodging her head in place with a folded pillow.

The drive to Chōshi was long and slow, with frequent stops for Cleo to vomit. They arrived a little before sunset. Passing through the city, though quake damage was visible everywhere, Iwata noticed how little had changed since they had lived here. It was still just a simple little city built on soy production and fishing. As he drove alongside the Tone River, he thought about the past. With his foreign police studies, only Chōshi had been prepared to take Iwata back then. Cleo joined him a few months later. She had joked about the city at first, not expecting anything more than just a backdrop to their new life. But then she had seen the coastline. Looking up at the lighthouse, she smiled.

It's home.

Cleo's eyes were closed now. In this light, she might have just shut her eyes momentarily, tired after the long drive. It struck Iwata then that, while he could picture her smile vividly, he couldn't recall her voice with certainty. He remembered its quality, its colour. The lilting between enthusiasm and playfulness. But he had gone so long without it, without a single word. It was inevitable he would lose it in time. Maybe that was the only way.

Inubōsaki Lighthouse came into view, piercing the orange fringe of the sunset.

Iwata stopped the car in its shadow and turned to Cleo. The absence of motion woke her. He unfolded the wheelchair and lowered her in again. When he manoeuvred her to face the lighthouse, she began to squirm in her chair, whimpering loudly. Iwata ignored it and pushed her to a nearby bench. The ocean sighed.

All around them, it was that perfect light – existing only at early morning or late dusk. It was at its most desperate and golden, casting shadows as long as they can be, so beautiful it seemed unlikely ever to return.

Iwata kissed Cleo on her cheek and she blinked. She used to have her own smell. Now it was wet-wipe lemon. He brought his face level with hers but there was no expression. He missed her concentration face. Even reading a newspaper she looked majestic. Or, if she were putting on mascara, she would make an 'O' with her lips. Lips he wished he could kiss.

'All right,' Iwata said. 'Enough.'

He walked to the cliff's edge and threw flowers over. He counted to three, then forced himself to look at the rocks below.

Finally, he saw them.

They were only rocks.

He went back to his wife, knelt before her and took her hands.

'I need to talk to you now, Cleo. I have this dream. A falling dream. Of you and the baby. And I can't have it any more. I just can't.'

He bowed his head.

'I still love you very much. I still love Nina very much. I will always love you both. More than life itself. But I have to start again, do you understand? If I don't, I'll always be stuck here. So I hope you can forgive me. For this. And for everything else. I'm very sorry. I truly am.'

Cleo closed her eyes. She seemed tired. Iwata sat back against her shins to watch the sunset.

The lighthouse looked down over them.

A chilly dawn, somewhere west of Miyama. Blue light was creeping over the mountainous horizon.

Iwata stopped the car. He didn't know what time it was but it didn't matter. He was accustomed to exhaustion by now. The road gave way to an overgrown field which sloped down to a deep valley.

All around Iwata, hills stretched out like green pyramids. There was a river cutting through them, silver in this light.

Iwata got out of the car, taking a bag with him. He made his way down to the river and followed it until he came to an old, familiar copse. He picked through the branches and emerged into the field he was looking for. But it had changed. There were no tall gates, no walls, no chapel. Iwata realized Sakuza Orphanage was no longer there, just some old foundations left in the grass. Bellflowers grew among the crumbled bricks. Sakuza was gone, like so much else.

Iwata crossed the field, into the denser forest. He was searching for the sound. The sound from his dreams. Sun pierced through the canopy. Birds chirped. A soft insect buzzing could be heard. He carried on along the ridge, tracing the stony spine from memory. The shape of the rocks, the rich smell of the leaves, the sound of the water – it all sparked old images in him – childhood echoes Iwata couldn't define. He couldn't grasp them firmly but they were unmistakably *there*.

And then he found the rock. The memory of Kei climbing it and preaching as Uesugi was vivid. He saw the tree he had fallen against laughing all those years ago. He closed his eyes and remembered the words.

'Let us not fear the bear,' he whispered.

Iwata tried to remember a time before the orphanage. There were only snatches. His mother putting on her perfume. Being left in the bus station. The first time he took the subway in Tokyo. That was a good, strong image. He loved that shabby Yamanote Line, rising up high over the city, the tracks running right past bedroom windows. The streets turned to scenery; blurry but sharp, with the melancholy of a child. Iwata remembered streaking past all that life he'd never know, all the life he'd never live himself. But Tokyo was never home. Not then, not now. Iwata looked around the forest. If anywhere had ever been home, it was here.

The ridge had narrowed and Iwata had to hold on to branches for balance. The sun cut white patches on the brown-golden carpet below. And then he heard the sound. The sound of the whirlpool. A crashing sound with a murmuring underneath that.

Ug.

Ug.

Ug.

Iwata followed it, feeling the temperature drop. The end of the ridge was very narrow, just wide enough for him to stand. He reached the end – a forlorn and wintry bluff. Iwata took a breath and looked down at it.

The eye of the whirlpool blinked up at him, the revolutions gleaming.

He opened the bag and took out the *Blue Light Yokohama*

LP Kei had given him all those years ago. He ran his finger over the faded stickers on the sleeve.

25TH DECEMBER 1968. EVERGREEN STANDARD. NUMBER ONE BEST-SELLER.

First, Iwata tossed the sleeve and Ayumi Ishida's beautiful smile went spiralling downwards.

Then she was gone.

He broke the record over his knee and threw it down too. Black fragments that glittered for a moment, then disappeared.

'I love you too,' Iwata said quietly. Then he walked away.

The whirlpool swirled.

It swirled.

It smiled.

40. Pavilions of the Sun

Kosuke Iwata was sitting out on the terrace across from Kyoto University's old camphor tree. It was a sunny, languid afternoon. Sipping iced tea, he listened to snippets of conversation. The first few students had returned after the long summer break. Frisbees zipped over the lawn. The skipping rope team were out practising. A circle of students sat on the warm concrete, playing cards. A young man rubbed sun cream into his girlfriend's shoulders. The KU newspaper editorial team were busy discussing their front page – the Fukushima nightmare, students still missing in the tsunami and a young Japanese woman swept over Niagara Falls. Iwata felt like talking to someone. On a whim, he dialled Professor Igarashi's number.

'Hello?'

'Professor. It's me.'

'Ah, Inspector. Congratulations are in order.'

'Thank you. Are you in Kyoto?'

'No, my classes begin next week. Why? You don't have another murder with an Aztec slant, do you?'

Iwata smiled.

'No. Although there is something I've been meaning to ask you. Something that has bugged me this whole time. When we first met and I shook your hand, you left a black mark . . .'

'Yes?'

'Professor, the killer was leaving behind sooty marks at the crime scene.'

Igarashi laughed.

'So that's why you suspected me?'

'. . . The thought crossed my mind.'

'Well, I suppose that is what you get paid for.' Igarashi was more amused than irritated. 'My indigestion, Inspector. I told you about it back in my office if you'll recall. The reality is pretty unexciting, I'm afraid. My doctor prescribes me charcoal tablets.'

'Charcoal tablets.' Iwata smiled ruefully.

'Another mystery solved, eh?'

'Someone once told me that if I hear hooves outside my window, I think zebras before horses.'

'Maybe that's why you're good at what you do.'

'I'll leave you alone now, Professor. I promise.'

'Not at all. Please call me if anything ever comes up.'

'Oh, I almost forgot to ask. What does "*ma'taali'teeni*" mean?'

'That's Mayan Yucatec, I think. It's an apology.'

'And what about "*hach k'as, eek*"?'

'Something along the lines of "filth, you disgusting filth".'

Iwata nodded.

'Well, then. Thank you for your help. Take care of yourself, Yohei.'

'Kosuke.'

Iwata hung up and a distant buzzer sounded. Students collected backpacks, bills were settled and goodbyes were said.

See you later on.

See you tomorrow.

See you again sometime.

In the cool gloom of a narrow hallway, Iwata stopped outside the door marked FORENSIC PSYCHOLOGY / SEMIOTICS.

Inside, quiet music that Iwata had never heard before was playing. He knocked timidly.

'Come in,' a woman called.

He opened the door and Emi Hayashi looked up from her papers.

'Hello again,' he said.

'Hello,' she replied.

Warm sunshine and silence between them.

'You're looking for David?' Hayashi prompted.

Iwata shook his head.

'Oh, I see.' Her face flushed slightly. She looked down at her papers. 'Shall we go for a walk?'

'I would like that.'

Iwata and Hayashi ambled along the Philosopher's Path, passing a bag of sunflower seeds between them. Tourists took photographs of the beautiful stream that flowed by the path and the overhanging trees. Hayashi was gesticulating enthusiastically as she spoke.

'Akashi was on a special brief, deep infiltration in the Children of the Black Sun. Sure enough, he worked his way up to become Takashi Anzai's most trusted soldier. But he was in too far, he got himself converted. He began to *believe* the doomsday myths. But trouble was brewing for the sect – they had already been stripped of their official legal religious entity status and they were close to bankruptcy. Akashi was especially tasked by Anzai with tracking down Keiko and anyone who might flip for state prosecution.'

'And now?'

'He's never let go of his mission. He's convinced that Anzai will rise again and he absolutely believes the god Tezcatlipoca will destroy the world without payment of blood debt.'

Iwata stopped at the vending machine and bought two cans of iced coffee.

'How can he live like that? Inhabiting the present day and some ancient mythology at the same time?'

Hayashi curled down both sides of her mouth like a shrug.

'Mythology has always been a way for people to explain the unexplainable.'

'Will we ever know what caused his break with reality?'

'It's hard to say. But he has been using LSD for a long time. It's not a drug you can easily form a dependency on but he is certainly suffering from HPPD. Hallucinogen persisting perception disorder. Essentially, the trips never really end. Information floods the cerebral cortex, the past and the present bleed together, things shimmer, appear or disappear. Akashi probably *interprets* reality rather than it being a fixed exterior world that you and I take for granted. It must be terrifying.'

'"Reality to survive, fantasy to live,"' Iwata said to himself.

A dog was barking in the distance. He pictured Akashi's face above him and felt the ripping of his own flesh. The memory caused Iwata no displeasure. He merely wanted to touch his own scars beneath his clothes.

They skirted a cluster of elderly tourists swarming around a particularly photogenic row of cherry trees. Hayashi crushed her empty can and put it in her pocket.

'Emi, I wanted to thank you. Your report really packed a punch in court.'

'I'm just glad they didn't put you in jail.' She smiled.

They walked in silence for a time.

'Can I ask you something personal?' She glanced at him. 'When you caught him . . . what did you feel?'

'I . . . don't really know. I just remember I was sitting in a hospital room, crying for no real reason. It was the strangest thing.'

'I don't think it's so strange. If you don't mind my saying.'

The stream below gurgled. Three cats were balanced on exposed tree roots by the water's surface, trying to fish for carp. Iwata and Hayashi paused for a moment to watch the cats.

'Kosuke?' She tried the name out for size.

'Yes?'

'Are you OK?'

'I think so.' He shrugged. 'I don't really know.'

'How do you feel towards Hideo Akashi?'

The cats abandoned their hunt, made nervous by observation.

'Not much. A sort of strange connection. Or just pity, perhaps.'

'Those on the precipice rarely judge the fallen.'

'Old proverb?'

'I just made it up, actually.'

'You mean it takes a screwball to catch a screwball?'

She threw a sunflower seed at him.

'You're not a screwball.'

They paused for a moment to stay out of a tourist's photograph and smiled at each other. Iwata thought about photographs. He remembered taking them. Taking photographs meant living, it meant continuing, it meant things mattered enough to record them.

'Have you ever thought that maybe it's just your job that's screwed up?' Hayashi asked.

Iwata's laugh was makeshift.

'I quit anyway.'

She looked at him, surprised.

'What will you do now?'

'Something else.'

'Good for you.'

They reached the end of the path as it met an old, cobbled hill leading back down to the city. Kyoto sprawled in black shadow and peach light.

'The lights of the city . . .' Iwata whispered.

'Pardon?'

'Nothing. Just a song I can't get out of my head.'

An old lady swept fallen leaves from her doorstep. Her house stood next to an old stone bridge which had been enveloped by thick moss. Low-hanging branches dozed over the stream, their leaves painting the water a fir green.

Iwata and Hayashi saw children letting off firecrackers for Obon, the Buddhist day of the dead. Gunpowder drifted past them like perfume. Parents hung lanterns on their houses to guide the spirits of their ancestors home. Graves would be cleaned, families would be reunited and food offerings would be made. When it was over, lit lanterns would be sent down the rivers, towards Lake Biwa. Huge bonfires would be set up in the mountains surrounding the city. Then the dead would go back to their world and the living would carry on living.

'Emi, do you remember when we met?'

'Yes.'

'You offered me coffee, which I declined.'

'Very rudely, too.'

'Can I buy you one now?'

She smiled.

'You already bought me one.'

'Dinner, then.'

Emi Hayashi checked her Mickey Mouse watch. The wind picked up and the cherry trees bled their leaves over the Philosopher's Path. The setting sun was at its most desperate, the horizon hungry for its light. Iwata closed his eyes for a moment and pictured Kei handing him half an orange.

Our glories float between earth and heaven like clouds which seem pavilions of the sun.

Iwata looked up.

There was hardly any light left on the horizon now.

The sun blazed on silently, in an ocean of emptiness, slowly dying alone.

Author's Note

The story of the story of Blue Light Yokohama

The beginning of my fascination with Japan is easy to determine – *Captain Tsubasa* – an anime series focusing on a football prodigy living in the shadow of Mount Fuji. For a star-gazing six-year-old growing up in a satellite town near Madrid, he was Doctor Doolittle, Robinson Crusoe and Captain Nemo all rolled into one. Aside from the fantastical on-field action, each episode would explore his friendships, his bitter rivalries and a sometimes tricky relationship with his parents (mother = concerned housewife, father = jovial, mustachioed seafaring captain). But what I loved most about his world was the mise en scène. Strange haircuts. Raw fish. Futuristic trains. Buildings with clean angles. The way people would become embarrassed at the most trivial things. Even the strange alphabet looked like a secret code. And, though the show was dubbed into Spanish, they couldn't fool me. I knew Captain Tsubasa's world existed a million miles away from mine. And that's precisely why it was so wonderful to me. Every episode was like a glimpse into another dimension where they looked and moved like us but in a place so completely *other*.

Naturally, I wanted to find out more. I went to the library to ask about Japan. The librarian came back with a book about tall buildings and big bridges. Sure enough, I came to a double-page spread of Rainbow Bridge, all lit up at night.

'You see those colours?' She tapped the page. 'They use solar power. In the day, the bridge stores up the power and then at night it lights up.'

And that was that, I was captivated. Gazing at those magical pages, I swore that one day I would cross that bridge.

Shortly after that, my parents divorced and I moved with my mother to London. I remember the alien feel of trousers on my shins. How different the cartoons were. Dole queues and spaghetti hoops. John Major's Britain, going back to basics.

By my mid-twenties, I was still in London and had fluked my way into a travel magazine. After a few years of writing articles on far-flung destinations such as Cardiff and Temple Cloud, I was finally given my first big assignment: Japan. Not quite believing my luck, I read a ton of books and planned my article meticulously. (It never saw the light of day, the magazine folded while I was out there.) I did, however, get to keep that promise to my child-self. I stood on the pedestrian walkway of Rainbow Bridge, fifty metres above the water, and watched the city sparkle in the cold. The bay below filled with party boats and skyscrapers stretched out in every direction, each one topped with red lights to warn off low-flying aircraft, like lighthouses. Lorries thundered past me on the bridge, their drivers maybe thinking I was a jumper. And to my shock, I felt tears in my eyes, sluggish and unfamiliar. The cityscape blurred into shifting hexagons of silver and gold and I blamed them on the cold. But I *had* made it to my bridge. I had kept the promise to my six-year-self.

It struck me then that Japan, or at least my idea of it, had always represented an escape. And the bridge had always been the physical expression of 'from here to *there*'. And I had finally reached *there*.

The beginning of *Blue Light Yokohama* is also easy to determine. During my first trip to Japan in 2010, I came across an article about the Miyazawa family murders. The case was unsolved and already ten years old. I remember looking at a photograph of the family. They were sitting on some stone steps, most likely on a day out. The father, Mikio, wearing an ocean blue polo shirt and moccasins, had let two fingers touch the shoulder of his son sitting below him. It was the only trace of visible affection. Yasuko, the mother, although almost smiling, looked more rigid. She wore a beige blouse, her hair neatly plaited, hands in her lap. She looked like a teacher, somehow. A good teacher but one who wouldn't have stood for any nonsense. Niina, cute, rosy face and Velcroed trainers, mimicked her mother's pose. Rei, legs apart, fiddled with his fingers and looked to camera open-mouthed. He wore sailing shoes, similar to his dad. Nobody was quite smiling. Nobody was giving away much. I gazed at them for a long time and asked myself: *who could murder an entire family with a sushi knife and a pillow, then walk out the front door in broad daylight?*

I cut out that image and put it in the book I was reading at the time. (I've never been able to find it.)

A few years later, I returned to Japan for my thirtieth birthday. It was 16 April 2014 and I was staying in a dated business hotel on the banks of the Ōta River. In my room, which had a 'no smorking' sign, I was unable to sleep. I put the shopping channel on and leafed through the newspaper from the day before. And that's when I stumbled across an article similar to this: http://www.japantoday.com/category/crime/view/setagaya-family-murders-remain-unsolved-15-years-later.

My breath caught. I was looking at the same photograph I'd seen years before. The Miyazawas on some stone steps surrounded by greenery. Maybe I want to remember it this way, but I felt it was as if they were calling to me. *Here we are again.*

I spent that night feverishly researching the case, by then fourteen years old. The upshot was that on 30 December 2000, a man broke into the Miyazawa home, murdered the entire family, then used the family computer, ate their ice cream and spent up to eleven hours in the house. He left the next day in broad daylight. There was no real motive but the killer did leave behind plenty of evidence – brand-new clothes, a hip bag, a bucket hat, sand grains from the Mojave Desert and powdered fluorescent dye (red and violet). In the pocket of the sweater were traces of bird droppings and Japanese zelkova leaves. The killer also left behind his blood at the scene. DNA analysis revealed a mother of European descent, possibly from a Mediterranean country. He left his faeces in the toilet, the stool revealing he was likely a vegetarian. He left behind the murder weapon, a sashimi knife which he bought that day costing him ¥3,500 (about £20). He left traces of French aftershave on a handkerchief.

It was approaching dawn in my hotel room. I looked again at the faces of the family. I had the shopping channel on – a limited-time offer for a music CD box set in the background. Ayumi Ishida was singing 'Blue Light Yokohama', smiling painfully as she sang. I looked at the lyrics passing along the bottom of the screen.

The lights of the city are so pretty, I'm happy with you. Please let me hear. Those words of love from you. I walk and walk, swaying, like a small boat in your arms. I hear your footsteps coming, Give me one more tender kiss. The scent of your favourite cigarettes, Yokohama, Blue Light Yokahama. This will always be our world.

And in that moment I felt it. Although intellectually I understood that the killer was still at large, it suddenly *hit* me. Fourteen years after this atrocity, the case was still unsolved. There was no ending. The person who did this was – and to this day, still is – free. Someone. Someone who travels. Someone who wears young, fashionable clothing. Someone who has contact with birds. Someone with a taste for spinach. Someone with a taste for French aftershave. Someone who, on the night of 30 December 2000, was walking through the streets of Setagaya, sashimi knife in his hip bag, bought with the purpose of slaughtering an entire family.

I went to bed unable to get that faceless man out of my mind.

The next day, I woke up still thinking about the case. I boarded the Shinkansen bound for Kyoto, still going over the countless odd details in my mind. Sitting in my comfortable seat on the climate-controlled bullet train, I went over the notes I'd made. And as I looked out of the window at Chūgoku countryside, streaking past watercolour fast, I thought about the lyrics to 'Blue Light Yokohama'. I wrote down the following bullet point:

Murder case involving a family of four. Blue Light Yokohama novel?

I knew I had to write a novel involving a family murder. I *had* to. It wasn't that I wanted to write about the family itself, that would be cheap, but the abhorrent fate that had befallen them wouldn't let me go. Perhaps it might sound crass but there were just too many haunting curiosities to ignore. Too many compelling questions. Too much mystery to explore. Ultimately, I wanted to write about facelessness. The agony of facelessness. Though I'd never seriously considered writ-

437

ing crime fiction, I'd always toyed with the idea of a Japanese detective. I would write little set pieces but he would always come off sounding like a bad marriage between Rick Deckard and Philip Marlowe. I could never decide who he was, so I wrote him as a tough guy by default.

I think it was an innocuous line from the *Japan Today* article that changed that:

Approximately 246,000 officers have been involved in the case to date . . . Forty officers remain assigned to the case full-time.

It was set next to an image of policemen dressed in black, respectfully lined up outside the Miyazawas' house, bowing before it on the anniversary of the murders. Where I was from, policemen didn't beg for forgiveness. I looked at their faces and wondered who they were. I pictured them waiting by the telephone, fourteen years after the murders. Handing out flyers at train stations. Endlessly bouncing around theories. Paying their respects every 30 December. It struck me then that my detective should be one of them. He wouldn't be wisecracking and he wouldn't be tough. He would be alone and full of sorrow, fighting the battles of the dead. I realized then that *Blue Light Yokohama* would be a crime novel only in façade. At its heart, I wanted to write about people in pain. About people who had lost something. So it was that Inspector Kosuke Iwata was born.

Nicolás Obregón
London, June 2016

Acknowledgements

I will be forever grateful to my parents, Gisèle and Álvaro. For my mother, who showed me limitless love and was the very example of bravery in the face of hardship. Even when we had nothing, she found a way to enrich my life. For my father, who taught me always to stand up for egalitarianism and whose wise counsel invariably found its mark. And I include Jack Canavan in that word – *parents* – may his songs be heard for ever. For Lela and Meme, and the memory of their husbands, all of whom lived through tribulations with utmost grace and created the patchwork family I love. For beautiful Camille, who believed in me, my first reader and my bro. Never-ending thanks to the superb people at Curtis – Melissa Pimentel, Richard Pike and, of course, my incredible champion, Gordon Wise, the smartest and funniest ally a writer could have. I'm blessed to have been able to work with the tremendous team at Penguin, Eve Hall, Jillian Taylor and my staggeringly lovely editor, Maxine Hitchcock – a veritable genius. To my friends who saw me through the grind, Kielan Thompson, Houman Barekat and Alexis Hercules, poet kings all three. To brave Kim, 感谢您的建议. To Benjamin Wood and his inestimable advice. To the Birkbeck Clique, wherever you go in life, we'll always have Kingsley. To my comrade, Chris Simpson, when your stories are known to all, I'll be able to say: *told you so*. And to my English teacher, Ms Kenney, who taught me the magic of words.

Lastly, I would like to acknowledge four people who should never be forgotten. Mikio, Yasuko, Niina and Rei Miyazawa. May they rest in peace and may the man who took them one day know justice.